Also by Patricia J. MacDonald:

THE UNFORGIVEN
STRANGER IN THE HOUSE
LITTLE SISTER

No Way Home

Patricia J. MacDonald

A Dell Book

To Jane Berkey—agent, friend, and fairy godmother

Published by
Dell Publishing
a division of
Bantam Doubleday Dell Publishing Group, Inc.
666 Fifth Avenue
New York, New York 10103

ISBN: 0-440-20665-0
Reprinted by arrangement with Delacorte Press
Printed in the United States of America

Published simultaneously in Canada

June 1990

10 9 8 7 6 5 4 3 2 1
OPM

Special thanks to my aunt, Ann Jambriska, who gave me the idea for this story, and to Jane Berkey, Don Cleary, Susan Moldow, and my husband, Art Bourgeau, for their considerable guidance in the telling of it

CHAPTER 1

For three days running the weathermen on the Nash-ville TV stations had been warning of a "storm watch" in middle Tennessee. And everyone in Cress County knew they weren't talking about a little rain coming. It was tornado weather, and country people weren't fooled by that network doubletalk. In order to forestall panic, the TV news never mentioned the word tornado until one had actually been sighted. But fast as a tornado traveled, by then it was too late anyway.

From the afternoon shade of her front porch, Lillie Burdette scanned the sky uneasily for a faraway funnel of dust and wind. Usually tornado weather came earlier, in late August. It was a little freakish this last weekend in September, but it was impossible not to recognize it. The air was humid and utterly still. Everything you looked at seemed unnaturally sunlit, and yet the sky was hung low with dark clouds. It was hot as blazes, but, now and then, a cold breeze would trickle over your skin and make you shiver.

Across the road from Lillie's front yard was a field, bounded by a split-rail fence, and an old horse liked to graze there. Normally the sloe-eyed beast would plant itself in one spot and scarcely lift its lazy head from its nibbling. Today the old farm animal paced the fence, head up, eyes fearful, as if it too were watching the skies.

Animals could always sense it, Lillie thought. It made them restless. She herself had never actually seen a tornado hit. She'd felt the rustle and seen the blackening of the sky that preceded it. And, as a child, she'd always hoped one *would* come, just for the thrill of it. Like all the other kids, she'd heard the tales of those who had survived one. Bessie Hill, who was old, used to tell about the one time she was alone in the house and a tornado struck. It was evening, and all the lights had gone out, as so often happened in Cress County given wind or rain. She'd decided to get into bed, since she had no lights, but after a while a huge gust blew her front door open, latch and all. She rushed out to the living room to try to push the front door closed, and when she was in the living room the twister lifted up a tree in her yard and put it right through the roof and her bedroom ceiling.

I must be getting old, Lillie thought with a shiver. I'd rather it didn't come anywhere near here anymore. A car passed by slowly, and the occupants waved. Lillie shielded her eyes with her hand and waved back, even though she did not recognize the passersby. It was customary, in Felton, Tennessee, to greet those you met, whether or not you had ever been introduced. There were more cars than usual today, passing on the road between her front yard and her neighbor's field across the way. But that was normal for a Founders Day.

Another Founders Day. She could remember attending that early-autumn celebration for the last thirty years, ever since she'd been a child of four. It was like marking another year of your life gone. *I suppose that's probably it, that, and the weather,* she thought, trying to account for the melancholy mood which had been with her since she awoke, anxious and sweaty that morning, in time to see the first pale streaks in the sky. *Another year gone and somehow the day never held the pleasure, the excitement, it had when she was young.*

"Mom, your timer dinged."

"Oh, thanks, honey," Lillie said. She picked up her watering can and dumped the last of its contents into the impatiens that hung in a basket under the rafters of her porch. "Could you do me a favor and pop those layers out of the pans. That's what I had it set for."

"Okay, in a minute. First, tell me how I look."

Lillie lowered the watering can and turned toward the front door. The face of her daughter Michele appeared suspended, like a luminous moon, behind the screen. Michele reached down, pushed open the door, and wedged the hoopskirt she was wearing through the doorframe.

The hoop sprang open and Michele twirled awkwardly out onto the front porch. Her long, shiny brown hair separated over her narrow shoulders and met the puffed sleeves of the old-fashioned dress. The rose-pink of the gown was too deep a color for her, and she did not fill out the lacy décolletage, but her eyes were bright with pleasure at her image of herself, and the skirt rustled pleasantly as she bounced it around her.

Lillie's spirits rose at the sight of her. "You look beautiful," she exclaimed. "You found it."

"Well, I could hardly miss it," said Michele, "hanging on the door to my closet."

"But it looks perfect on you," said Lillie. She reached down and plucked at the skirt, fluffing it out. "You look like a dream."

"I feel kind of stupid in it. And it's so hot. I can't believe they wore these things all the time in the old days."

"It's not usually this hot Founders Day," said Lillie. "I wish this weather would break. It makes everybody irritable. You know, this hoop skirt actually belonged to my great-grandmother—"

"I know, I know," said Michele, who had heard the old story about a hundred times, "and your grandma made this dress for you for the pageant when you were my age."

Lillie gazed at her daughter. The rose-pink had been shrewdly chosen for Lillie by her mother to emphasize the dark hair, cherry-stained lips and cheeks, and creamy complexion characteristic of some Southern beauties; her coloring made her look like something plucked from a chocolate box. Her mother had always prided herself on her eye for clothes and makeup. But it had been her grandmother, now long dead, who had lovingly stitched the dress for her. And now she felt an ache of happiness, akin to pain, to see her own daughter in that special dress. Her healthy, clear-eyed child, whom the doctors had said would not live to leave the hospital on the day she was born.

She did not understand the medical terms the doctors hurled at her as she lay recovering from Michele's birth in her hospital bed. A sympathetic nurse told her as gently as possible that her infant daughter would probably need a series of operations on her heart. The first weeks after Michele's birth were just a blur of anguish to her now. She remembered a frantic ambulance ride to Vanderbilt Hospital in Nashville, where a team of doctors operated all night on her baby. And then life formed into a pattern that would hold for years—a pilgrimage from one faraway hospital to another, one specialist after another, following an elusive trail of hope that had finally led to health, to normalcy, by the time Michele had reached her teens.

Michele held the bodice of the dress out in front of her in two dainty points. "I don't exactly do it justice," she observed ruefully.

Lillie smiled. Michele would always be on the small, fragile side. It was a legacy of her illness. But she was sturdy now, no longer frail. "Don't complain," said Lillie. "You never have to worry about getting fat. And with your cheekbones, you'll probably end up in a fashion magazine someday."

Michele grimaced but was pleased. She tossed her hair back off her shoulders. "I'm bringing my shorts to change into as soon as the dumb pageant is over. It's so sticky today."

"I know," Lillie said fretfully. "That sky looks mean."

Michele's eyes lit up. "Yeah. Maybe there'll be a tornado."

"Well, don't sound so darn pleased about it," said Lillie. "Now scoot. In the house. I've got to get those layers out."

"Oh, I forgot about them," said Michele, sweeping into the house in front of her mother, feigning annoyance as she gently lifted the skirt and hoop up so she could walk. She perched on a kitchen stool, fussily retying the bows on her sleeves as Lillie put her cake together for the picnic supper.

The back door opened and Pink Burdette came into the kitchen. He was dressed in a pale-green plaid jacket and tie, despite the heat. He was a large man whose waistline had gotten away from him now that he was in his midforties. His round, even-featured face was damp, and there was perspiration visible through the thinning strawberry-blond hair on his scalp. His glance fell on the cake Lillie was fixing. "What's this?" he asked in mock amazement. "Don't tell me we're giving food away. People could be paying good money for this."

"Look at Michele. Doesn't she look nice?" Lillie said, ignoring the jibe at her catering business. Pink had never wanted her to work, and he kept up a running line of jokes about it to mask—unsuccessfully, Lillie thought—his uneasiness.

"Let's see," Pink said.

Michele slid awkwardly off the stool and twirled around for Pink's approval.

"Right pretty," said Pink. "Just like *Gone With the Wind.*"

"Are you and Grayson about ready to go?" Lillie asked her husband.

"Yeah. I've just been out there tossing a few to Grayson. Warm him up for the big game. Goddamn, it's close out there today."

"Why don't you leave off the jacket?" Lillie asked, although she knew the answer in advance.

"There'll be people there I do business with," Pink replied. "I think they prefer to see a man looking a sight more dignified."

He walked over and tasted the frosting on the bowl. "Up, wait a minute. I think I owe you a quarter for this." He winked at Michele, who made a face. She had heard all the jokes before. Unlike Pink, she thought it was neat that her mother had a business.

"We'd better be going," Lillie said purposefully. "Why don't you call Grayson, see if he wants a ride."

Pink walked to the back door, opened it, and called out. "Son, come along. That team needs you over there to shape them up." He turned and announced, "He's coming." Then he turned back and gazed out the door until Grayson appeared and glided in past his father.

Grayson was actually Grayson Jr., although Pink had acquired his homely nickname in the cradle and no one, it seemed, had ever dignified him with the use of his given name. He vowed that his son would not meet the same fate, and he resisted using even the shortened version of "Gray" for his boy. He need not have worried. From the first, Grayson's elegant name suited him, and remained unsullied by pejorative nicknames. Despite the heat of the day, Grayson's uniform did not appear to be damp, and his thick, wheat-blond hair fell softly on his broad, clear forehead. He blinked his deep blue eyes a few times, to adjust to the relative darkness of the house, and then staggered backward, clutching his head.

"What is this?" he cried out. "A fairy princess."

"Shut up, Gray," said Michele.

"Michele is in the pageant," Lillie said.

"And you," Pink said earnestly, locking the back door and approaching his son, "are going to lead that team to the all-county championship today. Anybody who is anybody in this county is going to be there today. That includes the president of the bank, who just happens to be chairman of the Rotary scholarship committee."

"Oh, Pink, for goodness sakes," Lillie exclaimed. "He's only a sophomore. He doesn't need to be worrying about scholarships yet. Besides, the game is supposed to be fun."

"Lillie," Pink said patiently, "in case you haven't noticed, this is the game we've been working toward all summer. This is *it*. If we win this one we're all-county champions. Not to mention that Sterling Grisard, the bank president, just happened to play Grayson's position when he was on the Felton team years ago."

"Well, sir," Grayson said, "I do mean to win."

"You go up to Sterling after the game and introduce yourself. I'll be there to kind of smooth the way. We want him to know who the team's star player is."

Grayson nodded and flicked the ball lazily back and forth, hand to mitt, as Pink outlined his plan.

"Why does everything have to have a hidden motive?" Lillie asked. "Here, Michele, take this cake to the car."

Pink buttoned his snug sports jacket carefully. "We are only talking about being friendly and sociable, and presenting ourselves in the best possible light."

Michele picked up the cake gingerly and held it away from the rose-colored gown. "What if he loses?" she drawled.

"Catch, Michele," said Grayson, pretending to toss the ball at his sister.

Michele started and then wailed, "Grayson," but there was only feigned distress in her tone. At fifteen, Grayson Burdette was already the kind of boy that any girl, even his own sister, enjoyed being teased by. Grayson laughed, pleased with his joke, and tossed the ball into his own mitt, the muscles in his forearms working visibly under the olive skin covered with silky down.

"Yessir," said Gray. "I believe I'll just walk right up to Mr. Grisard, introduce myself, and tell him that I am the son of the busiest little caterer in Cress County, and his bank lent my mama the money to get started with." He winked at his mother.

"Don't say that!" Pink exclaimed.

"He's teasing," Lillie said. "Come on. Michele, are your clothes for changing in the car yet?"

"I have to get them," Michele replied.

"Well, go on then," Lillie said. "The pageant is on first. You best be there on time."

"Will you take this, Gray?" Michele asked, holding out the cake plate to her brother.

"Sure," he said, tucking his mitt under his arm. "Hurry up."

Although the site of the festivities was less than a half a mile away, they would never have thought of walking. In Cress County the sight of an adult walking down the road, unless he was carrying a gas can to or from a service station, was virtually an indication of mental illness. Pink kept his five-year-old Oldsmobile in mint condition, always washed and waxed, and it did stand out among the old pickups and battered sedans parked by most of the partygoers in the grassy field that served as a lot near the entrance to Briar Hill. They all got out of the car and stood for a moment, absorbing the festive atmosphere and sighting familiar faces. Then they started up the incline toward the Briar Hill House.

Despite its modest name, the mansion at Briar Hill was the pride of the town of Felton. The Briar Hill plantation had been one of the largest in Tennessee, but after World War I the family had been unable to keep the house, and no one who could afford to buy seemed to want to settle there. The old plantation house and grounds had gone steadily to seed until some ambitious town councilmen managed to reclaim it some years back and make a park out of it. The grounds were large and well kept by local volunteers, but the centerpiece was the house, which boasted pillars, balconies, climbing trellises, and French doors as well as a relatively new paint job. The town could not afford to restore the inside of the house, so various workmen had collaborated on rehabbing it to suit the needs of the many local groups that met there through all the months of the year in which central heating wasn't required. Their practical improvements included covering the old wooden floors with inexpensive burnt-orange carpeting of a particularly durable fiber, installing a cafeteria complete with folding metal chairs and long tables, and furnishing the rest with donations from people's homes and catalog pieces acquired after green stamp drives. Although the rooms of the old mansion bore little resemblance to the elegant salons of its antebellum glory days, the Briar Hill House was once again the seat of county society.

Lillie led the way through the open doors of the mansion into the cool, dark vestibule. She looked down at her watch. "What time does the pageant start?"

"Fifteen minutes," said Michele. "I have to go and line up."

"We'll get a seat," Lillie said. "Give this cake to one of the ladies in the kitchen when you pass it. And have fun."

Greeting friends and acquaintances as they passed, Pink led the way to the grand ballroom, which had been filled with rows of metal chairs facing a wooden platform that served as the stage. Pink found three seats together at the end of a row and they all sat down.

Every year the pageant was the official kick-off of the day's festivities. It was always the same from year to year —a short little play wherein boys dressed as Confederate soldiers and girls in antebellum gowns gave a loose reenactment of the founding of their hometown. Felton's founding actually predated the Civil War by many years, but recorded history of the place was scant, and everyone preferred the costumes of the Civil War era. Besides, no Southern celebration was truly complete without some evocation of the Confederacy, which, despite what most Northerners might be content to believe, was still cherished as the glory of the South.

The appearance of the high-school music teacher, Gay Jones, at the upright piano signaled the beginning of the pageant. A collective sigh emanated from the crowd as the first chords of "Dixie" were struck.

Lillie, who was wedged between Pink and Grayson, sat forward in her seat, straining to see Michele as the high-school girls streamed onto the stage in their gowns to the appreciative murmurs of the audience. Lillie waved to Michele, who just rolled her eyes and looked away from her family. Out of the corner of her eye Lillie saw Gray tug at the flounce on the gown of Allene Starnes, a pretty, red-headed girl in his class, as she passed by. Allene blushed, pretended to glare at him, and nearly stumbled on the steps leading to the stage. The boys came on stage from the other side, resplendent in their Confederate uniform reproductions.

Each of the girls was partnered with a soldier. Lillie beamed as she watched Michele cross the stage and take the arm of a tall, gangly boy whose brief, shy smile revealed braces on his teeth. Michele was perfectly at ease on the stage, speaking out clearly and deftly fielding the blundered cues of her mumbling partner, smiling all the while. She gets it from her father, Lillie thought. She looks like she was born on that stage.

From the audience, the rose-pink gown seemed to glow, giving Michele's young complexion the radiance of a magnolia blossom. Lillie could recall exactly how it felt to wear that gown. The weight of the skirts, the tickle of the lacy bodice, the narrow waist, the sense that you were transformed, a feast for the eyes, a rose.

Pink leaned over and whispered to Lillie, "Takes me back to the year you were in the pageant. You looked so pretty I couldn't take my eyes off of you."

Lillie flashed her husband a guilty smile, for she had just been remembering the admiring gaze in the eyes of her partner that long-ago day. Jordan Hill's deep-brown playful eyes had fastened on her with a yearning warmed by his sleepy dimpled smile.

"Everybody and his brother is here today," Pink said. "I think I may be able to drum up a little business."

Lillie nudged him in the side to be quiet and applauded

wildly with the rest of the audience as the self-conscious belles and their make-believe swains hurried through their lines and sang with rousing enthusiasm a Stephen Foster tune before clambering off the stage with considerably less dignity than they had claimed it. As the applause died away, Lillie felt a rush of foolish, sentimental tears filling her eyes. During all those years of doctors and hospitals, and Michele's tiny hand gripping hers, she had scarcely dared to think ahead to the next day, much less to dream that one day her daughter would be up there on that stage, a lovely young woman in her mother's rose-pink gown.

Pink got up and stretched. "Well, I've got to get out there and get to visiting," he said. To Pink, every gathering, no matter how social it might be, was a business opportunity. A real-estate salesman in a county where people spent generations on the same land, his oft-repeated motto was "I have to hustle."

Lillie wiped her eyes and stood up. She was used to him by now. He would grab a person's hand extended in greeting and cling to it, asking in a familiar voice about mortgage refinancing and whether they might not be better off letting just a corner of the farm go, especially when he could get them the best price for it.

They strolled together out the French doors and into the brightness of the afternoon. "You go ahead," said Lillie. "I want to find Brenda." Brenda Daniels, her oldest friend and her partner in the catering business, was a three-time divorcée who had used the settlement from her last, brief marriage to get the business going and lure Lillie into it. She had caught Lillie at a good time. Michele was finally healthy, and both children were past the age where they needed her constant attention. The business had been a perfect channel for her restless energy. Lillie could hardly remember a day going by in their lives when she and Brenda had not talked together at least once. She turned to Grayson. "What time does the game start?"

"In a few minutes. I've got to get over to the field and warm up."

"I'll be right over," said Lillie. "Good luck."

Pink cocked his hand as if it were a revolver and squinted down his forefinger at Grayson. "Knock 'em dead, shooter. I'm counting on you." Pink kneaded his son's shoulder with one large hand and then smacked him gently on the back to send him on his way, as he turned around to scout for a potential customer.

Lillie watched her son lope off in the direction of the baseball diamond. Allene Starnes materialized out of the crowd, still wearing her ballgown, and Gray stopped short to speak to her, one knee bent, his hat pulled down so that only his lazy, summery smile was visible under the shadow of the brim.

Lillie gazed at him a little wistfully. He seemed to have none of the insecurities and doubts so common to other boys his age. At least he never spoke of them to her. Perhaps he confided in Pink. From the day he was born and Pink scooped him up from her arms in the hospital and gazed hungrily down into his soft, innocent face, he had belonged to Pink somehow. Grayson had been the kind of child whose life seemed to unfold in a smooth arc of perfection. His was an easy birth, and he spoke his first words early and could point with clarity to what he wanted. He took his first steps, into Pink's waiting arms, when he was only eight months old. School was easy for him, and he was always one of those surprisingly coordinated children who got things right on the first try. What disappointments, what frustrations, he may have had, he brought them instinctively to Pink, who always was waiting. Their bond was a blessing to Lillie, who spent most of her time just trying to keep Michele from succumbing to one deadly episode after another in those days. But now, looking at her son, already so grown-up, she felt a sense of loss. Already he was taking up with girls, and soon he'd be a grown man and gone, and she felt as if she had never really possessed him.

Snap out of it, she chided herself. You're going to ruin the day with your moping. And it's just the oppressiveness of the air getting to you, the low sky weighing you down. Lillie began to walk slowly in the direction of the baseball diamond. She kept an eye out for Brenda, but there was no sign of her. Lillie thought she knew what that meant. Brenda had gone up to Nashville the day before to do some shopping, and like as not had looked up that married studio musician whom she had vowed never to spend another night with. Lillie secretly suspected that Brenda enjoyed the drama of these doomed affairs. Although she never came right out and said it, Brenda clearly regarded Lillie's life as far too humdrum for her tastes.

Lillie wiped her damp forehead and fanned herself with the program from the pageant. Everyone she greeted on her way to the ball field had the same thing on their minds. "Can't recall a Founders Day hot as this one," said Bessie Hill, brushing Lillie's cheek with her papery old lips.

"Twister weather if I ever seen it," intoned Bomar

Flood, the local pharmacist, as Lillie squeezed his damp hand and moved on. As she came up on the diamond, she saw Pink buttonholing an old farmer who was wearing overalls and the ubiquitous "Cat" cap pushed up on his forehead. They were standing just off the first-base line, and Pink had one eye cast on the game, which was just beginning.

Lillie felt a protective surge of warmth for her husband. It was true that he was not the kind of man who inspired poetry and fireworks. But he had come into her life at a time when she was desperate and frightened. He had promised to take care of her, and he had. He worked hard, he doted on the children, and he lived with her moods without complaint. She was grateful to have him for her husband. She knew plenty of women who wished they could say as much, she thought.

Pink spotted Lillie and waved to her. "Come on, our boy's about to get up to bat." Lillie walked up beside him and took a seat on the bleachers next to where Pink stood. The old farmer took the opportunity to excuse himself from Pink's importuning pitch. Lillie perched on the edge of the seat and shaded her eyes with her hand as Grayson stepped up to the plate.

Royce Ansley, the county sheriff, dressed in short sleeves and an olive-drab tie, walked up just then and stood beside Pink. In his fifties, Royce had the physique of a man half his age and the bearing of the soldier he had once been. He wore his graying hair in a crew cut, as he had ever since Lillie could remember. His black shoes shone like patent leather. "That's Gray, isn't it?" he asked.

"Number eighteen," Pink said proudly.

"Hi, Sheriff," Lillie said. Royce nodded and smiled at her. She could not remember a time when Royce had not been a law officer in Felton. When she was a young girl she had thought him sort of a romantic figure, gruff and silent. He had been an eligible bachelor until he was nearly forty, invited to many a home-cooked meal by mothers hopeful for their daughters. When he finally did marry, it was to a girl from Memphis, and for some years he was as happy as a boy. Lillie turned her attention back to the game. Gray was assuming his stance, squinting purposefully into the distance. Lillie noticed several girls, including Allene, lined up behind the cage, giggling and preening, their eyes on her son. As the pitch came toward him, Gray drew the bat back and swung it fluidly, his body moving with the grace of a natural athlete. The bat connected solidly with the ball, and it sailed out far into the field, sending the outfielders scrambling after it in a ditch below the railroad tracks that bordered the diamond. Cheers erupted as Grayson made his turn around the bases.

"He's a fine hitter," Royce observed as Pink pounded his fist into his hand in glee and restrained a war whoop.

"Yay, Grayson," Lillie called out as she applauded. As the cheers quieted and the pitcher from the Welbyville team tried to regain his composure, Lillie turned to the sheriff. "How ya doing?" she asked.

"Fine, thanks."

"Tyler playing today?"

The sheriff frowned. "He was supposed to play. I don't see him on the bench though." There was a tightness in his voice when he mentioned his son. The strife between Royce and his seventeen-year-old son was well known around town, having erupted in public on several occasions. Ever since Tyler's mother had died, when the boy was twelve, he had run a little wild.

Lillie decided to change the subject. "I hope the lawbreakers give you a rest today," she said, "so you can enjoy the festivities."

"Oh, I guarantee you I'll be busy tonight. I'll have every bunk at the county jail filled with drunk and disorderlies. People get to celebrating a little too hard," Royce said dryly.

"I suppose so," said Lillie.

"I can't get over that boy of mine," Pink interjected, tearing his eyes away from Gray, who had been soundly thumped on the back and had his hand pumped by every teammate. "If it was just baseball you could understand it, but I'm telling you, it's every sport he plays. And it's not just sports, either. He's got the brains too. Way to go, Grayson," Pink cried as the boy caught his eye and waved. "There is nothing that boy can't do, isn't that so, honey?"

"His daddy's pride and joy," Lillie said, almost apologetically, to Royce.

"He's got a right to be proud," said Royce. "Grayson's a fine boy."

"Mom, Mom, I need the keys to the car."

Lillie turned and saw Michele coming toward them, trailing her gown through the dusty grass. "Hello, Sheriff Ansley," she said politely.

"Hello, Michele."

"What do you want the car keys for?"

"To get my clothes. They're in that bag in the trunk."

"Oh, all right. Pink—"

"Hmmm . . ." Pink turned around. "Oh, there's the belle of the ball. You did real good in the pageant, honey."

"Thanks, Dad. I need to get in the trunk."

Pink handed her the car keys. "Bring 'em right back," he said. "You should have got here sooner. You missed it. Grayson just hit a homer."

"Oh, that's great," Michele said in a bored voice. She was used to her brother's accomplishments, and was even proud of them, but Pink's excess of enthusiasm always affected her adversely, so that she acted indifferent. She turned to the sheriff. "Is Tyler here?" she asked casually.

"He was supposed to play," said the sheriff.

"Oh, there he is, Royce," Lillie said. As soon as she said it, she wished she could take it back. Tyler was in uniform, but the shirt hung out of the back of his pants and the uniform looked as if he had rolled in the dirt in it. Tyler leaned over to select a bat, and when he stood up he staggered a little before he could catch himself. The coach came up to him and held his arm, speaking to him with a serious expression on his face, but Tyler waved him away with a limp hand and walked carefully toward the plate. He leaned over into his stance and licked his lips as he tried to focus his eyes on the pitcher. Tyler was a tall, well-built boy, nearly his father's size, with long dark hair and a fleshy, sensuous face that was usually creased into a scowl.

Tyler jerked his chin at the pitcher to indicate that he should go ahead. The pitcher wound up and sent one flying across the plate. Tyler swung wildly after the ball was already in the catcher's mitt, and nearly lost his balance. The coach came out to the plate, calling out, "That's enough." He grabbed Tyler by the arm and spoke quickly into his ear.

"He must be sick," said Michele.

Lillie held her breath. She could see the muscles in Royce's jaw working furiously as Tyler protested and tried to shrug off the coach. A couple of other players came up and surrounded Tyler, who was shaking his head with his eyes closed. Two of the boys took him by the arms, but Tyler angrily shook them off and walked unsteadily off the baseline.

"That's not fair," said Michele. "They won't even give him a chance."

Lillie marveled a little at her daughter's naïveté. It was clear to everyone from the silence in the bleachers that Tyler was high on something. But to Michele he was just another underdog to root for. It was Michele's natural tendency, Lillie thought fondly. Any runt of the litter, any stray cat, was her daughter's natural ally. She cried at the news reports on the poor and, to Pink's complete annoyance, wore black armbands whenever there was a prison execution. The troubled Tyler Ansley was a cause made to order for Michele.

Lillie did not want to look at Royce. She knew he would be pale from the disgrace of it. She wished she could make the whole incident disappear for him. The next batter got up and started for the plate. Lillie was trying to think what to say when she was saved by Wallace Reynolds, Sheriff Ansley's deputy, running up to the diamond with a grim expression on his face.

"Sheriff," Wallace said in a low, anxious voice, "you better get back to your car. Francis has been trying to reach you on the radio. There's been a break at the county jail."

A murmur went up from the people nearby and then a loud buzz as the news was passed down the bleachers. Lillie and Pink exchanged a glance of surprise, and Lillie put a hand on Michele's shoulder.

"All right, Wallace. You follow me up there," said Royce. Without another word he turned and hurried in the direction of his patrol car.

"What happened?" Pink asked as the deputy hesitated a moment to catch his breath. A group of people left their seats and had gathered around them.

Wallace shook his head. "I don't know."

"What did Francis say?" asked a man seated in front of Lillie. Francis Dunham, as everyone knew, was the dispatcher at the county jail, and had been for about twenty years. "Who was it?"

"I told you," Wallace said, "I don't know what happened. I got to get up there myself." Wallace began to shoulder his way through the crowd and was pelted with anxious questions, which he waved away.

"Folks, folks, the game," pleaded the coach, who had jogged over. The players, unaware of the cause of all the excitement, watched the knot of buzzing spectators in bewilderment.

"He's right," said a woman in red toreador pants. "The sheriff will get 'em. Nothing we can do about it." There were nods all around as the group of people dispersed and resumed their seats. The next batter stepped up to the plate.

Lillie looked across the diamond and saw that Tyler Ansley was gone. That was lucky timing for him, she thought. Saved by the bell. She turned her attention back to the game as Michele went off toward the car to retrieve her clothes.

The day's festivities went on without further incident, although the sheriff and his deputy did not reappear at the picnic. Various contradictory reports filtered back about who, what, and how many were involved in the jailbreak. Somewhere between the time that the Felton team captured the county championship from Welbyville and the women started serving up the plates of cornbread, ribs, and chicken, the sky darkened threateningly and then a wave of cool breezes began breaking over the picnickers, and the air cleared. The crowd, already cheerful, became buoyant. Everyone helped clean up, agreeing that the food was better than it had ever been. Then, since night was falling, a country band began to set up inside the grand ballroom, and the floor was cleared of chairs for dancing. As soon as the band struck up its first tune, Pink tugged Lillie by the arm.

"I think it's time we got on home, honey. I've got property to show tomorrow." He looked suspiciously at Lillie's tapping toe. "You don't want to stay, do you?"

Lillie watched the band for a minute and then looked away. "No, not really. You think it's safe to leave the kids with those convicts running around loose?"

"Sheriff's probably caught up with them by now. Anyway, they're not going to come around here, with all these people," said Pink.

"You're right," Lillie said. "We best tell them we're leaving though."

They did not have to look far for Grayson. He was already out on the dance floor, guiding an animated Allene

Starnes in the country swing. Pink caught his eye and the boy came over, still holding Allene by the hand.

"Your mother and I are going home now, son."

"Okay, I'll see you later."

"Not too late. Be home by eleven," said Lillie.

"Eleven-thirty," said Gray.

"All right," said Pink, beaming up at Grayson, whose blond hair was haloed by the light from the electric candles glowing in sconces all around the old ballroom.

"Walk home with your sister," Lillie said. "I don't want you walking home alone, either of you."

"Mom, don't worry," Gray said. "Where is she, anyway?"

"I don't know. I'm going to go find her," Lillie replied.

"I'll meet you at the car," said Pink.

Lillie wandered through the crowd still outside the ballroom doors. She saw Brenda, who had arrived in time to share supper with them full of tales of a wild evening with the musician in Nashville the night before. Brenda was talking now with Bill Mosher, a pudgy guy who worked at the bank. Lillie could tell by the glazed expression on her friend's face and her static smile that Brenda was getting ready to bolt for home to sit by that phone. Lillie smiled and moved on, knowing she would hear all about it tomorrow.

She caught sight of her daughter, standing alone and sipping a Coke.

"Michele," she said, "you all by yourself?"

"I'm waiting for Cherie. She's inside, in the ladies' room."

"Well, Dad and I are leaving now. Do you want a ride?"

"Nah. I'm going to stay. I put my dress in the car. Will you take it in for me?"

"Sure. Are you gonna dance?"

Michele shrugged. "Probably just watch. We're meeting Debbie and Bonnie inside."

"All right," said Lillie. "Have fun. But be home by eleven-thirty. Find Grayson and walk home with him. Or call us for a ride."

"Mom, I'm not a baby, for heaven's sakes. Here comes Cherie back."

"I'll bet some nice fellas are going to get you girls out there dancing," said Lillie.

Michele cocked an eyebrow at her friend Cherie. "Miracles do happen," she said. They both started to laugh.

Lillie had the impulse to hug her, but she didn't want to embarrass her in front of Cherie. "See you at home," she said.

"Bye, Mom."

Lillie walked slowly back to the car, savoring the cool, idle evening breeze brushing her face, riffling her hair. Pink already had the motor running and the air-conditioning on. The car was positively chilly. They drove home in silence. As they pulled in the driveway and got out of the car, Lillie could hear the strains of the Tennessee Waltz wafting up from Briar Hill. She gathered up the rustling skirts of Michele's costume from the backseat.

"Well, it turned out real nice this year," said Lillie, standing on the front lawn in the moonlight. "Thank heavens that storm didn't come."

"Yes, it was nice," Pink said. "And that was some game today. How about that boy of ours? He played like he was in the majors."

"He's a real good player," Lillie said. "But, Pink, you shouldn't be telling him all the time. He's going to get conceited."

"I can't help it." Pink sighed. "I just want everyone to know that's my boy out there. He's so darn good at everything. I tell you, honey, he's gonna have the world on a string someday. There were always a few boys like that in high school, or wherever you went. I used to always envy boys like that."

"You did all right for yourself," Lillie said loyally.

Pink sniffed. "Yeah, well. I don't kid myself. I do okay. I make a living for us."

"Come on, Pink. You're a respected businessman in this town. Why, I remember when you first started calling on me, how impressed I was with you in that jacket and tie, always on the go. Making one deal after another."

"I had a lot of dreams in those days," Pink said wistfully. "It's just that things haven't changed all that much since then."

"Why don't we sit up on the porch for a little while? We can still hear the music from the park," Lillie said gently.

Pink roused himself and shook his head. "Oh, I believe I'll go in the house and have a cold beer. The beer down there at Briar Hill wasn't cold enough to suit me. Warm as piss, if you must know. Besides," he said, "I wouldn't sit in those old rockers of your grandmother's on principle."

Lillie yawned and giggled at the same time, readying herself for the familiar tirade.

"They ruin the whole appearance of the front of the house. Here I buy you a house you could be proud of if you plunked it right down in the center of Nashville, and you put out these rickety old rockers that makes it look—"

"Like a bunch of country bumpkins live here. I know," she said.

Pink smiled ruefully. "You're used to me."

Lillie sat herself down in one of the rockers and let out a sigh of relaxation. "I guess I am," she said. "I'll be in in a few minutes. Will you take this dress in, Pink?"

Pink nodded and took it from her as he went inside. She heard the TV come on in the living room and she put her head back in the chair. The air smelled uncommonly sweet to her, and the night was still, except for the faraway sounds of the band. The long day in the sun made her feel tired all over. She closed her eyes and felt herself drifting off as she rocked. In a few minutes she was asleep.

She was awakened by Pink, shaking her on the shoulder.

"It's getting late," he said. "I'm going after those kids."

Lillie bolted up in the rocker, clutching the arms, disoriented and alarmed. "What time is it?"

"It's after eleven," said Pink.

"But we told them eleven-thirty," Lillie said.

"Well, I'm going anyway. I just heard on the news they haven't got that guy yet who broke out this afternoon. And he's a bad apple. Ronnie Lee Partin. Those kids have got no business wandering around at this hour. Especially Michele."

"No, you're right," said Lillie. She tried to force her foggy brain to focus. "Ronnie Lee Partin. Was he the one that held up that restaurant on Route 31 . . ."

". . . and pistol-whipped the manager and shot the

26

cashier. Right, that's the one," Pink said. "Besides, I just want to get them back in this house so I can go to bed in peace." He jangled the car keys.

Lillie knew from long experience that Pink was an alarmist when it came to the children. But it was a quality that endeared him to her. She realized that the night was silent, that the music had stopped from the park. "You're right," she said. "Do you want me to come with you?"

"No. You stay here in case one of them calls. Michele may have gone to a girlfriend's house. I'll be back soon."

Lillie watched her husband get into his car and drive off in the direction of Briar Hill. The kids will be fuming, she thought, when he shows up before their curfew, but it wouldn't be the first time. She opened the front door and went into the house. The TV was still on. She shut it off and sat down in her corner of the sofa. A stack of magazines were piled up in a basket beside her. It seemed as good a time as any to go through them. She and Brenda regularly culled recipes from women's magazines for the business. They were always looking for a good new casserole or dessert to try on their customers. Lillie put a stack in her lap, picked up the scissors from the end table, and began flipping and clipping. Her eyes roved restlessly over the pages until they lit, accidentally, on an article called "Soap Opera Dreamboats" in a woman's magazine she bought regularly at the supermarket checkout. Jordan Hill, "who plays Paul Manville on *Secret Lives,*" smiled out of the page, his deep-brown eyes still bright, although a little weary after all these years. She had read the article hastily when it first came out. An article about Jordan was always news in Felton. And people were quick to make sure she knew about it. She could see them looking for her reaction. Lillie stared down at the picture, her fingers poised to turn the page if Pink appeared at the door. There was gray at Jordan's temples now, and he had long ago grown a thick, well-groomed mustache, but he still looked young and careless to her. She looked up at the mantelpiece at Michele's picture, Grayson framed beside her, just as the clock on the mantel struck twelve.

Lillie turned the page and tried to focus on the recipes, but they all began to run together, the ingredients all sounding the same. Finally she set the magazines down. She rubbed her arms absently and stood up. She wandered down the hall to the kitchen, opened the refrigerator, and thought about having a glass of iced tea. Then she closed the door again. Her eyes went automatically to the clock over the refrigerator. It read nearly twelve-thirty.

"It's nothing," she said aloud. "It's Founders Day." It was a given that kids stayed out late on Founders Day. She remembered it from her own youth. She especially remembered the year she was seventeen. She and Jordan Hill had gone off and sat in the front seat of his father's pickup truck in the clearing by the Boy Scout camp until two-thirty in the morning. They would have been there all night if the superintendent of the camp hadn't heard his dogs barking and come out and shooed them away. Her father had hit her with his belt when she finally came home. The one and only time she could ever remember him hitting her. She didn't know it then, but the cancer was already in him, eating away at him. He knew he was going to die, and he was frantic about her. She bit her lip at the memory. Those last few months, those last rushed attempts at love and discipline, to try to leave an impression that would last while there was still time. All parents do it, she thought. When we finally know they're safe, we strike out at them for the worry they caused us.

She had walked back into the living room and now she returned to the mantel. She picked up the double heart-shaped frame. On one side was a photo of Michele, on the other, Grayson. She looked from one to the other, then carefully set the frame back down.

She sat down in Pink's chair with her back to the door and stared at the blank TV screen. The telephone was on a table beside her.

Lillie looked down at it now. Ring, she thought. Somebody call and tell me that everything is all right.

It's nothing, she reminded herself. Nothing. Any guy who broke out of jail this afternoon is long gone by now. Miles from here. And all the kids stay out late on Founders Day. Pink is probably just having a hard time rounding them up. He doesn't know where the kids go. And when he finds them they'll be humiliated to have their father come after them like that, herding them home. There was no reason to worry in a town like this one. This was the safest town in the world.

She picked up the county newspaper and tried to read it, but the words didn't make any sense. She threw it down again, stood up, and began to pace through the house. Every so often she would go to the front door and look out at the empty moonlit lawn and the quiet field beyond the street. Each time she came back and looked at the clock, it seemed that another ten or fifteen minutes had passed. She began to clench and unclench her fists as she paced, as if to mimic the beating of her cold heart.

"Please, God," she said aloud, "don't scare me like this."

Just then she heard the crunch of gravel in the driveway and the sound of a car's engine. Her heart lifted and she ran back to the living-room window. Then, through the gauze curtains that were closed between the open drapes, she saw a filmy blue light flashing out in front of the house and heard the faint squawk of a police radio.

Lillie stopped dead in the middle of the floor. The blue light went out, but the crackle of the radio could still be heard as well as the slamming of car doors. Pink's weary tread scraped the concrete slab of the front porch, and then the door opened. He looked up at her and then looked away.

Lillie did not scream or cry out. She stared silently as Pink came in, followed by Grayson, and then, his head bowed as if entering a church, the sheriff, Royce Ansley. Lillie's eyes darted from one to the other. She could see that Grayson was crying, ruddy tear tracks streaking the smooth face. Pink's complexion was a sickly gray. He was trembling all over.

"Where's Michele?" she asked in a hoarse, unnaturally calm voice that sounded strange to her own ears. "Couldn't you find her?"

Pink gripped his forehead with a sweaty hand, as if to still something clamoring behind it. He swallowed hard and licked his colorless lips.

"Grayson," Lillie demanded. "Where is your sister? You were supposed to walk her home."

Grayson lowered his head and tears splashed down on his shirt, and his heaving chest as he sobbed out, "I . . . know . . . I . . . was . . ."

Royce Ansley stepped forward and took Lillie by the arms. "You have to sit down," he said. He began to push her toward Pink's chair. She could see that his eyes were bright, as if with tears, but his voice was steady, his expression impassive.

"Why?" she said. But she knew why. Already she could feel the blood draining from her head, the lightness, the weakness in her limbs, a darkening around the edge of her vision as he propelled her backward.

"Lillie, I have something terrible to tell you. Michele is dead, Lillie. I'm so sorry."

"Dead," Lillie whispered. "No."

"Yes," Royce said firmly. "She was . . . apparently someone . . . killed her."

Crouched in the chair, Lillie tried to breathe, but the darkness was closing in on her now, and in the silence she could hear her heart pounding, pounding. Her arms were numb, her hands limp and cold in her lap. She could feel her eyes roll back, and then Royce was pushing her head down, lowering it between her knees.

"Breathe," she heard him saying from far away. "Breathe deep. Grayson, go get your mother a glass of water."

Lillie felt the tingle of blood returning to her head, but she did not look up. She kept her eyes closed and willed time to go back. It need only go back ten minutes. She would raise her head and see things as they really were. The door was opening and Pink was ushering them in, Grayson and Michele, scolding them. Slowly she raised her head. She saw the sheriff's somber face and catastrophe distorting the features of her husband.

"Pink," she whispered, for that was all the sound her weakened body could make. "Help me. Oh, my God. Say it's not true."

Pink tore his eyes from hers and stared at the back of the sofa. He had to tell it. He spoke carefully, but his eyes reflected the horror of what they had seen. "I found Grayson at Briar Hill with a couple of the boys, oh, a few minutes after I left the house," he said. "Grayson and the others, they hadn't seen her. I picked Grayson up and we went looking for her. I drove around and around. We looked everywhere. Finally we went down to the river over near the stone bridge, you know, Three Arches, and we . . . there we found her. Well, actually the sheriff had already found her. He was out looking for Partin. But instead he found . . . Michele." Pink's voice cracked as he spoke her name. "She was there, by the river, in some bushes. . . ." Tears began to fall from his eyes now, and his body shook violently. Pink looked up at his wife, his eyes and voice filled with tears. "I was too late. I'm sorry, honey," he said, his words slurred with sobs. "Too late."

Lillie pushed herself up from the chair and went to her husband. She buried herself against him. Grayson entered the room, carrying the glass of water. She reached out an arm and he came to her embrace.

"No, no," she said. "You didn't know. You couldn't have known. Oh, my God," she wailed, "how could anyone hurt her? She was just a baby. She never hurt anybody. My little girl." She had an image in her mind of Michele at the dance that night waving good-bye. She had failed to hug her in front of her friends. Her heart felt as if it was being crushed inside of her.

Pink struggled out of her embrace. "I feel sick," he said. "Let me sit."

Lillie clung to his arm and he fell heavily onto the sofa. She sat down beside him. Gray offered her the glass of water, but she turned it away. He stood helplessly by, with panic in his eyes.

Royce Ansley stood up. "I have to get back down there. There's a deputy with her now, and the coroner is on his way." He could see that his words were passing virtually unheard by the stricken couple on the couch. "I'll let you know when we know anything."

Lillie blinked up at him. "Oh, all right," she said in a numb, distracted voice. She got up from the sofa and started to shuffle toward the door as if to see him out.

"Never mind," Royce said quickly. "Please, please, sit down."

Lillie looked up at him. "Maybe it isn't Michele," she said.

"I'll be in touch with you," Royce repeated gently. "Meanwhile, somebody better call her daddy. Let him know what happened."

Lillie nodded. "I'll call him," she said in a dull voice. Jordan Hill had a right to know. He was Michele's natural father, after all. And in fact, he had tried to be a real father to her in the last ten years or so. Calling her. Sending her presents. Having her come to New York to visit him.

It was an hour later in New York City. Nearly two in the morning. Lillie wondered if she would be awakening him with those words. Michele is dead. For so long she had lived in fear of those same words. She had bedded down in cots beside Michele's hospital bed, and she had prayed that no one would waken her in the night with those words. And now, when the danger was long since past, when her guard was relaxed, the news had come, striking her, stunning her with the force of a whirlwind.

She would call Jordan. She would awaken him and say

the words, but they were not real. She could not feel the reality of it. Despite all the evidence around her, she thought she might look out the door again and see her daughter coming up the steps, dragging the skirts of a rose-pink ballgown, her child's face glowing like a bright oval wafer in the moonlight.

CHAPTER 2

It was two in the morning but Jordan Hill was not asleep, although he pretended to be. The girl in the bed beside him sat up and shook her head so that her abundant, wavy hair, the color of a brown-edged sugar cookie, resumed the windblown shape it had lost by being matted on the pillow. She reached down to the end of the bed for his shirt, which lay crumpled there, and pulled it on but didn't bother to button it. After climbing out of the bed, the girl walked gingerly across the bare wooden floor, past the waist-high bookcases that served as a divider between the bed and the combination living room–kitchen in the long, narrow studio apartment. Bending down to reach the half refrigerator below the sink, she suddenly let out a shriek.

Jordan propped himself up on one elbow and called out, "What's the matter?"

The girl came back to the bed, carrying an open bottle of beer. She took a swig and offered the bottle to him. Jordan smoothed the corner of his mustache and shook his head. "There's a roach in the sink," she said indignantly.

"Well, I hope you didn't scare him off hollerin' like that, Amanda."

The girl made a face at him and then sat down on the end of the bed. She lifted up one dainty foot and frowned at the grime that had collected on it in her brief trip to the refrigerator. The blue work shirt slipped becomingly off one shoulder as she twisted her shapely calf to examine her foot. She was in her mid-twenties and her body was without a ripple or a blemish. Jordan pulled the sheet up over himself, suddenly conscious of the gray hairs on his chest. "I'm not a great housekeeper," he admitted.

Still holding her foot, Amanda scanned the walls of the dimly lit apartment with a critical gaze. The room was neat, but he had never tried to decorate it. There were a few theatrical posters on the walls. He always meant to get them framed, but by now the edges were curling around the push pins that held them up. Otherwise, the sparsely furnished room was strictly functional. The walls, once white, were graying, and plaster bubbled beneath the windows and along the cracks in the ceiling of the ground-floor apartment.

Amanda looked back at him. "Didn't you used to have a series?" she asked.

"Two seasons," he said. "NBC."

The girl let go of her foot and picked up the beer bottle again, wiping off the bottom of it with the tail of Jordan's shirt. "You've been on the soap for a while, haven't you?"

Jordan had to think for a minute. "About three years now."

"Well, what did you do with the money?" she asked. "Snort it away?"

Jordan winced at the bluntness of the question. "No," he said. "I don't do that stuff."

Amanda nodded and looked around again. "Somehow I pictured you in something a little . . . well, you know, newer," she said. "Maybe a West Side co-op or something. That's what I'm going to get if I ever get a soap. I'm going to invest in real estate, right off the bat."

"They're a good investment," Jordan said politely. He hesitated a moment, taking a last speculative look at the lithe body displayed unselfconsciously in his old shirt, and then got out of bed and pulled on a pair of sweat pants. "I'm going to make some coffee," he said. "Do you want some?"

"At this hour?" she said. "I wouldn't sleep. I've got to look good tomorrow. I've got an audition. I told you, remember?"

"Oh, yeah," said Jordan, standing by the sink, running water into a kettle. "The Manhattan theater club."

He'd had a good time in bed with her. She was eager, expert, and businesslike in the way that younger women tended to be. But he didn't really feel like talking now, and he could tell that she was gearing up for the get-acquainted discussion that, in the old days, used to *precede* getting into bed. They had done a play reading together about a month ago, and then tonight he'd run into her having a hamburger with a couple of gay guys when he stopped for a beer at Montana's Eve over on Seventh Avenue.

"So, what *did* you do with the money?" she asked.

Jordan stifled a sigh and put a filter in the drip pot. "I've got a farmhouse up in Green County. I spend most of my free time up there. It reminds me of home."

Amanda got up off the bed and began to pad around the apartment, squinting at his book titles and giving his papers and playbills a desultory inspection. "I can tell you have a little accent," she said. "Where are you from?"

"Tennessee."

"Oh," she said. "I'm from San Diego. It probably seems funny to you, my coming to New York when I was so close to L.A. But I wanted to get into some serious theater and really learn my craft, you know. And I really like it here. I like the energy."

"You sure you don't want coffee?" Jordan asked, pouring himself a steaming mug.

"No," she said. She plunked the beer bottle down on top of one of his stereo speakers and shrugged off the work shirt. "I've got to get going." She picked up her silk top from the well-worn Persian area rug and shook it out. Then she slid it on. Jordan turned in time to see her small, perfect breasts disappear from view beneath the expensive fabric.

"You're leaving?" he said.

Amanda wriggled into her skin-tight stirrup-footed pants and sat down on a straight-backed chair to pull on her low lizard-skin boots. "That call is really early tomorrow and all my makeup and stuff is at home."

"Ah," Jordan said guardedly, not wanting to sound too relieved. "Well, I'm sure glad I ran into you tonight." It was true. He was glad. But he was also glad to have the rest of the night to himself, to know that he would be waking up without having to face any awkward conversation or careful euphemisms about what it all meant.

Amanda withdrew a round mirror from her purse and gazed into it, wetting her lips. Then she zigzagged her polished fingertips, like an Afro pick through her fulsome hair.

"You look great," Jordan said sincerely. He was suddenly aware of the slight thickening around his waist, and he crossed his arms over his chest.

"It was fun," she said. "Maybe we can do it again sometime."

"I'll give you a call," he said.

"I may have some free time this weekend."

Jordan felt her trying to steer him, like a rudder. He veered out of it expertly with the standard excuse. "I'll be out at my agent's house in the Hamptons. He wants me to meet a couple of people."

"Oh," said Amanda, nodding knowingly. She walked over to the bookcase and picked up the bracelets she had left there. She peered at a photo in a cardboard frame that was wedged between his alarm clock and an ashtray. "You like them young," she observed slyly.

Jordan's dark, almost sullen eyes lit up. "My daughter. Pretty, isn't she?"

"You were married?"

"Briefly. Years ago. Her name is Michele."

Amanda cocked her head to one side. "She is cute. But that hair. She needs to have a good haircut. I could take her to my salon. They'd really do her right. Let me know the next time she's coming in to town."

"I don't know," he said. "I usually take her fishing."

"Fishing?" Amanda laughed as if that were the most preposterous idea she had ever heard.

Jordan shrugged. "Up in the country. She likes fishing."

Amanda put the picture down and walked over to him. "With all those disgusting worms and everything? I can't believe it." She turned her face up to his, and her fingers played across his bare chest. Jordan's stomach felt suddenly sour from the coffee and the tension of their encounter. It was always awkward, once the urgency of the moment had passed.

He bent down to kiss her and felt her lips linger on his for a minute. He hoped she was not going to change her mind about staying. "Maybe you want to come back to bed," he said.

Amanda shook her head, content that he had asked. "Can't," she said. "I won't get any beauty sleep with you." She walked over to the door and he opened it for her, looking out into the hallway with its yellowed paint and worn linoleum.

"Have you got cab money?" he asked.

"Of course."

He kissed her again, more warmly this time. Now that she was actually on her way, he felt stirred again by the scent and the shape of her body. "Good luck tomorrow," he said.

She tickled his upper lip below the mustache with her tongue. "I'll let you know how it turns out."

"Why don't you wait a minute? I'll slip on some clothes and walk out with you. I want to make sure you get a cab all right."

"I'll be fine," she said. "I'm just going one block over to Sixth." He could see that she was pleased with the offer.

"No, you better wait," he said.

"Southern gentlemen." She sniffed, but she was grinning.

Some Southern gentleman, Jordan thought as he rooted through his pile of clothes on the chair for a pair of pants and a sweatshirt. It used to be that if you slept with a girl and didn't marry her, you were considered a bum. Now, if you had your way with her and walked her to the corner in the middle of the night, you were practically a hero.

"All right," he said, slipping into his moccasins, "let's go." As he pulled the door shut behind him, the phone in the apartment began to ring. He and Amanda looked at one another. Then he looked at his watch. "It's nearly two o'clock," he said, and a little frisson of fear ran through him. "I better get it."

Amanda shrugged. "I don't need an escort," she said coolly, hiking the strap of her pocketbook up on her shoulder as if it were a rifle.

"Why don't you wait?" he said, fumbling with the keys in the lock.

"Oh, it's probably some old flame," she said airily, but she stood there poised, waiting for a denial.

Jordan was already through the door. It's bad news, he thought. It could only be bad news at this hour. His first thought was of his mother. She was nearly seventy now. She lived alone in Felton, although his older sister, Jeni Rae, lived in Chattanooga, which wasn't far. His mother was healthy, but anything could happen at that age.

"I guess I'll head out," Amanda said uncertainly. She took a pair of sunglasses out of her purse and put them on, even though it was the middle of the night.

"Okay, okay," Jordan called out. He said a silent prayer

for his mother as he stumbled across the clothes on the floor toward the phone. Just as he lifted the receiver, his gaze fell on the picture of Michele. For a moment his heart froze. Then he dismissed it. She was young and, at long last, healthy and perfect. Her whole life lay ahead of her. No, he thought. Maybe it was a friend. Or somebody from the soap who'd had a few and needed to talk. Everybody had problems they wanted to unload. And for an actor, two in the morning wasn't that late. That's right, he reminded himself. That's right. It's not that late. "Hello," he said calmly into the phone.

Amanda thrust her lower lip out and looked at him with narrowed eyes behind her dark glasses. She gave a little huffy sigh, but he did not turn around. She slammed the door behind her.

Jordan held the phone to his ear and listened to Lillie's words. He asked a few questions and said he understood. And he thanked her for calling him. Then he fumbled, blindly, with the telephone receiver until he finally was able to hang it up, and he sat down in a chair in the corner of the room.

All night he sat there silent, alone, in a rage, in a sweat, and, finally, as the dawn came, in a fearful recognition of his loss. For the one good, right thing he was trying to do in his life was over. His only child was gone.

CHAPTER 3

S ometime during the night Lillie had lain down on her
bed for an hour or two, but she did not sleep. The
sheriff had forbidden her and Pink to return to the crime
scene with him or to go to the morgue. The doctor had
come in the middle of the night but she'd refused the
tranquilizer he prescribed. No one would allow her to
leave the house and so, at four in the morning, she began
to clean it.

Now the kitchen windows were bare. Stripped of their
covering, they glinted in the harsh light of the day. The
cotton eyelet curtains, still damp from the morning washing, were heaped in a plastic laundry basket on the kitchen
table. In the middle of the floor, Lillie bent over the ironing board, meticulously pressing the first set of valances

into crisp perfection. She heard the knock at the back door but she did not look up from her task.

"Grayson," she said.

"Yes'm . . ." Grayson, who was slumped over the kitchen table, his smooth forehead sunk in his hand, got up at once and headed toward the back door. Before he had a chance to reach it, the door opened and Brenda Daniels burst into the kitchen. Her frosted blond hair was blowzy, the lines around her mouth and on her forehead looked as if they had been dug with an awl. She was clutching a foil-covered plate. She stopped still and stared at her friend.

"Lillie, what on earth are you doing?" she exclaimed.

Lillie looked up at her almost fearfully, her dark eyes sunken in her pale face. The iron trembled in her clenched fist. Her dark hair stood out in wild curls around her head. "I'm ironing."

"She's been like this all morning," Grayson said tiredly.

"Put that away, honey," said Brenda.

Lillie set the iron carefully down on the trivet and walked to her friend. The two women clung together. Brenda sobbed while Lillie stared, dry-eyed, over her shoulder.

"Oh, Lillie-Lou," Brenda whispered, using a name she hadn't called her friend since childhood. "I can't believe it. I can't."

"Believe it," Lillie said in a soft voice.

"Sit down here," said Brenda, guiding a reluctant Lillie to one of the kitchen chairs. "Gray, are you all right, honey? That's buttermilk fudge," she said, pointing to the plate she had dropped on the table. "I know you like it, honey."

"Gray's been a good boy," Lillie said absently, as if she were describing a tot. "A big help to me. He helped me to get these curtains down. He's gonna help me get them back up when I'm done."

Lillie was drumming her fingers impatiently on the table. Brenda took her friend's restless hand and kneaded it. "How is Pink coping?"

Lillie shrugged. "I don't know. He's . . . he went back over to the . . . there this morning."

"Why? Oh, my God, how could he stand to be near there?"

"He wanted to see the sheriff. I guess he just wants to know if they've found anything. You know, you feel so helpless. You just can't quite believe that there's someone out there, you know, taking a walk, or reading the paper, or enjoying his lunch, that did this thing."

"I know," said Brenda, "I know. I'd kill him myself. So they still think it was that Ronnie Lee Partin. That's what the TV said."

"I don't know, Brenda. I suppose it's possible. But why? Why?"

"Because he's an animal," Grayson said, picking up a piece of fudge.

"Well," said Brenda, glancing apologetically at Gray, "was she . . . you know . . . molested?"

"The coroner examined her at the scene last night. He didn't think so, according to the sheriff," Lillie said in a tight voice. "They can tell more when . . . the autopsy. But no, probably not."

"Thank God," said Brenda.

"This is great fudge, Aunt Brenda," said Grayson.

"I'm glad, darlin'. You enjoy it. But what was she doing

45

over there at the Arches at that time of night? Grayson, do you know why she would have gone down there?"

Grayson put the fudge plate down on the table and stared into it. "She was supposed to come home with me. I was just hanging around with some kids. I didn't see her for a while. I figured she went home. I don't know why she went down there. It's in the opposite direction from home."

"Unless she was coming home," said Brenda, "and someone picked her up."

"I don't know," Lillie said wearily. "I can't think now."

"Of course you can't," said Brenda. "I'm sorry."

The front doorbell rang. "Gray," said Lillie.

"Yes'm." He was on his feet and out the door before she had finished. She smiled sadly at his disappearing figure. "He's running interference for me. I can't face people. And it started hours ago. I don't know how people found out so fast." Lillie gestured vaguely to the counter, which was dense with covered dishes and plates of food. "People want to help," she said.

"I know," said Brenda. "I had to come when I heard from Pink. But why didn't you call me last night, honey?"

Lillie smiled weakly at her friend. "I know you and your beauty sleep."

Brenda began to cry again, weeping into the soggy Kleenex in her hand. "It just can't be, Lillie. That little smidge of a thing. And all you went through. Before you married Pink you and I took her to that hospital in Pittsburgh, remember?"

Lillie nodded and her narrow shoulders started shaking. Tears twinkled in her dark eyes and ran down her cheeks.

Brenda clasped her friend's hands. "You go ahead and cry, honey. You have to cry. You need to."

"I need to finish these curtains," Lillie said, weeping.

"Oh, for God's sakes, you crazy woman," Brenda exclaimed. "I'll finish the damned curtains. Washing the curtains," she fumed, getting up and extracting the tangled wad of fabric from the basket.

Grayson appeared in the kitchen doorway, his face set in a stony expression. "You've got company," he said.

Lillie started to protest but Gray interrupted her. "He wouldn't leave."

Lillie looked up and saw the man standing in the doorway behind Grayson. The first thing she thought was how odd it was to see Jordan Hill in a tie. He never wore a tie, not even on the day they were married. His eyes were puffy, but his drawn, handsome face was composed.

Brenda slapped the curtain down on the ironing board and jerked the iron off the trivet. "Well, well," she said in a chilly voice. "Nice of *you* to come."

"Hello, Brenda," he said, but he was looking into Lillie's eyes. Then he shook his head and dropped his gaze to the floor. He shoved his hands into his pants pockets. "Lillie," he said in almost a whisper.

She could feel the inflection of his voice like a dark, silent bell, sounding all the way through her, her name spoken as if it were a plea. There was a blissful time in her life, a rapturous time when Michele was conceived, when she could deny him nothing if he spoke her name. The odd sense of déjà vu died away, and her heart felt wintry and gray again.

"Are you all right?" he asked.

Lillie shrugged and looked away from him.

"Is there any news?"

"No, nothing."

"My mama wanted to come but the doc made her take a sedative. She's taking this so hard."

"I know, I called her," Lillie said numbly. "I don't want her to get sick. The funeral will be bad enough for her."

"I need to know the arrangements," said Jordan. "Is everything settled?"

Lillie looked faintly surprised. In a cool voice she said, "If there's anything special you want for her . . ."

"No, no, whatever you decide will be fine."

The room fell silent and then Gray said in a loud, stilted voice, "My mother is tired."

"The funeral is tomorrow," said Lillie. "There will be no viewing. That's all we know right now. I'll call you with all the arrangements."

"Okay," said Jordan. "I'm over at my mother's." He looked from Brenda to Grayson, who had edged over to Lillie and were surrounding her like sentries. "I better be going."

"Give Miss Bessie my love," Lillie said stiffly.

Jordan nodded. "Her only grandchild."

"Don't," said Lillie, holding up a hand as if to stay him.

The back door opened and Pink came in. He stopped short at the sight of Jordan Hill in his house. The two men stared at one another, neither one sure whether to offer condolences or to accept them. Jordan broke the silence.

"Do we know anything yet?"

"They haven't caught that bastard yet," said Pink, "if that's what you mean."

"So the sheriff's pretty sure it was Partin," said Jordan.

"Of course it was Partin, for chrissakes," Pink muttered.

An uneasy silence fell over the room. Lillie glanced up at Jordan. "We'll be in touch with you," she said stiffly.

Jordan nodded and turned to go. Then he looked back at Pink. "You always took such good care of her, Pink," he said. "She always said so."

Pink looked as if he wanted to lunge at the other man's throat. "What's that? A sick joke?" he cried.

Jordan shook his head wearily and looked back at Lillie. "Never mind," he said. "I'll be at my mother's."

Lillie could feel his eyes on her but she did not look up. She understood what he meant. He had only been trying to console Pink. But there was no point in trying to explain it. His words of consolation were not welcome here. She thought how old and haggard she must look to him right now and was relieved when she heard the door close behind him.

CHAPTER 4

A steady drizzle began before dawn on Tuesday morning, and it was still coming down as people gathered outside the River of Jordan Baptist Church, patiently waiting their turn to be seated inside for the funeral service. It was a chilly rain, the first harbinger of autumn in Cress County, and it seeped under the collars of the waiting mourners, as church elders, soberly dressed in dark suits, directed the crush of people into the church and tried to figure out how to accommodate them all.

Allene Starnes solemnly approached the crowd of teenage boys and girls who were huddled under their umbrellas on the church lawn. She hugged a couple of the other girls who were already crying. The boys stood apart looking uncomfortable in their ties. All the high-school students had been officially excused today, and it looked to

Allene as if half of Cress County had taken the morning off from work to attend the funeral. Allene's stomach was in knots. She had agonized over what to wear. She didn't own anything black because her mother said it was too sophisticated. She had settled on a navy-blue Sunday dress, which her mother assured her was suitable. It was just so important to her to show her sorrow for Grayson. She hadn't known Michele too well. Michele was kind of quiet, and her girlfriends were not as popular as Gray's crowd. But it twisted Allene's heart to think of the anguish of losing a sister. She could not even imagine it.

After she had heard about the murder she had been almost too afraid to call. She wanted desperately to help him, to comfort him, but she didn't think she could find any words that would be right. Finally she had screwed up all her courage and ridden her bike over to the house to see him. He answered the door with a haunted, wary look in his eyes, and her heart ached for him. She tried to get him to talk to her but he went into his room and just sat on the edge of his bed, playing his radio and gazing vacantly past her, as if he were all alone. Her young body strained frantically toward him, as if she were a divining rod and Grayson were some hidden stream, but she could not touch him. He stared ahead, drumming his fingers to the music. Her mother told her, when she came home disconsolate, that everyone handled grief in their own way.

Now Allene stood among her friends, scanning the crowd for that beloved blond head, but she did not see it. She noticed, as she looked around, that a pretty girl with hair as dark and glossy as sealskin had walked up and was standing at the edge of the teenage group. Allene recognized her. It was a girl new this fall, a junior transferred from Chicago, named Emily Crowell. She looked uncomfortable and out of place. No one was speaking to her. It was nice of her to come, Allene thought. She excused herself from her friends and walked over to where the new girl stood. On a day like this, she thought, you have to remember how short life could be, how important it is to be kind to one another.

The service was due to start at ten, but because of the size of the crowd, extra chairs were being set up in the aisles and in the parish hall, where the service could be heard over a loudspeaker. From the kitchen in the church basement, the smell of warm ham and cooking greens wafted up through the building as the women of the congregation prepared food for the mourners. The knell of the funeral bells in the steeple seemed to urge haste.

In the backseat of the car across the road from the church, Lillie, Pink, and Grayson watched in silence. The hearse was parked in front of them. As they stared out the smoky windows they saw a long, silver-blue Cadillac with a Texas license plate pull up in front of the church and Pink's older brother, Haynes, and his wife, Elna, emerged from the front seat. When Haynes and Elna showed up at their house the night before, Haynes was wearing ostrich-skin cowboy boots and a turquoise ring with a nugget the size of a walnut. Haynes Burdette had made a fortune in the automobile business in Houston. He and Elna and their three children lived in a mansion with a heated swimming pool and a gazebo. Pink rarely saw his brother, but when he did it always had a bad effect on him, Lillie thought. He would talk compulsively for a few days about how smart and successful Haynes was, and then a period of depression was sure to follow.

"Look at that jacket," said Pink. "That's Ultrasuede. Doesn't he see it's raining?"

Who cares? Lillie thought wearily, but she didn't say it. It just seemed so completely trivial. She watched Haynes precede Elna up the steps to the church. In the rental car that pulled up behind the Cadillac Lillie saw her mother, Jo Evelyn, and her stepfather, Ron Henkle. They had flown up from Florida, where they lived in a condo at Cocoa Beach. Jo Evelyn was perfectly coiffed and turned out as always. People often flattered her by pretending to believe she was Lillie's sister, and Jo Evelyn never doubted their sincerity. Ron held an umbrella protectively over his wife's blond head as they climbed the steps. The crowd was somehow being squeezed into the country church and Shirley Lynch, Felton's female undertaker, decided it was time to start. She walked back from the hearse to the family's car and tapped on the window.

"I think we'll get started," she said gently. "Y'all ready?"

Pink looked at Lillie, who sat motionless, swathed in black. "Honey?"

Lillie nodded.

Shirley Lynch gave the car hood a thump, as if of encouragement, and returned to the hearse. The driver pulled it slowly around to the front of the church and then walked around to open up the back. Lillie watched as the young pallbearers assembled and the coffin was rolled out.

There had been no wake. The coffin had been kept closed. It was not that the fatal blows had so devastated the appearance of Michele's head. There had not been much blood at all. And Shirley had skillfully, painstakingly concealed the bruises. The deadly damage had been internal. But despite her pride in her cosmetic skills, Shirley had advised, in her kind, matter-of-fact way, that they keep it closed. "People are curious," she had said with a shrug. "It's human nature."

Shirley's advice had been unnecessary. Lillie had already decided that no one would have a chance to gape at her baby.

"Let's go," said Pink. He got out of the car and helped Lillie out. Grayson, his face drawn and tight, still looked stunning in his dark blazer, his blond hair bright against the gray sky. He crossed the street with his parents, and they all waited at the foot of the church stairs as the pallbearers lifted the coffin and bore it up the steps. From inside the church, the sad strains of "Precious Memories," sung by quavering voices, drifted out to them.

Lillie's gaze was fastened on the coffin, but she became aware of Grayson shifting restlessly at her side, muttering angrily. At first she tried to ignore it, but his words were like a persistent street noise, awakening her from sleep. She turned a blank face to him. "What?" she said.

"What do they think they're doing here?" Grayson demanded. "I don't believe this."

Lillie turned and looked. The family of Ronnie Lee Partin was approaching the church. Ronnie Lee's brother, Dwight, dressed in his Sunday clothes, held his aged mother, Ora, by the arm. Dwight's wife, Debbie, who was little older than Michele had been, walked beside them with her eyes downcast, holding together the front of a lavender raincoat that did not quite close around her stomach, distended by pregnancy. The Partins, including Ronnie Lee when he was not incarcerated, lived together in a trailer outside of town and were considered by many to be white trash, although Dwight held down a respectable job as a furniture delivery man, despite his lack of formal education. Dwight was a burly young man with an amiable personality. Unlike his brother, he had never been in trouble with the law, and most folks in town liked him. He was leading his family now, with a look of grim determination, toward the doors of the church. He pretended not to hear Grayson's remarks, although his wife looked up fearfully.

"They've got a nerve," Grayson said. "Coming here."

"Grayson, hush," said Lillie.

Dwight Partin's broad face flushed red, but he ignored the words. A stillness descended on the people outside the church. Pink, who was shaking hands with a couple of the other men, turned and looked as his son left Lillie's side.

Grayson approached Dwight Partin and stood in his path. Dwight gripped his mother's frail arm and looked into Gray's ice-blue eyes.

"You shouldn't be here," said Grayson. "If it weren't for your brother, my sister would be alive."

A little gasp rippled through the onlookers. "Grayson, stop it," Lillie demanded. But the boy remained stubbornly in Dwight Partin's path.

"You heard me," he said.

Dwight did not reply. His mother tried to pull him along but Grayson moved sideways to block their progress.

"Pink," said Lillie, "get him back here." But Pink was staring at his son as if fascinated and, at the same time, a little frightened. At that moment Jordan, his mother, Miss Bessie Hill, and his older sister, Jeni Rae, who had taken the bus up from Chattanooga, approached the cluster of angry people. Miss Bessie immediately walked up to the elderly Ora Partin and took her by the arm, speaking gently to her. Grayson was momentarily flustered by the friendliness of the two old women, who appeared to be ignoring him. Jordan spoke quietly into Grayson's ear.

"Let's try to get through this without any trouble," he said.

Grayson turned on Jordan. "Don't you try and tell me what to do," he said, his handsome face pale with anger.

Sheriff Ansley, who had just arrived with his son, stepped in. Tyler hung back, looking ill at ease and hung over. His dark, unkempt hair curled over the collar of a torn leather jacket.

"What's the problem here?" Royce asked.

Pink was standing at Grayson's elbow. "There's no problem. Let's go in," he said to his son.

Grayson answered the sheriff in a quavering voice. "They don't belong here. Not after what his brother did."

"I told you we shouldn't come," Debbie Partin wailed.

"Just . . . hush, Debbie," said Dwight. "He don't know what he's talking about."

"You keep your accusations to yourself," Royce said severely to Grayson. "These people are here to pay their respects. You just let them be."

Pink took Grayson by the arm and started pulling him away.

Grayson flung back an angry look at Dwight Partin and then straightened the sleeve on his jacket where Pink had tugged at it.

Lillie's teeth had begun to chatter as she watched them. It was partly from the rain, which ran like a cold finger

56

down her back. Mostly it was her nerves, vibrating like the strings on a fiddle, and it took all her effort just to stand still. She had refused to take a tranquilizer. She had a vague idea that it was imperative to feel everything, to be alert, to suffer everything, as if that would somehow keep her closer to Michele. Now, as the beleaguered Partin family resolutely mounted the steps to the church, she felt strangely pitying of them. It had taken courage to come here today. They must have known what people were saying about them.

Pink was speaking in a low voice to the sheriff as the last of the mourners was ushered inside. Lillie noticed Allene Starnes edging reluctantly into the church, her eyes bathing Grayson in a tender gaze of sympathy before her red head disappeared into the dark vestibule. Royce Ansley turned and gave his son a grim, meaningful look that seemed to propel the recalcitrant boy forward to where Lillie stood shivering.

"Sorry, Miz Burdette," Tyler mumbled. Royce's gaze was fastened on his son as he nodded at Pink's words.

Lillie looked sadly at the boy with his sickly complexion, his hands stuffed into the pockets of his jeans. His manner was gruff, almost rude, but he had an air of secret woe about him that touched her heart. Losing his mother at such a young age had wounded him badly, Lillie thought. It must be awfully difficult for him to attend another funeral. Kids that age were frightened of funerals anyway. She put a hand out and squeezed his. His hand was ice-cold. He jumped at her touch and looked up at her with fear in his dark, bloodshot eyes.

"It's all right, Tyler," she said quickly. "Thank you for coming."

The boy looked away. He nodded briefly to Grayson and Pink and retreated behind his father.

"Let's go in," said Pink. The people huddled in the vestibule parted to make a path for the family. Lillie leaned gratefully on Grayson's sturdy young arm and they walked slowly down to the front pews. As she went to sit down she looked across the aisle and spotted Jordan seated between his mother and Jeni Rae.

Their eyes met and an unguarded flicker of sorrow passed between them. Lillie withdrew her gaze at once and looked at Bessie. The old woman barely reached Jordan's shoulder. She peered with tear-filled, failing eyes at the order of the service in her hands. Lillie felt her own tears well up again as she looked at her. Bessie had been a true grandmother to Michele, spoiling her, sewing her dresses, letting her try to help in the kitchen. She had been the grandmother that Jo Evelyn had never wanted to be. She had reminded Lillie of her own grandmother.

Pink twisted around in the pew. "What a turnout," he said.

Lillie could hear the pride in his voice and immediately she knew what he was thinking. She knew him too well. He was hoping Haynes would be impressed. He wanted his brother to think that this large crowd somehow reflected Pink's importance in this county. Lillie bit her lip to keep from saying something mean. He can't help it, she told herself. Leave him alone.

Her gaze was drawn back to the coffin as the Reverend Dale Luttrall took the pulpit. The reverend was in his sixties now. He had baptized Lillie and her children, and many of the people who sat in this church. He began the service in his familiar, sincere tones. Lillie heard the ebb and flow of the voices around her, but she kept having the eerie sensation that she was alone in a silent room. Just herself, and her child, confined forever in that coffin.

All of a sudden she noticed Grayson, who was seated beside her, look at his watch and then sigh softly and look back up at the altar. Lillie's head snapped up and she stared at him. She could feel her heart hammering with anger in her chest. "Is this boring you?" she whispered angrily. "Is there somewhere you have to be?"

Grayson drew back and stared at her, as if baffled by her question. "Come on, Mom. This is all like a bad dream. I'm sorry but I just wish it were over. I can't believe it's really happening."

He's right, she thought. It is a kind of torture to sit here, staring at that casket, knowing that this is the end. She felt him reach over and take her hand. She squeezed his hand and gave him a pained, fleeting smile.

"When something like this happens to us," said the Reverend Luttrall, "we feel angry. We ask, 'Why did God allow this to happen to our family?' We want someone to pay for this. For doing this terrible thing to our precious child.

"My friends, I cannot tell you why, for the Lord works in mysterious ways. But I will tell you this. That as long as you feel hatred, you will suffer. Revenge is not the answer. Forgiveness is the answer. We must learn to forgive because we will never find peace in our lives until we do.

"Michele has found her peace. This child—" The preacher's voice cracked for a moment, but he waited, silently, until he regained his composure. The sound of muffled weeping could be heard from all corners of the church. "This child sits with God now. She sits lightly beside him, one of his angels, and she whispers forgiveness in our ear."

Lillie's tears splashed down on her cold hands. Wedged between her husband and her son she wept for herself, for the emptiness that lay ahead of her without her Michele. On her left, Pink's stout frame shuddered with sobs. On her right, Grayson's dry hand clutched hers as if to break it.

CHAPTER 5

The day after Michele Burdette was buried, the Reverend Ephraim Davis grimly contemplated his options. He knew very well what his duty was, but he was resisting it. He had spent most of his long life avoiding the business of white people, and it had worked out for the best that way. He didn't ask anything of them, didn't get in their way, and most certainly did not seek or desire their company. In fact, he didn't think very much about them at all, if he could help it.

But ever since Monday morning, when he had heard the news on the radio as he was saying grace over his breakfast, he had been preoccupied with the murder of a white girl, and the strain was beginning to show. His blood pressure was up. He could feel it. And his regular medication wasn't helping. He'd been sleeping poorly.

Yesterday had been the funeral and he had avoided driving in that part of town. This morning he felt as if he couldn't avoid the issue for another day.

If he could only talk to Elizabeth, he thought. She was sensible and, in her own shy way, she was strong. Through the thirty years of their marriage he had trusted her with many a tricky problem. But Elizabeth had decided to stay in Memphis when he was called to fill in at the Felton parish for a month. The Reverend Davis was one of a dwindling lot of circuit preachers. Like his grandfather and his father, he traveled through the great state of Tennessee, visiting one small black parish after another, spreading the Word and enjoying the hospitality of the good people of each town. Unlike his grandfather, who drove a horse and buggy, Ephraim drove a two-tone green Ford station wagon. Sometimes Elizabeth came with him, but on these long visits, when he was filling in for quite a while, she stayed in Memphis with their daughter and their grandchildren. Elizabeth was used to her husband's weekend travels. It had been that way from the very beginning of their marriage when she had always gone along, liking the traveling and the church people they met. But as she got older she preferred to avoid extended stays in other people's houses. She liked to be in the comfort of their own home, in her own bed with the rose-patterned spread, and spend every free minute with the grandchildren. With their African names and their boldness, she found them exotic. Secretly it gave her pleasure to see that they did not have the same fears in the world as she.

In a way it was just as well, Ephraim thought. It would worry her terribly to know the problem he was in. Anything that had to do with violence scared her like a little rabbit. He had thought about calling her, but Bill and Clara Walker, who were putting him up, kept their phone in the front parlor, and he couldn't very well outline the situation to Elizabeth without the whole household hearing about it. No, he had had to keep his own counsel. But now, the day after that poor girl's funeral, his mind was made up.

It was incumbent on him to tell what he knew. He had seen the girl and he had seen the fellow who was most likely her killer that night. Not that he had suspected any such thing at the time. If he had, he could have prevented it. But there was no way to know. And it was too late for "what ifs." He walked into the kitchen where Clara Walker was cleaning up after breakfast.

"May I use your phone, sister?" he asked.

"Of course, Reverend. Our house is your house."

The Reverend Davis went into the parlor and dialed the county sheriff's office. He had the number memorized by now from thinking about calling it. When Francis Dunham answered, he asked for the sheriff.

"Sheriff's not here," said the dispatcher.

"Where can I reach him?" the reverend asked politely.

"He may not be back for a while," Francis replied. "He's over at the murder scene."

"All right, thank you," said the reverend. He hung up the phone and stood there lost in thought, stroking his grizzled cheek. Clara Walker came into the parlor, wiping her hands on her apron.

"I've got to go out, Clara," he said.

"Will you be back for lunch?" the old woman asked pleasantly.

"Oh, yes. Long before lunch. I hope," said the reverend.

On the morning after his daughter's funeral, Jordan Hill awoke in his boyhood bedroom. He could smell biscuits baking in the kitchen and the tinny radio was tuned to the gospel show that his mother had listened to for as long as he could remember. Her clear, small, deliberate voice faltered on the words of "When the Roll Is Called Up Yonder."

Jordan lay with his eyes closed and let the bittersweet ache of the past envelop him. Here, in this bed, he had dreamed of fame and he had burned with love. He had crept home to this bed on the night that Michele was conceived, meadow clover still in his hair from where he and Lillie had rolled in the summer night. They hadn't dared to stay out the whole night. They were too young. Their parents would guess. It was a shame, he thought. He wished now that they had slept there, as they wanted to, in that sweet-smelling field, in each other's arms. Before they knew it they were married and had a child, and then he had left.

He heard his mother tap on his door. "Breakfast, honey," she said, as she always had. And now here he was, back in that same narrow bed. Not married. Not a father. Not a dreamer.

"I'm coming," said Jordan, and he got up.

Jeni Rae was already at the table finishing a cup of coffee. Jordan kissed his mother's dry cheek and sat down opposite his sister, who looked at him with sad, nervous eyes.

"I have to go back today," she said apologetically. She had a good job, working with computers in Chattanooga.

"I know," said Jordan. He unfolded a napkin and took a biscuit, although he did not feel the least bit hungry. "I didn't even get to ask you. How's the new fella? Burt, right? Mama told me about him."

Jeni Rae looked up at her mother in exasperation. Bessie continued to busy herself around the stove, oblivious to the conversation, her eyes distant and pink from the intermittent weeping.

"He's okay," Jeni Rae said cautiously. "He's divorced. Pretty nice guy."

She had never had much luck with men. She was too smart for most of the Felton boys when she was growing up and not pretty enough to be proud of it. She would have to be considered a spinster now, Jordan thought, but he still had hopes that she would find someone and get married. It would suit her now, much better than it would have when she was young.

"Well, you tell him to treat you right or your little brother'll come after him," he said.

Jeni Rae smiled. "Burt's first wife had a crush on you. She used to watch your nighttime series."

"Well, a woman of good taste. And one of the few, I might add," said Jordan. "Still, he's well rid of her."

Jeni Rae smiled. "You ought to come on down to Chattanooga one of these days," she said. "I've got a pull-out sofa bed. You could meet him then."

"That'd be nice."

Bessie walked over to the table and put a cast-iron skillet down on a trivet on the table. "Fried corn," she said gently. "I know you don't get this up North."

"No, ma'am," said Jordan, taking a heaping spoonful and ladling it onto his biscuit, although his stomach churned at the sight of food. It was little enough to please her.

"Jordan, will you drive me to the bus?" Jeni Rae asked.

"I sure will," he said. "I'm going out anyway." Maybe that's why his stomach felt so bad, he thought. The thought of going over there, where it happened, made him feel clammy all over, but he meant to do it anyway. It was almost like something he had to prove to himself he could do.

"You're a good brother," she said, and she patted him on his graying head as she passed him on her way to her room.

The Old Stone Arch Bridge, known alternately as Three Arches or just the Arches, was located at the end of a short dirt road, not too far from Bride's Mill. At one time the sturdy old stone bridge had been part of the main route used by local farmers, but by now the mill was closed and the farmers drove their trucks on smooth bridges over modern highways. Trees and vegetation had overgrown the base of the Arches and nearly hid the bridge from view as you approached it. It was normally a quiet, deserted spot, but today the rutted road was dotted with cars. Three deputies, two in uniform and one in dungarees and a sweatshirt, scoured the bushes and the decaying riverbank where Michele Burdette had died. The rain from the day before had left the area muddy, and their clothes were already dirty as they rooted through the area in search of a murder weapon. A number of cars came and went at intervals along the road as people arrived to look.

NO WAY HOME

This familiar, all but forgotten spot had taken on new interest now that a murder had been done there. People came to stare and to shudder, as they imagined the body on the riverbank, as it had been described in the county paper, a frail girl facedown in the muddy weeds, one leg twisted by the trunk of the weeping willow tree, arms outstretched to the bridge abutment, her head bashed by force of some blunt object not yet in evidence.

The Reverend Ephraim Davis slowed his Ford wagon at the top of the street and pulled over. He had not come to gawk or to speculate, and it bothered him to see the parade of people coming and going. He could see them shaking their heads and murmuring to one another as they returned to their cars, but he knew that beneath that display of dismay they found it exciting. Ah well, he thought, it's only human to be that way, and this is a small town. An event like this murder is not taken matter-of-factly.

All the Reverend Davis wanted to do was to get out of his car, walk down there, find the sheriff, and tell him what he had seen. Then he could go home with a clear conscience. It seemed simple enough, and yet the preacher remained in his car. Another car pulled up, a brand-new Mercury Marquis, and the reverend recognized the man who got out. He was the local pharmacist, Bomar Flood. The wiry druggist was wearing a bow tie and Wallabees, and he fairly bounced down the road toward the bridge. The reverend recognized him because he had gone into the pharmacy to get a refill on his high blood pressure medication, and when he had admitted to the inquiring druggist that he was under a lot of stress, the nosy but nonetheless kindly man had pressed upon him some vitamin samples that he recommended to help relieve tension. The reverend had tried the vitamins, but he knew there was no capsule that could relieve his symptoms.

The Reverend Davis sighed and chewed his lip. A family was emerging from the road now, the man in a flannel work shirt, the wife shepherding her two kids as if they had just taken them to an amusement park. Why, he wondered, had it been God's will that he should see what he had that night? He was virtually a stranger in this county, and a black man to boot.

He tried to imagine himself telling it to the sheriff the way it happened. Founders Day had been festive and tiring. The black people of Felton held their own fish fry to celebrate, and in this case, segregation was a matter of personal taste. The Reverend Davis had eaten his fill and then decided to take a basket of the leftovers to a shut-in from the parish who lived outside town. On his way home from seeing the old woman he was tired from the day, and her peach wine, and half indignant for her difficulties, so he was distracted and somehow got on a road he didn't recognize. As he drove slowly along, looking for a turn he was familiar with, he saw the white girl walking down the road up ahead.

Ordinarily he would not have stopped to ask a white girl for directions. It was the kind of thing that could start trouble. He knew better, but he was tired, and there was no one else around, so he pulled over and called to her, politely.

What he remembered most was that she smiled and didn't flinch when she saw that she was smiling at a black man on a lonely road. He was wearing his collar, and he was old. But that wouldn't matter to some. He explained quickly that he was lost and looking for Route 31. She told him to go up and turn in at the road to Three Arches Bridge and head back the way he came until he passed three lefts and then turn. He remembered that she leaned on the window of the car in a friendly, easy way, and he was struck by her eyes. They were calm and wise in the way of one who has known some suffering. He recalled thinking that about her.

Ephraim Davis shuddered. Maybe it had been a premonition about her. She had been murdered that very night. Even now it was hard to believe. She had been walking along, alone, in the direction of this very road, down to the bridge. Ephraim had thanked her for her help and he remembered that she said, "Good night, Reverend," and that had gladdened his heart. He was an optimistic man by nature and he found comfort in the ordinary, courteous exchanges between black and white people.

He had driven the car up to the entrance to this very road and turned in. As he was backing out, his headlights swept over a figure alongside the bridge, and he caught a glimpse of a startled face. A fellow taking a piss, he thought. He pulled out quickly and drove away, leaving the man to his privacy. Now, in retrospect, that brief moment took on a much more sinister meaning. She was a nice girl, a friendly girl, and someone had killed her that night, by that bridge.

A sharp rap on his car window made him jump and cry out. He looked up and saw a young deputy peering at him with narrowed eyes, preparing to rap again on the glass with the butt of his service revolver. The Reverend Davis stared wide-eyed at the man, who indicated that he should roll down his window. Reluctantly the reverend complied.

He stared at the deputy as sweat beaded in the folds of his coffee-colored forehead.

"Get out of the car," the deputy demanded.

The reverend licked his lips and opened the car door.

"Slowly," the deputy ordered him.

Ephraim Davis struggled out from behind the wheel and stood on the gravel beside the car.

"What's your business here?" asked the deputy, Wallace Reynolds. "You have some reason to be hanging around here?"

"Nosir," Ephraim replied automatically. "Just passing by."

"It looked like you were parked there to me."

Ephraim could feel his heart thudding arrhythmically. "I was just curious. Like these other folks," he said.

"If you've got no business, you just move along," said Wallace, ignoring the reference to the other onlookers, who seemed to be coming and going undisturbed.

The reverend immediately got back into the car and turned the key in the ignition. It did not surprise him. It was what had held him back so long in the first place. The reverend loved the South. He loved the people, and the weather and the beautiful, fruitful land. It was his home and he would never leave it. But he was not a naive man. He knew how things were here. People got along fine as long as everybody followed the unwritten rules. If he spoke up about this girl, he was crossing the line. He knew, with a sickening certainty, what they would think. He was a black man who had accosted a white girl on a lonely, country road. That was all they would need to hear.

The Reverend Davis pulled away from the side of the

road and did not look back, even though he caught the glint of the deputy's badge in his rearview mirror as he made his escape.

Jordan Hill pulled his rental car up onto the gravelly patch just being vacated by the two-tone green Ford. He could see that the deputy, Wallace Reynolds, was writing down the number of the station wagon's license plate as it pulled away. Jordan got out of his car and walked to the top of the dirt road. He hadn't expected to find all these cops and rubberneckers. Seeing it angered him. He had a sudden impulse to go up to people and shove them back, tell them to stop staring at the place where his daughter had been killed. At the same time he realized that he had become too used to New York, where murder came and went with the frequency of a newspaper. You cleaned up after them quickly, to make room for the next. People did not stop to linger and consider such a thing as a young girl's murder for long.

The deputy who had been copying the license number shoved his pad in his pocket and started past Jordan down toward the bridge. He glanced over at Jordan.

"Is the sheriff here?" Jordan asked.

Wallace nodded. "Down yonder."

Jordan thanked him and walked down the road. In the clearing near the bridge he saw Royce Ansley and Bomar Flood. Both men looked up at his approach. Bomar reached a skinny hand out and Jordan shook it.

"Well, Jordan Hill," Bomar said as he pumped Jordan's hand. "It's been a long time."

Royce just stared at him with tired gray eyes.

"I didn't get a chance to speak to you at the funeral,"

Bomar went on. "How are things going for you up in New York?"

"Fine, thank you," Jordan said grimly.

Bomar still gripped his hand. "Such sad, sad circumstances that bring you home, though," he said. Bomar's eyes twinkled with tears as he looked out across the shallow muddy river. Jordan had known Bomar all his life. He was a foolish, sentimental old busybody who was also one of the shrewdest, most capable businessmen in the county.

Jordan managed to free his hand and turned to Royce. "You found her," he said in a flat voice to the sheriff.

"Over there," said Royce. A huge weeping willow tree hung low over the bridge, its long slender fronds nearly touching the water's surface. The sheriff indicated the space between the tree and the bridgehead. "She was lying there."

Jordan looked at the spot. A deputy was squatted down there, using a flashlight to search the loamy riverbank beneath the willow.

"They're still looking for the weapon," Bomar offered helpfully.

"I see," Jordan said evenly. "Have you found anything else? Sometimes fibers or hairs and such can be useful . . ."

"We know about lab analysis, Mr. Hill," the sheriff said sarcastically. "The twentieth century has arrived down here in little old Cress County, Tennessee."

"That Ronnie Lee Partin," Bomar said nervously, shaking his head. "We knew he'd gone bad, but this . . ."

The sheriff looked sharply at the pharmacist. "Don't be adding to these rumors about Ronnie Lee. People are getting all worked up and we've got nothing that says it was him that did it."

Jordan looked at the sheriff in surprise. "You don't think he did it?"

Wallace Reynolds ambled over to where they stood and looked out across the river. Beside the young deputy, Royce looked haggard and weary even though, Jordan calculated, he was only in his mid-fifties. He was a far cry from the clear-eyed, broad-shouldered lawman Jordan had romanticized in his youth.

"She wasn't raped," said the sheriff. "That's the only reason I know of that a jailbird on the run would stop to bother about a young girl. Otherwise he'd just keep moving."

"That makes sense," said Jordan.

Wallace frowned at the sheriff's words. Then he said in a quiet, stubborn voice, "Well, I think he did it."

"A lot of folks agree with you on that, Wallace," Bomar said.

Royce sighed. "One thing's for sure. We better find that boy before he gets himself lynched."

A silence fell over them. Bomar turned to Jordan. "So, how long are you staying around with us?"

"I'll be here until next week," said Jordan.

"I heard you're going to give a little talk over at the high school," Bomar said.

Jordan marveled to himself at the man's ear for gossip. "Yes," he said, "the music teacher cornered me after the funeral."

"Oh, Miss Jones," said Bomar. "She replaced Lulene."

Lulene Ansley, the sheriff's late wife, had taught English and drama at the county high when Jordan was a student there. She had been his favorite teacher, a quick-witted, worldly woman. She had been the first to tell Jordan he had talent, to encourage his ambitions. She was pregnant with Tyler the year Jordan graduated from high school. Miss Bessie had sent him the clippings when Lulene died of cancer some years back. It seemed far too late now to say to Royce how sorry he had been.

"There was no replacing Lulene," he said sincerely.

Royce looked at him angrily, as if he alone knew that, and then he looked away. "I can't stand around talking," he said.

"Sheriff," said Jordan. "I just want to know if there is anything I can do to help. About Michele."

Royce looked at him coldly. "It's a little late for that," he said. "You should have thought of that years ago."

Bomar Flood coughed nervously and looked away. Jordan stubbornly stood his ground. He hadn't expected to be pelted with rose petals. "That's as may be," he said calmly. "But right now I am angry and I want to know if there's anything I can do."

"Nothing," Royce said stiffly. "We're doing all that can be done. Everyone in this town is angry today. Believe me, we'll find the one."

CHAPTER 6

"Lillie, no," said Brenda, physically forcing her friend down into a chair. "It's too soon to start working. Loretta and I just stopped by to see how you were doing. It's only been two days since the funeral, for God's sakes."

Lillie rubbed her forehead wearily. "Brenda, I thought you would understand. I can't just sit here."

"I do understand," Brenda said seriously. "It's just like the goddamn curtains. You're trying to keep busy, I know, but you're exhausting yourself in the process. You need to rest."

"I can't rest," Lillie cried. "When I try to rest I keep seeing her, lying there, on that riverbank . . ."

"Honey, you got to rest," said Loretta Johnson, the

black woman Brenda and Lillie employed part-time. "It's too hard on you."

"Pink is working. Grayson went back to school," Lillie protested.

"Well, it's a different thing," Loretta said mildly. "You the mother."

The three women were silent for a moment. Brenda's eyes filled up with tears. Lillie gripped her old friend's hand.

"I'm trying to think of what's best for you, honey," said Brenda.

Lillie looked away from Brenda, out the window, past the Home Cookin' van, at the gloomy gray sky. The dampness outside seemed to be seeping through the walls of the house. "I know you are," she said. "But you can't know how lonely it is here."

"I'll come by and see you after we're done this afternoon," Brenda said.

"Thanks."

"Are you going to be okay?" Brenda asked.

"I'll be okay."

Loretta put on her nubby green coat and buttoned it up. "I swear the weather turned just after Founders Day," she said. "My bursitis is hurting me already."

"That was the last nice day," said Lillie. She held the door open for the two women and watched them depart. When the van was down the driveway and out of sight, she turned back to the house and tried to think what to do. She had cleaned all there was to clean. She went into Grayson's room to see if any of his clothes needed sewing. She opened his closet door and looked in. New clothes she had never seen hung on hangers, the tags still on them. A tennis racket stood in the closet.

When did he buy this stuff? she wondered. When did he take up tennis? A buttery leather overnight bag was tossed carelessly on the closet floor and shirts still in plastic stuck out of it. He and Pink must have been shopping. She knew that Pink spoiled him, and it always annoyed her. He had treated both children alike in his love and concern for them. But he did tend to buy things for Grayson on impulse. Things the boy didn't really need. Or he'd take him on an expensive shopping spree. It was something he would never do with Michele.

Still, looking at the new things in the closet, she wondered how she could have been so oblivious to it. Maybe between the business and Michele, she had not been paying enough attention to Grayson's life. As if to confirm this, she noticed the pile of sewing in the corner of his closet. No wonder he had to get new clothes, she thought. Everything that he owns needs fixing. She thought guiltily of the long hours she had spent fixing the rose-colored gown so that Michele could wear it in the pageant. It had been fun to do that, mending the lace and enjoying the feeling of the masses of rustling fabric piled on her lap. She liked to picture Michele wearing the gown while she worked. It was much more enjoyable than replacing shirt buttons and darning socks. But there was no excuse for neglecting her son like that, she thought. She bent down and gathered up the pile of clothes in her arms. I'll do better, she thought. It was just that he was so busy with his young life. He never seemed to notice whether she was taking care of him or not. Maybe that's why Pink bought him all these new things. Because he *did* notice she was neglecting Grayson.

Not anymore, she vowed. She took the sewing to the living room and sat down with it. She was finishing the last of the missing shirt buttons when the call came from the hospital. For years now Lillie had volunteered some of her time to help out at the Cress County Hospital. She felt a deep debt to the strangers in the various hospitals they had known who had spelled her in the worst times, reading to a frightened child so that Lillie could get some sleep, bringing coffee or rolls or newspapers in those long, grim days. Still, when she heard Mary Dean Hesketh, the volunteer coordinator, on the other end of the phone, Lillie felt a shock of surprise. It almost seemed like a voice from another life.

"I know this is a terrible time for all of y'all," Mary Dean began apologetically, "but I've got a gal here who needs your help, honey. She's got a real sick baby, and she needs a little hope. And I thought of you."

Lillie did not comment on the irony of it. When you spent a lot of time in a hospital, you learned to be matter-of-fact about life and death. Mary Dean was right. Lillie knew what it was to need a little hope. She was the right person to provide it. She told Mary Dean that she would come, and put on her clothes and drove to the hospital. It was not until she was in the hospital corridor, walking toward the volunteer office, that she realized she had not been out among people since the funeral. She felt unnerved by the way the world was going on with its business, as if nothing had happened. She felt suddenly ill, abnormal. She checked her buttons and zippers with fumbling fingers to be sure she had remembered to fasten herself into her clothes.

Mary Dean, a hefty woman with flawless skin, was seated behind her desk drinking a diet Sprite. Mary Dean did not seem to see anything amiss about her, Lillie noted as she sat down. She must look normal.

"Honey, you're an angel to come. This little gal is up in maternity and she is just scared to death."

"What's wrong with the baby?" Lillie asked.

"He's got a little bitty hole in his heart. They've got him in the ICU. I think they're going to move him to Nashville."

Lillie stared into the arrangement of plastic geraniums on Mary Dean's desk. "It sounds familiar, all right."

"That's right," Mary Dean said firmly. "You've got experience, Lillie. You understand these things. Now I want you to go in there and tell her how great the surgeons are these days, and how tough these kids can be."

Lillie looked up at her with wide, anguished eyes. "And what if I start to cry?"

"That's all right," Mary Dean said matter-of-factly. "She knows you're a mother. She'll figure you're crying in sympathy. That's why I'm sending you. Because she's only going to listen to another mother who's been there."

"And what if she asks how Michele is now?" Lillie asked evenly.

"Well, honey, you're going to have to pretend a little bit. You're gonna tell her that Michele is fine. You tell her how Michele was even sicker than her own little boy, and how she survived, and got well, and turned out fine. That part is true, isn't it?"

Lillie felt an unexpected sense of gratitude toward

Mary Dean. It felt good to hear someone say how well and strong her daughter had turned out. She realized that ever since it happened, people referred to Michele in those same hushed, pitying tones they had when she was sick. As if she were somehow tainted. A victim again.

"Go on, now," Mary Dean was saying. "And let me know how it went."

Lillie took the name and room number and rode the elevator to the maternity floor. She hesitated outside the room, afraid for a moment that she would not be able to do it. But when she walked in and saw the terrified mother's face, she felt suddenly calm. She thought how Michele would be proud of her if she got through it without tears.

The new mother was too distraught to notice the pallor of the comforting hand on her own. Her spirits seemed to flare as Lillie told her seriously that they would have to fight, she and her son, but that they could win. The woman pressed Lillie's hand to her hot cheek before Lillie left the room, and thanked her sincerely.

The visit gave Lillie a little lift. Preoccupied with her thoughts, Lillie passed through the doctors' waiting area outside the maternity wing and pressed the button for the elevator. She thought she heard someone call her name, and she turned around to see a pregnant woman struggle up from her chair and lumber toward her.

"Miz Burdette," said the young woman.

Lillie frowned. "Yes?"

"I've been waiting for you. I'm here for my checkup." She placed a protective hand on her own stomach. "I spotted you going in there and I waited. I've got to talk to you." The girl saw from the puzzled look on Lillie's face that the woman did not recognize her. "I'm Debbie Partin," she said. "Dwight Partin's wife."

"Oh, yes," Lillie said in a wary voice. She had a vague recollection from Michele's funeral of a frail, very pregnant girl in a lavender raincoat flattening herself against the church steps as Grayson and her husband nearly came to blows. Lillie pressed the elevator button again.

"Could we talk for a minute?" Debbie asked. "Sit down somewhere out of the way? I don't want anyone to see me talking to you, 'cause if word got back to Dwight that I was talking to you he'd figure out why and he'd kill me."

"Look," said Lillie, "there's nothing for us to say." She could feel herself beginning to tremble, like someone who has gotten up from a sickbed too soon. She checked the floor light on the elevator. It was sitting still in the lobby. "I have to go."

"It's about Ronnie Lee," the girl whispered. "It's important."

Lillie looked up at the floor number lights, which had begun to change.

"Over here." Debbie pointed.

With a sigh more of worry than exasperation, Lillie followed the young woman as she waddled toward an alcove in the waiting area where no one else was seated. She settled herself into the molded plastic seat of a chair. Lillie perched on the chair opposite her and looked longingly at the elevator doors as they opened and closed again. "What is it you want?" Lillie asked.

"Ronnie Lee didn't kill your little girl," Debbie said earnestly.

Lillie pressed the heels of her hands against the hard

edges of the chair seat. "Well, I don't know about that," she said.

Debbie leaned over and tugged at her sleeve like a child. "I know I'm right," she said. "Oh, Miz Burdette, you don't know what it's been like for us since your daughter was killed. Everyone is treating us so bad. Nobody'll talk to us, and kids come and throw rocks at our trailer at night, and I'm afraid Dwight is going to get fired from his job. He works down there at the discount furniture place, doing deliveries in their truck. And now they're saying they might not need him. They say it's slow, but really it's not. It's their busiest season. And we've got a baby almost here," she said in a pleading voice. "Dwight needs that job."

Lillie could hardly believe that this girl could be complaining to her about her troubles. She felt like reaching over and shaking her and saying "Don't you know my child is dead? How dare you complain to me?" She recalled her father saying to her once, "Everyone thinks his own troubles are the worst." She took a deep breath and composed herself.

"That's a shame," she said dully. "People shouldn't be blaming your husband for what his brother did. But that's human nature, I guess." She looked at the girl's stricken face and softened. "I guess, if you want me to call his boss at the furniture store I could do that. If that would help."

The girl sat up in her seat as if startled. "That's so sweet of you. Why, thank you. Really. With all you been through." She shook her head. "That is sweet. But no, that's not it. You see, I reckon this is going to go on as long as people think Ronnie Lee did this."

"Well, it seems as if he did," Lillie said coldly. She

stood up. "If you want me to call that man at the furniture store, I will. I don't believe you can ask any more of me than that."

"Dwight could prove Ronnie Lee didn't do it, but he won't," the girl blurted out. "He's protecting his hiding place."

Lillie stared at the girl, who began shaking her head. "He'll kill me if he finds out I told you. He'll kill me. But it's not fair. I can't stand any more of this. No one'll even talk to me," she wailed. She started to sniffle and pulled a tissue out of the fringed cotton bag she was carrying.

Lillie sat back down in the chair and continued to stare without speaking.

"Dwight's a good person, really. He's kind and nice. Not one bit like that shiftless brother of his. But he has this notion that he's always got to protect him. And Ronnie Lee doesn't deserve it. He's always been bad and now he's ruining everything for us and Dwight won't say boo. But I have to think of the baby," she said earnestly, looking at Lillie with imploring eyes. "That's why I'm telling this to you. You're a woman. You can understand. I don't want people calling my baby names. Making a poor baby suffer when all the time Dwight knows where Ronnie Lee is and knows everything that happened."

"What do you know about my daughter's murder?" Lillie asked in a low, icy voice.

Debbie took a deep breath. "All right. Just please promise me you won't tell anyone where you heard it."

"I'll try not to let anyone know," said Lillie.

"Because if Dwight found out—"

"Please," Lillie said through gritted teeth.

Debbie hiccuped and was silent for a moment. Lillie

watched her solemn, childlike face as she waited, fearfully, for the girl's information. Debbie looked up at her with round, determined eyes. "Okay," she said. "The day your daughter . . . the day of the picnic, we were home 'cause I didn't feel good. The first we heard of the jail-break was when Ronnie Lee called Dwight. He was hiding out over at Caitlin's Crossing and he wanted Dwight to come get him. Dwight tried to tell him to go back but Ronnie Lee was cursing him and arguing with him. I begged Dwight just to leave him there, but Dwight said he had to go get him. I threatened to call the sheriff so he made me come with him. We drove over to the crossing and picked him up."

"When was that?" asked Lillie, feeling a tightness in her chest.

"About four o'clock," Debbie said. "He knew this woman in Kentucky who he met one time when he was out of jail. He called her up and she came to meet us, about three hours from here. He was drinking the whole way, singing these stupid songs." Debbie shuddered with remembered disgust. "He was so drunk by the time we got there we had to roll him into the backseat of her car. She was so happy to see him. I thought, good riddance, you're welcome to him. He even threw up in the back of her car but she was happy as a snake in a swamp. He's still there with her, although they're fighting like cats and dogs. He called us twice from there. I think he's getting ready to take off though. Probably find some other girl to sponge off of."

Lillie's mind was working furiously as the girl spoke. The girl was telling the truth. She was sure of that. But it forced her to think about something she had not wanted to think about. She had numbly accepted the idea of Ronnie Lee as the killer, and it made it seem like Michele's death had been almost accidental, as if she had been hit by a car. She had fallen into the path of an oncoming criminal, who was out to kill a girl. Any girl.

Now everything was different. If it wasn't Ronnie Lee, then maybe it wasn't accidental. Maybe it was deliberate. Maybe someone had killed Michele, her Michele, on purpose. She felt all her psychic wounds start to bleed again, all at once. Suddenly she remembered different things the sheriff had said. Different things she had heard. All along Royce had been saying that he didn't think it was Ronnie Lee. That he had no motive. That he wouldn't risk such a crime, that he just wanted to get away. But who, then? Why? She shook her head. Then she looked up at Debbie. "So, it couldn't have been him," she said.

Debbie shrugged. "It wasn't. We were with him."

"But why are you telling me? Why not tell the sheriff?"

"I told you," Debbie explained patiently. "Dwight would kill me. But you can tell the sheriff. You can give him the address where Ronnie Lee is, and they can get him and say they just tracked him down. Then the whole thing will come out and people will know it wasn't Ronnie Lee."

"Dwight could get in trouble for helping him to get away. Did you ever think of that?"

Debbie looked squarely at Lillie. "I thought of it," she said. "I'll say he forced us. With a gun." The girl pulled a piece of paper out of her bag and wrote on it hurriedly. "This is the address, where he's at."

Lillie looked down at the paper rattling in her hands. "Thank you for telling me," she said softly.

"It was the Lord's will for me to run into you today," Debbie said sincerely. "I just hope they catch who really did it."

Lillie exchanged a wondering glance with the young mother-to-be and then she shivered. "I have to talk to the sheriff," she said. "Right away."

CHAPTER 7

A deputy whom Lillie did not recognize sat with his feet up on Royce's desk, studying the latest issue of *Guns and Ammo* magazine.

"The sheriff's not here," drawled the young man in answer to Lillie's anxious request.

"Where is he? I need to talk to him right away."

"Out of town," said the deputy.

"Out of town!" Lillie cried. "There's a cold-blooded murderer loose in this county. Why isn't the sheriff here?"

The deputy suddenly recognized Lillie as the murdered girl's mother and took his feet off the desk. His cowboy boots hit the floor with a thud. "Deputy Reynolds is in charge, ma'am," he said respectfully. "He's over having lunch at the five and ten. He can help you, I'm certain."

"Well, I hope so," Lillie said angrily. She slammed the office door behind her in frustration, then strode out of the town hall. People came and went across the main square of Felton and the atmosphere in town was normal, business as usual. Shoppers visited the slightly shabby stores that bordered the square. A couple of kids sat on the base of the statue of Andrew Jackson in front of the courthouse, crushing the Virginia creeper vines that entwined it. Oh, people talked about the murder. She knew that. Every time she passed people she recognized and a silence fell, she knew that her daughter's death had been the subject of conversation. But soon it would just be gossip in town, an event that had once shocked them. For them there was no urgency about the whole thing. Not even for the sheriff. It was not their lives that had been changed forever, she thought, angry tears pricking her eyelids. She took a deep breath and composed herself. She could not wait for the sheriff. If Wallace Reynolds was all she had, then Wallace it would have to be.

She crossed the square to the five and ten, glancing into Flood's Pharmacy on the way. Bomar must have been out, for only his salesgirl was behind the counter. She was talking to a customer and all the while staring at herself in the mirror behind the soda fountain, examining her makeup with an intent expression. A couple of teenagers sat, as usual, at the soda fountain. Lillie walked on and opened the door to the five and ten. The familiar woolly smell of stale popcorn, sweetish candy and old cardboard boxes greeted her. She spotted Wallace Reynolds at the lunch counter and hurried over.

"Wallace," she said without preamble, "I have to talk to you right away."

The deputy set down his sandwich and looked up, surprised. "Miz Burdette," he mumbled, wiping his mouth. "Shouldn't you be at home?"

"Why should I be at home, Wallace?" Lillie asked. The deputy was a good four years younger than she, but he had a reproving manner that tended to make people feel as if they had to explain themselves. "I came to see the sheriff but it seems that he just up and left town," she said indignantly.

Wallace pushed a grayish pickled okra to one side of his plate and wiped his hands on a napkin. "It's not a pleasure trip, ma'am. He left this morning to take his boy off to the Sentinel. That's the military school over in North Carolina."

"Tyler?" Lillie dropped down on the stool beside the deputy. "How come? He never mentioned any such thing."

Wallace Reynolds shook his head. "Between you and me, Miz Burdette, that boy has been nothing but heartache to him." Wallace mimicked the motion of lifting a bottle to his mouth. "If you know what I mean."

Lillie nodded numbly. "I know," she said. "But military school . . ." She thought of Tyler at the funeral, disheveled and wild-eyed. Several years back, after Lulene died, Lillie had vowed to herself to try to help out. She had asked them to supper a few times, Royce and Tyler. But Tyler had been so silent and awkward, even around the kids, and Royce seemed to simmer with irritation at the boy. It made everyone uneasy, and after a while she stopped asking them. She wished now that she had tried a little harder. Apparently they had reached the point of no return.

"Military school'll be the best thing for him," said Wallace. "Straighten him right out. Anyway, you wanted to talk to the sheriff. What's the problem?"

Lillie turned her mind away from the sheriff's problems and back to her own. This could not wait for his return.

"Wallace," she said, "I have come into some important information. Someone—I can't tell you who, so don't even ask—just told me some things that prove that Ronnie Lee Partin was not responsible for my daughter's death."

Wallace smiled sadly at Lillie and pushed his beige plastic plate aside with one fastidious finger. "Miz Burdette," he said in a patronizing tone, "I think someone is playing a mean joke on you. Ronnie Lee Partin is a desperate criminal, and it is my best estimate that your daughter crossed his path at a very bad moment and became his victim. I believe that when we are able to apprehend Mr. Partin, we will have our killer."

"Well, go ahead and apprehend him then," Lillie said, thrusting the piece of paper at him on which Debbie had printed a Kentucky address. "This is where you'll find him."

Wallace took the paper from her and looked at it suspiciously. "Where'd you get this?"

"I told you. I can't say. I got it from someone who knows that Ronnie Lee did not kill Michele and only wants to prove it."

Wallace studied the address with a sour expression on his face.

"As I understand it, the sheriff never has believed that Ronnie Lee was the one," said Lillie.

Wallace shrugged. "With all due respect, ma'am, the sheriff is preoccupied with his own problems, he's overworked, and he ain't getting any younger. He may not be the ideal one to decide."

"He's just saying what makes sense," Lillie insisted. "Ronnie Lee Partin had no reason to kill my daughter."

"Miz Burdette," Wallace said, shaking his head. "You have to be around these people to comprehend what they are like. They don't need a reason for what they do. The best reason any of them need in this world is that they have consumed a bottle of whiskey and they just feel like it. Do you know," he continued, warming to his subject, "that not three weeks ago we arrested the Boynton brothers, and do you know why? Because they shared a bottle of moonshine and then they went out in Buddy Boynton's boat with shotguns and they went speeding across Crystal Lake, shooting at anything that moved on the shoreline. They thought that was a real good time."

"So maybe Buddy Boynton killed my daughter," said Lillie. "Don't you see what you're saying? It could have been anybody with the price of a bottle of bourbon."

"Now don't get all upset," Wallace said stiffly.

Lillie sighed in exasperation as the waitress, a chubby girl with bleached blond curls piled up on her head, came by. "Y'all want anything else?"

"Check," said Wallace. He peered at the piece of paper and then at Lillie. "If we do find Partin at this address, you're going to have to tell us where you got this."

"And you're going to have to come up with a killer," Lillie snapped back at him.

Wallace stood up from the counter stool. "I'll be in touch with Mr. Burdette or yourself on this."

"Good," Lillie said coolly. She knew the deputy was offended and she didn't care. She wished she could have spoken to Royce, but there was no time to waste. She didn't care what Wallace Reynolds thought. Royce would be grateful for the information, and he would be relieved to have Ronnie Lee Partin locked up again. But it was no wonder, she thought, that Debbie was afraid to talk to them. You could be treated like a criminal just for trying to help.

And, of course, it was no wonder Wallace resisted this new wrinkle. It put them all back where they started from. They had no killer and no information. If only someone would come forward, she thought, as Debbie had. And then she realized, as she thought about it, that perhaps there was something more she could do.

Lillie heard the anxious note in Pink's voice as he called out, "Lillie, I'm back. Where are you?"

"I'm in here," she called out. "In the den." Pink came to the door and looked in warily, as if reluctant to see what condition she might be in.

"Come on in," she said. She was seated cross-legged in the middle of the floor of the den on a hooked rug she had made one winter when Michele was in the hospital with pneumonia and she was sitting up with her. On the floor around Lillie were photo albums, and all of the recent photos of Michele were out of their sleeves and piled up on her lap.

"What are you doing there, honey?" Pink cajoled in the voice one might use on a distraught ledgewalker. "You don't have to sort those out now. This stuff'll be here." He squatted down beside her and began to close up the albums.

"Don't," she said. "I need a picture of Michele."

"What for?" he asked miserably.

She felt a little sorry for him. He was clearly worried about her mental state, and perhaps, she thought, she had given him reason. He would never come out and ask her, of course. Pink had a horror of any talk of feelings, and over the years she had come to accept it. He showed affection with gifts and avoided discussions by turning on the TV and arguments by driving around in his car.

"It's okay," she reassured him. "I need it for the paper. The newspaper. Pink, I came by your office today."

"I know," he said. "I found your note in the door. What'd you want?"

"Well, I'd just been talking to Wallace Reynolds. I wanted to see Royce but he's out of town. He took Tyler to military school. Did you know about that?"

"Oh, yeah," said Pink. "He told me he was going."

"He did? He never mentioned it to me."

"Maybe he thought you had enough to worry about. He's had nothing but trouble with that kid," Pink said irritably.

"Anyway," said Lillie, "this is going to come as a shock to you. I know it did to me."

Pink stared at her. "What are you talking about?"

Lillie told him about her encounter with Debbie Partin. Pink got up while she was speaking and sat down on the edge of the ottoman that matched his old club chair. He held the photo album on his lap and ran his fingers in and out of the embossed grooves on the cover.

"And these pictures?" he said.

Lillie got up and sat on the arm of the club chair. "I'm gonna put the best one we've got of her in the paper and ask people to call us with information. People who don't want to go to the police. Like Debbie Partin. You see what I'm saying?" She put a hand on Pink's shoulder. "There was somebody else. And somebody may be walking around town this very minute who knows about it. But they might be afraid to go to the sheriff."

Pink sat silently for a moment, his chest heaving, as if trying to catch his breath. "This is a nightmare," he whispered at last. "A goddamn nightmare." He shook his head and ran one freckled hand over his thinning hair. "Why did this have to happen to us?" He stood up abruptly, and shiny photos fluttered around him to the floor. He went over and opened the window. "How long have you been cooped up in here?" he asked.

"Pink," said Lillie. "We need to do something."

He turned back to her. "What can we do? We have to let the sheriff take care of it."

"Didn't you hear me? Don't you care?" she demanded.

"About my little girl being killed?" Pink cried, his wide face reddening. "Well, what the hell do you think? How could you ask that of me?"

"You're right, Pink. I'm sorry. You're right."

"We can't look for a killer. For God's sakes. It's all I can do to keep this family from falling apart. I come home and I'm afraid of what I'll find. Afraid I'll find you've gone off the deep end. You don't eat half the time. You don't sleep. Let the police take care of their job. You have to start taking care of yourself, Lillie. And what about Grayson? And me?"

"I'm home," came a voice from the kitchen. Pink's head jerked up, startled. Lillie frowned down at the fistful of pictures she was holding.

"We're in the den, son," Pink called out.

Grayson appeared at the door of the den and looked in at his parents. "What are you doing?" he asked.

"Gray," Lillie said stubbornly. "Maybe you can help. It seems as if that Partin boy didn't kill Michele after all. Maybe there was someone else. Someone who didn't like her, that you can think of. Maybe someone who was mad at her for something."

Grayson was taken aback. "I don't know," he said.

"Try and think, honey. Did she ever mention anything like that?" Lillie persisted.

"How do you know it wasn't Partin?" Grayson asked.

"It's a long story," Pink interrupted. "There's no proof of anything yet. Let's not get all worked up. How was your day at school?"

"Great," said Grayson. "I was nominated for student council vice president."

"That's wonderful, son," Pink exclaimed. "Won't that look fine on your record. And then, if you win this one, senior year you can shoot for president."

"I think I've got a good chance," said Grayson. "The election's in two weeks and all the kids are feeling sorry for me because of Michele."

"Grayson!" Lillie cried. "How can you say that?" She felt as if his words had slapped her in the face.

Grayson looked startled at his mother's tone. "What?"

"He's thinking like a politician," Pink said soothingly. "You've got to be a realist about these things, Lillie. There is such a thing as a sympathy vote."

Lillie stared at them both. "Is that all you can think about Michele's death? That it'll get you votes in a school election?"

Grayson shook his head incredulously. "Well, of course

not, Mother. I was just proud of being nominated. The only reason I mentioned it was because I thought it would make you proud, that you'd be pleased." He looked around the room at the scattered photos of his sister. "I thought you might be glad to have something else to think about, but I guess I was wrong. I'm sorry I bothered you about it."

"She doesn't mean it like that," Pink assured him hurriedly.

"Grayson," Lillie said in a trembling voice, "I did not mean that your news wasn't important. But to speak of your sister's death as if it were some kind of lucky advantage you have . . ."

"Sorry," said Gray. "I only meant that there are a lot of people who liked her at the school, and they'd probably vote for me just because of her. If that's wrong, I'm sorry. That's all I meant. I never dreamed you'd take it any other way."

"Well, maybe I misunderstood," Lillie said wearily.

"Come on, come on," said Pink. "We're all tired. We're all on edge."

"I've got a campaign meeting tonight," said Grayson. "I'm gonna make a sandwich. Unless you fixed something?" He looked back at Lillie expectantly. "Or shall I fix y'all one too?"

Lillie felt the familiar stab of guilt. She had been too absorbed in the revelation about Ronnie Lee Partin. And she had no appetite. But that was no reason to keep neglecting them like this.

"Stay put, son," said Pink. "I'll run down to the Country Kitchen and pick up some catfish and hush puppies. We'll sit down together and eat for a change." Grayson was poised in the doorway. Pink saw the expression in Lillie's eyes start to drift again. "Come on, Lillie," he said irritably. "We all have to eat."

Lillie looked at her husband helplessly. "I hate sitting down in there," she said. "Seeing her empty chair . . ."

"Grayson," said Pink. "Go take Michele's chair out to the garage. Go on."

"Yessir," said Grayson.

"Gray," Lillie said. The boy stopped and looked at her. "I didn't mean to spoil it for you. I think it's great you were nominated. Really I do."

Gray raised one silky eyebrow skeptically, but his voice was pleasant. "Well, I'm grateful."

Lillie looked at her husband. "Pink, I didn't mean to put him down. It's just that the way it came out sounded horrible to me."

Pink looked at his watch. "I believe I'll run get that catfish right now. Let's get this supper on the table."

He doesn't want to discuss it, Lillie thought. He never does. He just wants this whole ugly mess to go away. But it's not going anywhere. She looked down at the pile of pictures at her feet and suddenly felt exhausted. I'll clean them up later, she told herself. She heard Pink slam the back door. Dragging herself to her feet, she decided to go into the kitchen and put out the plates for supper. That way they could sit right down when he got home with the catfish. She walked to the kitchen and reached the door just in time to see the legs of Michele's chair disappearing out the back, leaving black scuff marks across the tiles where Grayson had dragged it away.

CHAPTER 8

Early the next morning, after a stop at the local dough-nut franchise, Lillie arrived at the office of the newspaper, the *Cress County Courier.* The office was located on Route 31 alongside a dozen or so other businesses with parking lots and neon-lighted signs that prospered on the highway strip between Felton and Welbyville. The newspaper occupied a one-story building with a tinted glass front and a broad-shingled eave. The adjoining business, which shared a common wall and a parking lot, was a Radio Shack, and the hum of the word processors in the newspaper office seemed to ride a constant, muffled bass line.

Pink had reiterated, loudly, his disapproval of the idea of a newspaper ad and gone off to work in a bad temper. After he left, Lillie had decided to call Brenda for moral support, but when Brenda answered she found herself talking about work and never mentioning the ad. She had a suspicion that Brenda would not approve either. Instead, Lillie chattered on about how she was feeling better and wanting to work, and Brenda finally agreed to let her try it on Monday.

Lillie looked down at the picture in her hand, took a deep breath, and opened the door to the newspaper office. She was greeted pleasantly by various staff members who recognized her. She often helped Pink out by placing his weekly ads for properties, and occasionally she and Brenda ran an ad when business was slow. Lillie walked directly to the classifieds and put the paper bag she was carrying down on the desk of a woman dressed in a turquoise-blue pantsuit and a ruffled blouse.

The gray-haired woman at the desk was on the phone, but she smiled and mouthed the words "You shouldn't have" as Lillie unpacked a paper cup of coffee, and a Krispy Kreme glazed doughnut on her desk. The woman said her good-byes, hung up the phone, lit a cigarette, and took a sip from the coffee cup. Then she looked down at the doughnut.

"I'm gonna save this for break," she advised Lillie in a deep, raspy voice. She moved the waxed paper to one side of her blotter with neatly manicured fingertips, never letting go of the cigarette.

"I know you like glazed, Rebecca Louise."

The older woman nodded and exhaled a smoke ring. "Oh, I do, I do. I get a craving for them that is positively irresistible about twice a week." She rested her deeply lined face in the palm of her hand, holding her cigarette out at an awkward angle. "How are you doing, sweetie? I have been thinking about you and Pink."

"I'm all right," Lillie said firmly. "But, Rebecca Louise, I want to put something in the paper."

"Well, I surely can help you with that. What have you got there?" Rebecca Louise reached into the file folders on the desk and pulled out the forms for a classified ad.

Lillie pulled a photograph out of her purse and handed it to the older woman. It was the best, most recent photo she could find of Michele. She had a natural-looking smile in the picture and it really looked like her, unlike the stiff eighth-grade graduation portrait the paper ran when she died. Rebecca Louise held the photo gingerly and blanched beneath her delicate pink face powder. When she looked up at Lillie her carefully made-up eyes betrayed every year of her age. "She was a pretty thing," she said.

"Thank you," Lillie said calmly. "Now, I want to run kind of a . . . well, a card of thanks, you know, with a picture."

Rebecca Louise took another drag on her cigarette. "Well, technically that would be obits, honey."

"I know," Lillie said. "But I want it to run in the classifieds, where folks will really stop and notice it." She rummaged in her purse for a piece of paper. "I worded it this way." She looked at the paper again and then handed it over. "Can you read my handwriting?"

The older woman frowned as she read it. Her lips mumbled the words as she read. "Thanks . . . kindness . . . information . . . the night of September 28, Founders Day, contact the sheriff or—Who's this number. Y'all's?"

Lillie nodded.

"You put this number in the paper you're gonna get all kinds of kooks calling you up, Lillie."

"Somebody had to have seen her that night. Somebody has to be able to tell us what she was doing down there. Who she was with."

"That Partin boy, wasn't it?" asked Rebecca Louise.

"No," Lillie said. "I don't believe so. Rebecca Louise, I want this to run every week until we get the one who did it."

"Did the sheriff okay this?" the older woman asked suspiciously.

"The sheriff's out of town. I want Monday's paper. Please."

"This is going to cost you, honey."

"I don't care," said Lillie.

"No, I don't guess you do." Rebecca Louise lit another cigarette from the one she was smoking. "All right. I'll get it in a good spot. Leave it to me."

Lillie thanked her and received a sage nod in reply. "I'll be in again soon," Lillie promised. As she headed out toward the front of the building, she saw the front door open and a familiar figure walk in. She tried to avoid him but Jordan stopped her as she hurried out.

"Lillie."

"Hello," she said. "What are you doing here?"

"Being interviewed about the show. Actors. We try never to miss a chance for some free publicity," he said with an awkward smile.

"Well," Lillie said briskly, "you ought to get plenty of mileage out of this murder, then."

"I'll pretend you didn't say that," said Jordan.

A pleasant-looking girl in glasses, wearing a University of the South sweatshirt, snapped off the glowing screen of her computer and ambled over toward Jordan and Lillie. "Mr. Hill," she said. "I'm the one who called you, Kendra Spencer. Glad you could make it."

Lillie had pushed open the front door and started out. Jordan turned to the girl, who was pushing her glasses up on her nose.

"Can you excuse me for a minute?" he asked as he followed Lillie out the door and into the parking lot.

"Lillie," he said. "Wait a minute."

"What?"

"Is there any news? About Michele. Anything I should know?"

Lillie sighed and leaned against her car. "There may be. I was just putting in an ad, to try to get more information. Right now, it just seems like Ronnie Lee Partin was not responsible."

"What? Well, if—"

"It seems like he has an alibi. That's all I know right now."

"Have they brought him in?"

"Not yet, I don't think so. Look, I don't want to go through it all again. It'll be in the paper. If you're around to read the paper, that is. What are you still doing here, anyway? Shouldn't you be back in New York or Hollywood or somewhere?"

"Well, I haven't been home in a long time. And I thought my mother might need me to stay around for a while."

"How thoughtful of you," Lillie said coolly.

"It takes time to absorb this," he said. "For all of us."

Lillie chewed on the inside of her mouth and avoided his eyes. "Well, that's true. I know Miz Bessie appreciates your staying."

"Lillie, I was hoping that while I was here, you and I could sit down and talk."

"I don't mean to be rude, but I don't see that there's anything for us to talk about," said Lillie. "The only thing we had in common was Michele. She's gone. What's there left to say?"

"Well, I'd like to talk about Michele," he said.

"What about Michele?" Lillie said defensively.

"Well, over the years, you know, I missed a lot of her growing up."

"And whose fault is that?" Lillie asked.

"It's mine, of course. But I find myself with so many unanswered questions about her. I'd like to hear about those early years. See pictures of her from those days."

"Kind of a capsule summary of her life," Lillie said with a flinty look in her eye.

"Look, Lillie, this may sound strange to you now. But I have memories of her too, and I have no one to share them with. If we could talk for a while . . . well, it would really help me to talk about her."

Lillie stared at his rugged face, his serious expression, in disbelief. "Oh, it would help you, would it?" she said. "Well, by all means, then. I'll just block out all the time you need. After all, you were such a great help to me and Michele. You helped us out a lot. Leaving me alone with an infant who was struggling just to stay alive."

"Well, you weren't alone for long," he said coolly.

Lillie glared at him. "How dare you?" she exclaimed. "How dare you even think to bring that up to me?"

"Lillie, you're right. I didn't want to start an argument. It just seemed to me that we should try to talk. To help one another along. For Michele's sake. For the sake of her memory."

Lillie shook her head, her jaw clenched. "For Michele's sake," she repeated. "You're unbelievable. Can't you even hear yourself? You know, Jordan, I hope it was worth it. I hope you found what you were looking for. But I sure don't want to talk about my daughter or anything else with you. I can hardly bear to think about it."

"All right, listen," Jordan said angrily. "I'm not going to try and justify my life to you standing here in the Radio Shack parking lot. All I'm asking you for is a little bit of your time."

"Well, I can't spare the time," Lillie said bitterly. "I've got to go and buy some cream cheese. I guess people don't have such mundane little errands like that to do in New York City. I guess you and I might just step on into some little café and have cappuccino and relive the good times, but I've got puff pastry to make for the Daughters of the Confederacy supper meeting. So, if you will excuse me, I have to get over to Kroger's. And I believe you are about to meet the press." Lillie looked back at the door of the Courier building. She could see the yellow sweatshirt behind the tinted glass as the young reporter peered out at them.

"All right," said Jordan. "Okay. You don't owe me any favors. I'll grant you that."

Lillie got into her car and slammed the door. She did not look back at him standing there. She pulled out on

Route 31 and drove carefully to the first red traffic light, where she was finally able to get a tissue from her purse and wipe away the angry tears that were making it difficult to see.

CHAPTER 9

First thing Monday morning Allene Starnes was at the high school, stapling up the posters she had made for Grayson's campaign. She had worked on them all weekend long, pleased that he had asked for her help. He had wanted to work on them with her, but he had to stay home most of the weekend. People were coming by to call because of his sister.

Allene understood. She told him not to worry and promised to make the posters perfect for him. And she did have an artistic eye, as Grayson said. She fussed over the lettering until it looked professional, and her father let her use the copying machine at his store on Sunday afternoon so they would be ready for Monday morning.

Now, as she hung the last poster on the bulletin board over the water fountain outside the auditorium, she could not help but imagine how grateful he would be when he saw them. The posters had turned out exactly the way he wanted them. She closed her eyes and pictured the smile dawning in his eyes, his warm breath whispering his thanks in her ear, his body pressed hard against her, maybe right here in the hallway. Her face flushed hot and tingly as she thought of it, and she felt her nipples standing up under the soft fabric of her shirt. Embarrassed, she picked up her notebook and held it against her chest and she bent over the water fountain, took a drink, and waited for the evidence of her excitement to subside.

The doors to the auditorium opened and kids began to trickle out. Allene greeted a few of them distractedly. She knew Grayson was in there, and she wanted it to look casual, as if she just happened to be passing by when he came out. That soap opera star who was his sister's real father was giving a talk and Gray had said he'd probably go.

Cherie Hatchett stopped and tried to engage Allene in a conversation, but Allene was not really able to pay attention to what the other girl was saying. She kept an eye on the doors, poised to cut Cherie off and saunter in Grayson's direction as soon as she spotted him. Suddenly the glimpse of a golden head at the far door made her heart turn over with delight.

"See you," she said to Cherie, and did not wait for a reply. She started toward him, mentally summoning up a calm, sexy voice to drawl out his name when she noticed that he wasn't alone, or with the guys. He was standing very close to Emily Crowell, the new girl from Chicago with the black hair, the one she had talked to at the funeral.

Allene stopped short and stared. An icy feeling gripped her. Grayson was not touching the other girl. But he had his head inclined toward her in a certain way that made Allene feel like there was something sharp poking her in the heart. Her face was flaming. She tried to turn away but Emily spotted her and nudged Grayson.

Gray looked up and gave Allene a brilliant smile. He and Emily walked straight toward her, and Grayson reached out and gave her a squeeze at the waist.

"Hey," he said. "How are you?"

His arm around her buoyed her like a life preserver to a person sure she was about to drown, but she was still shaken. "I'm okay," she said coolly.

"Do you know Emily?" he asked.

"We met," said Allene. As soon as she thought of the funeral, she felt immediately guilty for acting cold and jealous. It was so petty. "Hi, Emily," she said in a friendly tone.

"We just listened to Jordan's talk." Grayson dropped the name proudly.

"He was fabulous," said Emily, her shiny black eyes wide with excitement. "He told how he got his first part, and about learning to act and everything."

"Emily wants to be an actress someday," Gray explained.

"Oh," said Allene, feeling suddenly embarrassed by her often expressed desire to be an occupational therapist. It suddenly seemed a frumpy choice by comparison.

"So," said Gray, "I said I'd introduce her to Jordan. Maybe he can help her out."

Emily craned her neck to watch the door. "I cannot wait to meet him. He is so gorgeous."

"I finished putting up the posters, Grayson," Allene said.

"Oh, good," said Gray, keeping an eye on the door to the auditorium.

"Come and look."

Gray frowned slightly. "Can it wait just a second?" he said.

Allene felt the coldness creeping around her heart again. "There's one right here," she said, pointing to the alcove where the fountain was.

Gray glanced back over his shoulder and then followed her to the fountain. He gazed at the bulletin board. "Hey, that looks great," he said, and his eyes took on that gleam that Allene had imagined. The warmth of his smile enveloped her. "You did a great job, Allene. Thanks."

Allene nodded happily. "Don't you think? I put up two dozen around the halls."

Grayson stepped up to the poster and touched his picture with his forefinger as if smoothing down an errant hair. "I just wish I'd been wearing my blue tattersall shirt the day that picture was taken. That T-shirt doesn't look quite right."

"It shows off your muscles," Allene said loyally.

"Here he comes." Emily squealed. "Oh, Gray, I can't stand it. Come over here."

"Well, all right then," said Gray, feigning world weariness. "I may as well do the honors now."

Allene stared at Grayson as he ambled over toward Jordan Hill and Miss Jones, the music and drama teacher, who had just come out of the double doors. She thought briefly of marching up and demanding to be introduced to him too. But what for? She wasn't going to be an actress.

She turned away and walked toward her next class. She hoped maybe he would call out to her as she walked away, but she did not hear her name.

Jordan had enjoyed giving the talk. When he'd stepped up on that auditorium stage he had been overcome with nostalgia. The stage was so much smaller than he remembered it. It was narrow and kind of shabby, where once it had seemed grand to him. He remembered his hand trembling as he gestured with his pipe when he played the role of the narrator in *Our Town*. It was a character part that Lulene Ansley had insisted he should try, rather than the romantic leads he easily landed. He had been so proud of that role.

The audience was composed of high-school kids now, just as it had been then, but now they looked like eager children to him. In those days they had seemed like formidable critics. After the talk and the questions he had signed a number of autographs. Gay Jones twittered nervously by his side as they walked up the sloping floor to the auditorium doors. She blinked in the light of the vestibule behind her thick glasses.

"I can't thank you enough for coming," she said. "We all really enjoyed it. It's really an inspiration for these youngsters, seeing that you came from Cress County."

"My pleasure," Jordan replied. "A little encouragement doesn't hurt. It isn't a profession for the fainthearted."

"No, indeed," said Miss Jones. "Would you care to join me in the faculty room for some coffee and refreshments?"

"Hey, Jordan."

Jordan turned and saw Grayson ambling toward him, a

pretty girl with black hair in tow. Usually the boy treated him coolly, addressing him as "sir," like any polite Southern child, but putting a sardonic spin on it. Today, however, Grayson's face had the possessive, overly familiar look people wore when they wanted something from you. Deliberately, Jordan turned back to the music teacher. "That's very kind of you," he said, "but I've got to be getting back home."

Miss Jones smiled shyly. One of her front teeth overlapped the other slightly. "I really appreciate it. I know this was a bad time for you . . ."

Jordan shook her hand. "I'm glad I could come."

He turned back to Grayson, whose confident smile had faded while he had been forced to wait, unacknowledged. "Hello, Grayson," Jordan said. He smiled briefly at Emily.

"Grayson told me you're his stepfather," Emily said uncertainly. "I hope we're not bothering you. My parents used to watch your old show all the time when we lived in Chicago."

Jordan was surprised by the "stepfather" designation. Still, it would be hard to say exactly what he was to Grayson. These days family relationships could be difficult to define.

"She wanted to meet you," Gray said in a stiff, apprehensive voice, and Jordan immediately felt guilty for having snubbed him a moment before. The boy had only been showing off a little to impress a pretty girl. There was no harm in it. And they *were* virtually related. He had no cause to embarrass the boy. "Well, why don't you introduce me to her, Grayson?" he asked kindly. "I'd like to meet her too."

"This is Emily Crowell," said Grayson. "Jordan Hill."

Jordan shook the girl's hand. "Nice to meet you."

Emily beamed at Grayson as if the boy had pulled off a magic trick. Then she turned back to Jordan. "I want to be an actress someday," she said. "Can you give me any advice?"

"Be an actress now," said Jordan. "Audition for every production."

"Do you think I'm pretty enough?" she asked earnestly.

Grayson gave Jordan a sly, man-to-man smile. "I don't know, Jordan. I don't really think so, do you?"

"Grayson," she wailed, and punched him lightly in the arm.

Jordan felt his smile wearing thin. He wanted to like the boy, because he was Lillie's son, Michele's brother. But there was something about the boy that irritated him no matter how he tried. Face it, he thought. You just don't like him because he's Pink's.

"You're very pretty," Jordan assured her. "You just worry about learning to act."

"Well, we'd better get going," said Gray. He cocked a finger at Emily in a gesture that Pink sometimes made. "Come on, Emily. We've got class."

"So long," said Jordan. He watched Grayson walk away, shoulder to shoulder with the black-haired beauty. He realized that the boy had dismissed him, and it annoyed him. And he did not like Grayson to call him by his first name. He preferred the surly "sir." He felt like calling out to him and telling him so. Lighten up, he thought. Stop acting like an old curmudgeon.

A cluster of giggling girls approached him, shuffling closer as he turned and smiled at them. They extended pieces of notebook paper and he signed autographs dedicated to them and their mothers.

"How come you have a mustache?" one of them asked boldly.

"Makes me look younger, don't you think?"

They all giggled again and then scattered like little birds.

Jordan watched them go and then walked over to the water fountain in the nearby alcove to get a drink. As he stooped over he noticed that he was looking at one of Grayson's campaign posters. He felt his nose wrinkle as he studied it, as if he had smelled something bad.

Across the top it read "Grayson Burdette for Student Council Vice President." The picture on the poster had been taken in the summer. Grayson's hair was white blond from the sun, and he was leaning against the car with a mischievous grin on his face. His arm was draped loosely over Michele's frail shoulders, and she was looking up at him with laughing, admiring eyes.

That little prick, Jordan thought, staring at the poster. Of all the pictures he could have used, he had to use one with Michele. All the kids knew about Michele and what had happened to her. He didn't pick that photograph by coincidence. He knew that people would be touched by it, would feel sorry for him. It was probably Pink's idea, he thought disgustedly. No, it was too subtle for Pink.

Jordan took another swallow of water, but it tasted bitter in his mouth. Michele would probably have been proud as punch to appear on a poster with her little brother, he thought. She had adored that boy. Jordan recalled that whenever he saw Michele she had chattered happily about Grayson's accomplishments, about how handsome and popular he was. She bragged about his ability in sports. He was a star athlete, while she was delicate and the last one picked for every team. She marveled at his high grades while she labored to keep her average up.

And now her photograph would probably help him win another victory. If she knew, she'd doubtless think it was great. But he couldn't see it that way. It felt to him as if Grayson was capitalizing on her memory.

You're probably just jealous, he told himself, staring at the two teenagers in the picture. Jealous that Pink still has his child and you no longer have yours. Maybe that is all it amounts to. That's stupid of you, he thought. Michele was Pink's child too. But still he wished that he had Grayson in front of him at that moment. He would shake him until his teeth rattled.

Well, it was a satisfying thought, he had to admit, but impractical. The kid was long gone. Mind your own business, he thought. But before he turned away, he reached up and tore the poster off the board. He wadded it up in his hands as he headed for the exit doors. As he left the building, he threw it into a garbage can in the hall.

The arrest of Ronnie Lee Partin and the announcement of the establishment of his alibi, all of which had occurred during the weekend, had done nothing to soothe the nerves of the Reverend Ephraim Davis. The reverend had suspected all along that the escapee was not the one they wanted. He had seen the pictures of Ronnie Lee Partin on the news, and he was definitely not the one he had seen down by the Three Arches on that awful night.

"Do you want another slice of cake, Reverend?" Clara

Walker asked, her cake knife poised above the frothy coconut frosting.

Distracted by his thoughts, the reverend had not noticed that Bill Walker had left the supper table and Clara had been trying to clean up around him. He looked longingly at the cake, and then he lied. "No, thank you. I couldn't."

He got up from the table and went into the parlor, partly to get out of Clara's way and partly to get out of the way of temptation. In thirty years of marriage, he had never cheated on his wife, but he had lusted after the cooking of other women. His travels took him to the parishes of many excellent cooks, and he paid for his vice with tight-fitting vests and belts he had to punch holes in with a hammer and awl. He had sampled the chicken, the black-eyed peas, the turnip greens, and pork chops of women across the state. But in Cress County there were few treats that could compare with Clara Walker's coconut cake. The reverend eased himself down into a chair in the parlor and picked up the county paper, which lay on the table beside him. He could hear the hum of Bill Walker's band saw coming from the workshop. Bill was a quiet fellow who kept to himself, but he never seemed to mind the presence of an extra person in his home. The reverend picked up the paper and put on his glasses, feeling grateful, as always, for the goodness of the people who took him in. He opened the paper and scanned it with the perfunctory interest of an outsider. When he came to the back pages he stopped and stared at the picture of the girl.

She was an ordinary-looking girl, although there was something heartbreaking about her smile. He read the plea for information from her family and felt the heartburn beginning beneath his vest at the same time.

He remembered that smile. Maybe it only seemed heartbreaking now in light of what had happened. But it was ironic that he, who paid so little attention to the doings of the whites around him, should find his dreams haunted by the little girl's smile. He told himself that he had tried, that to do more was foolhardy, but the fact was that he was not sleeping well, not feeling well, and was not able to talk himself out of the shame and guilt he felt for keeping quiet.

He looked at the picture again. Maybe what he'd seen was not important, he told himself for the hundredth time. But maybe it was. And she was a good girl. And she had a mother and father who were suffering and who deserved an answer. Maybe this ad in the paper was just the solution. He could call the number and talk to them anonymously. It would be safer than calling the police. And it was certainly better than doing nothing at all.

Clara Walker wandered into the parlor and dropped down onto the velveteen settee with a sigh. "Anything interesting in the paper?" she asked.

The problem, he thought, was that the phone was in the parlor. He didn't want to ask Clara to move out of her own parlor. She was tired. She had worked all day.

"Nothing too much," he said. You're making excuses again, he thought. Just do it.

As if in answer to his thoughts, Bill Walker poked his head into the room. There was sawdust in his woolly black hair. "Hey, honey, come out and take a look at this, will you?"

Clara rolled her eyes at the reverend. "He's making me

a new table," she said. "I'm coming, honey." She heaved herself off the sofa with a sigh and waddled out the door behind her husband. The Reverend Davis was alone in the parlor.

He walked over to the phone and then hesitated. Despite the cool dampness of the night, he could feel sweat running down beneath his cleric's shirt. He picked up the phone and dialed the number in the paper. The phone rang three times, and then a young voice said, "Hello."

The Reverend Davis took a deep breath and began. "Hello," he said. "I'm calling about the advertisement in today's paper. Is this . . . I'm calling for Mr. or Mrs. Burdette."

"What about the ad? This is Grayson Burdette."

"This is about Michele. Uh, the murder. I might have some information."

"Who am I speaking to, please?" Grayson asked in a clipped tone.

The reverend was silent, and angry at himself for his silence. He was ashamed that he could not tell his name to a child.

"Look," the boy said in a brittle voice, "I don't know who you are, mister, but if you're some kind of a nut or a psycho—"

"This is very serious, I guarantee you."

"Then why won't you say your name?"

Once again the reverend was unable to answer. It was not exactly the reception he had expected.

"Do you know something about my sister's murder? How come you haven't told the police?"

"I saw the ad in the paper. It said to call—"

"Call Sheriff Royce Ansley, mister, and talk to him. *If*

you're for real," said Grayson. "Otherwise, stop bothering our family."

Ephraim Davis heard the phone click off at the other end. He gripped the receiver for a moment with sweaty palms and then he slowly put it back in its cradle.

Chapter 10

With the exception of Monday night, when she had agreed to help Brenda and Loretta with the Daughters of the Confederacy supper meeting, Lillie stayed in the house and waited by the phone. All day Monday her nerves were humming, so sure was she that someone would see the ad and phone. When she got home Monday night, Grayson admitted with distaste in his voice that one crank had called, but otherwise nothing. Tuesday seemed an interminable day. The phone rang a few times, never with any import, and by the end of the day she was amazed at how wearying it was to sit and wait. It put her in mind of those long hours outside operating rooms, where you did nothing except to focus your attention, your mental energy, on something you could do nothing else about. And you waited for a verdict. When Grayson got home on Tuesday night she questioned him more closely about the caller of the night before.

"How do you know for sure it was a crank call?" she said, delaying him at the supper table.

"I told you," Gray said patiently. "It was some black guy. He didn't have anything to say. He wouldn't give his name. He was just calling to hassle us. I told him to call the sheriff if he knew anything."

"But that was the whole point," Lillie insisted. "In case someone didn't want to go to the sheriff."

"Lillie," Pink said. "For God's sakes, stop this. Grayson did the right thing. He told the man to call the sheriff. If the guy knew anything, if he called Royce, don't you think we'd know it by now?"

"I know it," she said. "I know."

"Well, if you know, then why don't you cut it out?"

After they both had left the table, she remained behind, slumped in her chair, staring blindly at the mess around her. Pink was right. She was clinging to this idea of the ad as if it held some sort of hope for her. But hope for what? she wondered. Even if someone did call, it would not bring her baby back. It was all she could do to clean up and fall into bed.

The next morning when she awoke, the house was quiet, and she was alone. Like a boxer who had fought on, glassy-eyed and wobbly kneed, she was finally flattened to the canvas. She knew that she had to face her loss.

It took her a long time to get up. When she did, she forced herself to go to the kitchen and eat a piece of toast. Next she took a shower and washed her hair. Then she went back to her bedroom.

The sunlight was coming in through the bedroom win-

dow, falling across the pale green and rose patterned carpet that she had kept from her grandmother's house. She
looked at the bed, but then went instead to her dressing
table and sat in front of it, beside the open window. She
closed her eyes and breathed in the clear October air.
Autumn in Tennessee was never really crisp, the way
they said it was in New England, for example, but in those
early autumn days it had a silky coolness to it, and the
sky, through Lillie's lace curtains, was a baby blue. Lillie
sat quietly with her hands in her lap, letting the pain wash
over her, taking in her loss, accepting it in a way that she
had, to this point, avoided. It was the kind of day that
made you glad to be alive. Lillie brushed the tears off the
familiar tracks down the sides of her face. After a while
she knew what she wanted to do.

Slowly she got up and went to the closet. She took out
a pair of gray corduroy jeans and pulled them on. She
noticed, with a vague feeling of surprise, how they hung
from her narrow hips and bagged at the waist. Everyone
had been scolding her, telling her to eat. For the first time
it was apparent to her that she must have lost quite a few
pounds. She used a belt to secure the pants around her
waist. Then she went to her bureau and looked in her
sweater drawer. She was reaching for the drabbest
sweater she had when her eye was caught by a sapphire-
blue cotton sweater that Michele had bought for her on
her last birthday. It was a big, bulky sweater, the kind that
young girls favored these days. Lillie would never have
bought it for herself, but Michele had clapped when her
mother put it on, and Lillie had to admit that it suited her
very well. Michele had boasted that she knew it would.
Lillie pulled the sweater out and put it on.

Finally dressed, she sat down at the dressing table and looked at herself in the mirror. Her skin was the palest it had ever been. The sunlight seemed to kindle the ends of her dark, wavy hair as it dried in waves to her shoulders and even her eyes seemed lighter than usual, as if the sun were filtering through them, washing out their color. Although she was of a fragile build, Lillie thought of herself as a strong person, a healthy person. But the woman in the mirror looked evanescent, like a puff of smoke in the process of dissolving. Lillie reached into her makeup drawer and dusted a little pink blush on her cheeks. She could see now why Brenda had mentioned her lack of makeup. She looked ghostlike, even to herself. The pink blush helped. She put a creamy rose color on her lips, but she left her eyes alone. Tears would wash the makeup away anyhow. She pulled her damp hair back into a clip, although some of the clean tendrils escaped and curled around the taut, pale skin of her temples.

She got up from the vanity and walked out of the house. She went out into her garden and stood amid the withered summer blossoms and the bright, hearty autumn blooms. The day was even lovelier and more bittersweet than she had imagined. She went and got her garden tools from the storage shed, then returned to the garden. Bending over, she slowly began to clip. Candy-pink, gold and russet, the dahlias and zinnias fell into her basket. A few cream and peach roses still nodded in the breeze. She clipped them too and added them to her bouquet. She stood up and rubbed her back. Then she went into the house and filled a mayonnaise jar with water. She arranged the stems in the jar, and replaced her gloves, clippers, and basket in the shed. Then she picked up a trowel and the flowers and headed for the car in the driveway.

Across the street, the old horse was snorting in the field behind the fence. Lillie hesitated for a moment at the car door. Then she set the flowers down on the seat and crossed the road to the fence. She pulled up a handful of grass and offered it to the old beast. The horse lifted its nose over the railing and nibbled from her palm. Lillie ran her fingers over the horse's coarse mane and leaned her head lightly against its warm nose, which felt soothing on her cold skin. The horse quickly lost interest in the grass and turned away. Lillie walked back across the street and got into her car.

It was only about a two-mile drive to the cemetery, but the quiet roads of Felton had never looked more beautiful and tranquil to Lillie. She welcomed the pain that flooded her heart. The flowers in their jar sat upright on the seat beside her, like an obedient child.

She parked the car along the road and walked through the iron gate that was the only marker for the old town cemetery. They had chosen a lovely spot for the graveyard long ago. Trees sheltered it and farmlands surrounded it. Black-eyed Susans and bright-orange butterfly weed grew wild along the slope that led up to the graves. Lillie had not been back since the day of the funeral. It had been crowded that day, and the rainy atmosphere had been charged with anger and tension and tears. Now, as she walked to the spot where Michele was buried, she felt the peace and the imperturbable, endless quiet of the place.

She was still some distance from the grave when she suddenly saw that she was not alone. She was startled, so certain had she been that she was the only one there. She wondered if she had been speaking aloud to herself. But no, Jordan Hill was clearly unaware of her presence. He knelt on one knee at the gravesite, staring at the white cross that temporarily marked the spot until a stone could be placed there. The shadows of the branches above shifted across his stooped shoulders, and as Lillie came closer she could see that he was shivering as he knelt there, although the day was still mild. She did not want to startle him, so she gently spoke his name.

Jordan rose awkwardly to his feet and looked at her with glistening eyes across the crumbling stones of the cemetery. Lillie's heart turned over in a long-forgotten way at the sight of his sorrow. She tried to summon the old anger, but it seemed unimportant for some reason. She looked down at the flowers in the jar.

"I thought I'd put these on the grave," she said.

She could see him swallowing, gazing away from her. He cleared his throat and smoothed his mustache in a nervous gesture. "Well," he said in a hoarse voice, "I'll get out of your way."

"It's all right," she said. She walked over to the grave and crouched down beside it. She set the jar down and took the trowel from under her arm. "They're from the garden."

"Well, they're beautiful."

Lillie poked the trowel into the earth. The red soil was already getting a hard winter crust on it. After a moment, Jordan knelt down beside her.

"Would you mind if I did that?" he said.

Lillie looked at him for a moment. Then she handed him the trowel, leaned back, and held the flowers steady on her lap as he dug. She watched his hands work, and they seemed more familiar to her than his face. When he reached for the jar and their fingers touched, she felt a shock, as if she had not realized that the hands were flesh. It was as though she had been seeing them in her memory.

Jordan planted the jar in the hole he had dug and then patted the earth around it. He sat back and looked at the flowers and the cross. Then he bowed his head. Lillie did the same.

She had wanted to be here alone, to speak to her daughter in her heart. She knew Jordan's presence should seem a terrible intrusion, but it did not. She said her prayers, and her heart spoke freely. In spite of all that had happened, she felt oddly comforted that they should be there together, Michele's mother and father.

When Jordan reached his hand out to help her to her feet, she did not spurn it. The bitterness was not there. He has his own tears, his own pain, she thought. She let him help her up. The silence between them was awkward but not rancorous. He was looking at her in a strange way, and she suddenly wondered if perhaps her sweater might look too gay, too colorful to him, for he was dressed in the sober tones of mourning.

"I guess I should be wearing black," Lillie said, "but I wore this sweater because she gave it to me."

Jordan's grave expression turned to surprise, and then he smiled and his eyes filled up with tears. Lillie was reminded of a rainbow that appears while it's still showering. "She had your number pretty well," he said.

Lillie started to speak and then stopped. She might not feel bitter, but she still did not want to talk to him about

Michele. She turned her back on the grave and started walking toward the car. "Do you need a ride?" she asked. "I didn't see another car here."

"I walked over from my mother's," he said. "I guess I was coming to say good-bye."

"You going back?" she asked politely.

"This afternoon."

"Oh."

They walked sideways down the hill, through the gate, and back to where her car was parked. A hoary brown chicken-turtle was making its way slowly across the country road on crooked feet. Jordan walked over to it, lifted it up, and placed it on the other side as it paddled the air in alarm. Then he came back to where Lillie was leaning against the car.

"Life goes on, I guess," said Lillie.

Jordan frowned. "So they say."

"That's what everyone keeps telling me," she said. "I guess I've been a little deranged since this happened."

Jordan nodded. "Have you gotten any response to that ad you put in the paper? Did anyone call?"

"One crackpot. That's all."

"I was thinking of stopping by to see the sheriff before I left. Although he and I never did have much use for one another."

Lillie sighed. "I think you'd be wasting your time. All they know now is who *didn't* do it. Namely, Ronnie Lee Partin. I've been trying to . . . well, I can't. I can't keep thinking about it. It's out of my hands. Maybe I'm just focusing on the murder so that I won't have to think about the fact that Michele is gone. I've got to accept the fact that nothing, nothing is going to bring her back. Everyone's been telling me that and they're right."

Jordan shoved his hands in his pockets and let a deep breath out slowly. His dark brows formed a heavy line low over his eyes. "Lillie, I know that's true. But I still want the bastard caught and locked up and throw away the goddamn key."

Lillie looked up at him and their eyes met like two vigilantes acknowledging one another. Then Lillie shook her head. "I believe I've been flirting with a nervous breakdown. And I can't afford to fall apart. I still have a family to think of."

Immediately she regretted saying it. He hunched his shoulders in a way that said, more clearly than words, that he was completely alone. It's his own doing, she reminded herself.

Jordan looked out at their surroundings. "You know," he said, "I remember walking out here when I was a boy. The town cemetery. It was just a spooky place to run by on Halloween."

Lillie nodded and said nothing.

"You can go far away from here but there's nowhere else quite like it. It's in your heart, this country. I meet people all the time who have no feeling for their home, for the place they grew up. They really don't have a place that calls to them. Somehow, when I had Michele, I always felt that a part of me was still here. Still belonged."

Lillie looked out at the peaceful fields. "I don't know," she said. "I've never really been anywhere else." Then she scuffed one shoe along the road. A wild aster twisted in the laces. "Well, that's not true. I've been in the airports and the hospitals of a couple of big cities in fact."

Jordan looked at her, as if expecting anger, but there was only a faraway look of memory in her eyes.

"Well," she said briskly, "we'd better be getting back. What time is your flight?"

"Four o'clock. Out of Nashville," he said. He came and opened the car door for her. Then he went around and got into the passenger's seat.

Lillie looked back at the gates of the shaded cemetery. "She always looked forward to going up to New York to see you. She was so proud of that. That you were on TV. She loved that."

"I loved her," he said quietly.

Lillie turned on the engine of the car. She did not look at his face.

The Reverend Ephraim Davis stood on the steps of the town hall and breathed in deeply of the clear air. He felt light of heart and peaceful of mind as only a man can feel when he has done the hard thing, but the right thing, and he knows it. He had spent two sleepless nights after talking to that young boy, the dead girl's brother, on the telephone. His conscience told him to go to the sheriff and his instincts for survival told him to get in his car and head right back home to Memphis.

His sermon went unwritten, his Felton parishioners unvisited, while he pondered the problem. Perhaps he knew all along what he was going to do. He was a man who had dedicated his life to doing the right thing, and so he had thrown up his breakfast and then, with a fearful, prayerful heart, come to see the sheriff.

Now he felt buoyant, relieved, and even rewarded. It had been easy, in fact. The sheriff had been interested and polite. He was clearly a former military man, and the Reverend Davis, like many of his generation, had a lot of respect for soldiers. This was not some pot-bellied redneck sheriff. No, this was a gentleman who called him sir, asked him a couple of questions, and thanked him with a handshake for coming forward with his information. Now, he felt, he could go back to doing the Lord's business with a clear conscience. He had done his duty as a citizen and a man of God. He virtually skipped down the steps toward his car. He was hungry, and he was partial to the barbecue at Otis's Pit Stop, but this time he thought he would pass it up. He wanted to get back to the church and the work he'd been called here to do. As he walked off the last step he passed a rugged, handsome-looking white man in a dark-gray jacket.

"You look cheerful today, Reverend," the young man said as they avoided colliding on the step.

"Well, it's a fine day, son," said the Reverend Davis.

Jordan watched the minister go down the steps and get into a two-tone green Ford that struck him as somehow familiar. Jordan wished he felt half as cheerful as the old reverend. He opened the door to the town hall and ran into Francis Dunham, the dispatcher, who directed him to the sheriff's office. "He's not there, though," Francis said. "He's going out to a meeting."

"Has he left yet?" Jordan asked.

"I think he's in the men's room," Francis said brusquely.

Jordan hesitated a moment, and then walked down the corridor to the men's lavatory and pushed the door open. He swung the inner door back and walked inside. Royce

Ansley was zippering up at the urinal. His hat hung on a hook outside a stall.

"Sheriff," said Jordan. "Can I bother you a minute?" His voice echoed loudly off the tiles.

"Can it wait?" Royce asked, walking to the sink.

"No, not really," Jordan replied. "I'm heading back to New York this afternoon and I wanted to speak to you before I left. Francis said you were on your way out to a meeting."

Royce turned on the faucet, rolled back his sleeves, and dispensed a little liquid soap into his palm. "That's right."

Jordan could read the sheriff's dislike for him in his eyes as he squinted into the mirror above the sink. He pretended not to notice and went on.

"I've been concerned about the investigation. I know you have the whole county to think of, and I was wondering if it might not help to hire a private detective. Someone who could devote full time to the case. We don't want to let the trail get too cold here."

Royce lathered his hands carefully and then rinsed them. He turned to Jordan as he shook them off, and droplets of water splashed on his jacket. "Didn't you play a detective on a TV show one time?" Royce asked.

Jordan's face hardened as he returned the sheriff's gaze. "Yeah, I did. What has that got to do with anything?"

"Isn't that what they say on TV? Don't let the trail get cold?"

Before Jordan could answer, Royce pushed the disk on the hot-air dryer and began to rub his hands together beneath it. The dryer's roar made it impossible for Jordan to be heard. He waited until the dryer was finished and the sheriff began to roll down his sleeves.

"Look, Sheriff," Jordan said, "I'm not trying to step on your toes, but I want some results. It was my daughter who was killed."

Royce walked over and picked up his hat and jacket. His gray eyes peered off into the distance. "You know, Mr. Hill, I remember the day that child was born. Lillie went into labor, and she called me to come get her and take her to the hospital. Had you left for good by then, or were you just getting ready to leave them?"

"I was there," Jordan said coldly.

"Oh, that's right. You didn't leave until after you found out all that was wrong with the baby."

The door to the men's room swung open and the deputy, Wallace Reynolds, came in. He looked at the two men who were glaring at one another and then he greeted the sheriff. "Do you need me to come along on this, Sheriff?" he asked.

"No, you look after things here, Wallace."

"Okay, I will. I've just got to take a quick piss."

"I'll see you outside," said Royce. He pushed through the inner door and Jordan followed him outside.

"I don't care what you think about me, Royce," Jordan said. "But you better get the guy who killed my daughter."

"That's all I want," Royce said evenly.

"And I want to be kept informed," said Jordan.

"Feel free to call anytime," the sheriff said blandly. "Someone will fill you in. Right now I have nothing to tell you."

Jordan saw the futility of saying anything more. This man saw him as an outcast, almost as undesirable a being as the killer they sought. This was a town where people did not forgive and forget. He had once fled the responsibilities of a sick child and a young wife to chase a dream. Now all doors were closed to him here. No explanation would ever open them again. He could understand it in a way. It was too much to expect. He had once left his daughter's fate in the hands of others, and it was too late to want it back. Now he had no choice but to trust it to them. Jordan turned and left. He and the sheriff did not bother to say good-bye.

CHAPTER 11

In the weeks that followed Jordan's departure, life resumed something like its normal shape. Pink tried to sell off a corner of a large farm to a guy who wanted to start a rental operation for four-wheelers, but the seller backed out at the last minute. Lillie volunteered a lot at the hospital, and she and Brenda and Loretta had a full calendar of luncheons and dinners that required the services of Home Cookin'. There were no more calls about the ad in the paper. Royce came by occasionally to report that he was questioning one person or another, or to show them lab reports on minutiae collected at the crime scene. The murder weapon was not recovered, although the lab determined that it had been made of wood. Only Grayson had any positive news to report. He won the school election handily and quarterbacked the Cress County Cougars tʊ a winning game. Lillie tried to be excited for him, but it was difficult to feel enthusiasm. She was glad that her son's life seemed to be going forward. Often she felt as if her own was just going on.

On a Monday afternoon in late October, a pounding on the front door woke Lillie out of a sound sleep. The digital alarm clock read four-thirty, and Lillie could hardly believe that she had been asleep for over an hour. During the day she tried hard to keep a good attitude, but when it became too difficult, sleep was her escape hatch. The only drawback to the oblivion of sleep was that she awoke with a familiar, fearful feeling of emptiness and loss.

"Just a minute," she mumbled, and then called out louder, "I'm coming."

She stumbled down the hallway toward the front door, running her hands through her hair to push it back from her face and pinching her cheeks awake. She opened the door and looked out. At first she did not see anyone there. Then she noticed that Allene Starnes was seated on one of the porch rockers, wiping her eyes with both hands. Lillie walked out on the porch and shivered in the chilly October afternoon. She sat down on the rocker beside the girl.

"Allene?"

The girl looked up at Lillie with red, puffy eyes. "Hello, Miz Burdette."

"What's the matter, honey?" Lillie yawned and shook her head. "Excuse me." She drew her sweater tightly over her chest.

"I didn't mean to wake you," the girl said sorrowfully.

"That's all right," said Lillie. "I've got no business sleeping at this hour."

"Is Grayson home?" Allene asked.

"No. I don't think so. Maybe he came in while I was asleep." Lillie got up and opened the front door. "Grayson," she called sharply into the house. There was silence from inside.

"Do you know where he is?" Allene asked.

Lillie frowned. "He said this morning that he was meeting someone after school. I just assumed it was you."

"It was supposed to be me," Allene said. "He was supposed to meet me by my locker. Right after school."

"And he didn't show up?" Lillie asked, her voice rising.

Allene started to weep and shook her head. Tears flew off her face like rain off a wet umbrella.

Lillie's palms suddenly felt sweaty. There's some simple explanation, she told herself. He's practically a grown man. He can take care of himself. But no rationalization quelled the fear that suddenly gripped her. "I don't know," she said agitatedly. "Maybe he had to go somewhere with Russell or one of the other boys. He'll probably show up any minute."

"I knew it." Allene sobbed. "I knew it. He was planning this."

"Allene, what is it?" Lillie demanded.

"Everything," Allene wailed. "I've gotta go."

"Wait a minute," said Lillie. "Wait. If you know where he is, please tell me. I'm worried about him. If he said he was going to meet you . . ."

"I guess he changed his mind," Allene said in a small, hard voice.

"But where could he be?" Lillie cried.

"I have a hunch," Allene said bitterly.

And suddenly Lillie understood that there might be another girl involved. "When he gets home I'll tell him to call you," she said gently.

"Never mind," said Allene. "It'll be too late." Allene ran down the porch steps, got on her bicycle, and headed back down the road in the direction of town. Lillie watched her go. On the one hand she pitied her and hoped she would not end up broken-hearted. On the other hand she prayed that Allene was right, and he was safely keeping company with another girl. Allene's coppery hair looked like a little flame in the mottled brown of the autumn landscape. Love is so painful when you are young, she thought. Your heart is so vulnerable. The ringing of the phone interrupted her thoughts and her heart leapt. Maybe it was Grayson. She closed the front door and went in and took the call. The sound of the voice on the other end gave her a start. "Jordan?" she asked.

"How are you doing, Lillie?"

Lillie looked out the window and down the road, hoping to see her son coming. "I'm getting by," she said. There was a silence from Jordan's end. "Look, Jordan, I can't tie up the phone."

"Oh, sorry, I didn't mean to bother you." His voice was deep and he had the actor's ability to sound rich and confident, but Lillie could hear the worry and the distracted edge in his tone.

"Where are you?" she asked, more kindly. "Are you in New York?"

"Yeah. Back at work and all. I was wondering if there was any news yet. I didn't want to bug you but it's frustrating, not knowing what's going on."

"Believe me," she said, "you know as much as we do. I said to Pink, I think the sheriff is as discouraged as we are. But there doesn't seem to be much we can do about it."

"I guess not," he said.

Lillie heard someone coming down the hall and she turned around, hoping to see Grayson. It was Pink.

"By the way," she said to Jordan, "your mother came by to see me."

"She did? How did she seem to you? I've been concerned about her."

"She seemed all right. She's pretty tough. She's been through a lot in her time. As a matter of fact, she ended up making me feel a little better."

"That's good." There was real relief in Jordan's voice. "I was afraid that this might be too much for her." Lillie could hear a certain tone in his voice that she recognized from long ago. He was getting ready to settle in for a serious talk. Pink had gone out and returned to the room, carrying a bottle of Jack Daniel's and a glass. He poured himself a shot, frowning into the glass. She knew the frown was not intended for the whiskey.

"Well," she said briskly, "I'll let you know if we hear anything."

"Oh, okay," said Jordan, sounding a little surprised.

"Thank you for calling."

"Take care of yourself, Lillie."

"I will. Good-bye, now." She hung up the phone.

"Well," said Pink. "What did Romeo want?"

Lillie looked at him coolly. "Jordan was curious about the investigation."

Pink shook his head as he poured another shot. "What a golden opportunity." He sighed. "He's been waiting a long time for a chance like this."

"Pink," she said. "I'm worried about Grayson. He was supposed to meet Allene after school . . ."

Pink deliberately tossed off the shot. "After the day I've had, it's great to come home and find my wife getting cozy on the phone with her ex."

"Did you hear me?" said Lillie. "Grayson didn't meet Allene and he didn't come home . . ."

"For God's sake," said Pink. "He's sixteen years old. He probably found something better to do."

"What if he had an accident or something?"

"Don't be hysterical, Lillie."

"I'm sorry. I worry about him. I've already lost one of my children. I can't help worrying."

"Yeah. Well, I'm worried too. I'm worried about my wife and her ex-husband."

"Jordan called to find out if there's any news about Michele's murder. Does it seem odd to you that he would want his daughter's killer to be caught?" she said angrily.

"Oh, that's right. He's the real father. I forgot."

Lillie looked sadly at her husband. "Pink, you were the only real father Michele ever had. Nobody would ever say anything different. I'm just trying to explain to you why he is concerned."

"Father," Pink scoffed. "He was no father. He was a hard dick. That's all he was. And now he sees his chance to wave it around in front of you again." Pink raised his glass and drained it. "Here's to him."

"Oh, Lord," said Lillie, walking toward the door.

He followed her down the hall to the kitchen. "Don't you turn and walk away from me, Lillie."

She wheeled around and faced him. "Then don't talk like a pig!"

"I know," he said. "You're right." He put the cap back on the bottle and set it down on the counter. "I've had a bad day," he muttered.

Lillie opened the refrigerator door and looked inside. She did not feel like talking to Pink. She sighed and took out a package of hamburger steaks. Then she looked up at her husband.

"Do you think we should go out and look for Grayson?" she asked.

"It's not even dark!" Pink wailed.

"All right," Lillie snapped, still holding the package of meat in her hand. "I just wondered. Allene was so upset . . ."

"He's too young to be tied to one girl," said Pink. "He's got his whole life ahead of him. Lillie, I feel rotten. I'm gonna lie down."

"Go ahead."

"Call me when those things are cooked," said Pink.

"I will," Lillie said with a sigh.

Allene knew where to look for him. She knew it in the pit of her stomach. It was as if a little demon were alive inside her stomach, twisting and tormenting her. She knew it before she ever went over to his house. She got the idea when she was waiting for him outside school and she called out hello to Russell Meeks and asked him if he'd seen Grayson. Russell had blurted out that he'd seen him not long ago, talking to Emily Crowell. And then suddenly Russell looked away guiltily and Allene knew right then and there.

She was pedaling along, scarcely watching where she was going. She didn't really need to pay attention. She had lived her whole life in this town and she knew the way to the Millraney farm by heart anyway. They had been there a few times, she and Grayson. Each moment she had spent there glowed like burnished gold in her memory.

The first time she hadn't wanted to go there, but Grayson convinced her it was okay. Nobody was living there. It was a property that Grayson's father had for sale. Old man Millraney had died and his only heir was a nephew in Chicago who just wanted to be rid of the place. But nobody wanted to buy it because it was old and in bad condition. All the furniture and years of accumulated belongings were still in it. You didn't even need a key to get inside, Grayson told her. And he was right.

Allene felt as if she was pedaling through sorghum, so leaden did her heart and limbs feel as she rode along. Maybe there will be no one there, she told herself. Maybe you are blowing this whole thing out of proportion. You hear that he is talking to a pretty girl and the next thing you know you've already condemned him. She put on the brakes and wobbled to a halt. She balanced on one leg along the roadside, the other leg still on the pedal. If you just go home now, maybe everything will be all right. She stood there for a moment, staring, unseeing, across the road at the crisp brown ribbons of leaves that rustled on the dried-up cornstalks.

She had to know for certain, so she got back on the bike and rode on. She came to a bumpy, narrow road and pedaled past a large, empty field. Around the next bend was the old farmhouse. The last rays of the afternoon sunlight streaked the gabled roof and glinted off the dusty windows of the old place. Behind the house was a barn with a hole in its roof and a weathered split-rail corral. Not far from the back door of the house was an old stone well. The first time Grayson brought her here he had given her a penny and told her to make a wish. And then he had whispered what he wished for in her ear. It still took her breath away to think of the warmth of his breath on her, the brush of his lips against her ear, the feeling of his hand gripping hers, leading her, weakly protesting, faint with desire, into the house.

Emily Crowell's red sports car was parked in the driveway, outside the back door. She knew it was Emily's. Not many kids at school had a car, and Emily was old enough to drive. Her father was some big shot at the bank, so Emily had a red sports car that Grayson had often admired aloud. It glowed now, ruby red, in the driveway, and the sight of it sitting there was like a knife through Allene's heart.

She got off her bike at the foot of the driveway and balanced the bike against her trembling hip, gripping the handlebars with cold, sweaty hands. She knew which one was the bedroom window. She knew where they would be. She remembered the first time, when he had lured her in there with words of love and she had wanted to go, even though she knew it was wrong. When she closed her eyes she could still feel the nubby texture of the bedspread beneath her bare skin, and the fullness of him inside her, and see that beautiful face contorted with desire as he reared above her, moaning.

I don't want to go to the window and look in, she thought. The actual sight of them together could be no more vivid than what she saw in her mind. But some need to know beyond any doubt forced her forward. As she approached the window little fragments of prayers formed in her mind. The glass panes were dirty and reflected the fading light. She made her hand into a fist and carefully rubbed clean a spot in the low corner. All the while she said to herself that there might be nothing to see. Maybe they were studying. She knew he did some tutoring. He'd tutored Tyler Ansley before Tyler went off to military school. They used to meet up here. He told her so. Perhaps he was tutoring Emily now. The corner was rubbed clean and Allene gripped the grimy sill and looked in.

He was on top of Emily, the nubby spread tangled in their legs, her round white breasts flattened against his golden chest, her black hair fanned across the pillow. Their eyes were closed, their mouths open, and they moved together like a wave.

Allene jerked away from the window, feeling that she wanted to throw up. She could walk in on them if she wished. The back door would be open and they would probably not even hear her coming. But what for? Her humiliation was already complete. She had offered him her love, her body, her very soul. And it had not been good enough to keep him. Soon everyone in school would know it too. Her love for him would be a joke that everyone would laugh at.

And then another thought jolted her. Was it possible that they knew already? That she was the last to know? How long had he been lying to her? The night of Founders Day, when he said he wanted to hang out with his friends. Emily had been at the picnic. Allene vaguely remembered seeing her there. And how about the weekend when she worked on the posters, and he said he had to stay at home? Had it been going on all that time? The possibility of it overwhelmed her. Allene had never dreamed that you could feel so bad and still be alive. She turned the bicycle around, mounted it, and started back toward town, while, in a wretched whisper, she sobbed his name.

CHAPTER 12

"**Y**ou," Cyril Carty said as Jordan hung up the phone after talking to Lillie. "Into the makeup room. You messed your eyes up." Jordan obediently trailed the mincing steps of the makeup artist into his domain and sat down in the chair. Mark O'Connell, the network publicist assigned to *Secret Lives*, appeared in the doorway and announced to Jordan, between bites of a ham sandwich, that Walter Soames was here to see him. "You want me to get rid of him?" Mark asked.

Walter Soames was a furniture upholsterer from South Jersey who still lived with his parents. He was a well-mannered young man who enjoyed a certain status of familiarity around the studio on West 68th Street because he was the president of the fan club that Jordan shared with Lorna Maxwell. For most of his three years in the cast of *Secret Lives,* Jordan's character, Paul Manville, had been romantically involved with Lorna's character, Jennifer Taylor. In her private life, Lorna was married to an optometrist and had a two-year-old daughter. Jordan occasionally had lunch with Lorna, and every year he went to the open house that she and her husband gave in their East Side duplex at Christmas. Otherwise they were not inclined to socialize. But in the minds of the viewers, they were so enmeshed that it was inevitable that they should have the same fan club.

"You want me to tell him you left for the day?" Mark asked.

Jordan knew better than to shake his head when Cyril Carty was working on his eyes. "That's all right," he said. "Tell him I'll talk to him after the next scene. I'll be done for the day then."

"Hold still," Cyril commanded, licking his lips in concentration.

"He'll probably want to pump you about your daughter," said Mark, sticking the last of his sandwich into his mouth and pushing back his long hair with mustard-stained fingers.

"It's not a secret," Jordan said. He did not have much use for O'Connell, who was the biggest gossip of them all and yet maintained a cynical veneer that suggested he was above such petty concerns.

"The fans, you know. They love a story like that," Mark observed.

"Go ahead," Cyril said brightly, patting Jordan playfully on the backside. "Go."

Jordan checked his tie and his hair in the lighted mirror before preparing to go back on the set. "Their sympathy is more genuine than a lot of people who really know me," he said.

"Oh, puh-leeze, Jordan," said Mark. "No wonder they love you. You're so corny."

Jordan stifled a sigh. "Let him wait in my dressing room."

Walter Soames was seated in a swivel chair in front of the mirrored wall in the dressing room when Jordan finished his scene. Everyone on the show, except the original star, the venerable Margaret Clarke, shared a dressing room, but they often shared with people who taped on different days. So most often the dressing room was relatively private. Walter leapt to his feet when Jordan entered, and Jordan extended his hand to the sallow-skinned, overweight young man and told him to sit.

Jordan began wiping off his makeup and changing his shirt. "Walter," he said, "I was very touched by the wreath that the club sent. It was beautiful."

"You're welcome, Jordan. I took the liberty of buying it out of club dues because I knew it was what the members would want to do."

"Well, I appreciate it."

"I don't want to intrude on you in your time of grief," said the solemn-faced young man, "but I did want to express my sympathy to you in person."

Jordan had slipped into his street clothes by now. He ran his fingers through his hair to loosen the spray and mousse cement job that Cyril had done on him earlier. Then he sat back in his swivel chair and sighed. "Walter, she was my only child. And I was not much of a father to her."

"Oh, no," Walter said quickly. "I'm sure you were. You're a very good person."

You have me confused with Paul Manville, Jordan thought.

"Not Paul Manville," Walter said earnestly, as if reading his thoughts. "You. I know a lot of stars, Jordan. Believe me. I know what I'm talking about."

Jordan's sad eyes smiled at the boy. Walter was not dim, just politely persistent. He knew very well which actors snubbed him, which laughed behind his back as he pursued his enthusiasms for TV stars.

"Walter," Jordan said sincerely, "that means a lot coming from you. You brightened my day."

Walter smiled broadly.

"Look, I'm heading home. Do you want a lift downtown? I'll be going right by there." Jordan knew that the fan club president took the bus to the Port Authority for his visits.

"No, thanks. I'm seeing Lorna after the taping. She's got some new snapshots of her daughter for the newsletter. Thanks anyway."

Jordan shook Walter's hand, excused himself, and headed down the corridor, bidding those he passed a good night. He went out the double set of doors to the lobby and asked the security guard who he liked for the evening's football game.

"Giants, of course," said the guard.

"Of course," Jordan repeated, waving as he headed out into the street. He shivered when he got outside. It was cold and gray and the city had a kind of dreary, romantic gloom to it. Jordan hailed a cab and directed the driver to Sheridan Square. He bought a six-pack of beer and a TV dinner in a market on West Fourth Street, then headed for his apartment. He figured he would look at his script for a while and then heat up the dinner during the game. His heart sank as he came around the corner and recognized the girl seated on the stoop of his building. Amanda stood up when she saw him approaching and gave him a dazzling smile.

"I was having my hair cut on Christopher Street and thought I'd drop by. Like it?" Amanda gave her impressive curls a shake.

"Very nice," said Jordan.

"Feel like company?"

"Sure," he said with a forced smile. "Come on in."

He unlocked the outer door and the familiar musty scent of the hallway greeted him. He heard her chattering behind him but he was already trying to figure out what he was going to do with her. He had seen her twice since he got back and he knew it was going nowhere. He had hoped she felt the same, that she understood why he didn't call her. But she was clearly not ready to quit without an explanation. Well, he thought, he could take her out in the neighborhood for dinner and then put her in a cab. That way he might catch the second half of the game. The TV dinner would keep for another night.

He unlocked the door to the apartment and Amanda flounced in and made herself comfortable on the sofa. Jordan opened the refrigerator under the sink and popped the TV dinner into the tiny freezer. He opened a beer and offered her one. She played with the neck of the bottle with her tongue but Jordan pretended not to notice.

"I had an audition today," she said. "A household cleanser commercial. I don't think they'll give it to me though. I was the wrong type. They wanted a kind of frumpy housewife type. I wish my agent had told me. I would have worn an old kerchief on my head or something."

"No, that's not you," Jordan said politely, taking another swig.

"Listen," she said. "While I was sitting out there waiting for you I got a great idea."

"What?"

"Are you planning on going up to your country place this weekend?"

"I haven't made up my mind," he said warily. "Why?"

"I thought you said you went every weekend."

"I do usually."

"Well, I was thinking that I could go over to Balducci's and pick up some really nice food for us, and we could go up there together. We could relax and just hang out. I'd really like to see the place. And that's the kind of setting where I'm really at my best. Out in nature. You've never seen that side of me."

The idea of her invading his mountain place did not appeal to him. Under the best of circumstances it was not a place that had ever worked out well with women, even when he took them full of optimism and romantic plans. He knew without even imagining it that it would not work with Amanda. "Look," he said awkwardly, "my, um, storyline is heavy right now. I really need the weekend to study scripts and kind of regroup. The timing wouldn't be right."

Amanda studied him for a minute and then set the beer bottle down on the coffee table with a crack. Her voice had an edge to it. "You know, Jordan, I thought we were having a pretty good time together. What happened all of a sudden? I thought I turned you on."

"Amanda, it's not you, really. It's my fault. I'm kind of low these days, after what happened . . ."

"So let me take your mind off it."

"To tell the truth, I don't much want my mind taken off it," he said honestly. "I don't know how to explain that to you."

"I think that's just an excuse, Jordan. Are you interested or aren't you?"

Jordan hated this kind of scene. He didn't want to say anything to hurt her feelings. In fact, it wasn't anything she had or hadn't done. He couldn't explain it to her. He did not want to sit up all night with her, or hold her till dawn. He didn't see some depth in her eyes that made him want to live there. Maybe you only felt that way once in your life. Maybe you had to be young and innocent to feel it. He didn't know. It didn't matter. How cruel was she going to force him to be? he wondered. His stomach began to churn.

"I've heard about you," she said abruptly, standing up. "The word is out on you. You're conceited and hung up and no woman is good enough for you."

Jordan wondered briefly where she had heard that. But he didn't want to encourage this conversation, so he did not try to defend himself.

"Anyway, that's your problem," she said. "I didn't spend five years in therapy so some cowboy could ride roughshod over my self-esteem." She pulled her sunglasses out of her handbag and marched to the door. "When you get lonely enough, and I mean, really lonely— don't call me."

Jordan sighed. "I'm sorry, Amanda. You're right. It is my problem. There's no reason to keep on hurting you."

Tears sprang to the girl's eyes, and she quickly put on the sunglasses. "Hurting me?" she said hoarsely. "What about you? God damn it, Jordan, you don't even try." Jordan looked down and away from her. Amanda passed him and stepped out into the yellowed hallway. He felt an intense relief when she was actually out in the corridor.

Amanda shook her head. "Surely you could afford something better than this," she said coldly.

Jordan shrugged and gave her a wan smile. "I like it here."

"I think they call it 'stuck,'" she said archly. "I won't miss this dismal place." She clattered down the hall on the cracked linoleum floor. He watched her go. Once she was gone he closed the door and leaned against it. In the quiet of the empty apartment his thoughts were free to roam. There was no one to chide him as his mind drifted home again to Felton, to Michele, to Lillie, and to all that he had lost.

Chapter 13

"Where were you?" Lillie demanded the moment Grayson walked in the door. "You were supposed to meet Allene."

Grayson looked surprised and then he grimaced guiltily. "That's right," he said. "I forgot. Don't look so freaked out, Mom."

"I'm sorry," Lillie said lamely. "I was just . . . worried about you."

"Well, don't worry," Grayson said. "I'm a big boy. I can take care of myself."

"Supper's fixed," she said. "Wake your father."

The three of them sat down to eat in silence. Lillie reported to Grayson about Allene's visit, and he replied that he would call her later. The silence fell again over the table and Lillie felt somehow responsible. She had the sense that Pink and Grayson might be talking if she weren't there. She turned to Pink and asked him what was wrong with his day. All Pink would say was that he was never going to be able to sell the Millraney place. Grayson's head jerked up at those words and he stared at his father, but Pink just kept on eating.

"Grayson, what's that look for?" Lillie asked idly.

Grayson looked offended, as if she had been trying to invade his privacy. "Nothing," he said.

"I see," Lillie replied, and did not bother to try to start another conversation. After supper Grayson went to his room, and Pink settled in the living room while Lillie did the dishes. She stood at the sink, elbow-deep in soapy water, and remembered how she had almost enjoyed doing the dishes when Michele was alive. That was kind of a good time of day for them, when they would catch up on the day, on the things "the boys" wouldn't be interested in. They would talk over their plans for the next day, reminding one another of what had to be done, what they were looking forward to. You miss sharing those little things, Lillie thought. You miss having someone be interested.

She was almost finished with the dishes when she heard the front doorbell ring once and then, after a while, ring again. Drying her hands, she went out to the living room, ready to demand of Pink why he had just let it ring. Pink was slumped in his chair, the newspaper collapsed in his lap, a bottle of bourbon and an empty glass beside him. Drinking made him sleepy, especially after supper. These days, falling asleep in his chair was his regular pattern. Lillie hoped it was only temporary, until the worst of his grief had passed. He was very difficult to get along with when he had had a few. She shook his shoulder as she headed for the door. Pink awoke and looked at her through a fog.

Lillie turned on the porch light and opened the door. Betty Starnes, Allene's mother, stood in the arc of light, her eyes dark with worry.

Before Lillie could greet her, Betty said, "Allene didn't come home tonight. Is she here with Grayson?"

Lillie invited her in. "No, no, she's not. She was here earlier looking for Gray, but then she left."

"She always tells us where she's going," said Betty. "She hasn't even called. Bill is home waiting, in case she calls, but I had to come out looking for her. I couldn't just sit there."

"Pink," said Lillie. "Go get Grayson, will you? Maybe he knows where Allene is." She turned back to the distraught mother. "Why don't you sit down? Can I get you something to drink? Some tea, maybe?"

Betty shook her head. "I couldn't. My stomach is in a knot."

"I know," said Lillie. "But we'll find her. Don't worry."

"If anything happened to her . . ." Betty said, shaking her head. Her reddish-blond eyelashes were strung with tears, and her freckled face was drawn and splotchy.

Lillie squeezed the woman's cold hands. "I'm sure she's fine."

At that moment Grayson followed his father into the room. "Hello, Mrs. Starnes," he said politely.

"Hello, Grayson. I'm looking for Allene. Do you know where she might be?"

Gray shrugged his shoulders. "I haven't seen her since study hall this afternoon."

Betty let out a groan. "Oh, God. I've tried her other friends. You know what I'm thinking."

Lillie shuddered, but her voice was steady. "Don't even think it."

"I can't help it," Betty cried. "There's someone in this town who's crazy. He's still running around loose. He did it to your little girl . . ." She started to sob.

Lillie grasped her firmly around the shoulder. "Take it easy," she said in a voice that was calmer than she felt. "There's some good explanation. Come on. I'll help you look for her."

"Do you think I should call the sheriff?" Betty asked.

"I'm sure she'll turn up safe and sound," Pink said sympathetically.

"Do you want me to help look?" Grayson asked.

"You stay and finish your homework," said Lillie. "Gray, Allene was all upset when she came here today. Do you know what that was all about? Did you two have a fight or something?"

"No," said Gray, shaking his head. "It beats me."

"Where will you look?" Pink asked.

The two women looked at one another gravely. "We have to go down there by the bridge," said Betty. "Just in case."

"I don't want you going down there, Lillie," said Pink. "It's too much for you to have to be there. I'll go." He went to the hall closet and pulled out a jacket.

"I can go by myself," said Betty.

"Never you mind," Pink said. "That's what friends are for."

Pink picked up his car keys off the mantel and gestured

toward the door. Lillie frowned at her husband. "Are you okay to drive?"

"Don't be a nag," said Pink. "I know my own limits."

At that moment the phone rang.

"That could be Bill," said Betty, her eyes widening.

Lillie picked up the phone and spoke briefly to the person on the other end. When she turned back to face Pink and Betty, her color was ashen.

"What?" Betty whimpered.

"That was Bill. We have to get to the hospital. They found Allene unconscious in the balcony of the Felton movie theater."

"No," cried the girl's mother.

"Apparently she took a bottle of Sleep-Eze or one of those. They're pumping her stomach right now. Don't panic. She's going to be all right."

"Oh, my God," cried Betty. "Oh, my God."

"Come on," Pink said. "I'll drive."

When they reached the hospital they found Bill Starnes pacing the waiting area outside the emergency room. He was putting out a cigarette in a standing ashtray when they came in.

Betty rushed to her husband's arms and he patted her back soothingly. "I just saw the doctor," he said. "She's okay."

Betty began to weep and Lillie felt tears rush to her own eyes.

"Why?" Betty asked. "Why would she do this? She always seemed so happy."

"I don't know," Bill said grimly. "We're going to have to have a serious talk when she comes out of it."

At that a nurse emerged from the emergency room and

looked at Bill and Betty. "Are you the parents?" she asked. Betty nodded.

"You can see her soon. We're moving her up to a regular room. We just want to watch her for a day or two, and make sure there are no ill effects. But you can see her for a few minutes."

Betty thanked the nurse and then turned to Lillie. "You've been so good. Thank you."

Lillie nodded and then glanced at Pink and Grayson. "We'll be going now," she said. "If we can help in any way, please call."

"I will," said Betty, kissing her cheek.

"Tell Allene I said hi," Grayson said weakly.

"I will, dear." Betty returned to her husband.

Lillie trailed behind Pink and Grayson on their way to the parking lot. Before they reached the car Lillie called out to Gray. He turned to look at her. His wheat-blond hair glowed silvery in the harsh phosphorescent lamps that illuminated the lot.

"Grayson, where were you this afternoon?" she said. "Who were you with?"

"Mom, I told you I didn't see her."

"Were you with another girl?"

"Okay," said Grayson. "Okay. I was with another girl. I didn't know that was a crime in Cress County."

"Grayson, don't be fresh," Lillie exclaimed. "I'm just trying to figure out what happened. She was crying her heart out when she came by. Maybe that was why."

"So now it's my fault that she ate a bottle of pills. I don't believe this."

"I didn't say that," Lillie insisted.

Grayson's eyes flashed angrily. "Are you blaming me

for what she did? I want to know. Are you saying it's my fault she tried to kill herself?"

"That's ridiculous," Pink said grumpily.

"Grayson," said Lillie, "I know it's not your fault. Of course not. But she is your girlfriend. And you did break a date with her to go off with someone else."

"Look, Mom," Grayson said. "It's a free country. I'm not married to Allene." After a moment he added, "I'm sorry she did it, all right? How was I supposed to know she'd get so upset?"

Lillie shivered in the nighttime chill. Allene had done this out of anguish over Grayson. She felt sure of it. But when she looked into her son's eyes she saw an unsettling truth there. Allene's dramatic gesture had been in vain. This new girl must be something special. Because when it came to Allene, he didn't care at all.

It was late when they got home and much later still by the time Lillie went to bed. The whole incident made her nerves feel raw again. She kept thinking of Allene, huddled on the porch rocker in tears, and how she had not realized how close the girl was to doing something drastic. Lillie could not help wondering if she might have prevented it, if she had tried a little harder to talk to Allene. If she hadn't been so numbed by her own problems.

Pink was asleep when she finally climbed quietly into the bed beside him. He was breathing heavily, as if he had just been rescued from drowning. She lay still beside him, trying to force herself to relax, but her mind continued to race.

She understood the fierceness of young passions. In the darkness, as the night ticked slowly by, she remembered her own broken heart when Jordan left her, left town, left their sick baby, with only a brief note of explanation. She flushed hotly, lying there in her bed, when she remembered the feelings of embarrassment, of loss, of unbearable betrayal, and that was seventeen years ago. To her surprise, and irritation, she felt tears pricking her eyelids.

This is stupid, she thought, wiping them away. But she could still picture his young face and recall how once she had believed in him, as if his dark eyes held some answer she had sought all her short life. Pink began to wheeze and rolled over in his sleep, throwing an arm out across her. She looked over at him. He had been right there when Jordan left. In fact, he had been there for quite some time, but she had not seen him, so in love was she with her teenage husband.

Lillie shifted under the weight of his arm, but Pink only moved closer. She edged up under the covers so that the weight was off her chest, so she could breathe.

In the quiet of the night she ruminated on those terrible days when Jordan first left. She had not been much older than Allene at the time. Everyone told her that he wasn't worth crying over, that she had her whole life ahead of her. No one seemed to understand what she felt. I could have killed myself then, she thought. I can understand it. If it hadn't been for Michele . . . There was no telling what that kind of pain could make you do.

The thought of Michele brought its own painful ache again, and Lillie reminded herself that sleep was the only remedy, however fleeting. She closed her eyes and allowed herself to drift, to let the numbness come.

All of a sudden she started and was awake, her eyes wide in the darkness. Is it possible? she wondered. She sat up in bed, clutching the sheet tightly in her hands, and tried to think clearly. Could it be that her Michele had broken someone's heart? Had made him mad enough to kill her? She was still a virgin, according to the coroner's report, so no one was thinking about sex as a motive. But when you were young like that, passions ran so high, despite the lack of experience. Maybe someone had loved her. Maybe she had wounded him without even being aware of it. Lillie felt her own heart pounding at the idea, as if she might have stumbled over some answer there in the darkness. She wanted to wake Pink, to say it to him, but she knew instinctively that he would be angry to be awakened just to hear some suspicion she had dreamed up in the night. She forced herself to lie back against the pillow. She lay awake, staring, for a long time. When she finally slept, her dreams tormented her.

CHAPTER 14

In the morning light, Lillie cautiously examined her theory again. She thought about it as she made the beds and cleaned up the kitchen. It still made sense to her.

As far as she knew, there were no boyfriends in Michele's life. To her mother, she had been like a little girl. But she was surely old enough to have experienced love, and although they shared many problems, Michele did have a secretive, reflective side.

Lillie had not been able to go into Michele's room since the murder. Brenda had gone in and picked out the clothes that Lillie described to her for the funeral. The sheriff had searched the room, and Lillie had watched him carry out various papers and objects, but she had stayed outside in the hall. Thinking about it now, Lillie realized that the sheriff might have made the same assumptions.

He had never put the idea into words for them, but he was probably thinking that way. That's what he was searching for in Michele's room. Some clue to a boyfriend's identity.

But, Lillie reasoned, if there was some clue in there, it might not be apparent to the sheriff. It might well be something that only a mother would recognize. After all, who would know better than she what was normal for Michele?

She knew she was going to have to go into the room and look, to satisfy herself. But she hesitated on the threshold, filled with dread. Only the hope for some kind of answer enabled her to put her hand on the doorknob and turn it.

Lillie opened the door to the room and stepped inside. The look, the scent, and everything about it nearly knocked the wind out of her. The rose-pink dress still hung on the closet door. Trembling, she sat down on the bed and smoothed the cover with her hand as she let the memories break over her. The finality, the cruelty, the unfairness of it, battered her heart, but she did not run. After a while she felt more composed. She reminded herself that she was here to find something, although she wasn't sure what that something was.

Unlike many girls her age, Michele had no scrapbooks, and she did not keep a diary. Perhaps, Lillie thought, because a diary was for frivolous things, and Michele's life had too many days of needles in her arms and hospital rooms and green-masked faces hovering above her. Perhaps she knew she would never want to read about that again. When she was writing, it was always her schoolwork. She had to make such an effort to keep up.

Gently Lillie picked up the schoolbooks from the desk

and leafed through them. Lillie could picture Michele, the diligent student to whom nothing came easily, bent over them with a furrowed brow. Lillie turned the pages in her notebook. Michele had been an exceptionally neat person. There were no doodles on the page, no silly drawings, no indication of the impatience, the inattention of students. Lillie put down the notebook and picked up the student yearbook. The class that graduated this June should have been Michele's. She had been held back because of her long absences. Still, she had bought the yearbook, and many of her old classmates had signed it. There was a friendly impersonality to the inscriptions. To a sweet kid. To a nice girl. Lots of luck, remember homeroom. Remember gym.

Nowhere did it say Remember our great date, the fun party, the school dance. She had missed it all. It had all been shimmering ahead of her when some maniac struck her down.

Lillie replaced the book on the shelf and looked around the room. Everything in the room was neat and orderly. Was there no hidden side, Lillie wondered, to this child's life? She went to the closet and looked through the pockets of her clothes. She opened every shoebox, and each contained a pair of shoes. She moved on to the dresser, lifting the neatly folded clothes, the coiled belts and organized jewelry drawer. She was giving the bottom drawer a perfunctory check when her hand fell on something lumpy under the pile of cotton sweaters. Lillie reached back and pulled it out. It was a paper bag with a mortar and pestle printed on the front with the Flood's Pharmacy logo. Lillie opened the bag and pulled out a little stuffed dog with floppy ears, the kind of toy one might buy for a two-year-old. A little gold paper medallion still hung from the thread around its neck, but there was no price on it, and when Lillie shook the bag, no receipt fell out. She turned the toy over in her hand, examining it. Michele never bothered with stuffed animals, she thought. Maybe she bought it for some child she knew. Lillie sat back on her heels and tried to figure out for whom Michele might have bought a present. And then, as she was unsuccessfully reviewing a list of possible children, another idea occurred to her. Maybe the toy had been a present *for Michele.* Maybe a secret admirer had bought it for her. Maybe admiration had turned to hatred somewhere along the way.

Lillie put the toy back in the bag. It's too farfetched, she told herself. You're just reaching for something, anything, to make sense of a crime that was senseless. She looked at the pharmacy logo on the bag. There was probably some perfectly simple explanation for the toy stuffed into the drawer. Still, she thought, it wouldn't hurt to try to find out.

Lillie got herself ready to go out and then drove to the center of Felton. She parked on Main Street and crossed the square to Flood's Pharmacy. A bell jingled softly as she opened the door and went in. The blond girl who worked for Bomar was behind the makeup counter, fixing her cottony hair with the tail of a comb and studying her face in one of the round tilted mirrors that sat on the counter. Without lifting her gaze from the mirror she asked, "Can I help you?"

Lillie felt immediately self-conscious and hid the bag behind her back. This girl wasn't going to remember who bought a stuffed toy on some unknown past date. There wasn't even a receipt so that the date could be pinpointed.

Lillie pretended to be looking at the greeting cards so that it would appear that she had a reason for being there. Having performed her duty, the girl at the counter began applying tester eyeshadows to her lids.

Lillie walked over to the toy section and stared at the stuffed animals arranged there, as if they could speak and give her the answer she was seeking. Row upon row of round plastic eyes stared blankly out of furry faces. Go home, Lillie thought, this is a dumb idea.

"Lillie, my dear, how are you?"

Lillie jumped. She had not heard Bomar approaching on the soft soles of his Wallabees. His creased face shone above the plaid bow tie he wore. "Bomar."

"Is Kimberly helping you?" he asked sternly, casting a glance at the salesgirl, who suddenly busied herself by rearranging perfume bottles on the counter.

"I was just looking," Lillie said weakly.

"Well, I guess congratulations are in order," he said.

Lillie looked at him, confused. "For what?"

"Oh, there I go," said Bomar, "spoiling the surprise."

"What surprise?" asked Lillie.

"Well, I guess I have to tell you now," the old man said cheerfully. "The Chamber of Commerce had their meeting this morning over at the Sizzler Steak House, and they voted to name your Grayson as one of the winners of the leadership awards that they're giving out at the banquet next Friday."

"Oh, that's great," said Lillie. "He'll be so thrilled."

"Well, he deserves it, you know. He's a fine lad."

"Thank you, Bomar."

"Matter of fact, I nominated him," the druggist said proudly.

"That was right nice of you."

Bomar shrugged and rubbed his hands together. "Glad to do it," he said. "Now, what can I get you, little lady?"

Lillie hesitated, not wanting to spoil the good news about Grayson, but if anyone would know about the toy, she thought, it was Bomar Flood. She reached into the bag and pulled out the dog. She looked at it a minute and showed it to the druggist.

"I know this is going to sound kind of crazy, Bomar, but humor me if you would."

"I'll sure try," he said.

"I was going through Michele's things and I found this in her drawer, still in the bag. Do you sell this kind? I don't see one here."

Bomar squinted at the dog and nodded. "Oh, yes," he said. "Sure." Then he looked at her uneasily. "Did you want to return it?"

"Oh, no," said Lillie, "heavens no." The idea of returning the toy seemed so ghoulish that it made her errand seem innocuous by comparison. More confidently she said, "No, I'm just trying to figure out where she got it. I mean, who she got it from. If it was a present."

Bomar looked at her sadly. "Lillie," he said, "will you take an old man's advice and not dwell on things like this? It's not healthy."

"Bomar, I am not doing that. I am just trying to figure out if there was someone special in her life that we didn't know about. Some boy who might have liked her. Maybe someone she got mad at her. That might have had a grudge against her."

The pharmacist suddenly understood her implication. "One of these kids?" he asked incredulously. "Oh, no."

"Somebody did it," Lillie said angrily. "Why not one of these kids?"

"Well, all right, wait a minute." The druggist put his hands on his narrow waist and frowned down at the floor. "Well, she used to come by after school sometimes, like the other kids. With her girlfriends, usually. She didn't have a boyfriend. I can tell you that right now."

"No, I know," said Lillie.

Bomar took the stuffed toy from her hands and looked at it. "I'll be honest with you, Lillie. I don't rightly remember who bought it."

Lillie sighed. "It was kind of a long shot," she said.

"I do recall though," said Bomar, pointing a skinny finger at the toy's head, "I had a ruckus in here one afternoon over these animals. They were teasing one of the kids. Tyler Ansley it was. One of the boys caught him admiring one of these, and they got on him something awful. I remember 'cause it struck me odd, too. Tyler always acted so surly and tough. Anyway, he cursed the lot of them and I had to hustle him out of here before he started breakin' things." Bomar shook his head. "That poor boy. I hope he's better off in military school. Although he'd be a misfit anywhere. Now I can't remember if Michele was here that day or not. She might could have been. I just don't know."

Lillie stared at the toy. Tyler Ansley. She suddenly remembered the baseball game on Founders Day. Michele had been so indignant that everyone was being unfair to Tyler.

"Bomar," she said slowly, "did you ever see them together? Michele and Tyler?"

"Well," he said, "maybe I saw them talking a few times.

167

But he was real uncomfortable around girls. Tell you what, I think that she might have liked him a little bit. But I don't think he was interested. I hate to say this about that boy, because his daddy is a friend of mine, but the thing in this drugstore that interested him the most was drugs. Not that he ever stole from me. Don't get me wrong. But I kept my eyes open when he was around."

Bomar stopped talking long enough to notice the whiteness of Lillie's face. "Now hold on," he said. "Don't you start thinking any such thing about Tyler. I've been around a long time and I'm a darn good judge of character. That boy wouldn't hurt a fly. He's got his problems, but he's not that kind of boy."

"Well, thank you, Bomar," said Lillie. She suddenly felt a little light-headed. "I really appreciate your taking the time."

"I mean it now, Lillie. Don't start thinking crazy things. Do you understand me?"

"I do," she said, clutching the bag and backing out toward the front door.

"You take care now," said Bomar. "And I'll be seeing all of y'all at the banquet."

Lillie looked at him blankly. "The Chamber banquet. Grayson's award."

"Oh, right," she said. "I'll see you . . ."

"Friday," Bomar said.

"Friday."

The door jingled behind her as she hurried out to the street.

After she left the drugstore, Lillie got into her car and began to drive. She drove aimlessly for over an hour, preoccupied with her thoughts. When a pickup truck honked at her, she realized that she was not paying sufficient attention to the road. Lillie looked around and got her bearings. She was not far from Crystal Lake. She needed a chance to stop, and think and collect her thoughts. She drove in the direction of the lake and pulled into the empty gravel parking lot of a tiny bait and tackle shop that was closed on weekdays until spring, then parked her car.

Through the bare branches and the patchy bright foliage of the trees she could see a silvery sliver of the lake's shimmering surface. It was a place Lillie had come to all her life when she had something important to think about. She and Brenda had played at its perimeter with rocks and frogs and twigs, and later they had walked around it discussing boys. She and Jordan had skinny-dipped there in the moonlight on the loveliest of summer nights. She had walked the edge alone, trying to decide if she should accept Pink's proposal. She had sat under a tree there and prayed when she had to take Michele to Pittsburgh for surgery, feeling somehow that God hovered nearer to this lake than anywhere else in the county. Once she had come with Pink when he took Grayson fishing here.

Getting out of the car, Lillie walked down the road past a hazy lavender and brown field that skirted the lake and through a thicket of trees to the water's edge. She walked along the lakeside for a while, the water lapping gently near her as she bent over to pick up a stone and toss it into the smooth surface of the water. There was a motel on the other side of the lake, and a couple of trailers and cabins around its perimeter, but otherwise it was a quiet spot, a peaceful spot.

Lillie felt anything but peaceful. She walked along until she came to a long wooden jetty. After walking out to the end of it, she sat down and dangled her feet over the end. The water was low and her feet did not reach it.

She held the fur dog in her hand and gazed down at its plain, unthreatening face. Tyler Ansley, she thought. It couldn't possibly be. He was a troubled boy. Everyone in town knew that. But a killer, no. It couldn't be. She had known him all his life. He was young and confused and mad at the world. But not mean. Not vicious. It was just a rebellious phase he was in.

And Royce Ansley was her friend. One of the finest men she knew. He could never raise a boy to be a killer. Then an unwelcome thought came into her head. They always said that preachers' kids were the worst of the sinners. Maybe the same could be true of a sheriff's son. Maybe Royce was searching for a killer that would turn out to be his own son.

And then in the next moment, she had an even worse thought. Maybe he already knew. After all, hadn't he taken the boy off to military school not two days after Michele's death? No, she thought, it's not possible.

Lillie lay down on the jetty and felt a slight, lingering warmth from the wooden slats on her back. She covered her eyes with her hands but Royce's and Tyler's faces loomed before her. Maybe the boy had a violent streak, and Royce knew about it. It was well known that Tyler had problems with drugs and alcohol. Maybe he killed Michele and then confessed to his father and asked him to protect him.

Lillie sat up again. No, she thought again. No, there's still no reason for it. It doesn't make sense. If it was sex she could understand it. But Michele had not been touched in that way. There was just no reason for it. And besides, she thought. If Royce had wanted to protect his son, then why had he insisted on Ronnie Lee Partin's innocence? There he had a prime suspect he could shift the blame to, a ready-made scapegoat, and no one would even have blinked at it.

Lillie picked up the toy again and shifted it impatiently in her hands. It was a monstrous thought. And what did she really have to base it on? A toy dog like a million others. The faulty memory of a nosy drugstore owner? And what if Michele did have a crush on Tyler Ansley, a sentiment that he did not even return? Did that make the boy a suspect for murder?

Around the lake it was still light, but Lillie realized that she had been sitting there for a long time and that darkness was probably gathering in the town. She got to her feet, exhausted by the confusion of her thoughts, walked back down the jetty, and returned up the road to her car. As she suspected, the sky was turning a deep, violet blue. She threw the toy on the seat next to her and started for home.

When she arrived, Pink was in the driveway, washing his car by the back-porch light. Lillie shivered at the sight of the buckets of cold, soapy water. "Isn't it a little late for that?" she asked.

"Well, we've got to be spruced up for next Friday," said Pink. He gestured for Lillie to stand back as he ran the hose over the last of the soap on the hood.

"What for?" Lillie asked.

Pink turned off the water and, still holding the hose like a scepter, squinted at the streaks he could see in the lamplight. "I guess you haven't heard," he said proudly. "About our son."

"Oh, yes, the Chamber of Commerce Award. I did hear. I was at Bomar's place today."

Pink picked up a rag and started to wipe off the roof. "How about that?"

"I'm very proud of him," said Lillie.

"Proud of him?" said Pink, shaking his head. "I'll tell you, he's brought a lot of credit to us. He's our hope for the future, Lillie."

"I know it," Lillie said softly.

Pink attacked a smudge on the windshield with a soft cloth. "I know this is crazy doing this at night, but I've got a lot else to do between now and Friday. I promised I'd get him a suit for the banquet. Really, when you think about it, a boy his age should have a suit."

Lillie looked down at the toy dog in her hands. "Yes, I guess so," she said.

"I think things are looking up for this family," said Pink. "We just have to support our son's endeavors and put the past behind us. I think this award is some kind of a sign."

"Maybe," Lillie whispered.

"What?" said Pink. "What have you got there? What were you doing over at Bomar's today, anyway?"

Lillie opened her mouth to speak but Pink bent down to get his Turtle Wax. From behind the front fender he called out to her, "Did you know Bomar was the one who nominated him?"

Lillie knew he did not want to hear it. She knew before she said one word about it that he would be angry. He was so busy thinking about the good things he could find in life. Thinking about Grayson. And he was right, of course. There *were* things to be thankful for. Things to be happy about. But she said it anyway.

"I found this in Michele's room," Lillie said slowly, "and I think she might have bought it for Tyler Ansley."

Pink straightened up, the wax in one hand, the cloth in the other. Despite the coolness of the evening, he was perspiring from his effort. "What did you say? What about Tyler Ansley?"

She looked helplessly at him. What about him? she thought. A boy they had known all his life. The child of a friend. She tried to imagine herself explaining how he might have been the one. The one who killed Michele. It seemed absurd, even to her. But someone had killed Michele. It could have been Tyler.

"I think Michele liked him," Lillie said stubbornly.

Pink stared at her. "What if she did?" he said warily. "So what?"

"Pink," Lillie said, "do you think it's possible that he . . . ?"

"That he what?" Pink asked impatiently.

"That he was the one who killed her," Lillie blurted out.

"Now I've heard everything!" Pink shouted.

She looked sharply up at him. Although he was only partially visible in the lamplight, she could see him looking fearfully at the stuffed animal, almost as if he was afraid it would come alive in her hands.

"Pink," she said, "what's the matter? You look weird."

"*I* look weird," he said angrily. He daubed the wax on his rag and began to apply it to the car in jerking motions.

"That's a good one. For chrissakes, you're the one with the weird ideas."

She stared at him as he applied the wax to the car. "Pink," she said slowly, "have you been thinking the same thing?"

"Don't be a fool, Lillie."

"I know you, Pink. You think I might be right."

Pink straightened up and shook the rag at her. "Did you hear one word I said to you about this family?" he demanded.

"Pink," she persisted, "this is not just going to go away."

Pink was shouting again. "Can't you stop thinking about this for one minute," he cried, "and show a little interest in your own family? Do I have to do it all? Can I ever get a little help from you?"

The door opened and Grayson stepped out on the porch, a bottle of Coke in his hand. Lillie looked up at him guiltily. "What are you two yelling about?" he asked. Then he peered into the darkness at his parents. "Dad, are you washing the car at this hour?"

Pink's expression softened as he looked up at his boy. "I'm getting it ready for Friday," he said. "I don't want you showing up at the banquet in a dirty car. You're one of the winners!"

CHAPTER 15

Although Home Cookin' had been hired to cater the Chamber of Commerce banquet and Lillie had been planning to serve, she told Brenda early in the week that she was not going to work.

She had done a lot of thinking about Pink's complaints. No matter what suspicions, what ugly thoughts, might plague her about Michele's death, there was no excuse for neglecting her son or her husband. She thought about going to Royce and confronting him with her theory about Tyler, but when Pink asked her sarcastically what evidence she would hit him with, she realized what an impossible accusation it was to make with no proof of any kind. She still suspected that Pink harbored the same thoughts as she about the sheriff's son, but he denied it completely. He told her he was trying to concentrate on the present, and on what remained of their life, and Lillie realized that she had to try to do the same.

She found, however, that rejoining Pink and Grayson, trying to make a trio out of their duet, was easier said than done. Despite Pink's professed desire for her attention, she felt like an intruder between them. You've let them drift so far away from you, she thought. They don't even need you anymore.

Their major plan for the week was to go to the men's store in town and buy Grayson a suit. Lillie brightly suggested that she go along with them, and she tried to ignore the unwilling look that passed between them at her suggestion. "It's a men's store," said Grayson.

"That's all right," Pink amended hurriedly. "They allow women."

Lillie tried not to be stung by her son's reaction. It's your own fault, she thought. You have been so preoccupied with your job, with Michele, and then with Michele's death that they've come to prefer being without you. When the shopping day came, she was ready early and she chatted cheerfully on the way to town.

Once they reached the store, it required some effort for her to hold her tongue when Grayson chose the most expensive suit on the rack and Pink applauded his choice. She tried to be tactful, pointing out a few other options, but Pink announced grandly that he did not bargain-hunt when it came to his son. She decided not to protest when Grayson could not decide between two new shirts and Pink insisted that they buy them both.

When they got home Grayson tossed the expensive suit and shirts on his bed and went off to watch television. Lillie picked up the suit and hung it on the closet door.

Then she picked up the shirts and opened the bottom drawer of his bureau. When she looked in she saw a dozen new shirts, still in their bags, arrayed before her.

"Grayson," she cried.

She stood up as the young man entered the room and pointed to the drawer. "What are these?" she demanded.

"Shirts," he said pleasantly.

"What are you doing with all these new shirts? You haven't even worn them."

Grayson studied the bags in the drawer with an impassive expression. "In some cases," he said, "I don't have the right thing to go with them." He bent down and picked up a yellow pinstripe. "This really needs a navy blazer, I think. And the one I have doesn't look right in the shoulders anymore."

"Where did you get the money to pay for these things?" Lillie asked. "You don't even have a job."

"I tutor sometimes," he said defensively. "I told you that."

"And you made enough for all these? Or did your father get them for you? And why in the world did you need two more shirts today?" she insisted.

"None of these goes with the suit," Grayson said, closing the drawer with his foot. He turned and looked at his mother. "I thought you wanted me to look good for the dinner. I guess I misunderstood."

Pink, who had heard their voices raised, appeared in the doorway.

"I do want you to look good. But this is wasteful, Grayson. You've got a closetful of clothes . . ."

Grayson turned to Pink. "Mom doesn't think I need these clothes. Maybe we better just take them back."

"You're not taking anything back," Pink said angrily, gesturing for Grayson to leave. He turned to his wife. "Would it be impossible for you just once to say something to him without criticizing him? Good God, most mothers would be bursting with pride over a boy like that. All you can do is pick at him."

Lillie's cheeks were burning. "I didn't say he had to take the clothes back. I just wanted to know where he got the money for all these clothes in here. If he didn't get it from you . . ."

"He didn't get it from me," Pink said sarcastically. "He tutors. And he likes to be properly dressed. If you paid attention, you'd know that."

"But what does he need with so many?" Lillie protested.

Pink waved a hand at her in disgust. "Go back to your dream world, Lillie. I knew this would never work. Go back to your memories and your obsessions about Michele. Leave us be, will you?"

Lillie turned away from him, gripping the packaged shirts to her chest. Part of her wanted to scream at him, but another part thought that, in a way, he might be right. For such a long time she had not paid enough attention to her son, because of Michele, and now there was a lot about him that she didn't know. She promised herself to try, from now on, to concentrate only on loving her son. And her husband. What they needed from her was attention and interest, not disapproval.

In the following days, the effort she made seemed to pay off. She began questioning Grayson closely about his days at school. He was suspicious at first, but her lavish praise made him garrulous about each day's accomplishments. She learned from Grayson that he and Pink had had lunch twice together in the school cafeteria. If he was embarrassed to have his father come to school like that, he did not reveal it to her.

In keeping with her resolve, Lillie did not mention Michele's name. When thoughts of Michele and nagging suspicions about her death began to buzz in her head, she redoubled her focus on her family. Her living family.

The night of the banquet she was ready early and it was Pink who had to be hurried along. Grayson looked sleek and elegant in his new suit. Lillie admired him effusively and he seemed to bask in her compliments.

The banquet was being held at the Briar Hill House. As they drove up its winding driveway, the old mansion glowed warmly ahead of them. But Lillie shivered at the sight. They got out of the car and stood for a moment in the damp night air, which smelled of moldering leaves. Lillie looked over at Pink, wondering if he was thinking of their last trip to this place. He avoided her gaze, turning instead to Grayson and beginning to inspect the boy's tie, his collar and cuffs.

"He looks fine," said Lillie. "Very handsome." They started to walk through the decaying leaves on the lawn toward the brightly lit house.

"I've really been looking forward to this," said Pink.

"So have I," Lillie said. "Although I do dread going in there a little."

She was immediately aware of a chill in the atmosphere. Grayson stared stonily ahead, and Pink let out a noisy sigh. All week her silence on the subject of Michele had gained their tacit approval. She could feel that her remark had offended them, as if she had broken some unspoken agreement.

"Well," she said brightly, "this is a great occasion. May I take the arm of the guest of honor?" Grayson looked at her warily but proffered his arm. Lillie patted his cool hand as he led her into the foyer of the building.

The committee of wives had decorated the old mansion in a harvest motif, with arrangements of mums, pumpkins, and Indian corn. On the balcony, which overlooked the foyer, Gay Jones, the music teacher, was playing a piano. The love theme from *Romeo and Juliet,* which the spinsterish Miss Jones played with admirable flourish, wafted down and was picked up by many a hummer.

They each took a ticket for the door prize, hung up their coats, then joined the social hour, which was in full swing. Punch was being poured in the so-called library, which no longer held books but served as a perfect spot for a makeshift bar. Lillie peeked into the ballroom as she returned from the ladies' room and saw Loretta and Brenda putting the last touches on the round tables set up there. It was a longer walk to the kitchen, but it was deemed more elegant than the cafeteria dining room for a grand occasion such as this.

"This looks great," Lillie said to Brenda, who kissed her cheek. "I just feel guilty that I didn't help."

"Don't worry. We're not putting up with these excuses much longer, right, Loretta?" said Brenda.

Loretta giggled and congratulated Lillie on the award Gray was getting. "And you look real pretty."

"I'd better get back," Lillie said. "See you later."

She walked out of the ballroom and back toward the front rooms where the social hour was going on. As she came up from behind she saw a familiar stiff-backed figure standing in the shadow of one of the arched doorways. He was wearing a suit, and his short crew cut looked as if it had been starched.

"Royce," said Lillie, before she could catch herself.

The sheriff turned and looked at her with grim, unsmiling eyes. "Hello, Lillie."

She felt guilty looking him in the eye, given all the ugly thoughts she'd had about his son. At the same time she could not help but wonder. Was it possible? Did he know? He looked so uncomfortable and lonely standing there. He rarely went to social functions since Lulene died, unless, as in this instance, his presence was virtually required. Leave him be, she thought. He had always been such a decent man. But she couldn't help herself.

"How is Tyler doing at the Sentinel?" she asked in a voice that she tried to keep very neutral.

She noted the slight hesitation, the way he turned his eyes away from her. But his voice was calm. "Tyler is having difficulty adjusting, I'm sorry to say. But that's the story of Tyler's life."

It was the only time she had ever heard him refer, even obliquely, to his disappointment in his son. Although it was no secret. How could it be? It seemed cruel to press the point, but she felt as if she must.

"It was just so sudden the way you took him off to school. Had you been planning that for a while?"

Royce's eyes looked haunted in his leathery face. "Let's say it had been coming for a long time," he said evenly.

"You know, I never realized that he and Michele were close until recently." Lillie could feel herself trembling as she said it.

"Tyler and Michele?" he asked.

"Yes," Lillie said brightly. "I believe she was quite fond of Tyler."

"I didn't know that either," said Royce. "I wasn't aware of anyone who was fond of Tyler. Except for myself, of course," he added in a flat voice.

Lillie almost wished she had never spoken. She felt so sorry for him again, and she felt guilty for even thinking such terrible things of him and his only child.

"We haven't seen much of you lately," she said.

Royce looked into the crowded foyer, but his gaze was distant. "I have not forgotten Michele," he said, "if that's what you mean. She is always on my mind."

"I didn't mean that," Lillie said gently. "I know you've been working on it. Will you excuse me, Royce. I have to talk to some people."

"Oh, sure," said the sheriff. "It's a big night for Grayson." She thought there was a bitter note in his tone, and she looked back at him. He was pushing his way in the direction of the bar. With a son like Tyler, she thought, no wonder he was bitter.

She entered the room and, in a moment, was swept up in a welter of greetings and handshakes. The social hour passed swiftly, and then everyone surged into the ballroom and took seats at the assigned tables. Grayson was seated at the head table. Lillie and Pink found their seats near the front. As everyone took their places, the CC president, Sterling Grisard, tapped his glass for attention. The room quieted down and he thanked them all for coming. Promising speeches for after dinner, he introduced one of the two men in clerical garb at the head table, the Reverend Ephraim Davis, who would say grace.

After the black preacher stood up and delivered a brief prayer in a deep voice, everyone began eating. As the din of conversation rose, the woman beside Pink said, "How about that. A black preacher saying grace. He doesn't even have his own church here. He's just filling in over at Mt. Olive."

Pink drained the wineglass beside his plate and looked around the table for the bottle. "Well," he said, "you know the Chamber's got two black members this year."

"Who's that?" asked the woman.

"They own the Crispy Chicken franchise out on Route Thirty-one."

"Oh, yes," said the woman. "I guess I saw that in the county paper."

"They've got a Pakistani this year too," Pink said. "He and his wife own the motel out on Crystal Lake."

The woman buttered a hot roll and plunked it down on her plate. "Next year they'll be saying grace in Hindu." She sniffed.

Pink chuckled and then leapt from his seat as he saw Brenda passing by with a wine bottle in her hand. "Can I get a refill?"

Brenda came over and rolled her eyes at Lillie. "I gotta tell you, this is some job. I'll be glad when you're back. Grayson looks so handsome up there. Is that a new suit?"

"He just got it." Lillie nodded.

"I swear he's the handsomest guy in the room."

Lillie smiled and looked proudly at her son, who was conversing earnestly with the businessman next to him.

The dinner progressed pleasantly and soon it was time for speeches and presentations. They sat patiently through the introduction of new members, a memorial for a recently deceased Chamber "ambassador," a speech about economic growth in Cress County, and finally they came to the leadership awards. Pink, who had been refilling his wineglass at every opportunity, applauded loudly as Bomar Flood took the podium. Lillie could see that the back of Pink's neck was red, and beads of perspiration shone on his shiny forehead.

". . . a young man who has distinguished himself in his schoolwork, school activities, on the playing field, and in the family circle," Bomar said. "We are proud to present him with this award."

As warm applause rose and Gray stepped up to the podium, Lillie saw Bill and Betty Starnes get up from their table and walk to the door, their faces solemn. Lillie blushed with embarrassment as her son started to speak.

Grayson raised the plaque and took his time giving it an appreciative glance. Then he leaned over the podium. "Did I really do all that?" he asked in an ingenuous voice. The women giggled and the men in the audience shifted in their seats. "Well," he said, "I am deeply moved by this honor." His speech was brief and selfless, emphasizing service and duty. When he was done, Bomar patted him on the back, and they shook hands again, to more applause. Grayson sat down and Lillie felt herself relax. He had done well. He had sounded a little smug at first, she thought, especially after the Starneses' silent protest, but everyone seemed to like the speech.

Pink turned and looked at her, his eyes glistening in his florid face. "It's all worth it," he said, his voice slurred a little. "It's worth everything."

"What is?" Lillie asked as the woman next to Pink said, "You should be very proud of that young man."

"Yes, ma'am," Pink assured her. "We are very proud."

The remaining speakers droned on until Lillie thought she was going to doze off, and then, suddenly, it was over, and people were getting to their feet. Friends and neighbors came around, congratulating Lillie and Pink. At the edge of the group Loretta, still in her apron, stood talking to the clergyman who had given the invocation. Lillie noticed that no one else seemed to be talking to them. She excused herself and went over to Loretta.

"Loretta," she said, "excuse me. I just wanted to say how lovely it all was. You guys did a great job. You sure you two still need me?"

"Oh, don't be silly," said Loretta. "That was a beautiful speech your boy made."

"Why, thank you."

Loretta gestured toward the clergyman beside her. "Lillie, I want you to meet a dear old friend of me and my family, Reverend Davis. Reverend, this is Miz Lillie Burdette."

Lillie shook hands with the old preacher. "It's nice to have you here, Reverend."

"It's a pleasure to meet you, Mrs. Burdette. You're often in my prayers."

Lillie looked at the old man in surprise. "I am?"

"Your family, I mean. Your daughter."

"Oh, thank you, Reverend," said Lillie. "That's kind of you."

"Has the sheriff been able to make anything out of what I told him, do you know? I never heard back from him."

Lillie frowned and shook her head. "I'm not sure I understand."

The old man tried to brush it off, slightly embarrassed.

"Oh, it's nothing," he said. "It must not have been important."

"No, please tell me what you mean," Lillie insisted.

"Well, I simply told the sheriff how I saw your daughter that night—"

"The night she was killed," Lillie interrupted.

"Yes, walking alone toward the road to the Arches. I was lost on the road, you see . . ."

Lillie felt as if a fist were tightening inside her. "She was *alone*? Walking along alone?"

"Well, yes. But then I saw a young man down at the Arches. Didn't the sheriff mention this to y'all? He must have cleared it up right away."

Lillie's hands were icy and her knees felt as if they could scarcely support her. "What young man?" she asked quietly.

"He was down by the bridge. She was a lovely girl, Mrs. Burdette. She gave me directions on the road and then, as I turned into that dirt road to turn around, I caught sight of a young man down there."

Lillie struggled to keep her voice calm, casual. "What did he look like?"

The reverend rubbed a grizzled cheek nervously. "Well, I only saw him for a second. He looked to be a tall, well-built boy. Black hair. Kind of longish. Didn't the sheriff tell you all this?"

Lillie shook her head. Loretta peered into her face. "Honey, you don't look too good," Loretta said. "Why don't you come sit down."

"I'm sorry, Mrs. Burdette," said the Reverend Davis. "I shouldn't have reminded you of all that on this happy occasion."

Lillie squeezed the old man's hand as if she were gripping it for support. "No," she whispered. "Thank you for telling me."

"Here, sit," said Loretta, helping Lillie toward a chair.

Lillie turned a pleading face to the other woman. "Loretta, I've got to get out of here."

"Well, I'll tell your husband."

"No, I'm all right. I'll tell him." Lillie patted away Loretta's solicitous hand and walked in a daze toward Pink, who was standing in the middle of a crowd with Grayson. She gestured to him but he just smiled broadly at her.

"Pink," she pleaded.

Grayson heard her voice and turned, raising the plaque to show her. Pink had an arm draped over the boy's shoulders. Lillie nodded distractedly at Grayson and the triumph in his eyes faded. She indicated that she wanted to talk to Pink. Grayson spoke to his father and Pink came toward her, dragging the reluctant young man with him.

"How about this boy?" he asked.

Lillie nodded. "Pink, I have to talk to you. Have you seen the sheriff? Have you seen Royce? I have just heard something. I think there's something going on. I can't believe it myself . . ."

"What is this?" Pink growled. "What?" Grayson just stared at her.

Quickly, Lillie told him of her conversation with the Reverend Davis. "He saw a boy," she concluded, her voice trembling. "A boy who sounds a lot like Tyler Ansley."

Pink was looking at her with a grimace on his face, as if he had happened across a messy accident.

"Pink," said Lillie, "the sheriff never said a word to us about this. An eyewitness."

Pink looked over at the minister. "Why should we believe the likes of him? What was he doing out there anyway, talking to Michele?"

Lillie grabbed her husband's forearm and shook it. "Pink, for God's sake, I think it was Tyler he saw there."

"It could have been anybody," said Pink. "We all look alike to them. That's probably why the sheriff never mentioned it."

"Or it could have been Tyler, and the sheriff knows it," Lillie exclaimed.

Grayson was staring at his parents.

"Lillie, get ahold of yourself," said Pink. "Why would Tyler Ansley want to hurt Michele?"

"I don't know," Lillie wailed. "But it would explain why Royce hasn't found a killer yet. Why we don't get any information."

Pink glared at his wife. "I thought Royce Ansley was our friend. Is that what you suspect him of now?"

"Tyler is his son. Who knows what he would do for his son?"

"Well," Grayson interrupted with a rueful grin. "I guess it was silly of me to think I'd be the one in the spotlight tonight."

Lillie turned and stared at her son. She had felt the familiar stab of guilt at his remark, but all at once she felt something snap inside. "Stop whining, Grayson," she said. "I won't listen to it. I know this is important to you. But your sister was murdered, and that is more important than some award. Yes, it is."

Grayson drew back from her, angry surprise flickering

in his eyes. In the next moment he looked contrite, his face pale and downcast.

"I want to go home," said Lillie.

Pink looked at her indignantly. He reached into his pocket and handed her his car keys. "We'll get a ride from someone else," he said, dropping them in her hand. "Grayson can't leave yet."

Lillie felt her face blush hot with anger at his indifference. She grabbed the keys with a trembling hand and started for the door. Brenda called out to her as she passed by but Lillie kept on walking, out across the lawn into the damp night. She got into the car and drove off. The whole way home her mind was churning.

They were trying to punish her for caring, but it wouldn't work. Why didn't they care just as much as she? That was the real question. Pink had been hell-bent on getting Ronnie Lee Partin. But once she came up with the facts about Ronnie Lee, he seemed to lose interest. Now, when Tyler was a possible suspect, he didn't even want to hear about it. And Grayson was no better. All he seemed to think about was himself. All kids were self-centered. She knew that. But if he would only be a little more concerned, he might be able to come up with some information about Tyler. They had been in school together for years. Surely he could find out something about the boy. Well, she thought, if she had to do it alone, then she would. The important thing was to find the killer. She parked in the driveway and entered the dark, quiet house.

If it was Tyler, she thought . . . but what about Royce? Why hadn't he let Ronnie Lee Partin take the blame for it? She thought again of the sheriff, standing grimly on the outskirts of the evening's proceedings.

Would he have let Tyler get away with it? And then she wondered if Royce had noticed her talking to the Reverend Davis tonight. She had not seen the sheriff anywhere around. She assumed that he had left early. But what if he had been watching her, knowing what the old man was saying to her, wondering if she had made the connection? She had virtually revealed her suspicions about Tyler in their conversation tonight. Lillie shivered and turned on all the lights in the house.

Even as she did so, she chided herself for her fears. Royce would never hurt you, she thought. It just wouldn't be possible. But a crackling noise outside the window in the den made her jump. She would never have thought Royce capable of shielding a murderer either. Not even his son. If he would go that far . . . She walked to the window, holding her breath, and looked out. The yard was still, and apparently empty, in the darkness. She locked the window and pulled the curtain.

She walked to the door of Michele's room and pushed it open, snapped on the light, and walked in. Then she went quickly to the window and pulled down the shade. Lillie repeated her conversation with the sheriff in her mind. She had told him that she had learned of a friendship between Michele and Tyler. Did he know a lot more than that about what was between them? Could it be that there had been some shared, secret passion between her little girl and the sheriff's son? Some passion that had turned to rage? She had been bluffing when she said it to Royce, but perhaps it was true. Lillie looked frantically around the room, as if the room could speak. She tried to think where she could find her answer. After a moment she rushed to the bookshelf and pulled down the yearbook. She turned to the section on Juniors. With cold fingers she flipped the pages. His picture was on the second page. Tyler Ansley. Next to his photograph was a smudge. Lillie snapped on the desk lamp and held the book beneath it. The smudge was pale, pale pink and striated. It took her only a second to realize that it was a lipstick smudge. As if someone had kissed the picture. Lillie stared down at the photograph, her head thudding in time with her heart. The house was so silent she could hear her heart beating. Tyler, she thought. Oh, no.

The shrill ring of the phone sheared through her. She jumped and let out a cry, then slammed the book shut as if to hide her discovery. Her mind racing, she went out to the kitchen and picked up the phone. After a moment she held it to her ear. "Hello," she said warily.

"Lillie," said a faraway voice. "It's Jordan."

Lillie sank down on a chair. "Jordan," she whispered.

"What's the matter? You sound strange. Are you okay?"

Lillie licked her lips and tried to calm her breathing. "I don't know." She knew why he was calling. She didn't want to tell him. She could imagine the polite disbelief of his reaction. She thought about hanging up. "What do you want?"

"I've been thinking about Michele. What else? Is this a bad time to call?"

Lillie sat huddled in the chair, holding the phone in her shaking hand, her mind working feverishly, her caller silent on the other end. Suddenly she wanted to say it. She wanted to hear the stunned reaction and then the pity in his voice, the feeble effort to console her for losing her mind.

"I think," she said calmly, "that Tyler Ansley killed her. And that his father is protecting him."

She heard the expected sharp intake of breath and then there was a pause. "What makes you think this?" he said in a steady voice.

Lillie began to laugh. She could not help herself. The laughter, which was close to tears, rushed out of her in a jagged burst. "I must be crazy," she said. "I must be falling the hell apart."

"Not you, Lillie. You're the sanest person I know," he said. "Please, tell me."

"Forget it, Jordan. It's too long a story. I'm too tired, and there's no proof of anything. Not really. I have to go," she said.

"Lillie!"

"Good-bye." She hung up the phone and rubbed her freezing arms. Then she went back into Michele's room. It seemed chilly and unbearably lonely in the house. She kicked off her shoes and crawled under the flower-sprigged comforter in all her clothes. Then she switched off the bedside light and lay in the dark. She tried to imagine Michele, lying in this bed, fantasizing about Tyler Ansley. Innocently daydreaming of a boy she had a crush on. Planning to meet him perhaps. Never suspecting . . .

Lillie got up out of the bed and went to the door of Michele's room. She closed it tight and locked it. After checking to make sure the windows were locked too, she got back under the covers. In a few minutes, clutching her daughter's pillow, she was asleep.

CHAPTER 16

S he awoke feeling as if she had a hangover. Her head was leaden and stuffy, her eyes scratchy from tears she must have shed in her sleep. At first she felt a little jolt of alarm, finding herself in the unfamiliar room, and then she remembered. Michele. And Tyler. She forced herself to sit up.

The smell of coffee was coming from the kitchen. She looked at her watch. It was nearly ten-thirty. She wondered why Pink hadn't gone to work yet. Perhaps he was waiting to have it out with her about last night. She dreaded the confrontation, feeling as she did. But that was the least of her problems. What was she going to do about Tyler?

After opening Michele's bedroom door, she shuffled out

into the kitchen in her stocking feet. Jordan Hill was sitting at the kitchen table, drinking a cup of coffee.

"Good God," she cried. "What are you doing here?"

Jordan could not help but smile at the sight of her matted hair and wrinkled clothing and the makeup smudged across her face. "You always did look pretty in the morning," he said.

"Damn you, Jordan, I asked you what you're doing in my kitchen."

"What do you think?" he said soberly. "Unlike *you*, I couldn't sleep after that call last night. I got up at dawn, drove down from the mountains, and caught the first flight to Nashville. Then I drove here. Your back door was open." He offered her a cup of coffee. "It's still hot. I just got here."

Lillie stared at the mug in his hands.

"Go ahead," he said. "You always liked my coffee."

Lillie reached for the coffee mug with trembling hands and the steam rose from it, soothing her scratchy eyelids, her tense forehead. After a few moments she took a sip, and then she carried the cup to the window, warming her hands on it, and looked out at the gray, rainy day.

"Well, that was very dramatic of you," she said. "You picked the right line of work. You always did have that dramatic streak." She turned and gave him a thin smile, then took another swallow of coffee. "I feel a little like the boy who cried wolf. I was in a fever when I talked to you, but in the gray light of day here, I'm not sure of anything." She rubbed her forehead wearily. "Tyler is a nice boy. I've known him all his life. He's not a bad boy."

"Start from the top," said Jordan. "Tell it to me step by step."

Lillie sighed and tried to organize her thoughts. Then, slowly, she began to talk. When she got to the dinner and the conversation with Reverend Davis, Jordan stopped her.

"Wait," he said. "A black guy, right? A heavyset guy. Older. Kind of graying sideburns."

"That's him." She nodded.

Jordan got up and paced the kitchen. "I saw him, Lillie. The day I was leaving, he was coming out of the sheriff's office."

"I told you he talked to the sheriff."

"Yeah, but I mean as he swung the door out, I was going in. And yet when I asked Ansley if there was anything new, any new information, he said no. Just flat-out no."

"He'd probably say it was confidential. Police business."

"We've got to talk to that preacher again, Lillie."

"What for?" she asked. "I told you what he said."

"We'll show him the yearbook picture of Tyler. See if it's the boy he saw." He looked at Lillie, who was leaning over the sink as if she felt ill. "Are you up to it?"

"Yes," she said. "Just let me change." She started for her bedroom. Then she turned around. "Jordan, what if it is him? What do we do then?"

"Worry about that then. I'll do the dishes," he said, rinsing the two mugs out under the faucet and tossing them into the drainer.

Lillie called Loretta to determine the reverend's whereabouts, and then Jordan drove his rental car through the mist that hung over the fields of the town, while Lillie sat beside him, clutching the yearbook to her chest.

"Rain, rain, and more rain," Jordan said. "Tennessee in the autumn. And the winter."

"I guess so," Lillie said. "I hardly notice it anymore. Do you remember the way to Bell Street?"

"Sure," he said. "I think I still know every road in this county. Actually it rains a lot in the mountains where I have my house. It's just more likely to turn to snow in the winter."

"Michele told me about that sleigh ride you took last winter."

"That was fun," Jordan said wistfully.

They were silent then until they reached the Walker house. The house was quiet and dark. For a minute Lillie feared that Loretta had not gotten through to say they were coming. Then she saw Clara Walker open the front door and look out at their car.

Lillie and Jordan made a run for the porch through the rain and Clara invited them inside. The Reverend Davis was sitting in the front parlor, leafing through his Bible.

"Thank you for seeing us, Reverend Davis," Lillie said. "This is my . . . this is Michele's father, Jordan Hill."

They all shook hands and Clara Walker leaned over and said to Jordan in a conspiratorial voice, "I like to watch your program when I'm home on Tuesday afternoons. It's pretty good."

Jordan stroked his mustache, smiled, and thanked her. He turned to the man in the chair. "Reverend Davis, my wife tells me that you reported to the sheriff that you saw a young man down by the Three Arches the night my daughter was killed."

The reverend nodded wearily. Lillie opened her mouth

to say "ex-wife" and then did not bother. The minister looked as if he was anxious to be rid of them.

"Could you just look at this picture," said Jordan, "and tell us if this is the same boy you saw?"

Lillie looked up at Jordan and then opened the book. She handed it to the old preacher and pointed to Tyler's picture. Ephraim Davis studied the photograph in silence. Lillie thought that everyone in the room could hear her swallowing.

The old man raised his eyes from the picture. "Ansley," he said. "Same name as the sheriff."

"It's the sheriff's son," Jordan admitted. The two men stared into one another's eyes.

Then the reverend looked down again and closed the book. He handed it back to Lillie. "I'm not sure," he said.

"But you saw him," Lillie protested.

"I saw a young man," the preacher said. "It could have been this boy. But it was dark, and my headlights just passed over him."

"Oh, please," Lillie cried. "You're the only one who knows, who can help us. All you have to do is tell the truth."

The old reverend rose from his chair and glared at Lillie. "That's what I am doing, ma'am. I didn't want to go to that sheriff and tell him anything at all. But I searched my conscience and I did what I had to do. But I'm not about to accuse some young boy of murder who may be innocent just from looking at a postage-stamp-size picture. I'm an old man and my eyes aren't that good."

Jordan signaled for Lillie to stop, although she appeared to be ready to launch another plea. "Thank you for your time," he said politely.

"You're welcome," the preacher said stiffly. Clara Walker saw them out to the porch. They hurried to the car and slammed the doors.

"Well, that's it," said Lillie. "Now you think I was imagining it too."

"No," Jordan replied. "I think you're right."

She glanced over at his brooding profile as he turned on the car and started to drive. She did not ask where they were going. It felt strangely normal to be with him, to let him take control. They drove through the woods and country roads with only the *shush* of the wheels on sloppy, wet pavement to accompany their thoughts. She was not surprised when he turned down the dirt road leading to the Old Stone Arches Bridge. Wet branches slapped the car as they bumped down the rutted road and pulled off into a clearing. From where they sat they could see the rugged mass of stones that formed the bridge and the long, wet fronds of the willow that hung down over it. The narrow river that ran beneath looked like a dark gash in the earth. Jordan turned off the engine and they sat there in silence, Lillie still holding the yearbook to her chest.

The car was filled with the smell of their damp clothing, their hair, Jordan's aftershave, her cologne. Their eyes met, almost furtively, and they both looked away.

"What are we doing here?" Lillie asked.

"We're thinking."

Lillie nodded and looked out across the bridge. She began to shiver. Jordan shuffled out of his coat and draped it over her despite her protest that she did not need it. Then they stared out across the hood of the car again.

"The thing is," he said at last, "that it makes sense. It really does."

"I know it," said Lillie.

"We just don't know why. But everything else makes sense."

Lillie looked over at him. "Thanks for coming, Jordan."

Jordan shrugged and did not look at her. " 'Bout time I got here," he said.

"I try to talk to Pink but he acts like I'm a raving lunatic. He keeps saying to let the sheriff handle it. But how can we let the sheriff handle it if it is his son? I know Royce is a good man. But when it comes to your kids . . ."

Jordan turned to her with wide eyes. "Maybe Pink knows that it was Tyler, but the sheriff is forcing him to keep quiet."

"Don't be ridiculous," said Lillie. "That's impossible." But instantly she recalled Pink's furtive reaction when she mentioned Tyler.

"Why? Royce could have threatened him."

"Oh, think about it, Jordan. Could the sheriff make you keep quiet? Even with threats. It's not possible."

"Okay," Jordan answered. "You're right."

"You don't realize how much Pink loved Michele. He doted on her. How could you even say such a thing?"

"Okay, don't get mad," said Jordan. "I wasn't trying to cut Pink down. I thought maybe the sheriff was threatening his life or something."

"Royce isn't that kind of man," said Lillie.

"Who knows what kind of man he is?" Jordan asked thoughtfully.

Lillie put her head back against the seat as Jordan

opened the door of the car and got out. He stood looking up at the misty sky for a moment and then, with his head down and his hands in his pockets, he walked across the bridge and stood beside the willow, looking down at the spot where Michele died.

For a moment Lillie watched him as if he were alone. For years after she had married Pink, when people would ask her about Jordan she would say, "I don't hate him. I feel sorry for him." It was a good answer. It indicated that all was well in her life and that he was the one who had lost out. And half of it was true. She didn't hate him. She didn't have time to hate him. First there was Michele to care for, and then Pink and Grayson. There was no time to dwell on Jordan. But when she thought of him, whenever she did, when she looked at him now, head lowered, shoulders hunched against the rain, she thought the same thing: How could you leave me? We were everything to one another.

He glanced up, as if he had heard her thoughts, and looked solemnly at her. She opened the car door and walked to the foot of the bridge. Then she crossed over it, reluctantly, to where he stood.

Jordan turned his back on the willow and squinted around at the quiet spot by the river. "What happened here?" he said.

Lillie pulled his jacket close around her. "Do you think the reverend was lying? Did he recognize Tyler?"

Jordan shook his head. "I think he didn't want to make a mistake." They looked around at the desolate spot, the crumbling gray stones of the bridge, the muddy river. "She wouldn't have come down here by herself. She had

to be meeting him here." He shifted his weight. "All right.
I guess the next step is obvious."

Lillie wiped the rain off her face with the back of her
hand. "Not to me," she said.

"I'm going to go see Tyler Ansley."

Lillie's eyes widened. "And do what?"

"It's useless to go to Royce if he's covered up this far.
But if I can take Tyler by surprise—pretend I know more
than I do—I might be able to get him to tell me something."

"That's true," she murmured.

"We just have to make sure that Royce doesn't find out.
We don't want him warning Tyler that I'm on my way."

"Believe me," Lillie said grimly, "he's not going to find
out. When will you leave?"

"The sooner the better. This afternoon. The less people who know I'm even in town, the better off we're going
to be. Besides, it's five hours driving to get there. He's at
the Sentinel, right?"

Lillie nodded.

"I'll drop you at home. I don't think I'll even see my
mother. There'll be a million questions."

"And if he confesses? Then what?" asked Lillie. They
stared at one another, slightly aghast at the idea of facing
their daughter's killer.

"I'll take him to the police right there. Royce won't be
able to interfere," Jordan said resolutely.

Lillie chewed her lip. "It's a terrible thing to accuse a
young man of. Maybe he had nothing to do with it."

"Then a few questions won't bother him, Lillie. Come
on," he said. "I'll drive you back."

When they reached her house she looked around to

make sure no one was watching as she got out of the car. She shrugged off his sports coat and handed it in to him. She started shivering almost immediately. "Call me, will you?" she said. "Be careful."

"Go inside," he said, nodding. "I don't want you to freeze."

CHAPTER 17

O nce she got inside the house, Lillie went into her room and changed into a warm sweater and a pair of pants. She had worn a good knit dress to go and meet the reverend, as if she had been going to church. The dress was wet from the rain and she hung it up to dry. She looked in the dresser mirror. Her dark hair was curled up in an unruly mass from the dampness.

She felt relieved now, and strangely calm. Jordan was on his way to Tyler and, possibly, the truth. In a way, she wished she could go with him, but Tyler would certainly freeze up if he saw her and besides, Pink would never hear of her going off somewhere with Jordan. He was still suspicious of Jordan after all these years. Perhaps this, finally, would convince him that Jordan's motives were honest ones.

She thought back to how Pink had reacted when Jordan first contacted her, when Michele was about six, and asked if he could be allowed to see his daughter and possibly take her for short visits when she was well enough. In fact, she remembered, she had been cold to the idea herself at first. But Jordan's mother, Bessie, who had been steadfast as a grandmother from Michele's birth, pleaded her son's case, and Lillie had relented. For years Pink would grumble, or be silent, on the days when Jordan came to get Michele, and Lillie could see that Michele felt guilty about caring for her "new" father. But care about him she did, and Lillie had to insist that Pink put a better face on it, for Michele's sake. So Pink had learned to live with it. They all had.

The only time he had exploded was several years after the visits started, when Michele was twelve. Jordan asked if she could visit him in New York, and sent a plane ticket. They drove Michele to the airport in Nashville, and Grayson had cried and cried because he was not going to go. Michele had reported this to Jordan, and so the next time Michele was scheduled to visit him, Jordan called and offered to send tickets for both children, so they could both come.

Lillie shuddered, recalling the scene that ensued. Michele eagerly spilled the good news to her beloved little brother, and Pink hit the roof. He had punched a hole in their bedroom wall as he raged at her. "He could have you back any time he snaps his fingers," he shouted as she pleaded with him to lower his voice. "He's got my daughter, and now you want to give him my son. He will never, never get my son. Do you hear me?"

Lillie figured that the whole town had heard him, but

people were too polite to mention it. Grayson knew better than to cry that time in the face of his disappointment. The subject was never mentioned again.

Yes, Lillie thought nervously, Pink was going to resent this, when he heard. He might have felt it was his place to go. She felt a little dull headache start at the back of her neck when she thought about telling him. But he had no right to be angry, she reminded herself. He didn't even want to listen to her fears about Tyler. He was hell-bent on putting this blind trust in the sheriff. Well, someone had to help. And if Jordan wanted to take a hand in seeking his daughter's killer, who could blame him?

Lillie sighed. She knew who would blame him. Still, she thought, there was no avoiding it. Pink had to be told. Perhaps, she thought, she could make him understand it if she put it in the right way. They were not youngsters anymore. They did not have to compete with one another to prove their devotion to their children. They all understood that they were after a greater good.

Armed with her sanguine arguments, Lillie put her coat on and decided to go see Pink before her confidence receded. She got into her car and drove to town.

Pink's office was on the second floor of a building on the square. Downstairs was a shoe store that catered to older customers. The young people went to the mall for their running shoes and purple spike heels. This store was stocked with shoes of the Red Cross variety, sturdy, comfortable, and timeless in their lack of style. Lillie waved through the rain-splattered window at Ben Duvall, the proprietor, and opened the side door leading up the stairwell. There was a long hallway at the top of the stairs with a floor of well-worn brown-speckled linoleum. The first office on the left belonged to a lawyer, the aptly named Alvin Bickers. The green door was closed, and no light from within illuminated the frosted glass and the black letters that read ALVIN BICKERS, ESQ., ATTORNEY-AT-LAW. Probably in court, Lillie thought as she passed it by, or maybe working at home. Alvin wasn't getting any younger and he seemed less inclined to come into the office on cold, rainy days than he used to. There was a men's room next, and a women's room across the hall. The last door on the left was Pink's. A tarnished bronze-colored plaque beside the door read GRAYSON BURDETTE, REAL ESTATE, NOTARY PUBLIC. Lillie's sneakers squeaked softly on the old linoleum as she approached the open door to Pink's office. She walked in and looked around. There was no one at the front desk. Reba Nunley, a housewife who had recently passed her real estate exam and gotten her license, was sometimes there to field calls and welcome clients. In exchange, Pink let her use the extra office space and leave her answering machine there for prospective clients. Pink's desk was behind a partition that backed up to Reba's desk. Lillie knocked on the open door to the hall and called out, "Anybody home?"

Pink came out from behind the partition and looked surprised to see his wife.

"Hi, honey," she said.

"Hi," said Pink.

"Where's Reba? Out to lunch?"

"She had some errands to do."

"Pink, I've got to talk to you."

"Well, well. This is a pleasant surprise. After you spent the night locked in Michele's room I figured we weren't speaking."

"It was more like I passed out there," Lillie replied. "Honestly, I didn't mean anything by it."

"Well, you seem to have settled down a bit. That's a good sign."

Lillie shrugged. "In a way."

"You should have stuck around. The compliments for our son were quite impressive."

"He deserved them," said Lillie.

"He really wants you to be proud of him. He wants you to think about him."

"I do think about him, Pink. Come on."

"Well," said Pink, "you do a poor job of showing it sometimes. Excuse me." He went behind the partition and picked up the phone, which had begun to ring. "Burdette here. How may I help you?"

Lillie walked across the office and gazed at the bulletin board with the new listings and the property descriptions below grainy photos. There was not much for sale.

"You're in luck," Pink said to his caller. "I have exactly what you want. How about if I meet you here, at four say. We're talking about your dream house. That's right. Four o'clock."

Pink came out from behind the partition and Lillie turned to face him. "Pink, I've got something to tell you. That's why I'm here."

"Okay, tell," he said, folding his arms across his chest.

"Jordan showed up this morning."

Pink's fleshy face sagged. "Well, well," he said, "what a nice surprise."

"He called last night when I got home. I told him about my suspicions. I guess he thought it was serious. He decided to come down."

Pink smiled mirthlessly. "When you say 'jump,' he says 'how high?' Is that it?"

Lillie ignored his sarcasm. "We went to see the Reverend Davis today and we showed him Tyler's picture." She could see Pink stiffen at this. "He wasn't able to say positively that it was Tyler that he saw."

"That's just great," said Pink, lifting a set of keys off the pegboard behind him on the partition and jingling them from one hand to the other. "You two must have made a cute team. A couple of detectives."

"I wanted to tell you this in case anyone might have seen us and mentioned it to you," Lillie said awkwardly.

"Oh, nothing surprises me anymore," said Pink, the keys rattling in his hands. "He'll do anything to get to you and you love it. You just eat it up."

"Jordan has left for the Sentinel. He's going to try to question Tyler. We still think that he might be the one."

Pink slammed the keys down on the edge of the desk. "What?" he cried. "What the hell are you—"

"Pink," Lillie interrupted him. "We think if Jordan can take him by surprise, maybe Tyler will tell him something. It's worth a try."

"Oh, really," Pink said sarcastically. "That's what 'we think,' is it? Well, think about this. What is Royce Ansley going to say when he finds out that you're accusing his son of murder? What's inside that head of yours? Besides Jordan Hill. Cotton wool?"

"Jordan made an interesting suggestion," Lillie said coldly. "He wondered if Royce Ansley might be putting pressure on you."

Pink's florid, angry face suddenly turned white. He

stared at his wife with narrowed eyes. "What are you saying?" he demanded in a low voice.

She felt immediately guilty and wished she could take it back. "Nothing," she said. "He was looking for any explanation. I mean, it's apparent that Royce is doing nothing about this case. And look at the way he rushed Tyler off to that military school. He wasn't even supposed to go. Jordan just thought you might have suspected it, maybe even said something to the sheriff. You've got to realize that he's grasping at anything. We all are."

Pink began to pace the room as if he were in a trance. "He'll say anything to get what he wants," he marveled. "He accuses me, to make himself look good, and you let him do it. This is the opportunity of a lifetime for him. I love it." Pink let out a strangled laugh.

"Pink, this is not about Jordan. This has nothing to do with him."

Pink turned on her, his face contorted in fury. "It has everything to do with him. He's come back here to worm you away from me and you're so stupid you go along with it. I guess you've forgotten how he left you. You and Michele. Sick as she was."

"I have not forgotten anything," said Lillie. "I came over here to explain to you what we're trying to do, but I can see you aren't even able to listen."

"I suppose I should just sit back and let him wreck my family. Let him use my daughter's death as a weapon against me. That's right. *My daughter.* Not his. Mine. I paid the bills. I sat up nights with her. I sacrificed for her. *I did.* And now Sir Galahad comes along and it's *his* daughter."

"Oh, let's stop all this, Pink. It's petty. We haven't got time for it."

"Oh, well, pardon me, Miss Manners. He dumped you once and you settled for me. Don't you even have enough pride not to go kissing his ass the minute he walks in the door?"

"Go to hell," Lillie exclaimed, turning her back on him and storming out of the office. After slamming the door, she strode down the hall, berating her husband in her mind. When she opened the doorway to the stairs and started down, she was shaking with rage. She got as far as the landing and forced herself to stop.

Lillie leaned back against the wall and took a deep breath. The way he put everything was so ugly, so vicious, that it made her feel sick. But she could understand it. She could. He felt that she was turning to Jordan instead of him. And it was his greatest fear. He had always been jealous of Jordan. And, she thought with a stab of guilt, was he so wrong? There was no wrongdoing to accuse her of, and his fears that she would leave him for Jordan were unfounded. She had her life. Jordan was in the past. But he had been her one great love, and some memory of that still lingered, like an elusive scent, around her. Pink was not a fool. He could smell it, and it frightened him. But long after Jordan had gone back to New York, she and Pink would have to keep on with their lives together. It wasn't up to Pink to make amends, she thought. It was up to her.

Slowly she turned and climbed the stairs. She walked back down the hall. It did no good to run away from it, she thought. The door to the office was closed but not shut tight. As she put her hand on it to push it she realized he must have come running after her. He must have followed her out, maybe tried to cry out to call her back, but the words stuck in his throat. She felt a little rush of warmth for him. She pushed the door open and walked in. He was on the phone behind the partition. She wanted to surprise him, so she waited.

"Well, when will he be back?" Pink was saying. "Well, tell Sheriff Ansley that Pink Burdette called, and that it is very important that he call me back. Thank you, Francis."

He does care, Lillie thought. He cares more than he could ever show. Now he's taking matters into his own hands. He's going to assert himself about this. Well, fine, good. It's high time he started pushing on this. She felt the old warmth for her husband, who worked so hard, so uncomplainingly, for them, who had given his best. She wanted to apologize to him and to make him believe it. She *did* love him. He had always tried so very hard.

Before she could speak his name, she heard him dial again. And then she heard him say, "Yes, hello. I need to speak to one of your cadets, Tyler Ansley. Yes, well, I'm sure he is, but I need to get this message to him immediately. This is of the utmost importance. Please tell him to call Mr. Burdette at this number right away." Pink recited the office number. "Be sure you tell him *not* to call me at my home. That's my office number. That's right. At my office. Right away. It's urgent. All right. Good-bye." Pink put down the phone. He rubbed his sweaty hands rapidly together and clasped them against his forehead. Then he sat up and swiveled around in his chair.

Lillie was standing beside the partition, staring at him, her face as white as paper.

CHAPTER 18

"Oh, Christ," Pink exclaimed. He glanced guiltily at Lillie's shocked expression and then he looked away, scowling. The stuffy office was dead silent. "Don't look at me like that," he muttered. "I thought you were gone. Why the hell did you come back here?"

Sparks exploded in Lillie's stomach, searing her from the inside out. She blinked at him, as if she could not get his face into focus. A face she knew. Thought she knew.

Pink pushed himself out of his chair and the chair swiveled back and banged into a filing cabinet. Lillie jumped and let out a cry. Pink, who had stalked over to the office door, to close it, turned on her.

"Spare me the hysterics, Lillie." He sighed. "Just say what you're going to say."

"You *were* calling Tyler," she said slowly. But it was

almost a question, as if she still hoped she might have gotten it wrong.

"That's right," Pink said shortly.

"To warn him," Lillie cried. "To warn him."

"Yes," said Pink. "That's right."

Lillie stepped right in front of him, so that he was forced to look directly at her. She spoke each word through clenched teeth. "Don't you dare give me some little one-word answers. You tell me what the hell is going on here. Now."

Pink hunched his shoulders and grasped the back of his chair. "There's a good reason, Lillie," he said.

Lillie felt as if her breath were short, as if she could not spare even one unnecessary word. "What?"

Pink's eyes searched the corners of his office.

"No lies, Pink," Lillie cried. "Enough lies. I know that look. You've had it on and off for weeks but I thought I was imagining it."

"All right," he said, frowning at her. "All right. Shouldn't we go home and talk? This is no place."

"Tell me now," she insisted. "Why did you call Tyler? He killed her, didn't he? Have you lost your mind? Why were you calling him?"

Pink dropped wearily down into his chair and covered his pale, damp face with his hands. The phone began to ring on his desk and he started, then reached out and picked it up. Without a second's hesitation, Lillie leaned over the desk, jerked the receiver from his hand, and slammed it back down on the hook. Pink looked up as if to protest, but she stared back at him, wild-eyed.

Pink shook his head. "Lillie, I don't know how to tell you this. I hoped you'd never find out." He laid his trembling hands out flat on the desk in front of him. His finger-tips made dark splotches on the blotter. "Yes," he said. "It's true. You guessed right. He did kill her."

It didn't matter that she had guessed. That she had wondered and speculated and figured it out. The words from Pink's lips stunned her as if the thought had never crossed her mind. She groped for a chair and sat down.

"You knew this?" she whispered.

"I've known all along."

"And you never told. You bastard."

"Lillie, when I tell you—" he pleaded.

"You bastard," she spat at him. "You knew and you let him go? And now you . . . you were calling to warn him?"

Pink came around to where she sat and stood helplessly in front of her. "Lillie, listen to me. Hear me out."

Lillie leaned her head back and closed her eyes. She shook her head. "No," she murmured. "No, no, no."

Pink leaned over and shook her. Her eyes seemed to roll open, dulled and doll-like. "Your own daughter," Lillie murmured incredulously. "You lying bastard. There is no possible excuse."

"First of all," Pink declared, "it wasn't like you think. It wasn't a murder, really. It was more of an accident, I guess you'd say. They were horsing around. The way kids do. They'd been drinking."

"Tyler, you mean."

"I'm getting to that."

"Michele didn't drink."

"She did. She had some. Michele was not perfect, you know," Pink said defensively.

"I don't believe my ears!" Lillie jumped up from the chair.

"Sit down. I'm trying to tell you—" Pink began.

"I can't breathe. I think I'm going to be sick," she cried. "This boy murders your daughter in cold blood and all you can say is that *she* was drinking?"

"Don't make this worse than it is," Pink said. "I told you. He's just a kid. He didn't mean to do it."

"The coroner said she had been struck at least three severe blows to the base of her skull. Do you recall that, Pink?"

Pink drowned her out with his continuing explanation. "They were down by the bridge after the fair. They had some moonshine. And Tyler got drunk. You know what he's like. He's an alcoholic. He still had the baseball bat with him from the game. And Michele was teasing him. Just flirting, I guess, but she got him all worked up and he took a swing at her.

"Say it. He murdered her. He beat her head in."

"It all happened in an instant," Pink protested. "Before they even knew . . ."

"And you agreed to protect him?" Lillie cried. "Royce knows all this? And you went along with it? Are you crazy, Pink?"

"I had to," Pink shouted back.

"You *had* to!"

"It was an accident," Pink pleaded.

"Never, never," said Lillie, kneading her hands unconsciously as if she were freezing to death. "Never."

"I had to," Pink repeated. Sweat had beaded up all over his face, and his forehead was knotted, as if he was in pain. "It was . . . you see, Grayson was there."

Lillie stared at Pink. Her breath escaped her as if by a blow. She exhaled one word. "Grayson?"

"They were all three down there at the Arches," Pink said hurriedly. "Grayson had a few drinks in him too. And that Tyler is like a bear. Grayson never had a chance to stop him."

"Grayson?" she repeated. "Our Grayson?"

"Oh, Lillie, stop it. For chrissakes. The way you say it. As if he was responsible or something. I mean, it's alcohol. I know it's tragic, but these things happen with kids. It could have happened to anybody."

Pink stopped and looked worriedly at his wife. "Lillie, you look awful," he said. "I know it's a shock. That's why I didn't want to tell you." He reached out a hand to steady her. "Come on and sit down again, honey. You're wobbling like your legs are going to give out on you there."

Lillie snatched her arm away from him. He was right. For a moment she had teetered, craving oblivion to release her, but she was too angry to give way. "Don't you touch me," she growled at him. "Don't you dare."

"I knew it," said Pink. "This is what I was afraid of."

"Let me make sure I understand this," she said, forming each word as if her mouth were numb. "Tyler Ansley killed my daughter while Grayson stood by and watched it happen. And you decided not to tell me—just to let them get away with it."

Pink was sweating profusely. There were half-moons of perspiration under the arms of his shirt. "No. Not like that. Royce and I . . . He found them there. I don't know. It seemed like the best solution. Not just to let them get away with it. But what good would it do to ruin both their lives? It wouldn't bring Michele back. And they were sorry. Let me tell you. You have never seen two boys carry on so. It was just a horrible, horrible accident."

"Ruin *their* lives," Lillie exclaimed.

"Lillie," Pink said earnestly. "Believe me, I know how you feel. I wanted to kill them both with my bare hands when I heard. But we had to try and be rational. We had to think of the consequences. That's why we didn't tell you. We knew you'd be too upset to think straight.

"And then Royce came up with the idea of the military school for Tyler. And honestly, those places are almost worse than prison. Believe me, they can straighten that boy out, those tough old officers they've got there . . ."

"Stop it, Pink. Just stop it," she said furiously. "He's a killer. He killed our daughter. And you let him walk away for Grayson's sake. Don't pretend it's anything else. I'm not a fool. You did it so that no one would find out that he just let his own sister die and did nothing. So no one will know what a coward he was."

Pink's red face went suddenly pale, and he wagged a warning finger at his wife. "Don't say that about him, Lillie. He feels bad enough. Don't you call him a coward."

"No, no, you're right," cried Lillie, raising her hands in a gesture of surrender. "We mustn't hurt his feelings. Even though Michele lost her life and he just stood by and watched." Pink scrutinized her through narrowed eyes as Lillie stood trembling with fury, her mind racing.

"Well," she said. "We'll just see about that." She turned and started for the door. In an instant Pink was in front of her, blocking her path. When she reached past him for the doorknob, Pink grabbed her wrist.

"Where are you going?" he asked.

Lillie looked up at him fiercely, tears in her eyes. "I'm

going to find him," she said. "He is going to answer to me. How could you, Pink? You liar. All of you. Liars."

"Lillie, you can't tell anyone else."

"Why?" she cried. "Why, Pink? So I can be a liar too?"

Pink's face had taken on a strange, stiff cast, and his eyes had a smoldering, faraway look in them. "I knew you would react like this," he said, tightening his grip on her. "Now you're going to listen to me. I'm through apologizing to you. Grayson is just a young boy. He has his whole life ahead of him. I won't let you destroy him."

Lillie's eyes blazed out at him and she shoved him back with the wrist he was still gripping. "He's a liar and a coward and a . . . a traitor," she cried. "And I don't care who knows it."

It was only an instant that they stood locked together, glaring at one another, but it seemed much longer to Lillie. The bones in her wrist felt as if they were being crushed as she twisted it in his grip. It was with a sense of disbelief that she saw him raise his fist and by the time she realized what was next, it was too late to guard her face. Her teeth banged together and blood spurted into her mouth as the punch landed hard on her cheekbone. The blow buckled her knees. She felt Pink shove her away from him and she fell, hitting the wall behind her.

Her eye throbbed in the socket and for a minute she was too stunned to move, but then she saw him looming above her and she scrambled to her feet.

"I won't let you!" Pink cried, and then his voice broke. "I'm sorry, Lillie, but I can't."

"Yoo-hoo," came a voice from the hall and the doorknob rattled. "Pink, are you in there? It's Reba." Pink and Lillie did not move or speak. They both heard Pink's associate open her purse and begin to fumble for keys.

"Oh, me," Reba said in exasperation. "Where are they?"

As if in a trance, Pink turned, walked to the door, and unlocked it. He hesitated a minute and then he pulled it open. He looked blankly out at Reba.

"Honey," she scolded, "it's not good for business to keep this door locked during weekend hours. This is our busiest time." Still fussing about her keys, Reba bustled in past Pink, her arms full of packages. She gave Pink an indulgent smile and then her gaze fell on Lillie, who was standing with her body turned toward the wall, holding the side of her face. A yellowish bruise was already visible above her fingers and her eye was starting to swell shut. Reba's smile faded away as she looked from Lillie back to Pink.

"Oh, I'm so sorry," she said, as if she were somehow responsible for the conflict she had stumbled into. She hurried to her desk, her eyes lowered. Pink tried to catch her eye, ready to offer some jocular explanation, but Reba's face was grim and she kept her eyes downcast as her hands fluttered over the papers on her desk. "I'll be out of here in a minute," she said rapidly. "I just need the spec sheet for that house on Larkspur and the keys. Where are those keys?" The phone rang and Reba grabbed it up gratefully. "Burdette and Associates," she trilled with a false cheeriness. "One moment please. Who shall I say is calling?" She nodded and turned to Pink, the phone outstretched to him.

"This is young Tyler Ansley for you. The sheriff's boy."

Pink looked automatically at Lillie but turned immediately from the bitter accusation in her eyes. "I'll take it," he said. He stood holding the phone, his hand over the mouthpiece, as Reba quickly gathered her things.

She sidled out past Lillie, giving her a brief, embarrassed smile. "I'll close the door," she said.

"Thanks, Reba," Pink said as she pulled the door to behind her. He turned his back on his wife and spoke into the phone.

"Hello, Tyler," he said. "That's right. I did."

Lillie considered pulling the phone out of the wall. But what was the point? Pink would find another phone. The throbbing bruise on her face attested to his determination.

"Yes," he was saying. "There's a man who's been nosing around here. My wife's ex-husband, as a matter of fact, and he's got the notion that it was you. Now he's coming out there to try and make you talk, and you better watch your butt because he's out to get you."

Pink listened for a moment, an irritated expression on his face. "What I'm telling you is to keep your mouth shut. In fact, you'd be a whole lot better off if you didn't let him get ahold of you at all, because if you let something slip there is no telling what he's going to do. He's out for blood."

Pink listened briefly and then interrupted loudly. "No, no, listen here, boy. I'm telling you this for your own good. This guy is after you. What? Jordan Hill. He just left, so he could be there in five or six hours. I don't know. You figure it out. Tell the truth, I wouldn't care if he did beat your ass, but we agreed to keep this thing quiet and, by God, you better see that you do. All right."

Pink slammed down the phone. He turned to face Lillie,

his eyes defiant, in time to see the door shut behind her. She was gone. Pink's shoulders sagged, and he felt a weight, like a cannonball, on his chest. He wanted to cry, but instead he reached for the phone and dialed again. It was too late for tears. Grayson and Royce would both have to know. Grayson first. That was the call he dreaded the most. He had promised to protect his son and he had botched the job. In the state Lillie was in, there was no telling what she might do. They had to try to make her see reason before it was too late.

CHAPTER 19

She descended the stairs, almost running, but when she reached the sidewalk the cold air hit her like a slap, and she felt dizzy and dazed. Her heart was pounding out of control and she could not remember where she had parked. Passersby glanced at her and their glances frightened her, as if they all knew, as if they were incredulous that she had only now found out. Her frantic gaze fell on the comforting colors of her car and she stumbled toward it on wobbly legs, but once she was safely inside, she just sat, her hands trembling too much to turn the ignition key. She wanted to get to Grayson and leap at him like a wildcat and shake him like a rag doll and scream out at him "Why?" but her quivering fingers would not turn the key so she sat at the wheel and shivered, trying to think.

Grayson. Her baby. Her son. He had always been the

independent one. Pushing her away from her earliest memories of him. Wanting to do it himself. The opposite of Michele, who had turned to her, needed her so, welcomed her love. No, Grayson was the baby, but he was the strong, healthy, breezy one. Out the door and on the run, Michele watching adoringly as he piled up his successes. She idolized him. And he let her die.

Lillie put her hands on the wheel and smeared blood there from her palms, which she had punctured squeezing her hands into fists. She tried to think. Where would he be? There was a football game next week and this afternoon he would be at practice, leading the team as they practiced their plays. The captain of the team, the vice president of the student council, the leadership award winner. He had stood by. He had let Tyler Ansley murder his sister and stood by. And then the lies. The lies too. All of it. Lillie felt as if the weight of it could crush her. She was going after him. That was all she knew. He had never sought her advice, and from time to time, when she would offer it, he would fidget impatiently, that long-suffering look on his face. Well, he would listen to her today, by God.

She waited a few more minutes, until she felt composed enough to be able to drive safely, and then she headed to the high school and drove around back to where the athletic field was. The Cress County Cougars were out on the field, all right. It was muddy because of the rain, and the bright white-and-purple uniforms were streaked with rust-colored mud. The coach blew his whistle and shouted unintelligible instructions as the boys lined up to hurl themselves at the tackling dummy.

Gripping her car keys tightly in one still-bloody palm,

Lillie walked out to the front of the bleachers and stared at the tussling young men on the field. She craned her neck to peer at the various numbers on the uniforms but she could not spot number five among them. Usually she could recognize him by his brash, careless stance alone, but she could see no sign of Grayson among the players.

A voice called her name and Lillie swiveled around to see who it was. High up on the bleachers, a lone figure was hunched over against the chill, dressed in a pink dungaree jacket and cowboy boots. Instantly Lillie recognized the flame-colored hair of Allene Starnes. Lillie's heart flipped over at the sight of her. She felt a surge of unreasonable anger as the girl gave her a timid wave.

"Grayson just got called inside to the phone," Allene called down to her. "Some kind of emergency."

Lillie knew immediately who it was. Pink. Telling the boy she was on her way. "Allene," she demanded, "what are you doing here?" But she knew. She knew that this frail, unstable girl was waiting there for her son.

"I'm supposed to meet Gray after practice," Allene admitted sheepishly.

Ordinarily Lillie would have minded her own business, kept out of it. Ordinarily she would have trusted her son. But this was not an ordinary day. And her son did not deserve to be trusted. He did not deserve the attentions of a girl, any girl. Much less this fragile, vulnerable girl.

"Allene," she said sharply. "Come down here. This instant."

Allene started to protest and then slowly she gathered up her pocketbook and climbed down from the bleachers, her cowboy boots clattering on the wooden slats. As the girl made her way down the steps, Lillie glanced back out on the field. No sign of Grayson yet. He and Pink were no doubt still busily discussing their secrets, trying to avoid her wrath. But Grayson was not going to get away from her this time.

Allene reached the bottom seat. Lillie reached out a hand to her and helped her as she jumped off. The small-boned freckled hand was cold in her own, and Lillie felt as if she were guiding the girl down from a high ledge where she had gotten herself trapped.

Oh, no, Lillie thought furiously. Grayson was not going to have a chance to run roughshod over this girl, or any other girl, because she was not going to let him. He who had not even had the guts to defend his own sister. He was not fit to have a girlfriend. He was not going to hurt anybody else, ever again. She would see to that.

"Allene," Lillie said sternly. "Do your parents know that you're seeing Grayson again?"

Allene shook her head sadly.

"Well, you better just stop seeing him, or I am going to tell them. I mean it, Allene. Forget about Grayson. Don't waste yourself on him. He'll only hurt you. He doesn't care for you."

Lillie half expected the girl to be defiant but instead Allene shrugged and shoved her hands in her pockets. "I know, I'm sorry," she said.

"Don't you be sorry," said Lillie. "You just scoot."

"Grayson'll be mad," she said worriedly.

"I'll take care of Grayson," Lillie said grimly.

"Miz Burdette, please don't tell my mom."

"Not unless I catch you hanging around with him again. Now go."

The girl hoisted her pocketbook onto her shoulder and

said good-bye. Lillie watched as she disappeared around the corner of the bleachers. Then she turned and looked back across the muddy field. Grayson was coming out of the locker room.

He must have glanced up to see if Allene was still there admiring him because he had already spotted his mother and was on his way to her, loping toward the bleachers, his handsome face a study in feigned innocence.

"What happened to Allene?" he asked by way of greeting.

"I sent her home. Get over here," hissed Lillie. She could feel her heart thudding in her chest as she turned her back on him and started down the aisle.

"Mom, I've got practice," he said stubbornly.

Lillie turned on him, her eyes flashing. "Don't pretend you don't know why I'm here. I know that was your father on the phone. Now do as I tell you," she spat out at him. "I am still your mother."

Her tone silenced him and he lowered his languid blue eyes. A redness crept up his neck above the dirty uniform. He glanced up at her and saw the bruise forming beneath her eye and across her cheekbone. "Mom!" he exclaimed. "Where'd you get that?"

"Never mind that," she snapped.

"Sorry," he said with a shrug, and followed her docilely to the end of the bleachers.

Lillie, trembling with rage, did not turn around until she was satisfied that they were out of sight of the others. She wanted to say every vile thing that was on her mind. She had come prepared to rail at him, to vent her fury on him like a storm. She wanted to hurt him, humiliate him, accuse him. But when she turned and saw him standing there obediently behind her, his helmet on one hip, his fair hair mussed as if from sleep, his wide eyes on her, as if he only wanted to ease her mind, she felt the fury deflate inside her and what remained was confusion and disbelief. This was her son. Her little boy. Pink must have gotten it wrong somehow. He would never have deserted his sister that way. Maybe he wasn't even there. Maybe Tyler just said that. There had to be some other explanation.

"Grayson," she began, her tone severe, her voice shaking, "as I'm *sure* your father just told you on the phone, I heard what happened. That Tyler Ansley killed your sister and that you stood by and let him."

Grayson gripped his helmet and stared at her, wide-eyed, the flush gone from his neck, his skin now pale.

Lillie hesitated in the face of his silence. It isn't so, she thought with a sudden, wild hope in her heart. He'll tell me that it did not happen. That he wasn't there. That Tyler made it up. "Is this true?" she asked.

Don't answer that, she thought.

Grayson looked away from her, squinting out, unseeing, over the field, and then shifted his weight to the other hip.

"Well?" she said.

Grayson shook his head. His voice was small. "I'm sorry, Mom. I hoped you'd never find out."

To her surprise, his admission stunned her, almost as if she had never heard a word of this before. "Grayson," she whispered. "My God . . ."

"Mom," he pleaded. "Mom, I'm sorry. It was just . . . it was a freak thing . . ."

Lillie struggled to retain control. But she felt as if she couldn't breathe. "You tell me what happened," she said, and the words burst forth between gasps. "I cannot be-

lieve . . . what your father told me . . . was the whole
story. That you let him . . . kill your sister. Grayson, I
have to know . . . how could this be?"

His face was contorted and tears fell from his eyes.
"Mom, I know you're mad at me . . ." he said.

"Mad?" she cried, almost wanting to laugh at the inade-
quacy, the incongruity, of the word. "Grayson, look at me.
I know you. You're my son. You wouldn't . . . you
couldn't do that. Just leave her there. Let her die. I mean,
you and Michele, you loved her . . ." Her voice was
high, pleading.

"I did. You know I did," he cried. "But I swear, Mom. I
never thought Tyler would hurt her. I thought he was just
kidding around."

He looked at her miserably, waiting a moment for her
to speak, but she did not. "We were drinking," Grayson
said. "I know we weren't supposed to, but all the kids do,
you know."

She was peering at him as if it were a struggle to understand him, as if he were speaking a foreign language.

Grayson shifted uneasily under her gaze and continued
haltingly. "Michele actually . . . she wasn't supposed to
be there. I mean, she overheard us saying we were going
down there and she just insisted on tagging along. I tried
to tell her to go home but she . . . she liked him, you
know. I guess she thought it was a good chance to be
around him or something.

"So, anyway, we were drinking and she was teasing
him, and he was waving the baseball bat around, and Michele was laughing and then *bam, bam*. Before I knew it,
he hit her. And she fell."

"Stop it," Lillie shrieked, clapping her hands over her

ears. She could not stand to hear it. She did not want to picture her little girl struck down. She could not bear to hear her son recounting it, the way he would some incident at school.

"Mom, listen," he said urgently. "How did I know he would hit her?"

"You should have . . . You should have taken care of her," Lillie cried.

"Mom, I couldn't. Please." He stepped toward her. "Don't."

She was backing away from him, flailing one fist feebly at him, as if to keep him away. She bumped into the bleacher and grabbed on to it, tears blinding her again. She wiped her eyes angrily.

"So," she declared in a cold, cruel voice, "this boy killed your sister and you stood by like a complete coward and did nothing. Except to lie about it and protect him, of course."

"No," he yelped. "No. 1 jumped on him. I hit him. It was too late. Mom, you weren't there. I'm telling you. Nobody could have prevented it."

"That's all you can say about it? You were helpless?"

"Come on, Mom. Don't you think I would have done something if I could?" His eyes were bright with tears, and he wiped the muddy sleeve of his jersey across them, streaking his face with dirt.

Lillie shook her head furiously, her own tears choking her. "I don't know," she wailed. "I'll never know. You stand there and tell me this. As if you don't realize how you betrayed her. You betrayed Michele. And me. All of us. Aren't you ashamed?"

This seemed to prick him and his face hardened. "Look," he said, "I'm not the only one . . ."

"I cannot understand this," she said. "No matter how hard I try. How could you stand there? And do nothing? How can you sleep at night for thinking of it? How can you walk around each day as if none of this had ever happened?"

"I said I was sorry," he cried hoarsely. "Look, what do you want from me? What do you want me to do? Just tell me and I'll do it."

Lillie turned away from him and looked up at the steely gray sky. It was true. What else could he say? Michele was dead. Of course he was sorry. How many ways could he say it? His tears told her everything. For all the good it did, he was as sorry as could be.

Lillie shook her head and sank down on the edge of one of the bleacher seats, staring blankly out ahead of her. "I don't want to torture you with this," she said softly. "You're my son. I know you are sorry. And I know you have suffered too. But I can't just let it go. All these lies." She shook her head. "What about Michele? When you agreed to all these lies, to this silence, didn't any of you think of her?"

"What do you mean?" he asked warily.

"You know what I mean," she said. "Your sister is murdered and the whole lot of you just bent over backward to pretend it never even happened."

"Wait a minute, Mom," he said. "We couldn't tell. Once it came out that I was there too—"

"I know," she interrupted him. "You don't want to face the humiliation. Maybe even a trial. God help me, I don't want you to either. And now your father is involved. And the sheriff. But, tell me something, Grayson. Do you think this boy who killed your sister should just go free? Go unpunished? How can we live with that?"

Grayson stood silently above her, chewing the inside of his mouth absently as he stared out over the field. Then slowly, gingerly, he sat down on the bleacher beside her. "Mom, there's another reason," he said. "This is hard to tell you. . . . There's more to this than you really know about."

Lillie frowned at him. "Meaning what?"

Grayson licked his lips and turned his helmet in his hands, avoiding her eyes. He seemed to be concentrating on something, wrestling with it. Then he said, "There's something else that happened that night. Dad doesn't even know about it."

"Since when do you tell me and not your father?" she asked stiffly.

Grayson sighed. "I didn't tell Dad because . . . it's about Michele. I didn't want him to know this. I mean, you know how he is about her. I mean, in his eyes, she was just . . . you know, his little girl."

"What are you trying to say?" Lillie demanded. "I can't take much more, Grayson."

"Look, I know you think I'm a coward and that's why I wanted to cover this mess up, but I'm trying to protect Michele too, in my own way. So it won't come out what happened."

"Wait a minute," Lillie cried. "No. You can't think that you are going to turn around now and somehow blame this whole thing on your sister? Are you going to tell me maybe that she had a drink and she hit him first? Don't you dare, Grayson. Don't you dare try to blame this on her."

"Not a drink, Mom," he interrupted her. "We all had a drink."

"You stood there and you watched it happen and you did nothing. At least be man enough to admit it now, Grayson."

"I wasn't standing there. The truth is . . . I walked away," Grayson said. "I was leaving."

"We know that, Grayson," she said sharply.

"I had to."

"You did not have to. You chose to," Lillie insisted.

"I had to," he cried. "She . . . she took off her blouse."

Lillie stared at him. There was a bright pink flush rising up his neck to his cheeks. He did not look at her. Her own face felt hot. "She did not," Lillie said in a shaky voice.

"Mom, she did," Grayson said. "She liked him. She had a crush on Tyler. I guess she had some idea that it would make him interested . . . I don't know. She said it was too hot out and she took it off. I couldn't just stand there, Mom. It was too embarrassing. I had to leave."

Lillie was shaking her head. Not Michele, she thought, her cheeks burning with shame for her daughter. Not my baby. But she was not a baby.

"I guess she thought he'd like it, but he must have thought she was a tease or something." Grayson sighed. "Anyway, I went to leave and I heard it happen, and when I turned back . . ."

Lillie hid her face in her hands, humiliated, terrified, as if she herself were reliving her daughter's final moments.

"I put her shirt back on her after it was over," said

Grayson. "There was nothing else I could do. I didn't want anyone to find her like that."

Lillie squeezed her eyes shut but she could not blot out the image of her shy Michele, made reckless by infatuation and moonshine and moonlight, trying to be daring. Never suspecting . . . a victim of her own innocence.

Grayson interrupted her thoughts. "Don't tell Dad," he said earnestly. "Okay, Mom? I don't want him to know about this."

Lillie nodded numbly.

"What does that mean?" said Grayson. "Are you going to tell him or not?"

Lillie looked at her son with vacant eyes. "I don't want to talk to your father right now."

"I don't want anyone else knowing this about her," Grayson said. "They'll get the wrong idea about her. She really wasn't like that usually. She was kind of shy of boys. I still don't know why she did it."

Why? Lillie thought, more empty than angry now. Did she think, as young girls sometimes do, that no one would ever want her? She should have told me how she felt, Lillie thought bitterly. I could have made her understand that she never had to flaunt herself. That one day she would be loved, pursued, cherished. Lillie felt as if her head were spinning from this new revelation. You could have confided in me, Lillie wanted to cry out. We were so close. There was a sick churning in her stomach.

"I was trying to protect her, Mom," Grayson said urgently.

Lillie looked at her son as if he had awoken her from a trance, and she felt her heart soften toward him. She searched his troubled eyes as if from far away and then nodded. "I can see that," she said, reaching over and gripping his forearm for a second. Despite the renewed anguish she felt, picturing the clumsy attempt at seduction, the explosive consequences, she was glad he had told her. It was like a rickety bridge back to her son, reconnecting them. It was as if her heart had stopped completely, and now she could feel it, feebly beating again.

"Thank you for doing that for her," she said.

"I just wish I could have saved her, Mom," he cried.

"Oh, Grayson, so do I." Lillie moaned, shaking her head. Slowly she got up from the bleacher seat and brushed herself off.

Grayson scrambled to his feet. "When you get home—" he said.

"I'm not going home," Lillie interrupted.

"Where are you going?" he asked, alarmed.

Lillie looked around the playing field, empty now, the clouds low and smoky, the darkness gathering. "I'm going to Aunt Brenda's. I'm going to stay there tonight, if she'll have me."

He glanced at her bruised eye and nodded. "Because of that."

"Because of everything. I just can't. Grayson, I need to think. I don't know what to do next. I just need to be by myself and think about all this."

"Well, what *are* you going to do?" he asked anxiously.

"I don't know," she said. "I don't mind telling you that I have never felt so completely at a loss in all my life."

"It takes a while to get used to it all," he said. "But I don't think you should be away from home right now."

"Don't worry about me," she said. "You just go get dressed. I'll be fine."

Grayson glanced at her through narrowed eyes. "You're not going to tell Aunt Brenda about this, are you?"

"I am not telling anybody anything tonight, believe me. I am just going there to have some privacy. Some room to breathe."

This answer seemed to reassure him. "Listen, Mom," he said. "I *have* given this a lot of thought. And I *am* sorry."

"I know," she said dully.

"But it's too late now to start dredging it all up to other people. Everybody gets hurt that way."

"Everybody's already hurt," she said.

"Yeah, but now we have to think about the future. I mean, what good would it do to have to go through it all over again?"

"I have to go, Grayson." Lillie sighed. "Tell your father where I went, okay?"

She did not wait for him to reply. She had to get away from him. From all of it. She felt battered, inside and out. She had thought that Michele's murder had been the ultimate nightmare. She smiled bitterly at her own näiveté. It seemed now that her daughter's death had been just the beginning. She felt as if everything that held her world in place was coming apart.

Lillie walked slowly toward the parking lot and her car. When she reached the car, she turned and looked back. Her son was still standing there in the gathering dusk, feet apart, fists clenched, his eyes boring into her. His padded figure was silhouetted against the gray sky like some large, impossibly idealized sculpture of a man.

CHAPTER 20

In the gloom of a foggy evening, the cluster of dimly lit Georgian-style buildings of the Sentinel Military Academy looked like a fortress built into the North Carolina hillside. Jordan passed the sign that indicated the school had been founded in 1887 and drove slowly up the hill and down the driveway until he reached the parking lot beside the main quadrangle.

It was nearly seven o'clock and he was weary from his trip, but he wanted to accomplish his mission right away. He was edgy and anxious about how he was going to handle the boy, and it was best to just get it over with. There was an American flag, and a WWI vintage riding gun anchored in the center of a grassy island in front of the central building. Jordan figured that was where he was bound to find the person in authority. A couple of gray-uniformed cadets hurried past him on the walkway, their heads down, and some dried leaves rustled across the lawns, but otherwise it was quiet. Jordan climbed the steps to the main building, walked inside, and looked around.

The old mahogany woodwork gleamed like an officer's shoeshine, even in the dim light of the hallway. The building appeared to be deserted, but he followed a sign indicating the commandant's office and was relieved to see that there was a light coming from it. No one was sitting at the secretary's desk in the anteroom. The paneled walls were covered with plaques of achievement and bookcases holding military histories and Sentinel yearbooks dating back to the 1930s. The inside office door was ajar, and as Jordan walked up to it he noticed the plaque: Colonel James Preavette. Jordan tapped on the door. When a raspy voice ordered him to enter, Jordan poked his head in and saw a tanned, wiry man in shirtsleeves wearing silver-rimmed spectacles that matched his slicked-back silver hair. His glasses glinted as he looked up.

"I'm sorry to bother you, Colonel Preavette," said Jordan.

"No problem, come on in. You just caught me doing some piled-up paperwork."

Jordan could not help noticing, as he introduced himself, that the colonel's desk was immaculate except for two neatly arranged file folders and a framed photo of his family.

"What can I do for you?" the colonel asked.

"Well, actually I'm here to see one of your students. Ah, my name is Jordan Hill."

The colonel gave a sharp nod. "Well, I'm sorry, but you'll have to come back tomorrow. Sunday is Visitors Day around here. Are you a family member?"

Jordan hesitated. "A friend of the family," he said vaguely. "Actually, this is kind of important. It would really help if I could talk to this young man tonight."

"Is this a medical emergency in the family?" the colonel asked sternly.

Jordan felt like a soldier on the carpet. He did not try to lie. "No, but it's a matter of the greatest urgency to me. I believe this boy may have some important information concerning a serious crime . . ."

"Are you a policeman?" the colonel demanded.

"No, sir," Jordan admitted, acutely aware of his rumpled appearance, his longish hair, and his jacket, still redolent of Lillie.

"Rules and discipline are what make this institution work, Mr. Hill. The example we set for these cadets is all-important. There is a very fine motel not far down the road where most of our family members like to stay when they visit. Come back tomorrow, Mr. Hill," the colonel said, giving Jordan a fleeting wintry smile.

The dismissal was final and Jordan knew it. He also knew better than to try to persuade the colonel otherwise. He wished for a moment that he had thought to skirt the official channels. "What time tomorrow?" he asked coolly.

"Anytime after nine. What cadet was it that you wanted to see?"

Aha, Jordan thought. So the mention of a crime had registered after all. He's curious. "Tyler Ansley is the cadet's name, sir."

The colonel's eyebrows shot up behind the silver

frames. He reached for the pack of Camels on his desk and released a cigarette with one hand. Jordan waited patiently while he lit it and took a drag. The colonel nodded.

"I knew there was something wrong there," he said. "I can spot a boy in trouble a mile away."

Jordan did not reply. If the colonel wanted information, he was going to have to bend the rules. The colonel instantly understood the unspoken terms and took a moment to consider. Then he shook his head.

"Come back tomorrow, Mr. Hill."

Jordan thanked him curtly and walked out. Once he got out into the quadrangle he looked angrily around at the buildings of the school. It was possible that one of them housed his daughter's killer. But if he tried to determine which, without the colonel's permission, security would have him removed from the grounds, and he would not be allowed to return in the morning.

His weariness suddenly overcame him, and the thought of resting for the night did not seem unappealing. He could hardly believe that only this morning he had been up at his farmhouse in Green County. It seemed like a month had passed, not a night, since he had called Lillie and then decided to come down here.

Resigned to waiting, he got back into his car and drove down the side of the mountain to the motel the colonel had mentioned. He was given a room with a nubby turquoise and green carpet and brown plaid bedspreads. He unpacked his shaving kit and washed up in the bathroom, staring for a minute at his haggard face in the bathroom mirror.

Now that he was in a room, he wanted nothing more than to sleep, but he decided to avoid the inviting bed and head down to the motel restaurant before it closed. He left his room and walked back around to the front of the building, thinking all the while about his encounter with the colonel. The old officer had not been surprised to hear that it was Tyler he sought. On the contrary, it had somehow confirmed the colonel's own suspicions. Damn it, Jordan thought. Well, there was nothing for it but to wait until the morning. In the morning he would get his hands on the boy and find out what he wanted to know.

Jordan opened the double doors and walked down a short hallway to the restaurant. Across the hall in the lounge he could hear the muffled sounds of a country band and he wondered if they were playing to an empty room. There were only a few cars in the parking lot.

Jordan sat down in a maple captain's chair at a corner table and looked around the dining room, which was nearly empty. There was an exhausted-looking young couple with a baby in a high chair, and a pair of middle-aged couples finishing up their coffee and laughing while the men teased a good-natured waitress. Two tables away from him, an old man and woman were studying the menu and conferring. When the young waitress approached their table, Jordan could tell from their familiar conversation that these were local people here for senior citizens' night. The special dinner of fish sticks and macaroni could be had for three dollars with a coupon from the local paper.

The waitress excused herself politely from the elderly pair and came over to Jordan's table. Jordan consulted the simple menu and ordered a Jack Daniel's on the rocks and a steak. As the waitress left to put his order in, the old woman hailed the waitress back to her table.

She smiled up at the young woman, her face a patch-work of wrinkles, and said, "I'd like the tomato soup with that tonight, dear."

The waitress said, "That'll be extra. It doesn't come with the dinner."

The old woman looked over at her husband in alarm and he frowned down at the menu. "It usually comes with the dinner, doesn't it?" the old man asked.

"Sometimes," the young woman said patiently. "Not this week though. It's a dollar extra for the soup."

They can't afford it, Jordan realized suddenly, watching them.

The old man looked up from the menu proudly. "Bring my wife a bowl of tomato soup," he said.

But his wife was shaking her head. "No, honey, no. I don't really want it. I always eat too much when we come over here. If I eat soup I won't have room for the pudding."

"Are you sure?" her husband asked, a trace of relief in his voice.

"Positive," she said.

Jordan busied himself with a roll and pretended not to be eavesdropping. He did not want the old man to see the pity in his eyes. You probably promised her the moon once, he thought. And this is what it comes to. You can't give her a bowl of tomato soup. He looked up guiltily at the cocktail that the waitress was putting before him. Then he heard the old woman laugh, and when he looked over he saw her give her husband a little push on his wiry upper arm, as if to chide him playfully for a scandalous remark.

Jordan sipped ruefully on his drink. Here you are, he

thought, feeling sorry for them because they can't afford that bowl of soup. But they will go home together, pleased with their night out. They'll probably sit up in the kitchen talking about their grandchildren and fall asleep together in their old bed.

The waitress put the steak down in front of him, but he had little appetite for it. He forced himself to eat some, and by the time he was done and had left the restaurant, the band was in full swing in the lounge. He saw the middle-aged couples who had been in the dining room emerging from the lounge after an obviously brief stay. Ordinarily he might have gone inside and had a drink to pass the time, but tonight he did not feel like witnessing the earnest efforts of a local group. He knew they would be trying hard, dreaming of getting out of Beauville, North Carolina, and making the big time. He knew all about what it was to spurn your ordinary life and burn for fame.

Jordan walked slowly back to his room and opened the door. The emptiness of the place reminded him of coming home to his apartment. No one there, not even a pet. Once or twice he had thought of getting a dog, but he never really wanted the responsibility. Just like getting married again. He had always kind of assumed that he would, but it had never seemed worth all the trouble and aggravation it would require to change his life like that, to make room for someone else.

Michele was always on him about that. Whenever she came to visit him, she would ask him why he didn't get married again. And on those rare occasions when he brought a date along out to dinner in Chinatown or to a movie, Michele would sing his praises to the poor girl right in front of him, and pepper him with a million questions about her when they got home. Jordan smiled, remembering. Sometimes it was as if she were the adult and he was the mixed-up teenager. She would get that knowing look in her eye and tell him that one day he would find the right one. He had asked her once, "How come you're so anxious to marry me off?" And she had said, "Because I don't want you to be lonely when I'm not here."

Jordan's smile faded and he felt the pricking behind his eyes. "I can't think about her," he said aloud to no one. He turned on the TV and ran through the channels aimlessly. Then he flipped it off again. He was exhausted, but restless. He'd been on the road, on and off, the whole long day, driving at dawn to Kennedy Airport from Green County, and then from Nashville to Felton, and, finally, that long five-hour trek to the Sentinel. He realized that he was burned out from the strain of the day, and now he was just running on nerves and anxiety. But he would sleep lightly, knowing that the morning would bring him face-to-face with Tyler.

He glanced over at the phone and thought of Lillie. She was probably having supper with Grayson and Pink, trying to keep herself occupied while she waited for his news. There was no reason to call her tonight really. He sat down on the edge of the bed and looked at the phone. He had a sudden picture of her as she had looked that morning, her hair damp and curly from the rain, bundled in his sports coat. It was always amazing to him how unspoiled she looked. As if life had not hurt her at all.

When he thought about it now, it astounded him to remember how easily he had made the decision to leave them—Lillie and Michele—those long years ago. A promoter in Nashville had seen his picture, asked him to sing, and offered to arrange an audition for him for a musical in New York. To Jordan, it had seemed a miracle. A chance to have all his dreams. Love was a sweet but common thing compared to that golden opportunity.

He told himself to go, just go, and make the pain sharp and swift. Otherwise, he would spend his whole life regretting it. So he went, and he got the part, and before long he was in California, working on a TV series. But the pain, which *had* been sharp and swift, had ended up being long and lingering as well. He tried other women, but around them he felt hollow, and at night he dreamed of Lillie and his baby, and he woke up to the sunny California day in a cloud of dread. And one morning, after a particularly sweaty night, he finally understood that what he wanted was another chance.

Once the idea entered his mind, it began to seem to him that it had been his intention all along. He checked his shooting schedule, made reservations for home, and began to weave fantasies of their imminent reunion and how he would woo her. And three weeks later, just two days before his scheduled trip, a letter came from his mother, telling him that Lillie had remarried. That now she was the wife of Pink Burdette.

Jordan picked up the phone receiver and weighed it in his hand. Soon, he thought, you'll have no reason at all to call her. Michele is gone. This mess will be cleared up, and you'll be a thousand miles apart with nothing in common. Nothing more to say. At least tonight there was a plausible explanation for calling. He pressed for an outside line.

After one ring, Pink answered.

"Pink, this is Jordan."

"What do you want?" Pink said flatly.

He wondered if Lillie had told him about Tyler. About his trip to the Sentinel. She must have by now. But Pink clearly was not in any mood to discuss it. "Uh, can I speak to Lillie for a minute?"

"She's not here," said Pink. He did not elaborate.

"Oh. Okay. Can you just tell her I called?"

Pink was silent, as if he were gearing up to say something, but then he just said, "Yeah. Good-bye."

"Good-bye." Jordan put the phone back down. For some reason, he was happy she was not there. It didn't make any sense, but that was how he felt. For a moment he had the brief, absurd thought that maybe she had decided to come after him. He glanced at the door as if he expected her to knock, but then he shook his head, amazed once again at his own foolish imagination. After a few minutes he got up with a sigh and decided to give the tube another try.

CHAPTER 21

B renda Daniels had never exactly married for money, but she had made sure that she was adequately compensated for the heartache of all her divorces, and consequently, at the age of thirty-four, she had one of the most luxurious homes in all of Cress County.

As she turned her purring Lincoln down her tree-lined driveway, she felt a customary sense of satisfaction at the sight of her elegant pure white stucco house with the columns out front. She had spent the day in Nashville at a gourmet food show at the Opryland Hotel and had considered calling the married sessions guitarist she knew for a little evening honky-tonking, but at the last minute she decided just to head for the comfort of home.

She knew that a lot of women in this town whispered that she was a scarlet woman, but she believed that they were mainly envious of her house and her freedom. They would have been surprised to learn how tame her love life usually was. It wasn't for lack of suitors. She was as pretty now as she had ever been. And if she wanted to she could move in a minute to one of those Nashville condos with the pool and the tennis club and easy access to the string of restaurants and singles' bars that sprawled out over Nashville like the Vegas strip. But she liked her house, and her land, and the fact was that she wasn't really in the market for another husband.

Sometimes she longed for a family, like anybody else, but mostly she was skeptical. After marriage, the guy tended to cool off a lot, and before you knew it, he was being messy and drinking too much and not wanting to take you out to eat. She could not abide a sloppy house, ashes in the ashtray, a half-finished drinking glass scarring the pecan veneer of her imported French furniture. She liked to think of herself as understanding, but the fact was that men's habits made her queasy a lot of the time. Dirty socks stuffed into shoes and cigarette wrappers wadded up between the white leather seats in her car exasperated her. She liked things a certain way, and they never could understand that.

Nevertheless, this had all the earmarks of one of those lonely nights, and she was delighted to see Lillie's car parked in her driveway. She pressed the automatic garage door opener and pulled the Lincoln into the garage beside the Home Cookin' van. She had long ago given Lillie a key, so she knew she would be inside waiting for her. She gathered her packages out of the trunk, glad to be able to display her food show purchases to someone who could really appreciate them.

Brenda opened the door and called out, "Hey, Lillie," but there was no answer in the quiet house. She put her packages down on the kitchen counter and looked around. Her housekeeping was so immaculate that she could detect the slightest changes with ease. A glass washed in the drainer plus a drop of brownish liquid on the counter meant that Lillie had had a glass of tea. Brenda sponged up the drop and moved on through the house. One of her magazines was not aligned on the coffee table's marble top. Lillie must have been reading. She walked down the hall. An appliquéd linen hand towel had been used and refolded in the bathroom. In the adjoining guest room, a Chinese porcelain bedside lamp had been turned on. Brenda frowned, smoothed out the bed automatically, and proceeded through the house. There was no one in the den. The TV wasn't on. She came back out and then noticed that one of the outdoor lights was lit in the back.

It's too chilly to sit on the patio, she thought. But when she walked to the sliding glass doors and peered out, she could see the shape of a figure huddled on the white wrought-iron settee. Brenda pushed open the doors and stepped outside. "Lillie?"

Lillie looked up and turned around, her heart-shaped face shadowy in the darkness.

"Honey, what are you doing out here?" Brenda asked. "It's not summertime. How long have you been here?"

"A few hours," said Lillie. "Brenda, I need your help."

Lillie's voice quavered and Brenda did not like the sound of it. She could tell, even in the darkness, that Lillie's dark eyes were glassy with tears.

"Well, sure, anything you want. What happened, honey? I thought you were doing better?"

"I need to stay here with you for a while," Lillie said.

"Oh," Brenda said knowingly. She had always suspected that there was more unhappiness between Lillie and Pink than her friend ever let on, but this was the first time she had ever known her to walk out on him, even for the night. "What'd he do?"

"That's the other part of the favor," Lillie said, staring out into the dark expanse of yard. "I can't talk about it. Please, don't ask me, because I can't tell you anything about it. Not until I know . . ."

"Suit yourself," said Brenda, trying unsuccessfully to keep from sounding offended. She walked over and sat down in one of the wrought-iron chairs, and felt, with distaste, the damp, cold iron through her clothes. "I brought the cushions in weeks ago," she said. "I'll have to show you where they are in case you want to sit out again while you're here."

"Brenda, all I can tell you is that my life feels like it's falling apart. You can't know how much I wish I could talk it over with you."

"Well, if you can't trust me . . ."

"Oh, Brenda."

"You're right, that's not fair," Brenda admitted.

"If you don't want me to stay, I'll get a motel room."

"Don't be silly," said Brenda. "You stay as long as you need to."

"I knew I could depend on you."

"Well," said Brenda, "that's true. You can. And if you want to talk . . . After all, you know every rotten thing that happened with all my husbands."

Lillie shook her head. "I can't."

"All right, all right," Brenda said, standing up. "But let's go on into the house. It's cold out here. You'll catch pneumonia."

"I'm fine," Lillie said.

"Come on," said Brenda. "You can't sit here all night. And I want to show you what I bought at the food show. I tell you, that Opryland Hotel is so huge, I got lost today. I had to ask directions from two people."

Lillie stood up and followed numbly after Brenda, who led the way through the house to the cheerful kitchen, which was checkered with imported hand-painted ceramic tiles.

"I could use a drink," Brenda said, walking over to her glass-backed bar and reaching for the Southern Comfort. "Look in those bags. Those are the things I got at the show." She turned around. "Do you feel like a little splash?"

When Lillie looked up from the profusion of new kitchen utensils to refuse the drink, Brenda caught sight of her friend's face in the full light of the kitchen. She slammed the whiskey bottle down on the counter and glowered at Lillie.

Lillie looked at her, bewildered for a moment, and then her hand flew up to her face.

"What the hell did he do to you?" Brenda demanded.

Lillie backed away as Brenda strode around the center island and came toward her. "That son of a bitch," Brenda exclaimed. "Let me see that."

Lillie lowered her hand and exposed the swollen black-and-blue area around her eye and her cheekbone.

"Well, no wonder you left him," said Brenda, examining her friend's face. "Did you put ice on it?"

Lillie nodded dumbly.

"Lillie, there's no excuse for that. You know it, don't you? I don't care what the fight was about."

"I know," Lillie said quietly.

"Goddamnit," said Brenda. She picked up a glass, filled it with ice, and poured out some Southern Comfort. She added a twist of lemon and took a sip. "Divorce him," she said. "I'm telling you, Lillie. Once they start this kind of shit, it never ends. There is always a next time."

Lillie sat down on one of the cane-backed stools beside the island, her eyes far away. "There won't be any next time."

"There better not be. That bastard. I never liked him, Lillie. I don't care. I may regret saying this one day, but I don't care. I know he's been a good father to the kids and all that. But look at your face. It's purple."

Lillie walked over to the mirror behind the bar and gently touched the bruise on her cheek. She stared impassively at it, as if it were on someone else's face. All at once the front doorbell rang and both women jumped. They looked at one another.

"That is probably Pink," Lillie said calmly. "Will you send him away? I don't want to see him or talk to him."

Brenda banged the glass down on the counter and looked in the direction of the door with a vengeful gleam in her eye. "I'll do better than that," she said grimly. She opened the door of an antique oak server and reached inside. She rummaged for a minute and then pulled out a .38 caliber Smith & Wesson pistol from inside.

"Brenda!" Lillie cried. "What are you doing?"

"I'm running him off," she said.

"Is that loaded?"

"Damn right," said Brenda. "You'd be surprised how

handy one of these things is for a single girl to have around the house."

"Put it away," Lillie pleaded.

"We'll have to get you one," Brenda said, ignoring the plea. She started through the house toward the front door, her chin stuck squarely out, the heft of the gun like a natural extension of her manicured diamond-bedecked hand.

The knocking on the door had turned to pounding, and Brenda knew that sound very well. The irate husband. Well, she'd put a stop to that right quick, she thought. Brenda reached the foyer, threw the switch that floodlit the front yard, and pulled the door open, holding the gun low. When she saw who it was, she greeted him, barrel first.

Pink, who had been standing at the front door, nervously jingling his keys, spotted the gun and jumped back with a yelp.

Brenda looked at him coldly. "She doesn't want to see you."

"I have to talk to her," Pink insisted, glancing worriedly at the pistol. "This can't wait."

"Get lost, Pink."

"Come on, Brenda. Stop pointing that thing at me. Let me in."

"Why, so you can punch her around a little more?"

Pink scowled, but there was a sheepish look in his eye. "This is none of your business," he said. "Now just step aside there."

"Don't try it, Pink. I'll use it."

Pink looked in exasperation from the gun to Brenda's

flinty expression. "You probably would. You'd probably get off on it."

"I'm counting to three," said Brenda.

"Everybody knows you're a man-hater," Pink said.

"Wife-beater," Brenda retorted. "One . . ."

"I want to see my wife," Pink cried.

"Move," Brenda cried, rushing out the door after him.

"Lillie," Pink called out, backing down the steps between the gleaming white columns. "Lillie, come out here."

Brenda followed him down the steps, waving the pistol. Pink muttered something she could not understand and headed for the Oldsmobile, which was parked at the foot of the expansive front lawn.

"Don't come back," Brenda cried. She stomped back up the steps and slammed the front door behind her. She turned to Lillie, who was poised anxiously behind an antique commode that served as a telephone table in the hall. "I think he got the message."

"Thanks," said Lillie, a bitter smile curving her lips.

Brenda blew into the barrel of the gun as if she had fired it and smiled brightly at Lillie. "I enjoyed it."

"You should be more careful with that thing," Lillie said. "Put it away now, for heaven's sakes."

"I think you should take this with you, if Pink's going to be beating up on you. Do you know how to use it?"

"Sure, I know how to use it. But I don't want it. I'm not afraid of Pink."

Brenda arched her eyebrows and gazed pointedly at the bruise on Lillie's face. "Maybe you should be."

"Oh, Brenda," said Lillie, shaking her head. "This is the least of my problems."

"God, Lillie," Brenda exclaimed, "why don't you talk to me?"

"I have to try to sort things out in my own head. Figure out how our lives went so wrong. And what to do about it."

"Well, I hope it doesn't take all night. You need some sleep."

"All night is just the beginning," Lillie said.

"Well, go on to bed," said Brenda. "Try and rest."

"I think I will," Lillie said wearily.

Brenda chewed her lip and peered angrily after her friend, who looked as frail as a child to her, heading off down the hall. "If you need anything . . ." she called out.

"I'll be fine," Lillie replied, turning to wave good night.

Brenda drummed her polished fingernails against the top of the commode as she watched Lillie disappear into the guest room. Then she gazed down at the pistol she was holding and weighed it in her hand as if it were a decision. With a determined little nod of her head she marched back to the kitchen and looked around until she located the large leather satchel Lillie used for a handbag. After checking to be sure the safety was still clicked on, she dropped the pistol gingerly into the bag. Lillie, you're too trusting, Brenda thought. Once they get a little taste of that pushing you around and knocking you down, they learn to like it. They always have to try it again. She zippered up the bag and headed back for her own room, glad there was no man around to wad up wet towels on her bathroom floor tonight.

CHAPTER 22

E ver since childhood, Lillie had loved the sound of the church bells on Sunday morning, ringing out the old-time hymns through the town. It always made her feel as if she lived in the most peaceful, protected place on earth. But she had tossed, sleepless, in Brenda's guest room bed until dawn, and this morning the church bell's peal jolted her awake like an alarm.

She got out of bed, washed up, and dressed automatically. As she walked quietly down the hall she looked into the cream-colored Marie Antoinette–style bedroom and saw that Brenda was still asleep. She was lying still, wearing her lacy black sleep mask. Lillie wished that she could block this coming day out that effectively. But there was nothing else to do but to face it.

She had had a long night to think about all of it—her

PATRICIA J. MacDONALD

marriage, her children, and the impossible situation she
was in. But by the time the first flare of sun struck the
wall, she was practically feverish with anxiety. She had
made up her mind about only one thing that she had to do,
and that she intended to do right away. She went out into
the kitchen, put on her coat, and picked up her purse,
which was lying on the counter. The purse strap weighed
heavily on her shoulder, and she thought again of how
exhausted she was. She picked up her car keys from the
counter, looked around the room, and then let herself quietly out of the house.

It was a cool, dewy Tennessee morning, the trees bare
and chilly-looking, the air clear and silent except for a few
birds. As she started down the driveway toward her car,
she saw the black Oldsmobile parked out in front of the
house. Pink was slumped against the steering wheel.

Lillie hesitated a minute, feeling as if she should speak
to him. The leaden pain in her face reminded her that she
did not want to. She arrived at her car door and opened it
as carefully as possible, hoping he would not hear her. But
Pink suddenly sat up, as if the gentle *thunk* had been a
gunshot, and looked out at her. Then he clambered out of
the Oldsmobile and hurried toward her.

"Lillie, wait a minute."

"Be quiet," Lillie said sharply as he approached.
"Brenda's still asleep."

"We have to talk," said Pink. He was disheveled and
puffy-eyed from sleeping in the car, and nursing some
bourbon, Lillie suspected.

"I don't want to talk now," she said.

"Oh, honey, come on," he said, reaching out as if to
embrace her. Lillie shrank from him.

"Just keep away from me," she said.

"Honey, I just want to tell you how sorry I am. I didn't mean for things to get out of hand like they did," Pink insisted. "I never did that to you before. Now, you know that."

"And that makes it all right?" she said in a shrill voice.

"No," Pink said eagerly. "I know it was wrong. And I promise you, it will never happen again. Never. Now, darlin', don't be in such a hurry to rush off. Where are you going anyway?"

"There's someone I have to talk to," she said.

"Well, come on," he said. "I'll give you a lift."

"I'll drive myself."

Pink took her hand and tried to knead it in his own but Lillie pulled it away from him. "I just want for us all to be back together again. You and me and Grayson. The way it's supposed to be. That's the way Michele would want us to be."

Lillie stiffened at his invocation of her daughter's memory. "Don't you dare," she cried. "Don't you mention her name to me. Oh, God, what would she think of us? Leave me alone, Pink."

Pink stared at her in bewilderment and then in anger, as he realized that his apology was not having the desired effect.

"I *said* I was sorry."

"I heard you."

"It's just a bruise, for crying out loud. Where are you going anyway?"

Lillie looked at him with anguished eyes. "I am going to see Royce. His son killed my daughter, remember?"

"Look, there's nothing Royce can do about this now.

We made our decision," Pink said stubbornly. "Why stir the whole thing up again?"

"You decided, not me. All I knew about it were lies and more lies."

Pink shook his head incredulously and then slammed his palm down on the hood of the car. "Nothing I do is ever enough for you. I spend my whole life trying to satisfy you and for what? So you can turn on me. And our son."

"Pink, I'm not turning on you. You're my family. You and Grayson . . . you're all I have in this world. But this was *murder,* Pink. Not some prank. You're all pretending it never happened. Our daughter was murdered!"

"This is just for revenge, isn't it?" Pink demanded. "Because we didn't consult with you. You're going to start making a lot of noise about it. This is exactly why I didn't want to tell you in the first place."

"Oh, right, Pink," Lillie said sarcastically. "Absolutely. I couldn't be trusted with something like that. You just went ahead and made the most crucial decision in our whole lives and just lied through your teeth about it. Why, I should be grateful to you. I should thank you for that."

Pink eyed her obstinately. "Don't be so self-righteous. I was thinking of Grayson's future. Somebody had to. What do you think would happen to him if this thing got out?"

"I don't know," said Lillie.

"That's right. You don't know and you don't care. You'd think nothing of ruining his life to get your revenge on Tyler. Even though Michele is dead and nothing we do now can help her. You just always loved her more than you loved Grayson."

Lillie wanted to cry out in protest, make some nasty

reply, but the retort did not come readily to her lips. Pink's words winded her, like a low blow. Was it true? Michele had always been the vulnerable one, the needy one. The one who depended on her. Grayson had shaken off her help as soon as he could walk. And maybe that *had* hurt her a bit. Maybe she had drawn closer to the one who needed her the most. But it wasn't fair to say she loved one more than the other. She loved them both, each in her own way. They were her children, her little ones. She did not have to defend her love to anybody. But in spite of herself, Pink's words made her feel guilty. And she did not want him to know it.

"I'm sorry you see it that way, Pink," she said coldly. She reached for the car door handle, but Pink jerked her away from it.

She turned on him furiously and snarled, "Let go of me."

He loosened his grip. She pulled away from him and got into the car. She got out her keys and began to insert them into the ignition with a trembling hand. Pink hesitated, then reached in and tried to grab them away from her. Lillie cried out and rolled up the window. Pink snatched his hand out quickly, to avoid getting his wrist jammed in the window. Lillie reinserted the key, pressed on the gas, and started the engine. She put the car into reverse and let out the emergency brake. As she glanced into the rearview mirror, she saw her husband standing there, behind the car.

She rolled down the window and stuck her head out. "Get out of the way, Pink," she said.

"You can't do this," Pink said. "You can't just go out and destroy all our lives."

"I'm not trying to destroy anything. But I'm going to talk to Royce Ansley. Right now." She revved the engine and touched the gas. The car inched backward.

"Go ahead and hit me," he cried. "Why don't you?"

She blew her horn, but he stood still, blocking the car's path with his soft, aging body.

She looked at him incredulously. "Move out of the way," she cried. "I'm going out."

"Go ahead," he said. "I don't care."

And in that moment she knew that it was true. He would. For his misguided notion of shielding Grayson, he would stand in the path of a car. She didn't know whether it was pity or revulsion or even sympathy that twisted her heart.

She threw the gear shift into drive and the car jerked forward. She turned the wheel sharply and threw it into reverse, backing out at top speed over the emerald-green perfection of Brenda's lawn, leaving tire ruts in an area around the driveway. Pink shouted something after her, but she rolled up the window again so that she could not hear him.

Royce Ansley lived on a quiet street in a stone farmhouse that some returning soldier had modeled after a French country house after World War I. Lillie parked in the driveway and recalled what the now-shabby facade had looked like when Lulene was alive. Roses climbed up around the door and her flower garden was unrivaled in Felton.

After his wife's bout with cancer and her death, Royce's brown crew cut seemed to turn gray overnight, and he never did appear to recover. He had married late in life, and when a seemly amount of time had passed and people suggested that he date again, he would always say the same thing. "I had my wife." And the way he said it, it was as if he meant to say "my life" instead.

Lillie banished the sympathy that she'd always felt for him. She walked up to the front door, dropped the old iron door knocker, and waited. She heard footsteps and the door opened. Royce Ansley, still in his bathrobe, looked out at her with tired eyes. He did not seem surprised to see her.

"I thought it might be you," he said. "Come in."

Lillie closed the door and followed him into the front sitting room. "Do you mind if I get dressed?" he asked.

Lillie was tempted to refuse. Part of her wanted to humiliate him, to make him face this confrontation in that vulnerable condition. He was not the man she had respected all these years. He was a liar and a lawbreaker. But for some reason that she could not understand, she wanted to be fair to him.

"Go ahead," she said abruptly.

"Thank you. Make yourself at home."

Lillie nodded and looked around as Royce left the room. Who could feel at home here? she thought. The room was neat, everything perfectly in its place. But the yellowed curtains looked as if they had not been opened in years. Lillie could tell that Royce had not changed the position of one object, not even an ashtray, since Lulene's death. She remembered coming here with Jordan when he was in the school play *Our Town*. Lulene had served them tea and told Jordan about productions she had seen on Broadway. Lillie could remember how Jordan's eyes had shone, and she had not recognized the danger to her in that gleam.

She had felt only pleasure that he was so highly regarded by his teacher, that it made him so very happy. Lulene was pregnant with Tyler then. The house was neat then too. But it was also cheery with flowers and china teacups. She could not help but imagine, now, how dreary it must have been for Tyler growing up in a house like this after his mother had died. A house full of death and orderliness.

"There," said Royce, coming back into the room as he tightened the belt buckle on his civilian pants. "All right, Lillie."

"Did Pink call you?" she asked tartly.

"Yes." The terse word conveyed his readiness for her assault. She did not intend to disappoint him.

"Ever since I can remember, Royce, I always respected you. I always thought so highly of you. If someone had told me that you were capable of something like this . . ."

He did not try to adopt an aggressive posture. He sank down onto a worn brocade-covered chair and stared at his wedding picture on the table beside him. The couple in the photo smiled out at him, not young but still innocent.
· "I don't know how I can explain this to you," he muttered.

"You can't," Lillie said shortly. "I didn't come here for explanations or excuses. I've had it up to here with excuses."

Royce looked up at her somberly as she slashed a flat hand across her own throat. Then he shook his head. "It was Pink's idea to keep this from you. He said that you'd be so upset over Michele that you wouldn't be able to think clearly. I didn't see it that way, but then again, there was no good solution. I hated lying to you, Lillie. I don't expect you to understand, but I want you to believe that."

Lillie was not about to reassure him. "So," she said, pointedly ignoring his plea, "you and Pink went ahead and now we're all caught up in this pack of lies. And what are we going to do about it?"

"I don't know," said Royce. He got up from his chair and walked over to the writing desk in the corner. Lillie suddenly noticed his holster, lying on the desk, and for a moment her heart leapt in fear.

"Royce, don't!" she exclaimed.

Royce saw where she was looking and he frowned. Then he looked up at her with sorrow in his eyes. "Oh, Lillie, do you think I'm evil?"

"I don't know what to think," she said in a quiet voice.

He picked up a framed photograph of Tyler and studied it for a moment. Then he set it back down on the desk.

"How could you, Royce?" asked Lillie. "You've been a police officer all your life. Do you think you are above the law by now?"

Royce sighed. "Do you love your son, Lillie?"

"Don't give me that," she said impatiently. "I've had all I can stand of that from Pink. God knows I don't want my son arrested or publicly humiliated. I'm his mother. I want to protect him. Just as you want to protect Tyler. But this isn't a broken window we're talking about. Or even a stolen car. This is murder. My daughter lost her life. So don't give me this business about loving your son. We all love our children. But what is best for them? That's the question now."

"No, on the contrary," he said. "I'm not sure about that love. I don't know what a father should feel for his son.

When I think of Tyler . . . Lillie, I'll be honest with you—"

"It's about time," she said.

"I didn't really want any children. I was never good with children. Their games and so forth. And I was older than most. But she was so happy to have Tyler." He pointed vaguely to the wedding picture. "She just doted on him. I stayed away from him pretty much. I punished him when it was called for. When he got old enough for hunting, and sports and the things I knew about, he was never interested. His mother was gone, and I didn't know what to do with him. He was secretive and surly and rebellious. We never spoke that it didn't end in an argument. He was always in trouble, in school, everywhere. He was drinking. I knew it. And God knows what else. A year ago, money started to disappear from my wallet. I knew he was stealing from me. I warned him . . . I threatened . . . it was useless. He was everything I despised."

Lillie sat quietly, watching him. Royce sat back down and looked squarely at her. "When I found Michele that night, and the baseball bat. . . . That sweet little girl. . . . And then I came across those boys, and they told me what happened.

"I wanted to strangle my son with my own hands. You must believe me, Lillie. Protecting Tyler went against everything in me. Everything I ever felt, or believed in. If Pink hadn't showed up just then . . . Well, I won't say that. I won't lay my misdeeds at his feet. But I'll tell you this. I didn't do it for Tyler and I didn't do it for me. I did it for her. Because she loved him."

"I see," Lillie said bluntly. "And so that's the end of it. Tyler goes off to military school. And to hell with my daughter. And what about the next innocent girl who gets him angry?"

"I think the Sentinel will be the best place for him. I'm praying that they can straighten him out."

Lillie could scarcely believe how hard she felt. It was as if Michele was alive and she was fighting to save her again. "He killed my daughter," she said. "He belongs in jail."

"Justice." Royce sighed.

"All right. Yes," said Lillie.

"An eye for an eye," said Royce.

"Let's not play games, Royce. I have as much at stake as you do. Don't you think I'm in agony over this? I mean, the thought of exposing my husband, my son. I don't know what to do. But how can I let Tyler just walk away? He *has* to be punished for this."

"Do you want him to die for it, Lillie?"

"Don't be melodramatic, Royce. No jury is going to sentence a seventeen-year-old boy to death for a drunken . . . I don't know . . . I refuse to call it an accident. An incident. Not even in Tennessee. But he may go to jail for a while and I say he should. Military school is not punishment."

"I understand," said Royce. "But what *you* must understand is that when Tyler goes to jail, he will be killed. By the other inmates. He'll be killed because he's my son. Because I put a lot of those guys in there over the years. They'll have to keep him in solitary, all the time, but that won't save his life. They'll get to him. They have ways and ways."

Lillie sank back and gripped the arm of the sofa.

"That's why I agreed to keep quiet," Royce said. "Because I knew he would die there, and the reason he would die was because of me. Now, you may feel that he deserves to die, but I could not personally sentence my own son to death."

This isn't fair, thought Lillie. I don't want to hear it. But her mind was working furiously, realizing at once that what Royce said was true.

"You can see the problem," said Royce.

She could see it. The problem was that Tyler's life or death was now in her hands. And she did not want it to be.

"Lillie," Royce said earnestly, "I don't know of any good way. But I am asking you to be merciful and spare my son's life. Even though he did not spare your daughter's, and there is no earthly reason for you to show mercy."

"Maybe they wouldn't send him to prison," Lillie protested weakly.

"Why wouldn't they? This is Tennessee. You go to jail here for twenty years for possession of marijuana. And he deserves to be in prison, as you say. Anyone can see that. But, unfortunately, what you must decide is, does he deserve to die?"

Lillie stared up at him.

"You know what choice I made. But then again, he *is* my flesh and blood."

Lillie looked up at the sheriff's grizzled head and felt a wave of hopelessness. It was not fair. The responsibility was too great. It was one thing to send a boy to jail and another to mandate his execution. And to tear apart her own family at the same time. God knows what would become of Grayson and Pink, she thought. They might end up in jail themselves. They had lied. They had covered up a felony. Grayson had turned sixteen. He was old enough to face prosecution. She could not stand to think of him having to go through that. And for what? For trying to protect Michele in his own wretched way?

But what about Michele? Who was there to take her side if not her mother? Would her murder just be shoved aside, unavenged, as if she were some animal hit by a car on the highway? Oh, my baby, she called out to her lost girl from her heart, what would you want me to do?

And even as she asked it, she could not help but remember Michele, wearing her little protest armbands against capital punishment. A bleeding heart, Pink called her. Lillie had never taken her too seriously, for Michele was young and sheltered, and what did she know about criminals and murder, and victims wanting revenge? Although now, when she thought about it, Lillie realized that Michele had understood a death sentence all too well. In hospital after hospital, for most of her young life, she had steeled herself to face it. Death had hovered very low over her head.

Lillie's heart felt like a weight in her chest. It was not right to have to choose. On the one hand was her murdered child, and on the other, her living son, and Royce's son. Whom did you consider first, the living or the dead? And if she kept the secret, if they all kept the secret, would it torment them in the end?

"Will you think about it some more?" Royce asked.

Lillie stood up, numb. "I can't make any sense of it," she said.

Royce nodded his head in sympathy. "I know," he said. "It seems that whatever we choose, we can't win. Can we?"

They stared fearfully into one another's eyes.

CHAPTER 23

Jordan had requested a wake-up call from the motel desk, but he awoke without it and was almost finished shaving when the phone began to ring in his room. He walked over and picked it up, ready to respond with a curt thank you when a masculine, authoritative voice on the other end barked his name like a command.

Jordan frowned. "Yes?"

"Colonel Preavette here."

"Good morning, Colonel," Jordan said, surprised.

"Do you have Cadet Ansley there with you?" the colonel asked in an impatient, accusing tone.

"With me?" Jordan said. "No, of course not."

"You were here last night looking for him," the colonel asserted.

"Yes, that's right. And you told me to come back in the morning. I was just on my way up there."

There was a brief silence at the other end. "I have just been informed that Cadet Ansley did not return to his quarters last night. Do you know of his whereabouts at this time?"

"Goddamnit," Jordan exploded, and then quickly excused himself. "Colonel, did you tell him that I was there to see him?"

"No, I did not. I have not seen Cadet Ansley for several days."

Where the hell is he? Jordan thought. This isn't just a coincidence. How did he know I was coming?

"Mr. Hill!" the colonel demanded.

"I'm coming up there," said Jordan. "I'll be there in ten minutes."

He hung up, got ready, and checked out in record time, his mind working furiously as he drove the short distance up the road to the military academy. The Sentinel looked shabbier, less severe, in the pearly morning light. Even in the South, military schools did not enjoy the favor and prosperity they once had. Jordan parked the car and hurried up to the administration building, barely aware of the neatly uniformed boys he passed on his way. Maybe it was the old reverend, he thought. Maybe he had informed the sheriff of his and Lillie's visit. And the sheriff had called his son and told him to hide out until Jordan was gone. It was possible. Except that Jordan couldn't picture the reverend doing that. The old man didn't want to get involved in the first place. Why would he call the sheriff when he could just keep quiet? It didn't make sense.

Colonel Preavette was seated at his desk, calmly talking

on the telephone when Jordan arrived, somewhat out of breath, at his door. The colonel motioned for him to come in and take a seat.

Jordan dropped down into the visitor's chair and flexed his fingers impatiently while the colonel chatted amiably about Alumni Day with his caller. Finally he hung up and looked at Jordan.

"Well?" said Jordan.

"Apparently he has left the campus," the colonel said evenly, betraying none of the snappish urgency of his earlier call.

Jordan stifled an expletive. "How long has he been missing?"

"According to his roommate, he did not return after mess last night. The roommate assumed that Tyler had a special pass. He claims that Tyler was greatly upset by a phone call he received yesterday afternoon. Now, as you maintain that the boy is not with you—"

"He is not with me," Jordan said angrily. "I want to talk to this roommate."

"I don't think there's any need for that," the colonel said in a mild voice. "It's entirely possible that Cadet Ansley has spent the night with a young lady in town. This has been known to occur. There is no cause for undue alarm."

"What is the roommate's name?" Jordan demanded. "Where can I find him?"

"Look here, Mr. Hill. This is a disciplinary matter for the school and the boy's family. I regret that I involved you at all. I would not have called you except that I thought that Cadet Ansley's unauthorized absence might be related to your visit here last night." The colonel's eyes looked cold and gray as oysters behind his glasses.

"Oh, it is, Colonel. You can bet your rank on that," Jordan said sharply. "Now, I have to speak to this boy and find out who called Tyler and what this boy knows about it."

"I cannot allow you to harass my students, sir," the colonel said. "Is that clear? We are all concerned about the boy's whereabouts."

Jordan considered the colonel and knew that he must choose his words carefully. This was not a person who would respond well to threats and anger. This was a man who went by the rules, and believed in respect for authority and adherence to the law. Despite his stiffness, he struck Jordan as a good man, protective of his charges. And he was worried about Tyler, despite his bland demeanor. Why else would he be in the office on a Sunday morning? Part of him wanted to shake his fist at the old soldier, but he knew that was no way to approach the man.

"Colonel," he said. "I completely understand your position. And I have no desire to harass this young man. But I need most desperately to find Tyler Ansley. If this boy can give me any clue . . . Colonel, may I take you into my confidence?"

There it was again. That curious glint in the colonel's eye. There is really something very human about him beneath the military crust, Jordan thought.

"That might be useful," said the colonel.

"Sir, my daughter, my only child," said Jordan, "was recently murdered." He let the shocking words hang in the air for a moment and take their effect. The colonel winced at the bald disclosure. Jordan nodded toward the photograph on the colonel's desk. "I see you are a family man, sir. I'm sure you can understand what a blow this has been to me."

Colonel Preavette nodded. "Terribly sorry," he said grimly.

"I have reason to believe," Jordan said carefully, "that Tyler Ansley may have information about this crime. It is vital to me that I speak to him."

"This sounds like a matter for the police," said the colonel.

"I agree with you," Jordan said. "And my . . . wife and I have appealed repeatedly to the sheriff. But, as you know, the sheriff is Tyler's father."

"I see." The controlled expression on the colonel's face did not change, although Jordan thought he saw a tightening in his jaw. The colonel picked up the pack of Camels on his desk and shook one out. He lit the cigarette, clearly thinking over what Jordan had said. Then he sighed. "Mr. Hill, I have known Royce Ansley for years. He served under me in Korea."

Jordan felt his hopes sinking.

"When he brought Tyler here I took him in against my better judgment, because of our old association. I could see the boy had problems. And I could sense the tension between the two of them. But I have great faith in our program here. We can really help a boy if he gives it a good effort." The colonel took a long drag on his cigarette and stared thoughtfully at the family picture on his desk. "Sometimes, though, when a boy has a father like Royce Ansley, who represents something . . . the law, and is very strict— Well, it is particularly easy to shame a father like that."

Jordan nodded but did not speak, wondering where this was leading. The colonel took another drag on his cigarette and then put it out carefully in the clean ashtray on his desk. "Very well," he said. "I will let you speak to this boy, but I will come along with you to make sure that you do not abuse the privilege."

"Thank you, sir."

They walked together in silence across the campus to the door of Jackson House, the dorm where Tyler Ansley lived. The cadet at the front desk saluted the colonel, who returned the salute and nodded at him. A middle-aged couple, dressed in their Sunday best, emerged from the stairwell into the lounge, accompanied by their son, who walked stiffly between them. The mother was dabbing at her eyes with a hanky. The son saluted Colonel Preavette and his father beamed.

"Up these stairs," said the colonel.

Their steps echoed in the iron stairwell as they climbed to the third floor. Jordan noticed that the wiry colonel took the stairs easily, despite his smoking habit. The linoleum floors of the dorm were uncarpeted and their presence seemed to fill up the hall with racket. The colonel knocked on the door of one of the rooms and then said, "Cadet Fredericks, this is Colonel Preavette. Open up."

The door was opened immediately by a burr-headed boy with an anxious look in his eyes. "Yessir."

"Cadet Fredericks, this is Mr. Jordan Hill." The colonel pronounced his name Jerdan, in the old Southern way. "Mr. Hill, Cadet Fredericks."

Jordan shook the boy's damp hand.

"Mr. Hill has a few questions for you about Cadet Ansley, and I want you to cooperate with him and tell him whatever you can that he needs to know."

"Yessir."

Jordan stepped into the chilly cell of a room and made way for the colonel. The colonel shook his head. "I will be making an impromptu inspection of quarters up here." He looked significantly at Jordan. "I'll return for you in a few minutes."

"Thank you, Colonel." Jordan turned his attention to the cadet, who was standing stiffly in the doorway. "It's all right. At ease," he said. "Why don't you sit?"

The boy sat down gratefully on the edge of his bed and stared at him. Fredericks's side of the room was neat and orderly. Tyler's side was a mess. There were papers piled on his desk and clothes sticking out of the closet door. Jordan went over to Tyler's desk chair and sat down, facing the young man. "The colonel tells me that Tyler never came back last night," he said.

"No, that's right."

"Weren't you surprised that he didn't show up?"

The boy shrugged. "I thought he must have had a pass."

"I heard something about a phone call?" said Jordan.

"Are you a cop?" the boy asked.

"No," said Jordan. "I'm a . . . friend of the family. Was he worried about the cops?"

"I think his dad's a sheriff."

"He is. What about this phone call?"

"He got an urgent message to call someone. I don't know who it was. After we got back from the drill field. I just figured it was some family emergency and he had to go home or something."

"He didn't tell you who called him?"

"He didn't really tell me anything," said Fredericks. "We didn't talk very much. That was okay with me."

"You don't like him," Jordan said.

The boy shrugged and looked closely at Jordan, as if trying to figure out whether this guy was likely to spring to Tyler's defense. "He's kind of weird."

"What do you mean, weird?" Jordan asked.

"I don't know. Just weird," said the boy, avoiding his eyes.

He knew, all right, Jordan thought. He just wasn't saying. "So, he never told you who called him. Or why? Or where he was going?"

The boy shook his head. "Not to me."

"Anyone else you know that he might have confided in?" Jordan asked. "Did he have a girlfriend in town maybe? Did he ever stay out all night before?"

Fredericks snickered briefly at that.

"What's so funny?" Jordan asked.

"Nothing," said the boy. "He kept to himself. Most of the other guys stayed away from him. Look on his desk," Fredericks offered. "Maybe the message is still there. About who called him."

"A written message?" Jordan asked hopefully, swiveling around and lifting up the papers on the desk.

"Yeah," said Fredericks. "They give them to you at the desk downstairs when you come in."

Jordan rummaged quickly through the papers, which consisted of messy class notes, a stained take-out menu from a local barbecue place, and assorted doodlings. Jordan had the urge to settle down and read through every page, trying to find some clue about Tyler and Michele, but he knew his time was short. The colonel would be back before long. The desktop held no telephone messages. He shook the books piled haphazardly there, but no messages floated down.

Opening the desk drawer, he turned back to Fredericks. "Did he ever mention someone named Michele to you?" he asked.

"A girl?" the cadet asked. He smirked and shook his head.

Jordan peered into the desk drawer and began to rifle through it.

"He wasn't all that interested in girls," Fredericks said slyly.

Almost at the same moment Jordan picked up an open envelope. A photograph dropped out of it and fell to the bottom of the drawer. The photo was creased and dog-eared, as if it had been held and examined many times. It was a picture of a boy, his blond head thrown back, his eyes bright and knowing, his lips curved in a satisfied smile.

Jordan took out the picture and stared at it. Grayson. He looked over at Fredericks, who rolled his eyes and shrugged again. "There's another one of those taped inside his footlocker," he said.

Jordan continued to stare at the photo. What the boy was saying was clear enough, but it didn't make any sense.

Fredericks saw the confusion on Jordan's face and offered, "He'd put that inside his books and pretend to be reading, but then I'd look up and see him running his finger over it, just gazing away at it. It gave me the creeps to live in the same room with him. Knowing he was like that. I was afraid he'd start getting ideas about me."

Jordan felt dazed. Tyler and Grayson. It was possible, of course. But Michele didn't fit into it. It didn't make any sense. Still, he knew this boy had no reason to lie about it. No reason at all. Jordan studied the photo another moment and then slipped it into his pocket. He stood up on wobbly legs.

"Is he in trouble?" said Fredericks.

Jordan ignored the question. "You have no idea where he might have gone."

"I guess if he found out he was in trouble, he wanted to get as far away from here as he could."

"Yes, probably," Jordan said distractedly.

"I didn't mean to shock you," Fredericks said in a friendly way. "You'd never suspect it. He looks so macho and mean."

Jordan peered at the boy. "Do they keep a record of the messages downstairs? A log, do you think?"

Fredericks shook his head. "I don't know. You could ask."

Jordan nodded. "If the colonel comes back, please tell him that I've gone down to the lounge."

"I will," said Fredericks.

Jordan turned back to him. "Thanks for your help."

"You're welcome. I hope you find him. Just don't bring him back here."

Jordan looked up and down the hall but the colonel was nowhere to be seen. He clattered down the stairwell to the first-floor lounge and walked up to the cadet on duty.

The boy, recognizing him as the colonel's guest, turned a welcoming smile on him.

With difficulty, Jordan smiled back. "I was wondering if you could help me," he asked.

"If I can," the cadet said brightly.

"Do you keep a written log of the phone messages that come in here for the cadets who live here?"

The boy looked at him warily but was still eager to help the colonel's guest. "Yes. Why?"

"I need to know who called one of your cadets yesterday. The colonel suggested that I ask you." He hated to use the colonel's name after the man had tried to help him, but this was not a time for such scruples.

The boy looked at him expectantly.

"Yesterday. There was a message left for one of your residents—Tyler Ansley—to call someone. Can you tell me who that was?"

The boy took out the log book and began to pore over it. Jordan checked behind him to make sure the colonel had not yet entered the lounge. Then he turned his head to try to read the log as the boy examined it.

"I'm not finding it," said the boy.

"It was probably late afternoon, early evening," said Jordan anxiously. He could hear a brisk footfall on the stairwell. "Do you see it yet?" Sweat was popping out on his forehead.

"Here it is," exulted the cadet. " 'Call Mr. Burdette.' It says to call Mr. Burdette at his office. Not at home. And this is the number." The boy looked up at Jordan. "Do you want to write the number down?" he asked.

"Mr. Hill, what do you think you are doing with that

log?" The colonel had entered the lounge and was striding across the room to the desk.

The cadet looked in confusion from the colonel to Jordan. "Did you need the number?" he asked worriedly, closing the book.

"No," Jordan replied, turning away from the desk. "That won't be necessary."

CHAPTER 24

Having stretched and strained through fifty minutes of an exercise video, Brenda was rewarding herself with a cup of yogurt while she listened to a Crystal Gayle tape on her Walkman. She was sitting at her kitchen table, humming loudly along to the tape, when she looked up and saw a man pressed against the sliding glass doors at the end of the room, peering in. Yogurt splattered on her leotard as she jumped up with a shriek, and then her face relaxed into a scowl as she recognized her visitor.

She padded down to the doors and pulled them open angrily.

"Jordan Hill, didn't you ever hear of the doorbell? You about scared me to death."

"I tried it," he said. "You didn't answer, but I saw your car."

"Well, you're here now. Come on in," she said irritably. "What are you doing here anyway?"

"I'm looking for Lillie," he said. "No one was home over there so I figured I'd try your place. Have you seen her?"

"Oh, I see," Brenda said knowingly. "Well, she's been in and out. Don't ask me where she went. What is going on with you two anyway? Are you two getting back together? She won't tell me anything."

"Look, Brenda, I have to talk to her right away," he said.

"I'm sorry, I don't know where she is right now. She got up early this morning and went out—"

"She spent the night here?" Jordan asked.

"Oh, don't act so innocent," said Brenda. "Of course she did. She and Pink had a huge fight. I'm guessing it must have been about you." She pressed a long, orchid-colored fingernail into his sternum.

"No, I'm sure it wasn't," he mumbled. So, he thought to himself, Lillie must have found out that Pink called Tyler. She must have. Why else would they have had such a fight? What the hell is going on? he asked himself for the hundredth time since he'd left the Sentinel.

"When did you get back to town anyway?" Brenda asked querulously.

"Brenda, I can't talk," he said. "Do you have any idea—"

"Nobody will tell me anything," Brenda complained. "And no, I don't. She came back in a while ago and she was pacing around like a wildcat in a cage and then she said she had to go off somewhere and be by herself, to think. That's all I know."

"She didn't say where?"

"Nope. But she's in a state. I can tell you that."

Jordan frowned as if he were concentrating. "Well, thanks."

"Don't mention it. Hey, listen, Jordan. Don't go butting into this if you're just going to cause her grief. She doesn't need any more grief."

"Thanks, Brenda," he said wryly. "I'll keep that in mind."

Ever since she had arrived at Crystal Lake and walked out to the end of her jetty, Lillie had been aware of the family that was camping in a clearing about a quarter of a mile away from her around the shoreline. She had gone there, as she had so often in the past, to try to sort out her situation; but from the moment she sat down, it was as if nothing else in the world existed for her except those campers in the clearing. Her mind refused to focus on anything at all but the group huddled by the lakeside around their campfire.

It was late in the season to be camping. Most people had given it up months ago. This family seemed oblivious to the rawness of the day. They had their fire, and the father and son had spent a good part of their afternoon fishing while the mother, wearing a vest and a bulky sweater, did needlework in a folding lawn chair and kept her eye on her young twins, who were playing some imaginary scene out in the clearing. Now they were all gathered around the fire, cooking the fish, and their voices were like bells in the air. The smell of the food made Lillie's empty stomach yearn, and she had the idea that the woodsmoke from their campfire was causing her eyes to burn, even though it was too far off to reach her. But tears *were* forming in her eyes as she watched them. There was no doubt of that. Watching them was like watching people in a dream. Their words were indistinct and their actions made her feel heartsick, although nothing that they did was in any way strange or sad. She felt the exhaustion of the past day cornering her, seeping into her, and her eyelids began to droop.

No, she thought, shaking her head. You have to think. You have decisions to make. But it was no use. She felt herself getting limp, and she lay on her back on the jetty, the weak, waning sun still warm on her face. The drowsiness consumed her, and in a moment she was asleep. She slept lightly, the discomfort of the boards beneath her and the gradually cooling air around her contributing to her fretful, repetitive dreams. She dreamed that the campers were leaving, gathering up their things and going. The fire was doused and only a few wisps of smoke rose from the sodden ashes. They were scrambling into the RV, and the engine was running, although one of the twins was not in evidence, and Lillie wanted to cry out a warning to the mother, who seemed oblivious to this fact. In her dream Lillie could not understand why they were suddenly leaving, when they had seemed so comfortable there. She made her way over to their campsite and saw, to her anxious alarm, that they had left many of their belongings behind, although there was no rhyme or reason to the assortment of personal and household objects she found among the rubble of their brief settlement.

Lillie shifted uneasily in her slumber as the waters of Crystal Lake lapped beneath her, lulling her with a deceptive peacefulness. When the jetty began to vibrate beneath her, she did not awaken, but incorporated the movement, the heavy tread approaching her, into her dreams. Now she was alone, somehow capsized, and clinging to a spar in the turbulent lake. It was beginning to thunder. That's why they left, she realized in her dream. They knew this storm was coming.

A hand grabbed her shoulder and she jumped awake, letting out a cry. She sat up and looked into the somber eyes of Jordan Hill.

"Jordan," she cried. "My God, you scared me."

Jordan crouched down on the jetty beside her as Lillie fumbled to make sure she was properly buttoned and smoothed her unruly hair. She glanced automatically across the lake. The family of campers was still there, still seated around their fire.

"When did you get back?" she asked, awkwardly rising to her feet. "How did you find me?" Her heart had begun to pound. She was not ready for him. She had not yet figured out what to say to him. In truth, she had almost forgotten about him and the danger he represented.

Jordan stood up also. "I stopped by Brenda's and she said you went off to think, be by yourself. I had a pretty good idea of where to look."

"Oh," said Lillie. Despite her sense of danger and disorientation, something in her was oddly touched that he remembered where she liked to hide out. "What time is it?" she asked, looking at her watch. "I have to go."

Jordan wrapped his fingers around her wrist and detained her. There was no room around him on the narrow jetty. She looked down at the water, panic rising in her throat.

"Never mind what time it is," he said. "We have to talk.

What is going on, Lillie?" He suddenly noticed the bruise on her face and he grimaced. "Pink did that," he said. It was not a question.

"Why does everyone assume that?" Lillie asked defensively.

Jordan reached up and gently brushed the hair away from the ugly bruise, as if a cloud of hair might irritate it, might cause her discomfort. Lillie flinched at his touch, which felt hot against her cheek, but she submitted without protest to his ministrations, allowing him to touch her as if she were fragile, even though inside she was steeling herself against him, against his questions.

"Did you find Tyler?" she asked lightly.

"No, Tyler was long gone by the time I arrived. I suspect he's halfway to New York City or maybe Canada by now."

Lillie feigned surprise, as if this were news to her. In fact, she had still been at Royce's house when the call about Tyler's disappearance came in from the Sentinel. "So, you never saw him at all," she said carefully.

"No," he said.

She tried not to betray her relief. He still knew nothing. Now she could suggest that they might be wrong. That he should head back and she would keep him posted on any news. She remembered how grateful she had been when he showed up to help her. Now she only wished that he had never involved himself at all. "Well, that's a strange coincidence."

"Not really," he said. "Pink warned him in plenty of time."

"Pink!" she protested, but when their eyes met he was looking right through her. She looked away, feeling her face get hot again, this time from shame. And fear. He knew.

"Lillie, don't try to lie to me. You're no good at it. You knew it already. That's where this came from, isn't it?" he asked, nodding at the bruise on her face. "Why is Pink protecting him?"

Lillie stared stubbornly out at the lake. "I don't know what you mean."

"I asked you a question. Why is Pink protecting our daughter's killer?"

"*Our* daughter?" Lillie bristled. "My, you're awfully possessive all of a sudden. I don't remember you being around when she needed you."

"Don't bother," said Jordan. "The guilt trip is not going to put me off. Let me tell you something. I'm convinced now that you were right about Tyler. Now, I don't know how Pink is involved in all of this. You can tell me or not. But if you think this is an end to it, just because Tyler has bolted, you are dead wrong. I'm going over Royce Ansley's head. That boy can't run far enough."

She looked away from him, her heart leaden inside of her. "I envy you," she said dully. "It's so simple for you. It must be a great feeling."

Jordan looked at her in exasperation. "Lillie, I know you wish I would just disappear. But I'm in this, whether you like it or not. And whether you believe it or not, I want to help you."

"Help me!" She let out a bitter laugh.

"Yesterday you were glad to have my help," he reminded her.

Lillie turned and gazed at him. Yes, she thought. And today you have me trapped. If I don't tell you, you'll go to the newspapers or the county prosecutor and the whole thing will come out. And if I do tell you . . . "I didn't ask you to come here," she protested weakly.

"My God, are you protecting him too now? What is going on? Does Royce Ansley have something on Pink? I mean, since when is his son allowed to get away with murder? Don't you think he should be punished? Have you forgotten what happened to Michele?"

"No, of course not," she snapped.

"Why do I have to tell you this?" he demanded.

She sighed and shook her head, staring at her hands. "You don't."

"Well, then, what is it? What?" he pleaded. "Please trust me."

She studied his face, which was almost innocent with concern. He was seeing the whole thing in black and white, while her whole world had become gray. She had no choice, really, but to tell him. She had unwittingly drawn him into this. And now he would forge ahead, whether she wanted him to or not. All she could do now was to plead for clemency. She looked into his eyes, now feathered with lines of worry and the passage of time, and remembered how once she had believed in him with all her heart. She had been young and she had thought that if you loved someone, and he loved you, then you could trust him. All these years later and she was still learning the hard way how foolish it was to think like that. She would tell him, she knew. But not because she trusted him. It was because she had no other choice.

He met her gaze patiently, and waited.

Finally she spoke. "You're right," she said. "Tyler killed her."

Despite his certainty, Jordan flinched at the words. He took it in for a second, nodding. Then he looked back at Lillie. "You're shaking," he said. "Let's sit down." She did as he said, settling herself obediently beside him. "How did you find out?" he asked. "What does Pink have to do with all this?"

Lillie took a deep breath. She almost could not bear to say the words. It was like admitting to some terrible flaw, some guilt of her own. "Grayson was there."

"Grayson!" he cried. His face turned white and she could see the self-control at work in him. His hands gripped the edge of the jetty like a pair of vise clamps. "I don't believe it. My God . . . is that why you—"

"No, listen," she interrupted him. "Let me tell it." She hurried to explain it all, everything she knew about the killing, and the conspiracy between fathers and sons, her argument with Pink and her confrontation with Royce.

Jordan listened quietly, the muscles in his face flexing angrily, but he did not interrupt her. When she was done he shook his head as if he was trying to shake his words loose. Finally he said, through gritted teeth, "How could he have left her there? His own sister?"

Lillie blushed scarlet, as if it were her fault that he had, but she leapt to her son's defense. "I told you," she said. "They were drinking. And she took her blouse off. He had this idea that he was protecting her honor . . ."

"What? By leaving her facedown in the mud? Come on, Lillie. Michele wouldn't do that, anyway."

"But she did. He told me!" Lillie cried. "He must have panicked!"

"Bullshit, he's lying," said Jordan. "To make himself look good."

"He would not lie about that," Lillie said furiously.

"He lied about everything else," Jordan cried.

"Don't you dare say that about my son," Lillie exclaimed. "Don't you dare. He made a terrible mistake that will haunt him all his life. He should have saved her. He should never have left her. Don't you think I know that? Don't you think he does?"

"I hope so," Jordan shouted. "I hope it keeps him awake nights."

"And what about Tyler? What about him? He's the one who killed her. Why are you harping on Grayson?" She was shaking with anger.

Jordan struggled to control himself. He knew it was Tyler that he should be raging against. But the thought of Grayson abandoning Michele at the very moment when she needed him the most was like a white-hot poker in his gut. When she could not call on her father, either of her fathers, for help. The thought that he had done that, and then kept it from his mother, let her go on wondering and suffering . . . Don't make it worse for her, he told himself. Don't remind her of all this. He held his fury in and tried to concentrate on Lillie.

"I'm sorry," he said. He could not keep the bitterness out of his voice. "You've been to hell and back again."

"I'm still there," she said.

Jordan studied her, pained by how frail she looked to him. He wondered how much she could take. It was bad enough to lose your child. But now she had to deal with the news that her own son was involved, that her husband and her son had lied to her over and over. And he knew her well enough to know that somehow she would manage to blame herself. His own rage seemed like self-indulgence almost, when he considered the situation she was in. She wanted revenge on her daughter's killer. What mother wouldn't? But bringing Tyler to justice would mean exposing Pink and Grayson to public scorn and probably to imprisonment. It meant destroying what was left of her life. As hard as he tried, he could not put himself in her shoes. In his opinion, hell was too good for the lot of them who had been involved in his daughter's murder and their miserable little cover-up. But he could see by the look in Lillie's eyes that it was tearing her apart. He wanted to reach out and envelop her, protect her, but instead he said quietly, "What are you going to do now?"

Lillie looked at him in surprise. "What do you mean?" she asked. "It's more like what you're going to do, isn't it? I mean, that's the question here. I was just about to ask you for some more time."

"I'm going to honor your wishes," he said.

Lillie looked at him in disbelief. "Why?" she said. "Why would you leave it to me?"

Jordan sighed. "Lillie, I won't lie to you. I'd like to have Tyler hunted down and locked up and throw away the key. And if he got killed in some prison, I doubt I'd lose a minute's sleep. Just because he's the sheriff's son doesn't mean he deserves any special treatment. If that were true, there'd be a whole new class of criminals—law enforcement officers' children. No, maybe I'm cold-hearted, but that's how I feel. He killed my daughter. I want to see him punished. That's all that matters to me."

Lillie listened to him without protesting, her face tight and pale.

"But," he went on, "I also know that if Tyler goes to trial, so do Pink and Grayson. This whole mess will come out, and they could go to jail themselves. They covered up a felony, if nothing else. And I'd be lying to you if I said that I cared about them either. In my eyes, it would serve them both right."

The rational part of her listened and knew he was not being unfair. But her heart could not stand it, and hated him for saying it and making her feel as if she were guilty too.

Jordan took her hand in his and held it very tightly. "Lillie," he said, "if it were up to me, I'd say turn your back on them. They don't deserve you. Come home with me. Not that I deserve you either."

He looked boldly at her, glad he'd said it. Lillie stared back at him, shock and wariness in her eyes.

"But it's not really up to me," he said. "It's your life. It's your family. Only you can decide. I'll abide by your decision."

For one minute there was silence between them and he hoped against hope, and then her eyes filled with tears and she said exactly what he was afraid she would say. "Thank you, Jordan. I can never thank you enough."

He patted her hand awkwardly, then let it go. Lillie kneaded her hand absently, as if the circulation in it had been halted by his grip. "This has been a total nightmare," she said, wiping her eyes quickly. "Believe it or not, part of me wants to do exactly what you said. Make sure that Tyler is caught and punished, and damn the consequences for all of us. Believe me, there is an anger in me that is so deep. Sometimes when I think of all the lies, the secrets, that Pink and Grayson . . . well, I can hardly breathe.

"But then I think, this is my family. This is everything I have in this world—my husband, my son. For as long as I can remember, they are all I've cared for. Them. And Michele. I know this probably sounds selfish to you, but they are my life. I mean, I have a million memories of each of them. It seems like it was only a moment ago that Grayson was toddling to me, and Pink behind him, urging him on. And I think of that and I think of all the ways I really did let them down at times. I mean, I was so preoccupied with Michele's illness. I know I neglected them both, so many times. And then I went into business with Brenda, even though Pink didn't want me to. And I knew it. But I just went ahead. I wasn't there for them the way I should have been. And I keep thinking that if they didn't trust me with the truth, maybe there was a good reason. Maybe they deserved better than they got from me. Maybe I'm the one who should be asking for another chance."

I doubt it, Jordan thought angrily. But he kept his anger to himself. "This kind of secret will be a terrible burden to live with," he said at last.

Lillie nodded. "I know," she said. "And it's unfair for you to have to live with it for our sakes. I know that, Jordan. I wouldn't have asked that of anyone. You don't know how grateful I am."

"Well, I'll be back in New York," he said. "I won't have to look at them every day and be reminded like you will." His words came out sounding exactly as cold as his heart felt.

Lillie did not protest. "I'll never forget this, Jordan."

"That's all right," he said, as casually as he could. "I owed you one."

They sat in awkward silence for a few moments, and

then Jordan said, "I'll tell you something strange that I learned about Tyler while I was at the Sentinel."

"What's that?" Lillie asked.

"Well, our daughter may have been there that night to try to get next to Tyler," he said, and Lillie did not flinch at his use of the words "our daughter," "but Tyler was there because of Grayson."

"What do you mean?" Lillie asked.

Jordan fished around in his jacket pocket and pulled out the photo he had found in Tyler's desk. "It seems that Tyler had a mad crush on Grayson. He had Grayson's picture taped in his footlocker and I found this one in his desk." He handed the picture to her. "His roommate told me he used to moon over this."

Lillie studied the creased photograph in amazement. "My God. I'm sure Grayson had no idea."

Jordan nodded. But he was not so sure. He doubted if Grayson missed very many signals, but he was not going to say so to Lillie. His dislike for the boy was now akin to hatred, and carved in stone, but he could not expect her to see it his way. She was his mother.

Jordan could not stop thinking of Michele. Not for one minute did he believe that Grayson had tried to help her, or put on her shirt. He had run like a coward and left her there. Period. But Lillie believed his story because she needed to. If he tried to make her see Grayson for the self-centered little prick he was, she would hate him for it.

Lillie shivered and noticed for the first time how the light was fading from the sky. "Well," she said. "I guess I had better be getting home."

Jordan loathed the sound of those words, but he only

nodded. He scrambled up and offered her his hand. She took it and rose to her feet.

"What are you going to do?" she asked.

"Stop and see my mother," he said. "Then head back. Maybe I can get a flight out of Nashville tonight. I'm taping tomorrow morning."

Lillie nodded. She was trembling—from the cold, he suspected—and he went to put his arm around her but he stopped himself. There was no use in pretending that she still needed him. The ties between them would be severed after this day. From now on he would only be an uncomfortable reminder of something that she would be trying to put into the past and out of her mind.

"I'll walk you to your car," he said.

"Jordan," she said, and then she pressed her lips together and looked away from him across the lake. "Don't hate me for this."

"Never," he said. "Don't hate yourself. Come on. Let's go."

CHAPTER 25

Lillie's stomach was churning as she pulled into the driveway of her house. She sat in the car, trying to compose herself, and looked out at her home. She had not liked the house that much when they bought it, but at the time she was much more concerned about Michele's illness, and Pink had insisted it was a good deal, so she had agreed to it without deliberation. She did not have time to go house-hunting for a dream cottage. She had just accepted it. But over time she had done her best to fill it with comfort and make it inviting. Everywhere she looked was the evidence of her labor, her life. The shrubs she had planted framed the walk and her grandmother's rocker sat on the front porch. The curtains she had sewn softened the windows. Through the years she had made a home.

Lillie got out of the car, approached the front door, and hesitated. She felt as if once she walked in, there would be no turning back. She would join the betrayal of her little girl in order to protect what was left of their lives together. She had never felt more like turning and running. She could not dismiss or pretend she had misunderstood what Jordan had said to her. After all these years, after all that had happened, he still had feelings for her. The irony of it was almost painful. So many times she had pictured him saying just such words to her, and she had imagined herself scorning him. Then at night, her dreams would betray her and she would dream of the same scene, and instead of mocking him, she would accept him passionately. But it all seemed so unimportant now. When he had finally declared himself to her, all she could think of was her family and how grateful she would be to have another chance. He could not be expected to understand. He had walked out on his own family without a backward glance, and to him it probably seemed simple. She knew, even as she tried to explain it to him, that she could never make him fathom it. But now that she had denied him and made her choice, she felt lonelier than she ever had in her life. Go ahead, she thought. No looking back. She reached for the doorknob, took a deep breath, eased the door open, and went inside.

Pink was sitting in his chair, holding a glass. He was staring at the TV, although the set was not turned on. Lillie could tell that he'd had a few, but he was not yet drunk. When the door opened, his head snapped around and he stared at her. The whites of his eyes were bloodshot, whether from whiskey or tears she could not tell. His florid complexion was unusually bright and she wondered briefly about his blood pressure, worried, by long habit, about him.

"Lillie," he said hoarsely, "are you back?"

Lillie closed the door behind her. "Hello, Pink." She hung up her jacket in the closet and walked across the room. Pink followed her with wary eyes. "Is Grayson here?" she asked.

"No."

"Where is he?"

Pink picked up his glass again. "I don't know. I went down to the office this morning after I saw you. I just needed to keep busy. Keep my mind occupied. He wasn't here when I got back. I haven't seen him all afternoon."

"I wanted to talk to both of you," she said.

"Well, you'll have to settle for me," Pink said. "That shouldn't be too hard for you. You've done it before." He saluted her with the whiskey glass.

Lillie ignored the barbed remark. She sat down in the chair opposite him. "I talked to Royce," she said.

"I heard," said Pink.

"And I saw Jordan. He's back from the Sentinel."

Pink turned suddenly pale. "Great," he said. "And I suppose you told him all about it."

"He already knew, Pink. He knew you were the one who warned Tyler. He'd figured most of it out."

Pink slammed his glass down on the coffee table and rubbed his hands over his face.

"So, that's it," he said. "We're all screwed. You and your lover are going to crucify us." Pink jumped up out of his chair and his glass tipped over as he jarred the table. "I might have known. This was just the excuse you needed."

"Pink," Lillie cried. "Shut up. Listen to me. Nobody is going to crucify anybody."

"Come on," Pink said, leaning toward her so that she could smell the bourbon on his breath. "Do you think I'm stupid? Do you think I was born yesterday? What are you up to with him? This is ideal for the two of you. You're probably enjoying this. You two can tell the world what a bum I am. For trying to protect my boy. Oh, I can just imagine how righteous you'll be. Lillie's revenge. For putting up with me all these years. When everybody knows you only married me for my money and to put a roof over your brat's head!"

Lillie recoiled from him, from the venom in him. She was trembling all over. She forced herself to speak calmly. But her tone was hard and bitter. "I'm sorry you feel that way, Pink. We've both had our share of disappointments."

Pink grimaced, shame and regret mingled in his eyes. He sat down heavily in the chair and covered his face with one hand. "I didn't mean that about Michele," he said miserably. "She was the sweetest child in the whole world. My little girl. She thought her daddy was the greatest. All I ever wanted was for you to think that way too."

Lillie heard the need, the plaintive question in his voice, but she ignored it. "Pink," she said, "you can calm down. I did not come here to persecute you. I have been trying to tell you that I think that I understand what you did. For whatever reasons, you felt that you couldn't trust me with the truth—"

"It wasn't that," Pink bleated. "I wanted to spare you, Lillie. And I had to think of Grayson. Of his future."

"Well, believe it or not, I love my son too. I don't want to hurt him. Or you."

Pink emitted a sound that was somewhere between a laugh and a sob. "But . . ." he said, as if prompting her next remark.

"But nothing," she said quietly. "No buts. I've come back home to stay and we'll keep this only to ourselves. Jordan has given me his word that he will not interfere. Or tell anyone."

Pink looked at her in amazement and then his eyes narrowed. "I don't buy that, Lillie. Why should he keep quiet? He'd love to get me."

Lillie looked at him steadily. "Because I asked him to, and because he felt that he owed that to me. For past grievances, you might say."

Pink looked at her skeptically, but she could see that he was starting to believe it.

"He's on his way back to New York," she said, and she was embarrassed by the note of regret in her own voice. "He's probably already gone," she added as briskly as she could.

"How do we know we can trust him?" Pink asked.

Lillie looked at him, her eyebrows raised as if in mild amazement at his question. "How do we know we can trust anybody really? We'll just have to."

Pink shook his head. "Oh, God, Lillie. I don't know what to think."

"What else can we do?" said Lillie. "We'll go on."

Pink looked up at her and for the first time there was a wisp of hope in his expression. "You're not going to change your mind about this?"

"I already told you," she said.

"I know," Pink said hurriedly. "I know you did. I kind of wish I had told you everything in the first place. Then

Jordan wouldn't have gotten involved in this thing." He tried his best not to put a sarcastic spin on Jordan's name.

"Well," Lillie said with a sigh. "I think we should make an effort to tell each other the truth from now on. I've had enough lies to last me a lifetime."

"We will," Pink said eagerly. "From now on." He came over and crouched awkwardly beside her chair, resting a puffy hand on her knee. "And I'm sorry I did that to you," he said, eyeing her bruised face. "I'll never do that again. I swear it. Life is going to be better for us. For all of us, from now on."

Lillie studied his earnest face sadly for a moment and then looked up as she heard the front door opening. Grayson walked in, his cheeks pink, his eyes almost feverishly bright. At the sight of his parents, he drew back tensely, like a cat in a corner. Pink clambered to his feet and beamed at him. "Grayson," he called out. "Look who's home!"

"Mom," said Grayson, at once surprised and a little wary.

"Your mother finally sees that we did the right thing, son. About, you know, Tyler and so forth. So, she's come back to us. The whole thing is settled."

"Well, great," said Grayson.

Lillie felt herself recoil from the way Pink had expressed it, but she did not correct him. Pink was cheerful and full of hope.

"What about Jordan Hill?" Grayson asked.

"He's out of our lives," Pink exulted. Then he added, more soberly, "He's agreed that it's none of his business and he is going to keep quiet about it. In fact, he's gone back to New York."

"Better late than never," Grayson said brightly, the tension in his shoulders relaxing at Pink's announcement. "Good going, Mom."

Lillie tried to smile, but inside she was offended by their pleasure and approval. "I don't think this is really something to be happy about," she said stiffly. "Jordan didn't want to let the matter drop. He just felt that our family had suffered enough."

"Well, that was right decent of him, considering all the suffering he caused in this family in the first place." Pink snorted.

"Pink, if you start again, I swear . . ." said Lillie.

"Oh, come on, you two," Grayson said cheerfully. "Let's just be glad he's gone."

"Amen to that," said Pink. "The important thing is that Mom is home and everything is going to be all right again."

"Yeah," said Gray. "We can just forget this whole thing ever happened."

Lillie was about to protest when the phone rang and everybody started. Then Grayson, who was closest to the telephone table, walked over and picked it up. He spoke for a second and then held the receiver out to Pink. "It's for you. It's Miz Nunley."

"What does she want, for chrissakes?" said Pink. He walked over and took the phone from Grayson and started to speak to Reba.

Grayson and Lillie exchanged a glance, serene on Grayson's side and grim on Lillie's. Then the boy looked away.

"Oh, all right," Pink said angrily. "But they better be serious. Calling me out this late on a Sunday . . . I was there half the day. They should have come by then. All right. All right."

Pink slammed down the phone and went to the hall closet. He pulled out his sports jacket and shrugged it on over the velour shirt he was wearing.

"What is it?" Lillie asked.

"Oh, there's this couple I showed a piece of property to a while back. They just showed up at the office wanting to look at it again. It's practically dark. I don't know how they expect to see anything. I wouldn't even bother to go, but usually when they want to look a second time it means they're serious. And we're gonna need the money to send this kid to Harvard, right? I'll be back soon."

"Take your time," said Lillie.

"Well, I hate to break up our reunion like this," said Pink.

"I'll be here when you get back," Lillie replied.

"Attagirl," Pink said. "Grayson, you help your mother get supper. I'll be back in a jiffy."

The door slammed behind him, and Lillie could hear Pink whistling as he trundled off to his car. She turned to Grayson. "I have something to say to you," she announced brusquely.

Grayson looked at her with a boyish, bewildered look on his face. She could not deny to herself that she felt a desire to punish him. He can't go around weeping forever, she thought. But she wondered how long it would be before she could look at him and not feel a lingering resentment toward him. "Look, Grayson," she began calmly, "a lot has happened. I haven't absorbed it all yet."

Grayson studied the cuff of his shirt and tucked it back

neatly into the rolled-up sleeve. "I know," he said seriously.

"Just because I have decided to keep this within our family does not mean that this is all going to be forgotten and swept under the rug. Do you understand me?"

Grayson frowned and looked at her quizzically. "I thought you said everything was settled."

"Well, yes. I suppose you could say . . . officially, it is settled. I mean, as far as the law is concerned with it. But that doesn't change the fact that your sister was murdered. This is not something you just accept in a day. This family will never be the same after this."

Grayson lifted his chin and brushed his blond hair back off his forehead. "I know that," he said.

"Grayson, come here and sit down. I want to talk to you."

Lillie sat down on the couch and Grayson, after a moment's hesitation, sat down on the edge of the couch cushion. Lillie patted his knee and then clasped her hands together.

"Do you know that Tyler ran away from the Sentinel?" she asked.

Grayson combed through his hair with his fingers. "Yeah," he said. "The sheriff called this morning."

"Does that bother you?" she asked.

Grayson looked at her blankly. "No. Why should it?"

Lillie tried to choose her words carefully. "Son, I know these last few months have been hard on you. Maybe harder on you than on anybody in a way. You had to keep a lot of things inside. I think you've probably got a lot of grief bottled up in there. Probably a lot of guilt over what happened. That would only be natural. And it does no good to pretend you don't care. You can't just ignore something like this. None of us can. It can just eat away at you after a while."

Grayson shifted his weight and stared thoughtfully ahead of him. Lillie studied his face and wondered what was going on behind his eyes. It amazed her sometimes how little she knew him.

"Well, it seems like a long time ago that it happened," he said at last. "I try not to think about it too much."

"That's what I'm saying, Gray. I think it's better if we *do* think about it. And talk about it. Here, at home, I mean."

Grayson looked at her a little suspiciously. "Well, we all know what happened. It doesn't change anything to keep going over it. I thought we were going to start fresh around here."

"We are," Lillie said wearily. "That's right."

"Mom, I don't mind talking about it if you want to," he said in a conciliatory tone. "But I have some homework right now. Is it okay . . . ?"

Lillie nodded and looked away from him. "Go ahead," she said.

As he left the room she sank back against the sofa cushions. She was overcome again with that feeling of being alone. Stop it, she chided herself. Stop feeling sorry for yourself. You have your second chance. Now make the best of it. Things are not going to change overnight. You'll have to be patient and draw Grayson out. Earn his trust. Get him to tell you about it in time. He went through a great trauma, and he's not used to confiding in you.

But at the moment, she did not feel strong or purposeful. She felt as if she'd been flayed, and everything stung. Guiltily, she thought again of Jordan, his grave eyes studying her, his dry hand hot on her own. Forget the past, she thought. Only the future matters. But a few tears escaped from her tired eyes as she sat there. For a minute she let them run down her face and then, when one drop made its way down her neck and beneath her collar, she reached down into her purse on the floor beside her and rummaged for a Kleenex.

As she sought the tissue her fingers fell on something cold, metallic, and unfamiliar in the depths of the leather satchel. Lillie reached in and pulled out a small pistol.

She stared at it for a second, completely baffled at how it might have gotten into her purse. Then, all at once, she remembered. Brenda had been telling her how she needed a gun. That was yesterday. It seemed like a year ago.

Lillie wiped off her tears with her fingers and smiled grimly. There was no need for this. Pink was contrite. It was a once-in-a-lifetime thing. Still, for an instant she felt warmed, and a little less lonely, thinking about Brenda pigheadedly going ahead and stuffing that pistol in her purse, determined to protect her from afar. Maybe finding the gun was a little sign, through her sorrow, that she was cared for, that she was important to the ones who loved her.

With a sigh, Lillie stood up and carried the gun over to the mantelpiece, where she laid it down among the framed photographs. It was almost as if she wanted to keep it out of the reach of children, even though there were no little ones around to be endangered by it. I'll return it to her tomorrow, Lillie thought. I'm sure she'll give me a right good scolding for bringing it back. Lillie smiled. What else were friends for?

CHAPTER 26

"You don't have to do that, son," Bessie Hill protested as Jordan picked up a dishtowel and began to dry the dishes from their supper. "You just relax. You've had a long day."

"We'll do these up quick and we can both relax," he said. He had told his mother very little about his unexpected visit here. He had said only that Lillie had asked him to come and look into something for her but that it had not amounted to anything. Bessie could tell that he was keeping things to himself, but she did not ask him too many questions, for which he was grateful.

Bessie put a hand, damp from the dishwater, on his forearm and squeezed it. "I wish you didn't have to go back tonight," she said. "Couldn't you wait and go in the morning?"

Jordan smiled at her. "I wish I could," he said, "but I've got an early call."

Bessie resumed her dishes quietly for a moment while Jordan moved around the kitchen, putting up the plates and bowls he had dried. "Don't look so glum," he said to her. "I'll be back before long."

"Well, your idea of long and mine are two different things," she said a little reproachfully.

He knew what she said was true. He had not always been the most reliable of visitors. It was not until the last few years, when he began to realize how much he looked forward to his own child's visits, that he had revised his ways and become a bit more attentive as a son. "I know, Mama," he said. "But my intentions are always good."

"Well, you're mighty busy with the show," she said. "I know that."

"Don't be so understanding," Jordan teased her.

"I know you mean well," Bessie said, lifting up a plate to rinse it.

Jordan wiped up a spot on the counter with the dishtowel and gave his mother a sidelong glance. "You always gave me the benefit of the doubt."

"Well, I tried to," she said.

"It mustn't have been easy sometimes," he murmured.

Bessie nodded. "There were times . . ."

"Like when I left Lillie and the baby," said Jordan.

Bessie stopped her rinsing and cocked her head to one side, remembering. "I guess that was the time I was the most upset with you. Yes. I don't mind saying that it hurt me quite a lot. I was deeply disappointed in you."

"Yeah," he said, "but when I got to New York you sent

me little checks, and socks and care packages. And you called me."

"Well, of course I did," said Bessie. "I love you. I was worried about you. What happened with Lillie didn't change that. Besides, I felt like you must have had a good reason for what you did. I figured they were better off with you leaving than with you staying and resenting them both every minute of your life. People do sometimes have to fulfill their destiny or whatever."

"What if I just did it to be rotten?" he said.

"But you wouldn't do that," she said simply. "I know you."

Bessie took the towel from him and wiped her hands. "I just always thought it was sad because she was really the right girl for you. Very few people get a second chance to have a love like that."

He met her eyes and acknowledged the truth of what she said. "That's for sure."

"Well, it's chilly tonight," she said. "I'm going to get me a sweater."

"You want me to fetch it?" he asked.

"You don't know which one I want," she said, gently moving him aside and heading for her bedroom.

Jordan smiled at her and then walked over toward the porch. The night had fallen, quiet and starry, and he marveled at the peaceful self-absorption of his old hometown. He remembered how stifling it had once seemed here. He had imagined the world to be such a beautiful place away from here. And it had been beautiful, he thought. But not better.

Bessie came back into the living room, sat down at her end of the couch, and picked up her half-glasses from the end table. She opened the newspaper and began to look it over.

Jordan turned away from the door. "There's somebody I have to see before I leave."

Bessie looked at him questioningly, but he just bent over and kissed her cheek. "I won't be long," he said. "I want to leave here for Nashville by eight o'clock."

Jordan was surprised at how easy it was for him to find Royce Ansley's house. It was eighteen years since he had been there last, and then it was only a couple of visits. But those visits had made a deep impression on him. It was here, in this house, that he had first gotten the idea that he was special, talented, and that he might find fame and fortune in the world. He had walked out of the door of this house with stars in his eyes. Now he pounded on the dry wood of the door and a splinter gouged his fist.

No one answered, and the house was dark inside. Royce's car was not even in the driveway. Jordan stood on the step for a minute but there was no sign of life. He got back into his rental car and drove to the center of town, parking in the square. It didn't seem likely that Royce would be at work on a Sunday night, but then again, criminals didn't confine their activities to weekday, nine-to-five hours, he reasoned. Jordan ran up the courthouse steps and tried the massive double doors, but they were locked. There were a couple of side doors to the building and Jordan went around to each of them, figuring Royce would have his own set of keys, but the whole building appeared to be closed up tight.

He decided that his best bet was to head over to the county jail. That was never closed for business, and they would surely know where to locate the sheriff. Jordan crossed the quiet square toward the jailhouse building. Bomar Flood was just locking up the dark pharmacy while a woman customer thanked the old druggist profusely for opening up on a Sunday night.

"A person's got to have their insulin," said Bomar, dismissing her gratitude.

"Hello, Bomar," Jordan said.

The old pharmacist looked around and could barely conceal his surprise. "Well, hello there, Jordan. What brings you back to town?"

"I'm looking for Royce Ansley," Jordan said. "He's not home and he's not in his office. I thought I'd head over to the jail and check there."

Bomar tried not to appear too curious, although he seemed to be mulling over more than Royce's whereabouts. "Let's see," he said. "Well, it's Sunday night. He's probably over at the Winchester Hotel. He has supper over there every Sunday night. He has done for years."

"Thanks," said Jordan.

"You know where that is?"

"Sure do. Much obliged."

Bomar watched him intently as he got back in his car and pulled out. Jordan figured this would give Bomar and his wife, Charlotte, fodder for a whole evening's conversation. Jordan drove through town, across the railroad tracks, and up the hill to the Winchester Hotel. It was a grand old Southern hotel, once the pride of the county, that had endured some lean years. A three-story brick building with a white balcony and a columned porch, the old hotel had limped along through Jordan's boyhood, but then a young couple from Atlanta had bought it several years back and had slowly restored it to its former genteel charm. Jordan had never eaten there under the new ownership, but his mother always asserted that it had the finest green beans and squash pie in the county.

A number of cars were parked in the small dirt lot across the street from the hotel, including the sheriff's car. Jordan parked his own car and went in through the lobby. The parlor was hung with heavy draperies and lace and filled with stiff, ornately decorated Victorian furniture as it must have been in its glory days. The main desk was carved mahogany and behind it were the pigeonholes for the guests' mail and messages. From the number of empty mailboxes hung with keys, it appeared that the hotel had precious few overnight guests, but the dining room was doing a lively local business.

Jordan walked up to the hostess and was about to ask for the sheriff when his gaze fell upon a solitary figure at a corner table. The fringed lamp on the tabletop weakly illuminated the face of Royce Ansley.

"I'm joining the sheriff," Jordan explained as he entered the dining room and crossed over to where Royce was seated. A waitress approached with a wicker basket of fresh hush puppies just as Jordan arrived at the table. Royce thanked the waitress and looked up at Jordan impatiently.

"May I join you, Sheriff?" Jordan asked.

Royce looked at him steadily. "It appears that you're going to."

Jordan pulled out the chair opposite Royce and sat down. The base of the table was an old sewing machine. Jordan rested his feet on the wrought-iron treadle. "I've got a few things to say to you," he said.

Royce ate a hush puppy and wiped his greasy fingers deliberately on a napkin. "Well, get on with it."

"Look, let's be frank," said Jordan. "You know that I went up to Tyler's school. Well, I found out that Pink warned him. And Lillie has filled in the rest. About my daughter's death, and the cover-up you and Pink concocted."

Royce's face was very white in the lamplight, but he did not respond.

"And much as I'd enjoy seeing you suffer," Jordan said, "I may as well tell you that I have agreed to keep quiet about this and let you handle it among yourselves."

"Well," Royce said calmly, "I think it is a good idea for you not to involve yourself."

"I *am* involved," Jordan said coldly. "It's my daughter we're talking about. I've just agreed to it because it's what Lillie wants."

"I'm afraid I don't think of you as Michele's father," said Royce. "Despite this recent show of zeal on your part."

Jordan smacked his hand down on the table and the hush puppies jumped in their basket. "Well, I *am* her father whether you like it or not. And you are a liar. Now don't tempt me to change my mind." The other diners turned to stare at the sheriff and his companion.

"Don't bother showing your temper to me," Royce said in a low voice when the hum of conversation had resumed in the dining room. "I'll tell you right now, with all that's gone on, I'm not about to be intimidated by the likes of you."

The two men stared defiantly at one another. Then Royce picked up his iced tea, took a long sip, and put it down again. "Thanks to your meddling," he said slowly, "my son has left school and run off to God knows where."

Jordan did not flinch. "Oh, I suppose I should have just stayed out of it and let the sheriff do his duty as he saw fit."

"Yes," said Royce, "you should have stayed out of it. I know why you're here. You think I don't? You searched me out so you could look down your nose at me. Make yourself out to be some sort of hero in this whole thing. Well, I'll tell you something, mister. My opinion of you hasn't changed one whit. You come storming into town here, the avengin' father, and stick your snout into everyone's business where it doesn't belong and now you're going to make the grand gesture and ride out again. Well, you don't impress me one bit. Leaving is your specialty. Being a father—you don't know a thing about it. And don't bother threatening me with telling. You won't tell. You couldn't stick around long enough to see it through."

"Wait a minute, wait a minute," Jordan said loudly, and then lowered his voice as the other diners turned to stare again. "Since when is my character the issue here? You're the one who abused your office. You're the one whose son is a murderer," he whispered through gritted teeth.

Royce's eyes were stony. He avoided Jordan's gaze and began to look for the waitress. After a moment Royce looked back at Jordan. "I don't owe you any explanation," he said. "You can sit there till you rot. You'll get nothing from me. I will tell you this. My son is out there somewhere, on the run, nowhere to turn, and it's because of you and your interference. God knows where he went. He may be out of the country by now. And if I am unable to find him, I hold you responsible for that."

Jordan sat back in his chair. "You're unbelievable," he said. "I mean, I know that the best defense is a good offense, but aren't you carrying this a little far? Now you blame me for Tyler's disappearance?"

"You're goddamned right I do," Royce said grimly.

The two men sat in awkward silence as a waitress appeared and placed a platter of fried catfish and vegetables in front of Royce.

"Do you want anything?" she asked Jordan.

"He's not staying," said the sheriff.

Just then an agitated Wallace Reynolds appeared at the door of the dining room and hurried over to the table where Royce and Jordan were seated.

"What is it, Wallace?" Royce asked irritably.

"Sheriff," said the deputy, "I just got a call over to the jailhouse. Some woman seen a body out at the Millraney farm. In the well. We got to get a rescue team up there. Somebody's got to go down there and try and bring him up."

"Is he alive?" asked the sheriff.

"Don't know. It's too dark to see down there. He's not answering though."

The sheriff sighed and lifted his napkin off his lap. "All right. Call up Estes Conroy. His jeep's got a winch on it. Better call the ambulance."

"I did," said Wallace.

Royce looked down at the plate of food. "It's just as well. I've lost my appetite." He looked unsmilingly at Jordan. "Don't you have to be leaving town?" he asked.

"Tonight," said Jordan. "It can't be soon enough to suit me."

CHAPTER 27

Pink went back again to the rim of the well and looked down into it, as if drawn by a magnet to the ghastly sight. It was dark now, and the flashlight he had found in his car's glove compartment was too weak to illuminate much, but when he angled it just right he could see the twisted legs and a torso wedged down there in an awkward position. There were dark stains on the clothes, which Pink figured must be blood. It looked like the guy was only wearing one shoe. The other one must have ended up on the bottom of the well when the poor soul went down. Pink couldn't see a face, or even the head. For one awful moment he hoped the body still had a head attached. Then he chided himself for the gruesome thought.

The young couple who had wanted to look at the farm,

the DuPres, sat huddled on the back steps of the old farmhouse. Pink had urged them to go inside and make themselves comfortable while they waited for the police to come. After all, the house was fully furnished. But the woman absolutely refused. She said she never wanted to go into that house again.

So much for that sale, Pink thought as he lingered by the well and strained to hear if anyone was coming down the road. It was lucky the phone still worked up here, so that he was able to call for help. The guy in the well might possibly still be alive, but Pink doubted it seriously. Pink and the DuPre fellow had called down repeatedly, their anxious voices echoing off the stones, but there had been no response.

Pink could hear the woman complaining to her husband, "I just want to get *out* of here," and the young man was placating her, promising her they would leave as soon as they talked to the police.

"I'm cold," she grumbled.

Well, go inside, for chrissakes, Pink thought. Nobody told you to sit on those steps. That's what you get. Actually, he felt unreasonably angry with her anyway. He hadn't wanted to go out there this evening in the first place. He was exhausted and he just wanted to relax at home, especially now that Lillie was back. But he had gone anyway, and they had seemed to be making some real progress. The man was definitely interested, and she had warmed up a lot toward the old place since their first visit. She kept mentioning things that she liked and acting as if all the repairs were minor, although Pink knew better. But he could tell that the husband had her three-quarters convinced that this was the place for them, and

Pink was getting that old optimistic feeling that he was going to be able to close the deal. And then she had asked about the well.

"Is it dry, or does it still have water in it?" she had asked, as if she was familiar with the uses of a well. The fact was that Pink didn't really know. No one had ever gotten that far along in an inspection of the Millraney farm. They usually just came and went after a cursory look. One woman, in fact, had refused to get out of the car, much to her husband's embarrassment.

It was the women, Pink reflected, who always caused trouble in these things. The men noticed the good things about a place and always acted vaguely apologetic for wasting Pink's time, as if showing houses was somehow inconvenient for him. But the women picked at everything. They were always the negative ones, criticizing the taste of the previous owners and always acting suspicious, as if you were trying to cheat them of something.

It was just the way Lillie had been when they bought their house. She'd had that dissatisfied look on her face that gave him a sick feeling in the pit of his stomach. He had explained to her over and over why it was the best deal for them, but he could tell she wasn't exactly delighted with it. As long as he could remember, it had always been that way with Lillie. No matter how hard he tried to please her, she always had that skittish look in her eye. And it always gave him that knot in his stomach.

Pink glanced down the road again. What was keeping them? He could hardly believe the way this day had turned out. Well, the important thing was that Lillie had seen the light and come back. And Grayson's future was secure. Pink had actually felt pretty good by the time he arrived at Millraney's with the DuPres. Pretty fortunate. He never saw this thing, coming out of left field, as it were. The woman had gone over to the well and, using his flashlight, looked down it, and before she had time to straighten up, hitting her head against the bucket, and start screaming, the deal for the property had been queered.

The bucket had begun to bounce crazily from side to side, and Pink had to steady it with his hands before he and the fellow could look down the well and see what it was that had set her off. Then he couldn't blame her for screaming. He felt like letting out a yell himself when he saw it.

The sound of a siren and the rumble of cars on the dirt road made Pink look up. He rushed out to the edge of the property with his flashlight and began to gesture importantly toward the driveway.

The ambulance was the first to arrive, its pulsating red light a blur against the evening sky. Pink indicated a spot next to the Oldsmobile as the DuPres jumped up from their seat on the steps and ran out anxiously to greet the medical team. Two attendants in white jackets spilled out of the van, and there was a general commotion as Pink and the DuPre couple tried to explain to them about the well and other cars began to appear down the road. The attendants began to prepare the equipment in the van for any contingency. Pink ran down the driveway and called out to Estes Conroy, who was coming slowly up the road in his Bronco.

Pink led the slow-moving Jeep across the lawn, and the driver parked it about ten feet from the well. Two police cars pulled into the driveway. The sheriff, still in his Sunday clothes, was in one, and Wallace Reynolds and another deputy, Floyd Peterson, were in the other.

Royce got out of his car and walked up to Pink. The DuPres hurried over to the sheriff as if he were a warm fire on a cold night. Pink and the sheriff nodded perfunctorily. "What happened?" Royce asked.

"My husband and I were looking at the property," the distraught woman blurted out, "and I was just checking the well and I saw him."

The driver of the ambulance, a red-headed fellow in a blue uniform, joined them. "Do we know if he is still alive?" he asked. One of the attendants, whose white smock seemed to glow in the darkness, leaned in to hear the answer.

"I doubt it," said Pink.

"We called to him repeatedly but no answer," said the DuPre fellow.

"How will you get him out?" Mrs. DuPre asked in a shrill voice.

Royce walked up to the well and examined it calmly. He could see the twisted legs dimly inside, but nothing else. He turned around and called out to Estes Conroy, who was winding a rope around the winch on the front of his Bronco. "How are you coming, Estes? Hurry up with that winch."

"Almost ready, Sheriff."

Royce turned to Wallace and the young deputy. "Floyd," he said, "will you do the honors?"

The young deputy nodded grimly. "Yessir."

Estes, a burly man with a cigarette hanging out of his mouth and a Cat cap on his head, approached them with the rope in his hands. "Who's wearing the loop?" he asked.

Floyd Peterson stepped forward and Wallace helped Estes to secure the loop around the young man's chest. The ambulance driver checked the knot and then made a loop at the end of another length of rope for Floyd to take down the well.

"If he is alive," said the male attendant, "try to find out where his injuries are. We'll have to be very careful bringing him up."

Floyd nodded quickly, eager to begin his mission of mercy.

"It'll be slippery in there," Royce advised him. "Keep a good foothold on the sides. Wallace, you hold the other rope."

Wallace nodded and took his position at the side of the well as Floyd, his athletic silhouette lit by the headlights of the gathered cars, climbed up and lowered himself into the well. Estes returned to the Bronco to prepare to operate the winch.

A silence fell over everyone as the young deputy began his descent and then, all at once, the onlookers erupted into nervous chatter.

Pink, who was still standing beside Royce, rocked back and forth on his heels. "Not much of a way to spend Sunday night," he said uneasily.

Royce walked away from Pink and the others and folded his arms across his chest. Pink followed after him. They were out of earshot of the crowd.

"Lillie came home," Pink said eagerly. "She decided we were right."

"I heard. I just had a visit from her ex-husband."

"That bum!" Pink exclaimed, and the sheriff glared at him so that he lowered his voice. "What did he want?"

"Oh, he tracked me down at the Winchester." Royce sighed. "He just wanted to threaten me a little bit."

"That son of a bitch," cried Pink. "He told Lillie he'd stay out of it. I hate that son of a bitch."

"You all right?" Wallace yelled anxiously down the well.

"What happened?" Royce called out, stepping forward.

"He slipped against the side," Wallace said. "He's okay."

Mrs. DuPre clung to her husband, who whispered reassuringly to her. They did not want to see what was going to come out of the well and, like everybody else, they could not turn their eyes away.

Pink sidled up close to Royce, wanting to discuss this news about Jordan, but the sheriff seemed to be absorbed in the rescue effort. Pink tapped him on the arm persistently, and Royce turned and stared at him, his face drawn and gray in the weak illumination of the gathered headlights.

"I thought he left town," Pink complained. "How come he is still hanging around?"

"Because he's enjoying himself," Royce said wearily. "Anyway, he says he's leaving tonight. He claims he'll keep quiet."

"He better keep quiet," Pink fumed. "I swear, if he comes back here and starts to bother my family . . ."

People were leaning over the edge of the well, shouting encouragement to Floyd, who had reached the body and was attempting to maneuver it.

"Is he alive?" the ambulance driver called down.

Floyd's voice drifted up, faint and hollow. "Blood everywhere. Dead." A sorrowful hush fell over the spectators and then, one by one, they began solicitously to urge the deputy on, directing him as he tried to shift the dead man's weight to secure him.

Royce gazed unseeing at the commotion by the well. "I don't think he'll bother anymore. He was only in it for the excitement. You know, he probably thought he could get some publicity out of it."

"Well, he sure managed to get Lillie all worked up about it. I think I've finally got her calmed down, and I just want to put this whole mess behind us," said Pink.

A weird, strangulated cry went up from the deputy inside the well, but it was drowned out by the advice of bystanders.

"Haul him up, Estes," Wallace Reynolds called out as Floyd signaled from below.

"Tell the sheriff," they heard a weak voice call out.

"Tell the sheriff what?" the ambulance driver called down as the sound of the motor and the whine of the winch muffled any response.

"It was all Jordan Hill's doing," Pink insisted.

"It was all our doing," Royce said in a dull voice.

The rope on the winch creaked, and the motor hummed and people shouted directions as Floyd Peterson, his face white and sweaty, appeared above the edge of the well. His eyes scanned the waiting crowd and clamped onto Royce.

"Okay," cried Wallace Reynolds, "help him down. Attach that other rope."

Floyd clambered over the edge of the well and collapsed against the side, hiding his face in his hands. The other men hurried to unwind his rope and attach the second rope to the winch. In a few seconds it was done, and Estes started the motor to begin to raise the body. Royce freed himself from Pink's urgent grasp and walked over to where the deputy was huddled, gasping for breath, against the side of the well.

"Sheriff, I'm sorry." Floyd sobbed.

"That's tough duty," said Royce, leaning down and putting a comforting hand on the deputy's shoulder.

"That's right," cried Wallace. "Here he comes. A little more."

Slowly the bloodied, lifeless body rose out of the depths of the dark stone pit. The DuPre woman screamed at the sight of it and pressed her face to her husband's chest. The groans of dismay in the group were followed by a shocked silence, as one by one they recognized the corpse.

"Oh, my God," breathed Wallace Reynolds. Then the sheriff turned to look where they were looking, at the broken body, the lolling head, the bloodied face.

Pink, who had hung back, did not understand for a moment. He could see that blood had run in dark rivers across the dead man's face. The guy was gone, all right, he thought. They could send that ambulance home. He noticed that the crowd was hushed, as if stricken. The sight of the corpse seemed to have shut everybody up. Well, it was a grisly sight, all right, Pink thought. But he could not understand why they were all staring at the sheriff. As if they were a little fearful of what he was going to do. That seemed strange to Pink. The sheriff had seen plenty of dead men before. More than any of them, Pink figured.

No, he did not understand until he saw them release the

repulsive, twisted body from the rope and lower it gently to the ground. And then suddenly, sickeningly, he knew, as he saw Royce fall to the ground beside the body and tenderly gather it up into his arms.

CHAPTER 28

Lillie went through the house, turning on all the lights, as if light would somehow banish the chill she felt in the quiet rooms. You're home, she told herself. Everything is the same. But nothing felt the same. The last time she had been in these rooms she had been innocent, she had been in the dark. Pink and Grayson had shared their secret knowledge of Michele's death and had let her stumble blindly in her grief.

Stop it, she thought. You must not think that way. You must do the normal things. Start getting supper. A reunion supper. The start of a new era.

She knew that thought should make her feel better, but it did not. Everyone around her seemed to feel that the time for grieving was over and that better days had arrived. But inside Lillie felt the loss of Michele more keenly than ever. I wonder if it will ever go away, she thought. I wonder if I will ever have a normal day again.

She moved around the silent kitchen, pulling out plates and pots and bowls, automatically going about the familiar process of fixing a meal. She took out some chicken, already cooked, from the refrigerator, made a salad, put some water on for rice. All the while she felt the weight on her heart that would not lift. She thought of putting on the radio, but the idea of music made her nerves feel jumpy. She preferred the silence.

After she had finished making her salad, she went to the hall and called out for Grayson. In a few minutes he appeared in the doorway.

"What?" he asked.

"How about setting the table?" she asked.

"Sure," he said pleasantly. Then he looked around. "Where are the placemats?"

"Boy, you really don't know your way around here," Lillie said, meaning to tease him. "Michele always claimed that you helped her."

The smile seemed to flatten out of Grayson's face, and the remark hung in the air between them. It was as if he did not want any reminder of his sister.

"Left-hand drawer," said Lillie. Grayson went to the drawer.

Ordinarily Lillie would have let the subject drop, but she was resolved that she was going to be more honest and end the uneasy silences in the house. She had to start somewhere. "Grayson," she said. "It bothers me. I mean . . . it seems like you . . . and your dad . . . don't even want me to mention Michele around here. Is that true? Does it make you uncomfortable to even hear her name?"

Grayson set the placemats on the table and smoothed them down. Then he thought a moment. "No," he said at last. "I don't mind you mentioning her. Now that you know what happened. I guess that was just a habit from before. Not wanting to talk about it."

Lillie sighed with relief. She felt as if they had just made a little progress. "That's good," she said. "I don't want to feel that everybody flinches when her name is mentioned. I mean, we're always going to be reminded of her, in a million ways around this house." Her voice caught on the last word, but she cleared her throat.

Grayson examined the tabletop. "Do we need spoons?" he asked, looking up at her with an implacable gaze.

"Do you understand me, Grayson?" she asked.

"Yes," he said a little indignantly. "You want to talk about Michele sometimes. That's fine with me."

"Or you or your father might want to talk about her," Lillie said emphatically.

"Right," said Grayson. "What about the spoons?"

Lillie's heart sank. I shouldn't be surprised, she thought. He's just like his father. Avoid the subject. Keep your feelings inside. He was just following his father's example. Grayson, don't be that way, she wanted to cry out. Share the pain with me. But she knew that wouldn't work. It would only scare him farther away. "Yes, we need spoons," she said. "We have banana pudding."

"Oh, good," he said. "I like that."

Lillie poured herself a glass of wine as Grayson finished up with the table. She watched him out of the corner of her eye. Maybe, she thought, I'm asking for too much, wanting him to dwell on such a terrible time. He had spent the last several months absorbing it and trying to get it as far behind him as possible, and now this whole business with Tyler had brought it all rushing back. Watching the graceful movements of her handsome son, she could not shake the image that Jordan had planted in her mind of Tyler, mooning over Grayson, carrying that picture with him, even after all that had happened. She wondered how Tyler could still think he loved Grayson after he had murdered his sister. She knew that what she wanted to say was like picking at a scab, but she could not prevent herself.

"I heard something strange about Tyler today," she said.

Grayson stopped short but did not look at her. "I know," he said. "He ran away. You already said so."

"Not that," Lillie said, taking a sip of wine and putting the glass down on the countertop. "Did you ever hear from anybody that Tyler might be . . . interested in boys rather than girls?"

Grayson looked at her calmly. "Sure. He was queer as a three-dollar bill. Everybody suspected it. I've heard that he was paying a guy at school to have sex with him. Paid pretty well too. He was stealing the money from his father."

Lillie looked at him incredulously. "You knew about this?"

"It was just a rumor," he said. "What's the big deal?"

"Well, you never mentioned it. Michele didn't know it."

"No," he said soberly. "She was a little naive about Tyler."

"And I'm sure Royce didn't know any such thing. Come

to think of it, he said Tyler was stealing from him. And he didn't know what he was doing with the money."

"Mom," Grayson said abruptly. "Do we have to wait for Dad? I'm really hungry now."

"Well, I thought we would all eat together. Kind of a reunion dinner," she said.

"Look, you know what he's like when he gets started. He could be gone for hours. I don't really feel like waiting."

Lillie's stomach tightened. So much for reunions. "All right," she said. "If you're that hungry."

"Can I take it to my room?" he asked.

"No, Grayson," she said sharply, hurt that he seemed to want to get away from her. "You can eat right here at the table. Don't be dragging food all over the house."

Grayson shrugged, picked up a plate, and filled it by the stove. Lillie sat down at the table with her glass of wine. "I'll wait for your father," she said.

The boy sat down opposite her and began to eat.

Lillie rolled the wine around in her glass, staring into it. After a minute she said a little spitefully, "If you knew Tyler was like that, how come you went down to the Arches that night?"

Grayson raised his eyes to the ceiling and then gave his mother a patient, long-suffering look. "He had some moonshine. You know all this," he said. "We went down there to try it."

"But who asked Michele to come along? You or him?"

Grayson resumed eating. "Neither," he said through a mouthful of chicken. "She just tagged along."

"But Reverend Davis saw her walking down there alone."

"Reverend Davis," he scoffed. "Look, we were meeting there. I don't remember who showed up when."

"Grayson, don't be smart about this. I mean, this may all be old business to you, but try to remember that I just found out about this a day ago. I still have a lot of questions in my mind," Lillie insisted.

A strange expression came over Grayson's face as he stared down into his plate. For a minute she thought she had touched a nerve, that he was going to lash out at her. Then, suddenly, he looked up and said, "Mom, there are cucumbers in this salad. You know I don't like cucumbers."

Lillie stared at him. "Grayson, why are you talking about cucumbers?"

Grayson lifted up a limp cucumber slice with a look of distaste on his face. "I've told you again and again I don't like them," he said.

Lillie got up from the table and stood with her back to him, staring out the window, as Grayson removed the offending cucumber slices from his salad and pushed them off his plate. When he was satisfied that his salad was free of the unwanted cucumbers, he looked up at her. "Everything else is good," he said encouragingly.

Lillie turned and studied him soberly. She had read enough articles and seen enough TV programs and experienced enough of life to know that people often denied their feelings and tried to bury them under a normal facade, and that sometimes only the help of a psychiatrist could give them relief. She could not help but wonder if maybe that was the answer for her son. Outwardly he seemed perfectly fine, but she was his mother, and she could not take any chances with his welfare. There were people right here in Cress County who might help. She could get a referral from Mary Dean over at the hospital.

"Mom, stop staring at me," he complained. "I'm trying to eat."

"Grayson," she said, "I was just thinking that maybe what we ought to do is find someone for you to talk to— you know, in confidence. A professional . . . to help you deal with this whole thing."

Grayson's eyes narrowed. "What do you mean? A shrink?"

"Honey, you have been through a terrible experience . . ."

Grayson clenched his fork in his fist. "I'm fine," he said evenly. "I don't need to talk to anyone. You're making a problem where there isn't one."

Lillie sat back down at the table. "Grayson, what you went through . . . to see your own sister cut down. And then to have to live with that knowledge . . . in secret. It was a terrible thing." Her eyes filled as she spoke. "That Founders Day was the worst day of your life. Of all our lives . . ."

Grayson smiled and patted her arm. "Hey, it wasn't all bad. I won the ball game, didn't I?"

Lillie jerked her arm away from his hand as if he had burned it.

"Hey, Mom, I'm just kidding," he said, noting the stunned expression on her face. "Don't get all bent out of shape."

At that moment the phone rang. Lillie turned and started down the hall, dimly aware of a desire to silence it, to stop the ringing in her head. She felt numb and slightly ill all over, as if she had pulled open a drawer and seen a rat staring up at her. It might turn and dart off in an instant, and she might shut the drawer and tell herself that it would never come back, but she could not pretend that she had not seen it.

"Come on, Mom," he said. "I didn't mean it."

"Then why did you say it?" Lillie cried, her voice shaking. She did not give him a chance to answer. She picked up the phone, grateful for the distraction.

Pink was nearly hysterical on the other end. She could tell it was him, but she could not understand his words.

"What is it, Pink?" she said. "I can't hear you."

"Tyler," Pink blurted out. "He's dead. They just found him."

"Tyler Ansley?" Lillie's legs buckled beneath her and she sank down on the seat of the chair beside the phone table. "It can't be. What are you talking about? What happened?"

Her body was abuzz with shock. She was vaguely aware that Grayson had come into the living room and was standing in the doorway, his whole body poised in a tense attitude of interest.

Lillie glanced up at him, her indignation dissolved by this news, automatically grateful that he was safe and there with her. That it was not her son who was dead.

"At the Millraney farm," Pink cried. "I was showing the place. He's been murdered, Lillie. Somebody pounded his head for him with a hammer."

"Oh, my God!" Lillie exclaimed. "Oh, my God. Does Royce know? At Millraney's? What was he doing there? Jordan said that he ran away."

"Royce was here. He's the one who found him. Lillie, I

can't talk. I just wanted you and Grayson to know. He's there with you, isn't he?"

Lillie gazed at her son who was standing in the doorway. His eyes were worried and questioning. He looked young and vulnerable to her as he waited for her to explain. "Yes, he's here," she said faintly. "Oh, God. This is so terrible. Who do they think . . . ?"

"Killed him?" Pink finished. "Isn't it obvious?"

"What do you mean?" Lillie asked.

"Jordan Hill. Who else? He goes after Tyler, and suddenly Tyler disappears and then turns up dead. He was out to get him, Lillie."

"Stop it, Pink, that's ridiculous," Lillie cried. "Jordan would never—"

"Look, Lillie, I can't stay on this line."

"No, Pink, that's impossible. You have to tell Royce."

Pink chuckled. "Hey, I'm not telling Royce anything. He's gone, anyway. He left here a little while ago with blood in his eyes."

"He didn't—" Lillie heard the phone click. "Not Jordan."

Lillie sat with the receiver in her hand, and then she let it drop into her lap. Her heart was hammering in her chest. Tyler dead. Murdered. It couldn't be. Her hands were icy cold. She fumbled with the receiver to replace it on the hook.

"What is it?" Grayson asked. "What's going on?"

Lillie looked up at him feeling dazed and frightened. "Tyler Ansley. He's dead. He's been murdered." Her voice was incredulous.

"I gathered that."

Lillie stared at her son. "I'm afraid that Royce has the idea that Jordan did it."

"Well, what if he did?" Grayson said with a shrug. "Good riddance, I say. He deserved it."

"Grayson!" Lillie exclaimed.

"Hey, look. He killed Michele, remember. Why should anybody be surprised if Tyler got himself killed? He was always in trouble. He was always drunk, hanging out with sleazy guys. It could have been anyone that did him in. Maybe he was into drugs or something."

Lillie nodded, reassured. "That's right," she said. "It's crazy to point the finger at Jordan. Royce is just upset. He's lost his child." She went over to the front window and looked outside the house. There was no one out there. Only the night sounds of the rustling trees, a far-away train whistle, and the occasional rumble of a passing car. "Poor Royce."

"This could be messy though," Grayson went on. "I mean, if he starts putting the pressure on Jordan, Jordan may decide not to keep quiet after all. Tit for tat."

"He promised me," Lillie said vaguely.

"Yeah, but if he wants to make trouble for us, he can do it."

"If he said he won't, then he won't. Can't you think of anyone but yourself?" Lillie said irritably, still staring out into the night. "Tyler is dead. I still can't quite believe it. Well, Jordan didn't do it, so there's no way they can arrest him. Royce just probably needs someone to blame right now." She spoke calmly, but in her heart she knew how desperate Royce must be feeling. She just prayed that he did not catch up to Jordan in that state of mind. "It must have been such a shock," Lillie said, "finding his child like that."

"Where'd they find him?" Grayson asked offhandedly. "I heard you say something about the Millraney place?"

"Yes," said Lillie. "Your father was out there showing the place to some clients and they discovered him."

"Leave it to Dad," said Grayson.

"Well, it's hardly your father's doing."

"I know. But he couldn't just show them the house and leave well enough alone. He has to show them the well too. Like that's going to make them want to buy the place."

Lillie turned and stared at her son.

Grayson looked at her questioningly, his eyebrows raised.

All the color had drained from Lillie's face. She was squinting at Grayson as if her vision were blurred. Her mouth hung open like a gash.

"What?" Grayson cried. "You want me to pretend I'm sorry about it? I'm not. He was a creep. He deserved it."

"What do you mean about the well?" she said.

Their eyes locked, and his widened, and then he looked away, silently scanning the room. "The phone," he said triumphantly. "You mentioned it when you were talking to Dad. You probably don't remember."

"No, I didn't," she said slowly. "He didn't say anything about a well. I didn't know there *was* a well."

"I don't know," Grayson said irritably. "I must have just imagined it. But I'm sure you said it."

The room reeled around her. She ordered her mind to be a blank, but she could not stop the thought that was mushrooming inside her head. An icy feeling of fear clutched her heart, squeezed it.

"Grayson," she whispered. "You have to tell me the truth. You didn't have anything to do with this?"

Grayson looked at her in frustration, as if she were a dimwitted child. "Of course not. Are you going to start hounding me about *this* now?"

"If you did, you must tell me."

"I told you. No. How many ways do I have to say it?"

"Son, I—I want to believe you. But why did you say that about the well?"

Grayson stared at her stonily. "I don't know what you're talking about. I didn't say anything about the well. It's all in your head."

Lillie was about to cry out in protest and then she stopped herself. "All right," she said, her voice shaking. "We'll settle this. I'll just call the sheriff's office and ask where they found the body."

"No, you don't," Grayson barked, stepping in front of her. "Just get back."

As he blocked her way to the phone, Lillie was suddenly aware, as if for the first time, of his size and his strength. He was not a child. He was a man. An angry man. Capable of hurting her if he chose to. She forced the awful thought from her mind. This was her son.

"You don't tell me what to do," she said. "Get out of my way."

Grayson hesitated for a moment and then, almost to her surprise, he gave way, letting her pass. He stared into the distance, as if preoccupied with something.

Lillie glanced at him and then she walked unsteadily toward the phone. Her insides were jumping wildly, but she tried to appear calm and resolute. Grayson had turned away from her and kneaded his fist with his other hand. "All right," he said impatiently. "All right. Put it back. You don't have to call them."

Lillie gripped the receiver. "Why?" she asked faintly, without looking at him.

"Because . . . he was in the well."

There was a roaring in her head. "How do you know?" she said.

"How do you think?" he asked.

"Oh, my God."

"You wanted me to tell you. So I'm telling you," he said angrily.

"Oh, God, no," Lillie breathed.

Grayson circled her, forcing her to look at him. "Wait a minute, Mom. Don't act now like it's some tragic thing. It's Tyler we're talking about. It's what you wanted me to do. Wasn't it?" He looked at her imploringly. "Wasn't it, Mom?"

She stared at him, her heart thudding wildly in her chest, her face bright, as if it had been seared.

"Avenge Michele," he cried. "That's what you wanted. You practically accused me because I didn't do it before. That *is* what you wanted. Don't deny it. If I did it, I did it for you. And for Dad."

Lillie's legs wobbled, and she grabbed the back of Pink's chair for support. God help me, she thought over and over. Did I do this? Is this what I made him believe? Tears filled her eyes and she began to shake her head. "No, darling, no."

Grayson began to pace back and forth across the room. "This morning, after Dad left," he said, "Tyler called me.

He wanted to meet me. At first I didn't want to see him but then I thought, well, maybe I should. Here's my chance. I'll do it. I'll do what they want. So they can be proud of me again. So that there will be some justice for Michele."

"You killed him?" Lillie whispered.

"He killed Michele," Grayson cried.

"Oh, baby, I know I said he should be punished." Lillie moaned. "But when I said that I didn't mean . . . not to take his life. That was never what I meant."

"Wait a minute," Grayson protested. "You can't start saying that now. You were the one who wanted an eye for an eye. You were screaming at me, saying I was a coward. So, when he came back I decided I'd make him pay, for once and for all."

Lillie's head was pounding. Her mouth was almost too dry to form the words. "Darling, oh, God, I was angry and I yelled at you. And I said some things in anger . . . but I never . . . I would never want you to kill another human being. Not for any reason, my God." She tried not to picture him dealing the blows.

"Don't you start backing down now, Mom," he said. "It's too late for that. I did what you said."

Lillie shook her head helplessly and reached out to him but he backed away from her. "Grayson," she said. "You are right. I feel as guilty as if I had killed him myself. I'm not trying to deny that, son. Believe me." Her breath was short, and her heart ached so that she wondered, for a moment, if she was having a heart attack.

"Good," he said.

"It doesn't matter what I said. You understood that that was what I wanted you to do."

"That's right," he exclaimed.

"I will tell them that, Grayson. Your father and I both are at fault here. All I can tell you is that people will understand. After all we've been through, I know that they'll see what happened here." I pray they will, she thought. Although she wondered if God heard her prayers anymore.

Grayson stared at her with startled, diamond-hard eyes. "Wait a minute," he said. "You're not telling anybody else about this. I didn't tell you this so you could throw me to the wolves. You're responsible for this. You have to cover for me."

"Oh, son," Lillie pleaded in a strangled voice. "You have to believe that I love you and there is nothing I wouldn't do for you. But we can't cover this up. It's gone too far. We have to tell the truth about this. There are other people involved here."

"Who? Like Jordan Hill? We covered up about Michele," he shouted. "And you thought that was fine."

"That was different," said Lillie, although for a minute she could not think why. "She was ours. We were the victims," she finally managed to say. "But that's not the point. We have no choice here."

"The point is," he shouted, "that I did this for you and you have to protect me."

"Don't you see?" she said. "That's what I'm trying to do. What's next, Grayson? What's next? This whole thing has gone too far. Do you think Royce Ansley won't know it was you, sooner or later? And then what? You're walking home from school one day and you get hit by a car? And no one is ever arrested? So Royce gets his revenge. And then what? Where does it end? I'm trying to protect you the only way I can. I have to stop this thing." Her eyes were blind with tears.

"Okay, Mom, look. You're losing it. You're not making any sense," said Grayson. "Now Dad's going to be home before long. He'll know what to do. We'll just tell him about it and let him decide."

Lillie shook her head sadly. "Oh, I know," she said. "I know what your father will decide. He'll think that more lies are the answer. That's why I'm not going to wait for Dad. We can't live like this. It seems easier to you now, but you have to believe me. These lies will destroy us. There is no other way."

She turned her back on him and walked to the closet. She opened the door, reached inside, and pulled out her coat.

"What do you think you're doing?" Grayson demanded.

"I'm going to the police station," she said calmly. "And I want you to come with me."

"Are you crazy?" he cried. "I'm not going there. Why are you doing this to me? I thought you said you *loved* me." His voice was sarcastic.

"I do love you," she said. "That's why we have to go. It's the only way I can think of that you'll be safe." She turned back to the closet rack and pulled out his jacket. "Put this on. You'll need it tonight. It's chilly."

"No, I won't," he said.

She turned, holding his jacket, and saw him facing her, his eyes glittering with hatred. In his hand he held Brenda's gun, trained steadily on her.

"You're not telling anybody," he said.

She could not believe her eyes. "Grayson, for pity's sake," she breathed.

He drew back the hammer. Staring her down, his eyes were cold, murderous. Her child's eyes. She wanted to scream, but no sound came out. The words "too late" came to her mind.

"Get away from the door," he commanded. "You do as I say now. Or I'll kill you too."

CHAPTER 29

Easing himself from his mother's embrace, Jordan kissed her dry cheek, then headed for the car. "I'll call you soon," he assured her as he turned back to wave. She stood on the front steps, holding the front of her coat together with one hand and waving with the other.

He threw his overnight bag in the backseat of the rental car and drove off on the road out of town. There was only one short detour he wanted to make before he headed to the airport. It was hardly even out of his way.

He turned off the main street onto the road to the cemetery. After parking his car along the roadside, he climbed the hill to the iron gate. There was moonlight enough to see by, but still it spooked him a little to be there at night by himself. He hesitated for a moment before approaching his daughter's grave. Then he thought of his little girl,

344

buried alone here for eternity, and his atavistic fears shamed him.

Dead leaves crunched beneath his feet and rustled against the granite markers as he found his way to her. The bare, black tree branches seemed to reach out over the graves, and the mown fields glistened beyond, almost like snow in the moonlight. Jordan sighed and gazed down at her headstone. For a moment he said a silent prayer, and then he shook his head. The sheriff's words still nagged at him: Leaving is what you do best.

The creak of a gate reached his ears, and Jordan turned around. At first, when he saw the shadowy figure looming over the graves, he thought his senses were deceiving him, that exhaustion was making him see and hear things. But suddenly he felt a chill.

Someone was entering the graveyard and coming toward him. Jordan peered into the darkness, his heart racing a little at the sight of the intruder. As the dark figure came nearer, Jordan suddenly recognized its familiar size and contours, and he exhaled, as surreptitiously as possible, when he saw that it was the sheriff, Royce Ansley. Then, just as suddenly, his apprehension returned at the sight of the sheriff's face.

"Royce," he exclaimed more heartily than he felt, "we meet again. What are you doing here?"

Royce's eyes were flat black and looked sunken in his head. His face seemed wizened, like an old man's, and his expression was still and forbidding. "I was on my way to your mother's to get you when I spotted you pulling up here," he said.

Jordan did not like the sound of the phrase "to get you," but he was curious all the same. "I decided to stop here on my way out of town. Just to say good-bye, I guess," he explained.

Royce looked down at Michele's grave. "Wanted to gloat a little bit, eh? Let her know you'd taken care of Tyler?"

Jordan peered at the sheriff in the darkness. "I thought we already had this out," he said.

"You almost got away with it," Royce said slowly. "Not quite."

"Look, Sheriff," said Jordan impatiently. "I think we said all we needed to back at the hotel." Jordan glanced at the dial of his watch, which glowed green in the dark. "I know you're ticked off, and maybe you wanted to finish this in private, but I've got a plane to catch."

Royce gave Jordan a mirthless smile. "Thought you'd found a perfect spot for him, didn't you? Never figured we'd find him so soon. My, you must have been surprised when Wallace came along to the hotel tonight."

For the first time Jordan was genuinely confused. "What are you talking about? Find who?"

Royce's dead eyes suddenly came to life with a spark of fury. "I ought to kill you myself," he said, taking a step toward Jordan.

Jordan jumped back, still trying to comprehend what was going on. Then, all at once, Royce's words began to register. He stared at the sheriff. "My God, Royce. Was it Tyler you found?" he croaked. "What happened to him? Is he all right?"

"Spare me the performance," said Royce. "Save it for someone who'll really appreciate it. Like a jury. Come on. I'm taking you in." As he spoke, Royce had removed some handcuffs from his belt. He reached out and snapped them on Jordan, twisting his arms roughly behind his back, before Jordan had a chance to protest.

"Taking me in?" Jordan cried. "Wait. What the hell are you doing? Royce, is Tyler dead?"

Royce prodded Jordan roughly from behind, and Jordan stumbled forward. Pushed by the sheriff, he staggered along through the cemetery. "Oh, he's dead all right," Royce drawled. "What'd you figure? You'd beat his head in and toss him down the well just to teach him a little lesson for the future?" Despite the fury in his tone, the sheriff's voice cracked on the last words.

They had reached the gate and Royce shoved Jordan forward so that he fell down the slope and landed hard on his face, without the use of his arms to break the fall. Rolling onto his side, Jordan managed to get up on his knees just as Royce unlocked the back door of the cruiser. He pulled Jordan up by the elbow and pushed him inside, as hard as he could. Jordan's cheek cracked against the opposite door handle and he slumped down onto the seat.

He struggled to sit up as Royce went around and got into the front seat. Jordan could feel the blood trickle down the side of his face. "Royce!" he cried.

"Shut up," said the sheriff. He pulled away from the roadside, leaving Jordan's rental car parked forlornly in front of the graveyard.

"What happened? What happened to Tyler? My God, I told you I never even saw him."

"That's what you said," the sheriff agreed bitterly.

"I swear it," said Jordan. "He was gone when I got to the school. The colonel called you. He can tell you."

"You claimed he was gone," Royce corrected him. "That must have been after you killed him. Then you brought him back here and dumped him somewhere you figured no one would ever look. Well, surprise, Mr. Movie Star."

Jordan fell back against the bouncing seat and licked the blood as it dribbled into his mouth. He closed his eyes and tried to think. He had to get through to Royce somehow. Calm down, he told himself. Use your head. Of course he suspects you, he reminded himself. You went after Tyler. Tyler was fine until then.

Tyler dead. Jordan gasped again as he thought of it. It was unbelievable. Yesterday he'd gone looking for him and today he was dead. Jordan could not help but realize that it would not appear coincidental. But you know the truth, he reminded himself. The truth is that Tyler *had* run away. Which means that he must have come back to Felton on his own. He must have had a reason to come back.

Jordan suddenly opened his eyes and sat up. You know why he came back, he thought. You know something that Royce doesn't.

He leaned forward to the wire mesh grid that separated him from the other man. "Sheriff," he said.

Royce ignored him.

"Royce, I'm sorry about your son. I am. Please believe that. But I didn't have anything to do with it."

"That little visit to the hotel tonight. Now that was a nice touch. You wanted to see if you could make me kiss your ass after you'd already killed my son. I wish I could skin you alive. I almost don't care what they'd give me for it. Just as long as I could make you pay."

"Look, do you want to make threats or do you want to talk about the truth?" Jordan shouted over the sheriff's ravings. "I didn't bring your son back here, dead or alive.

He came back here to see someone, and I know- who it was."

Through the cage that separated the seats, Jordan could see that Royce's shoulders were hunched as if to keep out the sound of Jordan's voice. Jordan leaned forward, close to the metal grid. "Grayson Burdette," he said. "He came back here to see that kid."

Royce shook his head and drove on for a minute, but then it was as if he himself, instead of the car, had run out of fuel. He slowed down and then pulled the car over to the side of the road, where it bumped to a halt. He sat there, refusing to look back at Jordan, not moving.

Jordan's lips were so dry, he could hardly speak. He couldn't see Royce's face and had no idea what might be going through the sheriff's mind. The road was lonely and desolate, and his heart felt a little sickening thud of fear. But deep inside he was calm, a certain conviction steadying him. The lies had begun to unravel inside his head.

As he looked out the window of the patrol car, he suddenly recognized the spot where they were stopped.

"Royce," he said to the silent, unmoving man on the seat in front of him. "We're right near the entrance to the Arches. I want to go down there. I want to see the place where Michele died again." He waited anxiously, half prepared for the sheriff to turn on him with a gun. Instead, after a moment, Royce got out of the car and opened up Jordan's door. He did not speak, and, in the darkness, Jordan could not see what was in his eyes. Jordan struggled out of the seat, and the two men tramped toward the dirt road that led to the Arches. Jordan glanced at the sheriff but Royce kept his eyes ahead as he walked. They reached the dirt road and began to make their way down it, toward the Arches and the river below. Jordan's arms ached from being bound by the cuffs but he did not complain. As he walked, his mind worked furiously. There was only one person Tyler would have risked his safety to see: Grayson. Grayson, the only other witness. The only other person who knew exactly what happened to Michele. Therefore, he was the one person who might have the best reason to kill him.

Jordan judged by the heavy tread and the preoccupied scowl of the man beside him that perhaps these same thoughts, in a slightly different form, might also be occurring to the sheriff. But there was a piece missing for the sheriff. A piece he would not want to hear.

A low-hanging branch snapped across Jordan's face in the dark and he let out a cry. The sheriff stopped and stared at him. Jordan calculated the effect of his next words. He was cuffed and helpless. He steeled himself for a blow and spoke quickly, before Royce could react.

"He came back to see Grayson and I'll tell you why," Jordan said in a low, deliberate voice. "Your son was in love with Grayson Burdette."

Royce lurched forward as if to throw himself upon his prisoner. Even in the darkness his face was purplish with rage. But he stopped short of striking Jordan. "You lying scum," he exclaimed.

Jordan could feel the sheriff's breath on him but he did not draw back. "I found out at the school. Tyler loved him. He would do anything for Grayson. I think Tyler was protecting Grayson." Jordan stared into Royce's blazing, tormented eyes. "I think Tyler admitted to murder for Grayson."

"Goddamn you," Royce growled. His face was darker

than ever, his voice hard. But Jordan could hear it in his voice. A hopeless note of admission.

"You know I'm right," Jordan said. "You know this is no ordinary boy."

Royce wheeled away from him and stumbled forward in the rutted road like a wounded bear. Jordan followed after him, seizing his opportunity. He began to say aloud all the things that were buzzing in his head. "Don't you ever ask yourself," he rushed on, "how come Grayson never took any blame for Michele's death? How come, if he was there, he didn't try to stop your son? It was his own sister. Did it really happen too fast? I don't believe it."

"They said so," Royce bellowed. "Tyler said so."

"Now," Jordan said softly, "Grayson claims his sister took off her blouse, and he put it back on after she was dead."

Royce stopped in his tracks. "He said that?"

Jordan nodded. "That's what he told Lillie."

Royce continued to walk on. He reached the bank of the river and stood still, gazing across the Arches.

Jordan stepped up beside him. "You saw the body," Jordan said urgently. "She was facedown in the mud. And he says he put her blouse on. What, and left her like that? I say she never took her blouse off. It's another of Grayson's lies. What kind of person leaves his own sister lying facedown in the mud?" The two men stared across the riverbank, one remembering the sight, the other imagining it with the familiar horror.

"Why did he run?" Jordan went on. "Why did he agree so readily to protect a boy who beat his sister to death? I don't buy it. And what about you? Why were you so ready to believe that your son was the guilty one? Is it easier to believe that than to admit he might be protecting another boy, a killer, because he's in love with him? Is it?"

"You son of a bitch," Royce muttered.

"Only Tyler knew who really killed Michele. As long as Tyler stuck by their story, Grayson was safe. When I went after Tyler, Grayson realized that the lid might come off," Jordan cried. "And then Tyler played right into his hands. He showed up here, probably seeking Grayson's help, and Grayson saw his chance to silence him. To protect himself."

"No," Royce said furiously, turning on him.

"Yes," said Jordan. "Think about it."

"No, that would mean Grayson killed her. His own sister. She was just a sweet, harmless girl. Why would he kill her?"

"Because she stumbled onto the truth that night. I'll tell you what I think," said Jordan, staring defiantly into the sheriff's anguished eyes. "I think *your* son lied out of love. But Grayson . . . well, I think Grayson would do *anything* to avoid humiliation. Anything."

CHAPTER 30

Lillie clasped the boy's jacket to her chest as if it were a shield and stared at her son.

"Come over here to this chair," he said, "and sit down."

Lillie did not budge from the spot where she stood. "Grayson," she said in a quavering voice, "put that gun back where you found it this minute and I will try to forget this ever happened. This minute."

Grayson smiled but his eyes were cruel. "Sorry, Mom," he said. "You shouldn't have left it there."

A white-hot rage erupted in Lillie and she started toward him. Grayson leveled the gun at her chest without flinching.

"Get back," he cried. "Do you think I'm kidding?"

Instantly she knew that he was not. There was no uncertainty in his eyes, no inclination to retreat, to pretend that it had all been a game. Lillie's stomach tumbled over and the floor felt like sand beneath her feet. She sat down in the chair he indicated.

"It's your own fault," he said. "You brought this on yourself. You came back here pretending that you wanted everything to be fine, to get back to normal. But the fact is that you wanted to make trouble for me. Admit it," he demanded. "You were looking for something to get back at me. The first chance you got, what do you do? You can't wait to drag me to the police. Drag me through the mud."

"Drag you through the mud?" Lillie repeated incredulously. "Grayson, I was afraid for your life. I don't want to see you hurt. Grayson, put that gun down. You don't mean any of this. Put it down and we'll talk this out. Please."

"Talk!" Grayson exclaimed. "That's all you've been doing, all night. Lecture is more like it. Interrogate me. Michele this. Michele that. What happened? Where were you? Who was there? How many times did Tyler pass wind? I mean, what difference does it make? Who cares? It's over. Done. Forgotten. But no. You have to talk about it, talk about it, talk about it. God.

"And now you want to talk about Tyler, right? What happened to poor Tyler. You want to talk to the whole world about it. What did mean old Grayson do to poor little Tyler? You'd think *he* was your son instead of me."

My son, she reminded herself over and over. As if that thought were a mantra that could protect her from his hail of words that were like stones he was pelting her with. My son. She shook her head helplessly. "It's you that I'm concerned about. Only you. I was trying to help you. I know you don't see it that way but it's true."

"You're a liar," he said. "I knew we could never trust you. I told Dad that from the beginning. He wanted to tell you everything about Michele. He was ready to come home and blurt it all out to you. It was just because he was all worked up, he wasn't thinking clearly. I had to warn him. I knew you would take her side against me because you always did. She was like your little lapdog, always yapping at your feet. Well, I'm not anybody's lapdog. I am not going to buckle under and be told what to do by people who are not as intelligent as me. People who don't have the looks and the class in their whole bodies that I have in my little finger. It's not right that I should."

Lillie stared at her son. His words made her cringe inside and she wished she could shut the sound of the injured, remorseless tirade she was hearing. Where did this come from? she wondered. Was it always there?

He saw the despair in her eyes and nodded slyly. "I know what you think. You think I sound conceited, don't you? Naturally you think that because you are too limited to admit it might just be the truth. It makes sense that you preferred Michele, now that I think about it. She was more ordinary and simpleminded. More your type."

He waved the gun as he spoke, and Lillie kept her eye on it as if it were an undulating snake. He was enjoying holding it, enjoying having a prisoner and tormenting her. She had to ignore his words and maintain her composure. Be the adult. Try to soothe him. "Grayson," she said as calmly as she could, "I'm sorry that you thought that I favored your sister. It was only that she was sick. I love you both more than you know, and now you are all I have left—"

"Oh, I don't care," Grayson said impatiently. "I don't

imagine it was any great privilege to be preferred by you. More of a burden actually."

"Do you hate me so?" Lillie blurted out, although as soon as the words were out of her mouth the answer seemed ridiculously apparent to her. He was holding a gun on her. He was threatening her life.

Grayson looked at her in surprise. "No," he said, as if genuinely desiring to reassure her. "You've been pretty good as a mother, all in all. I would say you haven't been exceptionally good, but you haven't been exceptionally bad either. I'd say you did a fairly decent job. You've been a good cook, and the house is pretty clean, and you still look quite young for your age."

His indifferent assessment landed like a cold blade in her heart. She would have preferred hatred. It was becoming undeniably clear to her, although she could not really grasp it, that no emotional appeal would move him. She might have been a stranger he encountered in an alleyway.

She shuddered and took a deep breath. "Grayson," she said. "What is it you want from me?"

Grayson pressed his lips together and shook his head sadly. "Something I'm afraid I just can't have. Your loyalty. I need to know that I can trust you. But I just don't see that as possible."

Tears sprang to Lillie's eyes in spite of herself, and she wiped them away angrily. "How dare you?" she said. "I only tried to do what I thought was best out of love for you."

"You see," he said. "We just don't see eye to eye. You'll always be getting in my way. Always trying to drag me down in the name of mother love. I have to get rid of you."

Get rid of you. The matter-of-fact threat jolted her like a live wire, but when the jolt subsided it was not so much fearful she felt, as piteous and ashamed. Her own son. He's mad, she told herself.

Part of her did not want to live another moment with this knowledge, but the will to survive surfaced and guided her. Fear returned, making her alert. Say something to him, she thought. Keep him talking until Pink arrives.

"Your father will be here any second," she said.

"That's what I'm waiting for," he said equably. "Then I can say that he killed you."

Lillie stared at him.

"Well, everyone knows that you've been fighting. Everyone in town has seen that shiner he gave you. We'll say it was an accident, more or less. I'll say I tried to stop him, and I'll come out looking pretty good. Dad will take the blame," he said. "He'll do anything for me."

She could not look at his face. There was a roaring in her ears, like the ocean. She looked at the gun. Stand up and lunge for it and take it from him. If he kills you, so what? What is there to live for?

But she was frozen to the seat, paralyzed by trying to select the last moment of her life. Grayson was looking out the front window. "Look who's here," he said. He opened the front door a crack and held the gun low. "Come on in."

Grayson stepped back and pulled the door open, and Pink walked inside the house.

"Close it," Grayson ordered.

Pink shut the door, turned, and saw Grayson holding the gun on Lillie. For a minute his face sagged, his eyes widened, and he jumped back. But immediately he collected himself and acted as calm and disinterested as if he had just come home from work and this was the most natural thing imaginable, to find his son training a weapon on his mother. The only sign that betrayed him was the sweat that broke out all over his face.

Lillie saw and understood that Pink was making a terrific effort to maintain that unflustered posture, and she felt a stab of appreciation for him. At the same time, Grayson's words ran like an awful jingle in her mind. Dad will do anything for me.

"What's going on here?" Pink asked his son. "What is this?"

"She started it," said Grayson. "Ask her."

"I asked you," Pink said irritably. "Where'd you get that gun?"

"It was over there," Grayson said, nodding toward the mantel.

"Well, what was it doing there?" Pink demanded, as if the gun itself were at fault.

"I don't know," said Grayson.

"It's Brenda's," Lillie whispered. "She put it in my bag."

Pink shook his head and sighed. "Brenda," he said. "I might have known. All right, Grayson. Give that thing to me. And tell me what this is all about."

Lillie saw a flash of anger in the boy's eyes, a contemptuous sneer at his father's authority, and then he seemed to think better of it. He held on to the gun but his tone was confidential. Here was his ally, his friend. "She thinks

I killed Tyler. She threatened to go to the cops and tell them that."

"What?" Pink said incredulously. He turned on Lillie. "I've never heard anything so crazy."

"He told me he did it," Lillie said. "I caught him in a lie and he admitted it."

"I did not," said Grayson. "She made it up."

"Lillie, you must have misunderstood what he said. That's just plain outrageous. Everyone knows who the guilty party is." Pink looked at Lillie with disappointment in his eyes. "Why did you start this, Lillie?" he asked. "We're just getting this family back on the right track and you go and say something like that. What does he have to do to prove himself to you? Why must you always think the worst of this child?"

The small hope that Lillie had felt at her husband's arrival dissolved inside her. He was chiding her for her transgressions, meanwhile apparently accepting the idea that Grayson had turned a gun on his mother. She looked helplessly at her husband. It was almost as if he were enchanted by his son. His faith was leaden, impenetrable. He would rather believe that his wife was a liar than disturb that magical glow around his son.

"Pink," she said stubbornly, "when you called he already knew that Tyler's body was in the well. When I confronted him, he said he had killed Tyler for revenge."

Pink's brow furrowed, and he bit his lip. "Revenge. Well, that I could understand." Pink turned to Grayson. "Is that what happened?"

"No," Grayson said after a moment's hesitation. "She made it up."

Pink looked from one to the other. "Somebody's lying

here. Are you sure, Lillie? Are you sure you didn't just imagine this?"

"Oh, God, Pink," Lillie cried, turning away from him.

"Well, don't act like it's my fault." Pink bristled. "I walk in on this and get two different stories. I'm just trying to figure it out."

"Do you see what he is doing?" Lillie cried.

"He is defending himself," said Pink. "Look, why don't you get out of here, Lillie. Go take a walk or something. Grayson and I will talk it over among ourselves."

"Wait a minute, wait a minute," said Grayson. "Hold it. She's not going anywhere."

"Hey," Pink said. "We don't need her here. We'll put our heads together. Talk this thing over."

With anyone else, Lillie thought, it might have been a clever ploy, a virtually heroic way to obtain her release. To set her free and take the burden on himself. But she knew better. It was no such thing. It was the all-too-familiar pattern of their lives. She studied Pink's bland face, wondering what gave him such blessed blindness. One thing was clear though. Grayson was not about to agree to this plan.

"No," said Grayson. "She stays here."

"Look, son," Pink said patiently. "I don't blame you for being upset. Being accused like that. It stands to reason. But you also can't just pick up a gun and hold it on a person. Number one, it's dangerous, and number two, it really gives the wrong impression."

"Dad, I can't let her go. She'll run right off to the sheriff and tell him I killed Tyler and that I held a gun on her."

"She won't, I guarantee you," said Pink. "This is family

business, strictly between the three of us. Isn't that right, Lillie?"

It frightened her to speak, to defy that loaded gun, but she could not let it go. "Not anymore," she said.

"You see?" said Grayson.

"Goddamnit, Lillie. Hasn't there been enough damage done to this family? Do you have to create more? I thought we had agreed that we were going to handle our own problems in our own way."

"That was before," she said in a dull voice. The two of them were aligning against her, preparing to mow her down. Somehow, she did not care anymore.

"Wait a minute," Pink said suddenly, his eyes narrowing. "Wait a minute. I think I am beginning to understand something now." He looked balefully at his wife. "Tell me I'm wrong about this. Tell me this can't be. Oh, my God. No wonder. . . . This is about Jordan Hill, isn't it? You're figuring that he's going to get nailed for this, so you decided to come up with another solution. God, is it any wonder Grayson is acting like this?"

"For pity's sake, Pink," Lillie cried. "Do you think I would accuse my own son . . . to protect anyone?"

"Look, Lillie," said Pink, pressing hands to his chest. "I don't know what you would do. You're a mystery to me. All right? But this is my son. My own boy. And I won't have you or anybody else slandering him and accusing him. If you don't love him, well, that's your loss."

"It's not a question of love . . ." Lillie cried, but he turned his back on her. He waggled his hand like a traffic cop, as if to call Grayson forward.

"Okay, son. Give me the gun. Everything is going to be fine."

"She's going to tell them I did it," said Grayson. "She's going to tell the sheriff."

"Don't worry about her. She's not going to tell anybody anything. Believe me."

Grayson shook his head. "No, we can't trust her. She'll go to the sheriff."

"And we'll tell the sheriff she's lying," Pink said patiently. "He'll know she's lying. No matter what she says, I'll take care of it."

"Dad," Grayson said almost gently. "We can't take the chance. It's going to be her and Jordan Hill against me and you. Jordan Hill is important. He's on TV. You just have a little rinky-dink business. Who do you think people are going to believe? They're going to listen to him. And he'll say whatever she wants him to. You know they're just looking for a way to screw both of us."

"Well," Pink blustered, "I may not be on television but I guess I have some influence in this town. Anyway, I don't see what else we can do."

"Well, I don't think we can just let them get away with it. I think the best solution might be if she could accidentally be killed. By this gun."

Lillie was almost glad that he had finally said it. Slowly she lifted her head and looked up at Pink, as if to say "There. Now do you understand?"

Pink looked at Grayson in amazement and then at his wife. His jaw slackened and he blinked a few times, as if newly awakened, and then he looked back at his son with the most chagrined expression on his face that Lillie had ever seen. She felt tears of pity for him spring to her own eyes, watching him. He had staked everything on this child. Now he had to somehow reconcile this murderous statement with this perfect embodiment of his hopes and dreams, this son.

"Grayson," Pink said at last, his voice quavering, "I know you don't mean that about your mother. You're just upset."

"Dad," Grayson said eagerly, "I've been thinking about it. It wouldn't be that hard. First of all, it's Brenda's gun, so Brenda will have to admit that Mom had it."

Pink was staring at Grayson as if stupefied, a lost, haunted look in his eyes. "Son, don't say any more."

"Will you listen?" Grayson demanded. "It's a good plan. We say you two got into a fight, and she pulled the gun on you. It'd be only natural for you to try and take it from her and then, it could go off, and that would be it. She'd be, you know, gone."

Pink was trembling and his usually florid face was pale. Lillie buried her face in her hands, overcome at her own child's imaginative rendering of her execution.

Pink cleared his throat. "Grayson, we all get carried away at times, imagining that we want to hurt the people that hurt us. It's just a harmless . . . harmless thing to do. It's just . . . it's something everybody does. It doesn't mean anything."

"We can do it, Dad," Grayson said evenly. "You and me. No one ever will know."

"Okay," Pink said abruptly. "That's enough of this nonsense now. Give me the gun. No one's going to shoot anyone."

"Hey, wait a minute," said Grayson. "I thought you and I stood together. That's what you always said."

"That's right," Pink said, avoiding his son's eyes. "And

I'm telling you I will take care of everything. No one is going to lay a hand on you. I promise you."

Grayson narrowed his eyes and then he began to slowly shake his head. "Don't give me that, Dad. What makes you think you can take care of it? You have no authority in this town. You're not anybody. You don't even have a new car. Why should they believe you over her?"

Pink's face flushed at the cruel assessment. "That's my problem," he said. "Look, I'm your father. You'll do as I tell you."

"Don't argue with him, Pink," Lillie said in a low, warning voice.

Pink glared at her, as if outraged that she would align herself with him. "Stay out of it," he said bitterly. His eyes were full of rancor toward her, as if she were entirely to blame for this destruction.

"Don't give me that 'I'm your father' bit," said Grayson. "What about all my plans and my future? You're the one who's always saying what a great life it's going to be."

"It will be," Pink cried. "It's going to be everything we always said."

"Not if you're going to let her sell me down the river. You know, all these years no matter what I did, you'd be there, taking credit for it. Always clapping a hand on my shoulder so you could get into the newspaper pictures, always putting your greasy fingers on my trophies, always trying to make it seem like you were behind it somehow, no matter what I got. When I won a game, you'd claim you were the coach. When people say I'm handsome, you beam like it was your doing. And on the best day of your life you never looked one bit as good as me," Grayson said scornfully. "Well, let me tell you something. I let you get away with it. I let you take the credit. But fair is fair. Now you have to take the blame. It's your turn."

Grayson hefted the gun and started toward Lillie. For a moment Pink was frozen, as if Grayson's words had drained the life from him. Then suddenly he sprang between Grayson and his mother.

"Grayson," he pleaded, his voice tearful. "Maybe you don't think much of me. And maybe all you said is true. I don't know. I have been proud of you. And I guess, it seems, you haven't been all that proud of me—" Pink's voice cracked and he stopped and looked away, his body trembling. "But," he continued, "I can take care of this one, Grayson. I'll prove myself to you. You just hand that gun over to me and I'll show you."

He reached out his hand imploringly, but Grayson raised his head like an animal sniffing danger. "What's that?"

Lillie heard it too. It sounded like a car door slamming outside. "It's the wind," she said.

"Is there someone here?" Grayson said.

Pink seemed oblivious to the sounds outside and to his son's agitation. He stepped forward and shook Grayson's arm. "Son, you have to give me that gun," he insisted. "You have to trust me. Believe me, you'll see I'm right. Trust me. Please, son, please. Do it for me. I can save you."

"I should have known you'd be too weak," said Grayson.

Lillie saw the loathing in Grayson's eyes as his father reached clumsily for the weapon in his hand. She jumped up from the chair. "No, Pink, don't," she pleaded. "Get back."

But Pink would not stop. He was concentrated on his task, a dogged expression on his wide, wounded face. Grayson endured this interference for a moment, but that was all. "You're in my way," he said.

"Pink, let him go," Lillie cried, knowing the truth. "He'll shoot you."

But her voice was drowned out by the roar of the gunshot that exploded into him. Lillie screamed and rushed toward her husband. Pink stood still for a moment, his eyes wide with innocent surprise. He clutched the bloody gap in his chest as Grayson lifted the smoking gun. Pink held out one hand and then pitched forward toward the taut, unyielding figure of his son. Grayson grimaced and stepped to one side, and Pink fell, first to his knees and then to the floor.

In the next instant the front door slammed back. Jordan Hill leapt across the room and tackled Grayson, who was caught off guard and went down. The gun dropped from his hand as they struggled. Grayson clawed, kicked, and furiously grappled with Jordan, whose skill and weight gave him only a slight advantage over the boy's ferocious resistance.

Lillie screamed, and then screamed again as Royce Ansley appeared in the doorway, his gun drawn. The sheriff looked at Pink's body, glanced at Lillie, and then turned in a continuous arc to the boy that Jordan had wrestled to the ground.

In that moment Lillie saw the intention in his eyes.

She scrambled across the floor and shielded her son with her body. "No, Royce," she cried. "Don't kill him. Don't. Please."

Royce Ansley hesitated, vengeful and tempted. And

then he holstered his gun. "All right," he said. He walked across the room and roughly dragged Grayson to his feet. Jordan willingly let him go. He went to Lillie and took her hand. She gripped it tightly and clung to him. After a minute she let go of his hand and went over to where Pink had fallen. She knelt down beside him and felt for his pulse. Then, shaking her head, she gently touched his lifeless face and began to weep. Jordan crouched down beside her and drew the eyelids down over Pink's startled expression.

"Let's go," said Royce, and he led the handcuffed Grayson toward the door. Royce's black eyes were smoldering in his haggard face as they approached Pink's body.

"Is Dad dead?" Grayson asked, his voice sounding young and wistful.

Lillie turned and looked up at him, wiping her eyes. "Yes, Grayson," she said. Jordan helped her to her feet. She was trembling almost uncontrollably.

"I didn't mean to shoot him," Grayson said. "He grabbed the gun and it just went off. It was an accident, really."

She did not turn away from him. She looked steadily into his eyes. "No, it wasn't," she said. Her voice did not break. It was firm and patient, as if she were correcting a child's mistake. One that would require correcting, again and again and again.

EPILOGUE

D r. Carl Lundgren finished the notes he was making and then leaned back in his chair and looked out through the barred window of his office at the bleak, rainy afternoon. The winters were like one continuous gray, damp day down here, but they did not depress him. He figured it must be his Scandinavian heritage, something in the genes, that enabled him to actually enjoy Tennessee's dreariest season.

He pushed his notes aside and rummaged through the disorder on his desktop for the folder he wanted. He did not really have to read this one. He had studied it many times in the last three years. It was one of his favorite cases.

The fact was, although some thought him warped or ghoulish for it, Carl Lundgren loved his prison work. He had plenty of cases in his regular practice, but prison work was ruining him for the run-of-the-mill neuroses of the general public. He was a family man, an even-tempered man, whose idea of reckless disregard for the law was occasionally to park too close to a fire hydrant, but he was fascinated by the people he met inside these walls. And the prisoners liked to talk to him because he was so interested in them and the bizarre lives they had led. So who does it hurt? he asked himself cheerfully.

The guard appeared at the cellblock door and told Carl he had someone waiting for him in the visitors room.

"Okay," said the doctor. "I'll be right there." He opened the file he was holding and perused it again, so that he would have his information fresh for this visit with the prisoner's mother. He knew she would have a lot of questions. She always did. There was just so little that he could really explain to her.

After locking the folder back in the file drawer, Lundgren left the Health Services cellblock and made his way through a series of gates, which had to be unlocked for him, until he came to the visitors area.

He looked inside but did not see her. There were a couple of lawyers conferring with their clients in the beige and gray carrels, under the watchful eyes of the guards. Carl went out to the coffee machine, deposited his quarter, and obtained a paper cup of coffee. He looked at his watch. He was supposed to meet Lillie at two-thirty. She must have stepped out for a minute. When he looked up again he saw her coming down the hall toward him.

As she approached him, smiling hesitantly, he was struck again, as he had been the first time they met, by what a pretty woman she was. It had not surprised him, given the physical beauty of her son. These things tended to be genetic. But he had been eager to meet her from the first, because he knew from long experience that appearances were not the only things handed down in families. He had been most interested in knowing her, studying her, unearthing the influences that had created an aberration like Grayson Burdette. Their meetings over the last three years had proved puzzling and even frustrating to him. He had come to like her.

"Hello, Lillie," he said, extending his hand to her.

She smiled as she shook his hand, although her worried eyes never really cleared. "Thank you for seeing me today. It means a lot to me. Did you meet with him already?"

"Just a little while ago." Carl nodded. "I'm sorry. He hasn't changed his mind about seeing you."

Lillie sighed and Carl gently led her to the door of one of the meeting rooms and ushered her in.

Lillie sank down into a chair and absentmindedly twisted her wedding band.

"Did your husband come down with you this time?" Carl asked pleasantly.

Lillie looked up. "Yes. My best friend is getting married in Felton this weekend. We're staying at my mother-in-law's for a few days."

"That should be nice for both of you," he said.

"Yes," Lillie murmured distractedly.

Carl took a seat and sipped his coffee. "I'm sorry," he said. "Did you want a cup?"

Lillie shook her head. "If he would just agree to see me. Even one time . . ." she said.

"He doesn't want you to come back. He means that, Lillie. I think that you're torturing yourself unnecessarily, coming here again and again."

She was always upset when she came here, but today she seemed more distressed than usual. The doctor blew on the surface of his coffee and studied her anguished face sympathetically. "You know, he's really doing very well."

"Meaning what?" Lillie asked bluntly.

Carl knew her by now. She was one of the few mothers he had met behind these walls who actually wanted the truth. But he still had to temper it. There were certain things she was better off not knowing. "Well, he's studying and progressing very quickly with his courses. He's physically strong, healthy."

She looked at him ruefully, as if his words were almost a taunt. "He's thriving, eh?"

Carl sighed. "He's a strong boy, Lillie. He's learned the rules here. He'll survive. In fact, he'll do better than most."

Lillie looked at him with bright, frightened eyes. "Are you treating him?" she asked. "Is there any improvement?"

Carl put his coffee cup down and looked at her directly. "I see him occasionally. But no, he's not in treatment. He cannot change, Lillie. He doesn't believe there is anything wrong. If he were 'treatable,' he would be in a hospital, not a prison. He doesn't belong in treatment. He has . . . adapted perfectly to his environment. Believe me, he'll be fine."

"I know what you're saying," she said. "There's only one way people manage to get by in a violent place like this. Much less thrive."

Carl shrugged and sipped his coffee.

"Oh, God." Lillie groaned. "Where does it all end?"

"Bottom line?" Carl asked. "He will probably never be

granted parole." He looked solemnly at Lillie. "You should be very relieved to hear that."

Lillie's eyes filled up. "I'm numb. I don't know what to wish for anymore." She seemed lost in her private anguish.

Carl looked at her kindly. "It doesn't get any easier, does it?" he said.

Lillie shook her head.

"Now, why don't you tell me why it was so important for you to see me today?"

Turning off the highway exit for Felton and retracing the familiar roads, Lillie thought as she drove along how it always made her heart ache to be in this place. Even now, after a long, bleak winter, it had its own special beauty. The fields were lavender-hued, and beneath its low bridges, the wide creek twined sluggishly through the town. Smoke rose from the farmhouse chimneys, gray against a gray sky, and it was as peaceful as she had always remembered it.

She drove on, past the cemetery, where the bare tree branches leaned out over the lonely graves. She would stop there and bring flowers for Michele, and for Pink too, before they went back up North. Bessie tended to the graves between their visits. Lillie knew that it was silly to care about that. It made no difference to Michele if there were flowers or not. But Lillie felt better knowing that her grandmother visited. They had buried Pink beside her, and, in an odd way, that comforted her too. No matter what else he had done, she had never doubted his love for his children.

She passed the street that led to her old house, but she

chose not to drive by it. She continued on past the sign for Royce Ansley's old road, but she did not go down it either. She had heard from Bomar Flood when she stopped by the drugstore that Royce had moved to Houston, and had a job as a security guard there. Lillie had testified on his behalf and been relieved that he had not had to go to prison. He lived inside his own prison, she thought. Enough was enough.

Lillie glanced at her watch. Brenda had asked her to come over and see her wedding dress if she got back in time, but Lillie did not feel up to prenuptial gaiety and girl talk this afternoon. She was truly happy for Brenda, who was marrying a young restaurateur from Nashville about ten years her junior. Lillie and Jordan had liked him right away when they met him. And, aside from her professed fear of looking like the groom's mother in the wedding pictures, Brenda had never seemed happier. Lillie smiled, thinking of her old friend. I'll go over tomorrow, she thought. Maybe I'll feel better then.

She slowed the car as she reached the fork that led to Bessie's house, but at the last moment she turned the wheel and took the other road. She did not want to go back to her mother-in-law's house. She did not want to face Jordan and the questions he would surely ask. She found herself driving, almost automatically, in the direction of Crystal Lake.

Because the trees were bare, she could see clear through the woods to the surface of the lake. It looked like pewter-colored silk, its shores deserted and undisturbed. Lillie got out of the car and walked through the crunchy ground cover of cold, brittle leaves to the edge of her lake. The damp air seeped through her wool coat, making her shiver, as she traversed the edge until she came to the foot of her jetty. She stepped onto the weathered boards and looked out. All her ghosts seemed to crowd around her.

She hesitated for a moment and then she walked out to the end of the jetty and sat down. The boards beneath her were cold and damp and she wrapped her coat more tightly around her. You shouldn't be sitting here, she thought. You can't afford to catch a cold. You're pregnant.

It had been more than a suspicion on her part when she went to the doctor in Manhattan. She had experienced it twice before, and she recognized the first slight symptoms. Today, before she left for the prison, she had stopped at a phone booth and called the office in New York. The doctor had been delighted to make it official, removing any doubt, any hope, she might have had that it was not so.

A hawk circled in over the lake and then swooped up and soared out of sight. Lillie watched it go, envying its flight. She felt weak, and earthbound, and unable to face what lay ahead of her. Jordan would be happy to hear it. She knew that. They had agreed that they would try to have a family, but even as she had agreed to it, a secret voice inside of her was whispering no, never again.

Lillie sighed and looked despondently out at the soothing, familiar waters of Crystal Lake. She had always treated those waters as if they were a crystal ball, holding the answers she needed. But today they were dark and opaque under a lowering sky. "Grayson. Oh, Grayson," she whispered. He was all she had thought of since she first suspected she was pregnant. Living out his life in a jail cell, cursing her, if he thought of her at all.

She went back over her conversation with Dr. Lundgren in her mind. She had told him she felt responsible for what had happened to Grayson. That she was somehow to blame. And she confided to him her greatest fear—that she would have another child and that she might bring about this same sort of nightmare all over again.

Carl had answered her kindly. "You have a different husband," he said, "and these are very different circumstances. We can never completely understand how these disorders come about, but I don't think you should be fearful. I'll give you the best advice I know. Don't try too hard to be a perfect parent with this new child. When you feel afraid, ease up a little. Give yourself a break. Get some pleasure out of the experience. Nothing you can do will change the course that Grayson is on now. I know this sounds brutal, but he can't be saved. This is clinically true. Believe me. Send him money for his expenses in here, write to him if you want. Maybe he'll relent and see you one of these days. But there is little else you can do for him. Go ahead with your own life, Lillie, and don't be afraid."

Lillie sighed and shook her head. It was easier said than done. She could never convey to the doctor, or to anyone, how terrified she felt, how undeserving she felt of having another child. One of her children was dead, and the other was living out the rest of his life in prison. She had no right to try again, no reason to believe that she would do better, that her child would not suffer from her mothering.

Lillie shivered in the damp air, and she knew she should get up and go back. Go back and tell Jordan the news, that they were having a baby. That he too was being given another chance.

She could not help but remember the first time she had told him that she was pregnant. That first, frightening time, she recalled, they had been so young and so naive. He had tried to be brave and reassuring, and had said it was perfect, because they wanted to be married anyway. And then Michele had been born, so beautiful and so sick.

What would *she* think of all this if she knew? Lillie wondered. And almost as if in answer to her question, an image of Michele, bright-faced and laughing, pierced her gloom like a sunbeam over the lake. No, Lillie thought almost angrily, you were sick, and you suffered so. But the happy image refused to fade. And it gave off a glow that warmed Lillie from inside. She does know, Lillie thought. She's up there on some heavenly cloud and she does know. And she's happy for us. Lillie pressed her lips together and held back the tears. There seemed to be no end to the tears she could shed over her lost girl. Her perfect, wonderful girl, with her kindness and her loving heart. That was your child too, she reminded herself. How dare you deny her? You made a child who was as good as could be.

The sound of a car door slamming echoed out over the quiet lake. Lillie turned around and saw a pale-blue Ford through the bare trees. Bessie's car. Jordan had come looking for her.

She got to her feet, feeling a little guilty, knowing that he would have been worried about her. He hated for her to go up to the prison alone, but she always insisted on it. And now, when she hadn't come home right away . . . She peered through the trees and then she spotted him coming down the path, the collar of his leather jacket turned up against the chill. Jordan saw her at the same moment and waved. Lillie waved back. The worried frown on his face was replaced by a smile.

"You found me," she called out.

"I saw the car," he called back.

He was coming toward her, making his way around the lake, his jacket open, his graying hair disheveled by the breeze. His face was alight as he rushed to reach her, to get to her. He always knew where to find her. He always had.

Here comes your father, she thought. And for a second she did not know whether she was speaking in her heart to Michele or to the baby inside her. Both, she decided. She placed her hand gently over the child within her. Here he is, come to get us and take us back home.

And as she walked down the jetty, she could not help but smile at the sight of him. He was so eager to protect her, envelop her. He would cherish this baby, this second chance. They both would. Believing it would be all right was half the battle.

"I was worried," he said. "You were late."

"Don't be worried," she said. She reached out her hand to meet his. "Darling, come closer. I've got some good news."